SHIVAJI
MAHASAMRAT
• VOLUME ONE •
THE WHIRLWIND

Vishwas Patil is one of the most acclaimed Marathi writers today. He has written iconic novels like *Mahanayak, Chandramukhi, Pangira, Zhadazdati* (A Dirge for the Damned), *Panipat, Sambhaji, Nagkeshar* and *Lust for Lalbagh*. He has also written a literary biography of Anna Bhau Sathe, the founding father of Dalit Literature in Maharashtra, titled *Annabhauchi Dardbhari Dastaan*, which is considered an outstanding work by critics. He has received the Priyadarshini National Award, the Bharatiya Bhasha Parishad Award (Kolkata) and the Sahitya Akademi Award for *Zhadazdati* and the Gadkari Award for *Mahanayak*. *Panipat* has received thirty-eight awards since its publication in 1988. *Panipat, Mahanayak* and *Sambhaji* have been published in English by Westland Books. Patil's novel *Nagkeshar* has been adapted into a television serial. In 2020, he was awarded the prestigious Dr Indira Goswami (Mamoni Raisom Goswami) National Literature Award. The *Shivaji Mahasamrat Series*, a quartet of novels on the Maratha Empire, is his most ambitious work so far.

Nadeem Khan has been a teacher of English since 1973. He retired as Head, Department of Languages, Shivaji Science College, Amravati in 2010. In 2011, he became the founding director of the Western Regional Centre of the Indian Institute of Mass Communication run by the Ministry of Information and Broadcasting, at which post he remained till 2018.

Other than translating three other novels by Vishwas Patil, he has also brought into English the novels of the young Marathi writer Avadhoot Dongare, as also the works of celebrated writers like Bhau Padhye, Rangnath Pathare and Anant Deshmukh. His translation of the Marathi autobiography of Dr. Savita Ambedkar, *Dr. Ambedkaraanchyaa Sahavaasast*, has recently been released by Penguin Random House, India.

OTHER BOOKS BY VISHWAS PATIL

Mahanayak Subhash Chandra Bose
Panipat
Sambhaji

VISHWAS PATIL

TRANSLATED FROM THE MARATHI
BY NADEEM KHAN

SHIVAJI MAHASAMRAT

• VOLUME ONE •
THE WHIRLWIND

eka

eka

First published in Marathi as *Mahasamrat: Zanzawat – Khand 1* in 2022 by Mehta Publishing House

First published in English as *The Whirlwind* in 2022 by Eka, an imprint of Westland Books, a division of Nasadiya Technologies Private Limited

No. 269/2B, First Floor, 'Irai Arul', Vimalraj Street, Nethaji Nagar, Allappakkam Main Road, Maduravoyal, Chennai 600095

Westland and the Westland logo are the trademarks of Nasadiya Technologies Private Limited, or its affiliates.

Copyright © Vishwas Patil, 2022

Vishwas Patil asserts the moral right to be identified as the author of this work.

ISBN: 9789395073790

10 9 8 7 6 5 4 3 2 1

This is a work of fiction. Names, characters, organisations, places, events and incidents are either products of the author's imagination or used fictitiously.

All rights reserved

Typeset by Jojy Philip, New Delhi 110 015
Printed at Parksons Graphics Pvt Ltd

No part of this book may be reproduced, or stored in a retrieval system, or transmitted in any form or by any means, electronic, mechanical, photocopying, recording, or otherwise, without express written permission of the publisher.

CONTENTS

Dramatis Personae		vii
1.	The Craving For Struggle	1
2.	The Flaming Battlefield of Bhatwadi	18
3.	The Commander-in-chief of Bijapur	48
4.	The Resolve for Sovereignty	58
5.	The Plough of the Donkey	69
6.	Tears on the Bank of Kukadi	83
7.	In the Kingdom of Pemgiri	102
8.	Here Shahaji, There Shah Jahan	118
9.	Our Sun, Our Earth, Our Resolve	136
10.	The Chains of Mahuli and Externment	152
11.	In Bengaluru—Under the Tutelage of His Father	165
12.	Training for the Mission	187
13.	Assault against Slavery	204
14.	The Suvarnakumbh of Freedom	217
15.	On the Jinji Front	233
16.	The Battle of Purandar	248
17.	Assault on Jawali	267
18.	Prabalgadh—the Goddess of Wealth	289
19.	A Challenge in the Durbar	295

20.	'If you go, you will never return'	304
21.	Afzal Khan at the Threshold of Swarajya	318
22.	Netaji Palkar	334
23.	The Diplomats Meet	345
24.	The Treacherous Trail of Radtondi	359
25.	Afzal's Camp on the Koyna Bank	376
26.	Priming the Spring Traps	389
27.	The Challenge and the Battle-obsessed Champions	402
28.	The Confrontation	411
29.	Funeral and Felicitation	428

DRAMATIS PERSONAE

Afzal Khan	supreme commander of the Adilshah of Bijapur
Ali Adilshah	Mohammadshah's son and successor
Ankush Khan	captain of the Bijapur army under Afzal Khan
Badi Begum	queen and wife of Mohammadshah
Bahirji Naik	commander-in-chief of Shivaji's espionage network
Baji Prabhu Deshpande	general in Shivaji's army
Burhan Nizamshah	the king of Nizamshahi sultanate of Ahmednagar
Dadaji Lohkare	Shahaji's companion from Bijapur days
Dadoji Kond'dev	Shahaji's lieutenant and friend
Daulat Khan	prime minister of Bijapur; also known as Khawaas Khan
Deepa Devi	Shahaji's mother
Dundey Khan	general in the Bijapur army under Afzal Khan
Girijabai	Jijabai's mother
Gomaji Baba Pansambal	clerk and assistant to Jijabai
Hanumantrao Morey	Shivaji's wife Jaishri's father; also younger brother of Yashvantrao, jagirdar of Jawali

Ibrahim Adilshah	Sultan of Bijapur, Mohammadshah's father
Jayantibai	Shahaji's elder son Sambhaji sr.'s wife
Jijabai	Shahaji's wife and Shivaji's mother. (Also referred to as Jijausaheb, Jiu, Aausaheb, Matoshri and Masaheb)
Kanhoji Jedhe	lieutenant of Randullah of Bijapur; later a captain in Shahaji's army
Khelkarn Bhosale	alias Babaji Bhosale, son of Shahaji's cousin Kheloji Bhosale
Kheloji Bhosale	Shahaji's cousin, Mambaji's elder brother
Koyaji	Shahaji's son from a concubine
Krishnaji Bhaskar Kulkarni	Afzal Khan's emissary
Ladli Begum	Afzal Khan's favourite wife
Lakhoji Jadhavrao	Raja of Sindhkhed, father of Jijabai
Malik Ambar	chief secretary to Nizamshahi rulers of Ahmednagar
Maloji	Shahaji's father
Mohammadshah	Ibrahim Adilshah's son and successor
Moropant Peshwa	prime minister of Shivaji's kingdom
Mambaji Bhosale	cousin of Shahaji, son of Vithobaji
Murari Jagdev Pandit	lieutenant of Daulat Khan, the prime minister of Bijapur
Netaji Palkar	Shivaji's close companion and also a warrior in his army
Pantaji Gopinath	administrator in the Lakhoji household; later moved with Shahaji
Prataprao Morey	brother of Yashvantrao, jagirdar of Jawali
Putlabai	Shivaji's wife from the Palkar household
Raghunath Ballal Sabnis	an administrator in Shivaji's goverment

Randullah Khan	general in the Bijapur army and a friend of Shahaji
Rustam-e-Zamaan	general in the Bijapur army and son of Randullah Khan
Sayyad Banda	Afzal Khan's bodyguard
Sambhaji Kavaji	Shivaji's bodyguard
Sambhaji sr. (also referred to as Shambhu)	Shahaji and Jijabai's elder son
Shahajiraje Bhosale	powerful Maratha commander of South India, son of Maloji Bhosale
Shah Jahan	Mughal ruler of India
Shaista Khan	captain in the Mughal army and Aurangzeb's uncle
Shareefji Bhosale	Shahaji's younger brother
Shivaji	Shahaji Bhosale and Jijabai's son; founder of Hindavi swarajya. (Also referred to variously as Shivba, Shivraya, Shivajiraje)
Shivaji's wives	Gunvantabai Ingale, Kashibai Jadhav, Lakshmibai alias Jaishribai Morey, Sagunabai Shirke, Saibai Nimbalkar, Sakvarabai Gayakwad, Soyrabai Mohite
Tanaji Malusare	trusted captain of Shivaji
Vishwasrao Dighe	commander in Shivaji's espionage network
Vithoji Bhosale	Shahaji's father Maloji Bhosale's brother
Vyankoji	Shahaji's son from Tukabai
Yashvantrao alias Chandrarao Morey	jagirdar of Jawali

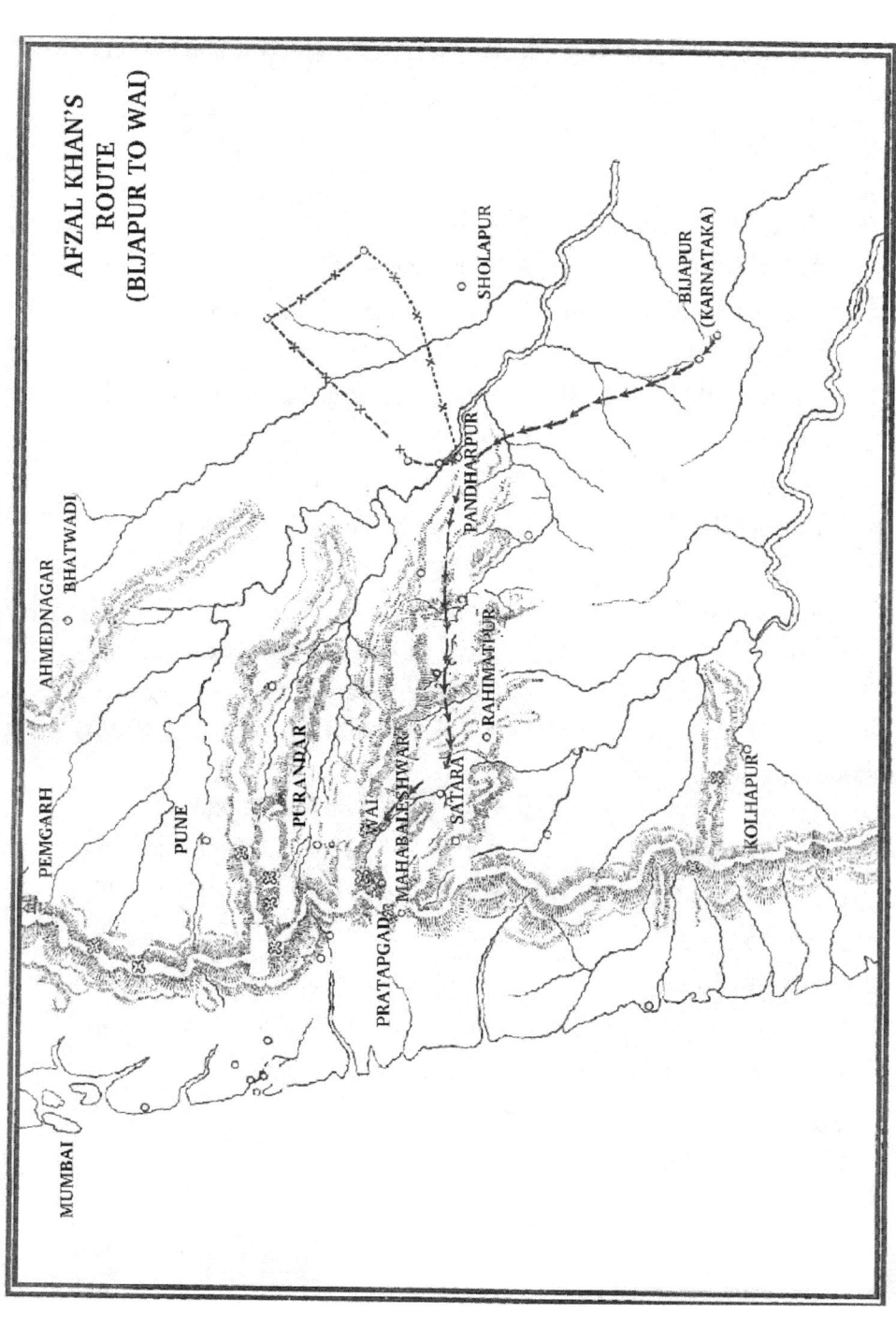

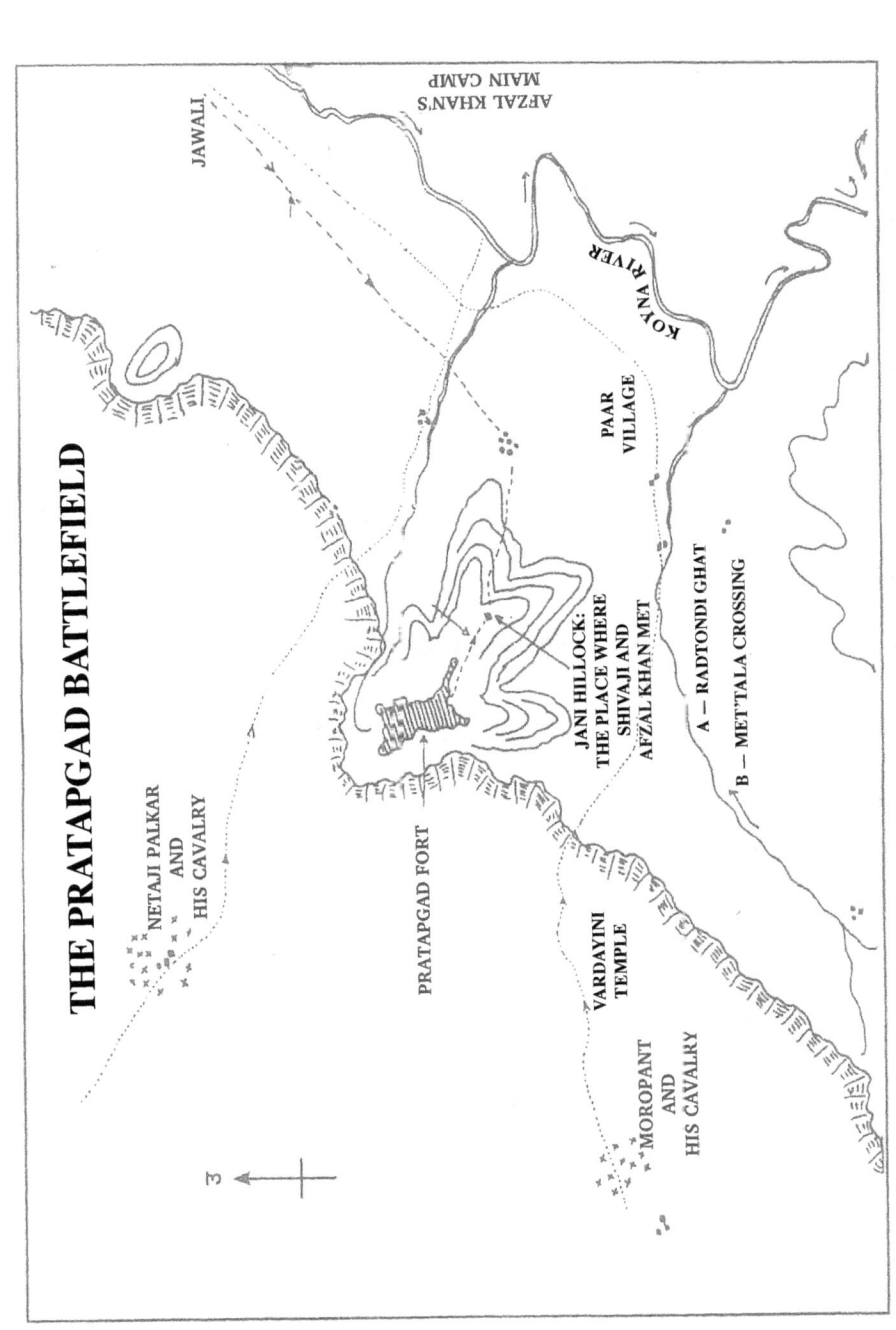

1

THE CRAVING FOR STRUGGLE

JULY 1629

The palaces that Malik Ambar had built in the town of Khacki, the manors of the chieftains, the newly constructed temples, the Ambar canal that supplied water to the town, the windmills that turned the huge wooden pails for drawing water, the mosques, the inns that took care of traveller comforts—they had all been left far behind. What lay in front now was dense vegetation and a range of mountains on the other side.

A dozen or so well-built palanquin bearers were moving with their load at a quick sprint, their dark, lithe bodies bathed in perspiration. Two hundred horses galloped ahead of the royal palanquin and another two hundred followed. A squad of twenty camels had been placed in front of and behind the caravan that shuffled along like graceless old hags, their backs loaded with small cannons like 'shaaheens' and grenade-launchers. The caravan was adequately armed to seriously scotch the fancy of a passing enemy or a bunch of wayside robbers.

The occupant of the palanquin was no ordinary royalty of the garden variety. She was somebody special.

Whenever one shoulder began to tire, the bearers would lower the palanquin, move over to the other side and resume their brisk lope. The ebony palanquin was decorated with gold and silver tassels and carried diaphanous silk drapes. The lady inside was about twenty-five years old. Singularly beautiful, she was fair and delicate as a lotus stem. Her head of lush, silken hair swayed across her face like monsoon clouds flitting over a lustrous full moon. Her delicate features, straight, sharp nose and pearly teeth had the resplendence of a finely tempered sword.

A jewel-inlaid pendant travelled down along a delicate, jewel-studded chain through the parting of her dense black hair to rest on her luminescent brow. Gold bracelets on her upper arm, gem-laden bangles, toe-rings, tinkling anklets gracing her feet and her brocaded saree—she could have been an artist's imagination of a goddess.

Jijau pushed the half open drape further aside and peeped out at the blue sky with satisfaction. Her gaze then travelled down to the dense green earth racing below her. The regions of Khadki and Daulatabad were particularly known for the absence of rains. However, the previous two months had seen unaccustomed rainfall, and now it was the month of Shraavan. The swaying crops in the fields were smiling; the farmers were smiling too. Streams and rivulets had sprung up everywhere, and they were gurgling with a new awareness of life.

Four days ago, Jijau had taken the carpenter of Paranda to task. She had got him to remove the door of the royal sandalwood palanquin, hinges and all. All she wanted was a gossamer curtain for protection against the sun and cold winds. She had often declared as a matter of principle, 'No curtain should ever separate the ruler from the ruled. We need to get as close to our subjects as possible.' Jijau now tied a light knot to the curtain and pushed it to one side. As she turned a corner and looked out excitedly, she was immediately greeted by a gust of wind.

Her attention was drawn towards the top of the mountain that loomed in front. The grand city of Nizamabad at a distance, the Daulatabad fort inside, the multi-layered, elephantine bastions and the pill-boxes atop them were now clearly visible. The small, rapidly moving cavalry unit crossed the streamlet in front and the hillock beyond it and descended to the other side. A long distance had been covered. The inaccessible Daulatabad fort on top of the mountain, palaces alongside it, mansions, feudal manors and posts of armed soldiers had now fallen comfortably within view. Swaying before the main gate stood squads of elephants, camels and horses.

Jijau's gaze travelled beyond the bastions and palaces right up to the very top where, standing atop the ancient fort, she espied a flag-post silhouetted against fleeting white clouds. The green pennant with the crescent moon and stars fluttering on the post set her temple throbbing and her eyes flashing with anger. She thought of the numerous conversations she'd had as a child with her distinguished father Lakhojirao, the king of Sindkhed. After all these years, she still remembered the bitterness of his voice when he would say, 'Pori, this fort of Daulatabad was once the capital of our ancestors!'

'Capital? Ours?'

'Yes, we Jadhavs are the Yadavs of Devgiri of some three-hundred-odd years ago; Devgiri, the city of gold. Horses and elephants would set off from this very fort to journey, for months together, right up to Delhi-Agra in the north and Rameshwar-Madurai in the south.'

These mountains of Devgiri were theirs! The holy land of Verul that lay beyond the hills in front was theirs too! It was the land ruled by the ancestors of her husband Shahaji. As a matter of fact, it was for setting off for Verul forthwith that Lakhojirao had sent the camel-squad over to Paranda.

It was the first day of the month of Shraavan, and the patriarch had wanted to use this auspicious occasion to take his family along to pay obeisance at the temple of Ghrumeshwar. Why would this thought of taking his entire brood with him have struck him, she wondered. The next thought sent a pleasant tingle down her spine: could her father have somehow heard of the glad tidings? But, no, how was that possible?

So many pleasant memories sprang to her mind at the sight of this place. So deeply intertwined were they with the most unforgettable events of her life. It was inside the walls of that fort visible up there that the Nizamshah had got the huge marriage pandal erected. That was where she had first set eyes upon a husband of the eminence of Shahajiraja. The sensation was quite similar to pulling a pot out of an abandoned well and finding it full of gold.

Seven-year-old Jiu was sitting on the steps of the Sindkhed palace, applying henna to her soft little hands. The wedding date had been decided, setting off a spate of sprucing-up operations among her friends under the watchful eye of senior matrons. Around that time, she'd heard the administrators telling each other: 'This injunction of love has arrived from Nizam Padshah to tell Lakhojirao that even if the daughter is his, the king himself will be standing in as the bridegroom's uncle. The marriage, therefore, will take place in his capital city of Daulatabad with royal fanfare. Elephants, camels, horses, cannons, all will be arranged by him. He has mandated that he will bear the entire expenditure.'

The Padshah Nizam Burhan Shah had lived up to his word. If it had been his own daughter getting married, he couldn't have improved on the fanfare and pageantry that accompanied the occasion. Jijau had been brought over from Sindkhed to Daulatabad in a marriage procession that consisted of twenty-one strong, handsome elephants belonging to the finest Assamese and Malabari breeds, richly caparisoned and decorated right up to their toenails. The lead elephant carried a canopy that stood on posts of the purest gold. Under that canopy sat the bewitchingly beautiful princess of Sindkhed.

It was from this canopy, later, that she first sighted the man who would be her husband and her destiny as he rode in from under the main arch of the Daulatabad fort. Smart, handsome, well-built, the sixteen-year-old Shahaji was the epitome of youth, energy, valour and heroism. He came riding atop a horse that could only belong to the king of gods. Tall, broad-backed, fiery and sparkling white with black ears and tail—an animal such as this had never before been seen in the land of men. The bride wasn't the only person to swoon at the sight. The guests who had gathered from as far away as Jaipur, Delhi and Bhaganagar also watched in goggle-eyed wonderment at the arrival of this gorgeous prince astride his magnificent steed.

When Jijau had settled down in the Bhosale waada,[1] Shahaji related the story behind the acquisition of that superlative horse. His younger brother Shareefji was two years junior to him. There was this town called Sarangkheda, beyond Khandesh in the east. The horse market there enjoyed such prestige that buyers and sellers from far-flung lands like the Arab countries, Turkey, Russia, Burma, Ceylon, Java and Sumatra would attend. The dealers would put their Arab, Turkish, Russian and Paanchaali animals on exhibition for the indulgence and delectation of kings and emperors, soldiers and sportsmen. Many of the horses on display often cost as much as a decent-sized palace, and their true worth could be

---

[1] manor

estimated only by the most knowledgeable dealers, stable owners, grooms and other hippophiles.

The market that had assembled at Sarangkheda some time before Shahaji's marriage overflowed with thousands and thousands of horses, but there was one animal that had become the centre of all conversation: a Turkish thoroughbred called Dilpaak. The trader to whom the horse belonged was relishing all this talk and attention, like the father of a beautiful princess shooing away pedigreed princes lining up at his palace gates for his daughter's hand. Kings and emperors, barons and grandees were willing to empty out their treasuries to buy the magnificent creature. They just wanted the trader to name the price, but the good man simply refused to oblige. 'How do you put a price on Allah's creation?' he would respond cryptically. 'My horse is beyond pricing and beyond prices.'

The moneybags had begun to tire from paying visits to his stable. They simply couldn't gauge what the trader wanted. It was after a long while that the man finally announced, 'My Dilpaak is not for sale like all the other animals in the market. I shall hand my darling over to the man who I believe has the love, skill and resources to take care of it.'

Visitors in thousands would weave circles round the handsome horse, but the trader remained unimpressed. Not a single worthy person could he locate among the hordes that came ogling. Then, one day, a bunch of young lads came and gathered round the animal. A twelve-year-old lad among them, the handsomest of them all, couldn't restrain himself and began caressing the horse's back with great tenderness. Dilpaak too, who had resented and vigorously shaken away such endearments from others, reciprocated the boy's warmth in equal measure, rubbing its muzzle against his chest. The young boy was in a state of stupor when he muttered, 'I'm not going without this horse …'

'Look, son,' came a voice from behind him, 'this horse is not for sale.'

'Understand, chaachaa, that I too am not stirring without taking this prodigy along with me.'

The trader gazed carefully at the boy's resolute face and divined that this was blood of the highest order. Satisfied with what he saw, he shot out, 'Who are you?'

'My name is Shareefji, and I am the younger brother of Shahaji of the Bhosale clan.'

'So, how did your attention zero in on this frightfully expensive animal?'

'I can see that my brother will blaze like the sun when he goes riding on this horse for his wedding.'

'But I am not selling this horse! Why did you think I would?'

'If you don't, chaachaa, you will be the loser!' responded the lad cheekily.

'Hmmm? How's that?'

'You will know when you actually cast your eyes on my brother, Shahajiraje.'

The trader let out a loud laugh, gathered the details of his address and packed the boys off home with a few kind words.

On the fourth morning after this meeting, when Shareefji got up as usual for his morning ride, he was flabbergasted at finding the trader poking around the stables. It appeared that he had begun this operation quite early. He had already taken a round of all the stables on the campus and checked out every little detail—the stakes to which the horses were tethered, the racks where the fodder was stored, the quality of the grams and oats served, even the place where they were taken for a bath and scrub. Amazingly, he had also found the time to make friends with his brother Shahaji.

The trader returned after a couple of days with Dilpaak in tow and handed over the reins to the awestruck Shareefji. The completely overwhelmed Shahaji offered to pay whatever price the trader named, but the man was adamant. All he was persuaded to take was the travel expenditure from Turkey and back, and a little bit more for sundry expenses. The entire Bhosale court was bewildered at this unprecedented magnanimity.

'Why do you want to suffer this loss?' Shahaji couldn't help exclaiming.

'Loss? It's no loss at all, huzoor. For a long time, I've been looking for a good master, a good house for my Dilpaak. And now my wish has been fulfilled. It's found angels for masters and heaven for a home.'

'This sounds great to hear, huzoor, but what have we done to deserve this praise?'

'Huzoor, I can see that you Marathas love your animals as much as you love your own children. I've been around the world but have yet to come across any other people like you who are as devoted to their animals.'

This legend that the horse had brought with itself helped it ease its way into Jijau's affection. This was the horse that, on the day of her marriage, had put the lavishly caparisoned royal elephants in the shade.

Jadhavrao's huge tent had been erected right in front of the main gate of the fort. The massive pavilion was generally used during campaigns. A dozen or so smaller tents were for the servants, with horses frisking around on the open space in front, elephants happily tucking in their fodder, and the children of the Jadhav household running between them playing hide-and-seek or frolicking on the trees nearby.

Suddenly the clip-clop of hoof-beats and the arrival of the palanquins sent an electric current in the atmosphere. The bearers lowered the lead palanquin and Jijau stepped out promptly. When she saw four caparisoned horses along with their grooms all decked up and waiting in regal finery, she understood that her father and brothers were preparing to leave for the court on an urgent matter. As she advanced towards the pavilion, a bunch of excited little girls rushed out giggling and clapping and shouting, 'Taisaheb's arrived! Taisaheb's arrived!'

The sound of the excited chatter brought Lakhojirao outside, dressed in formal court wear, and behind him emerged Jijau's mother Girijabai. She rushed forward and took her daughter in a tight, long embrace. Then, without releasing her, she moved her a little back and looked admiringly at her slim, comely form. Her two brothers Raghavrao and Achalojirao and nephew Yashvantrao—ranging from ages seventeen to twenty-five—then stepped out, and with unconcealed joy, bent low to salute her: 'Mujra, Taisaheb.'

The camp had suddenly come alive. Everybody was buzzing and swarming around their darling Jijau like bees around a hive. The senior among the *choli-parkar* clad girls broke in, held her hands and asked point-blank in a loud voice, 'Speak, Jiutai, what do you feel like eating?'

'What do you mean feel like eating?'

'We've collected everything you may require. So, what's it you want—tamarind or amla?'

This triggered a roar of laughter among all present—parents, brothers, their wives and children and the assembled servants, causing Jijau to blush deeply. She ran up to her father, placed her head upon his chest, and thumping it with her fist, she said in mock complaint, 'What's this, Aabasaheb, why have you people decided to make fun of me?'

'Pori, I'm your father!'

'Ishh! What other gossip have people been feeding you with?'

'Look, girl, the slightest whiff of a whisper in the enemy's camp reaches me within no time. And when it's the news of a grandchild soon to swing in my arms, how can I possibly not know?'

'So, the very winds serve as your couriers, do they?'

'What nonsense you talk, girl!'

'How else could this news have reached you at such speed?'

Low stools were laid to one side, with colourful rangolis around it, indicating that Girijabai had performed the ritual of *aukshan* for her husband and three sons before they set off for the king's court. This act of swirling the holy flame round the face was performed to neutralise the evil eye and ward off misfortunes of all kinds. The men were in an obvious hurry to leave, but the temptation of having a quick chat with his darling daughter was too much for Lakhoji to resist. He seated himself on the stool and said, 'Pori, this time round it's going to be a really big affair with you.'

'What are you talking about, Baba?'

'I have this strong premonition that the child in your womb this time may well be a rare phenomenon! An incarnation of some divinity!'

'You are turning quite clairvoyant, Aabasaheb, aren't you?' Jijau turned towards her mother and said, 'Aai, this is my sixth conception, after five earlier abortions, but this time the portents are so sharply different. I'm deluged by all kinds of fantastic images: I see enchanting arches in the rainbow, golden canopies seem to make my heart sway, all of this interspersed with the loud eructation of ferocious carnivores.'

'These really are strange presages indeed!'

'Strange, isn't it, that this urge for sour foods should spring up in me just when both my husband's house and my father's house are preparing for the battlefield? The signals behind these omens are perplexing!'

'But tell me, Jiu, why did you come alone? Where's my son-in-law?'

'He said he'd ride directly to Verul.'

As they sat chatting, the topic of politics sprang up. The conversation turned towards the strange and eccentric nature of the person who presently occupied the Nizamshahi throne. As long as Malik Ambar was alive, the kingdom was in safe hands; he was a man of his word. As Lakhojirao began turning impatient to leave, Girijabai chipped in, 'How can it hurt if you are not present in the durbar today?'

'Whatever for?'

'Well, we could all set off together for Verul as we had decided.'

'Look, it's neither fear that drives me nor greed. I'm the master of my sword.'

There was an intangible worry, however, that seemed to have insinuated itself. Raghavrao's voice was loaded with concern when he said, 'Circumstances are not good, really, Aisaheb. Looks to me that we Jadhavs were in too much of a hurry to abandon service with the Delhi Mughals and cross over to Daulatabad.'

'Why do you say that, boy?'

'Nothing seems to be much right with our patron Nizam Padshah. He has taken to drinking heavily these days and has become awfully distrustful. And now we have Hameed Khan's wife who has him eating out of her hands.'

Stress lines sprang upon Lakhojirao's brow. 'Well,' he said as he cleared his throat after a moment of silence, 'Hameed Khan and I had had quite an open conversation before I'd renounced my fealty to the empire at Delhi. I've returned to my service with the Nizamshah with an open heart and without any preconditions. And then we have my son-in-law Shahajiraje too in the Nizam's service!'

'That's where the problem lies, Aabasaheb!'

'Why should this be a problem, pori?'

'Shouldn't it? A distinguished warrior like you and an equally illustrious son-in-law coming together to serve the same durbar, won't that make you a powerful team and tilt the scales heavily in your favour? And if this power equation can be a cause of envy to our own relatives, what do you think rank outsiders are going to read into it?'

'Oh, come on, Jiu, how's that going to make a difference?'

'How is it not, Aabasaheb? People have already seen in the battle of Bhatwadi how the entry of Shahajiraje changed the course of the battle within a short time. The coming together of an accomplished son-in-law and a seasoned father-in-law will seriously disrupt the interests of some others. Many seniors will find the space for their intrigues shrinking, petty administrators and clerks will find their channels of underhand dealings getting blocked!'

'Hmm! You do have a point. However big the palace, there are bound to be drainages underneath, and where there are drains, rats and mice are bound to flourish in their filth.'

Trumpets are not blown and kettle-drums are not beaten in the Nizam's palace of mirrors, the Aaeena Mahal, unless there is a special occasion. In recent times, in terms of grandeur, the Nizamshahi durbar had begun to be regarded as next only to the Deewaan-e-Khaas of Agra. Its pomp and splendour had been scrupulously maintained. When the musical instruments began playing in its portals, the city of Daulatabad knew that something grand was afoot.

Verging on eighty, the strong, well-built Lakhoji Jadhav entered the outer arch with commanding steps, like an elephant on a stroll. Following him were his three princes exuding equal grace and dignity. The foursome were a sight for the Bhaganagari people to ogle at. The pipes broke out into loud music.

The centrepiece of the Aaeena Mahal was a six-foot-high dais made of sandalwood, on which rested the peacock throne embellished with the most intricate carvings and inlay work. On this stunningly beautiful seat sat Burhan Nizamshah. On either side of the throne were tall lamps, lit up for the occasion. Next to them stood comely adolescent girls fanning the monarch with hand-held fans and sprigs of fragrant flowers. The ceiling of the hall was artistically done in Persian wood. The numerous pillars holding up the ceiling were also inlaid with colourful Persian mirrors, and when they reflected the lights of the lamps, they seemed to fill the entire durbar with effervescent energy.

The ostentatiously carved doors of this magnificent hall would open only for very special occasions. As Lakhoji and his handsome boys stood in the front row, they wondered along with the other courtiers what special occasion could have prompted this assembly. They were pleasantly surprised at the new chamber for the royal ladies that had lately been added to the right of the throne. Right in front sat Hameed Khan's handsome, beautifully proportioned wife, Noorani Begum. Her steadily increasing interference in state matters and her intimacy with the Nizam were subjects that carried great entertainment value in marketplace gossip.

The pipes and drums on the other side began their music as the heralds and court-criers announced the commencement of the durbar. Nizamshah swept his imperious gaze over the assembled courtiers. Now in his fifties, he wore an elegant silk pagree with intricate designs embroidered in threads of gold. At the front end of the pagree was pinned a golden crest in the shape of a peacock's graceful neck, encrusted with pearls and precious stones. He wore a loose, deep-red, full-sleeved robe, and the red arrogance of his eyes indicated that he was still working at absorbing the alcohol he had been imbibing across many a night.

The deliberations began with an officer loudly announcing the name of Lakhojirao Jadhavrao, the Raja of Sindkhed, and inviting him to step forward for felicitation by the Nizam. Lakhoji felt a great sense of satisfaction and pride at being publicly commended in this manner. A spontaneous smile flashed behind his lush, white side-whiskers as he took four steps forward with great dignity. The assembled nobles gazed respectfully at this doughty Maratha warrior who, for the past sixty years, had been a force to reckon with in the politics of the Deccan. He stood respectfully, holding his sword and shield against his chest.

'A lion's brood are lions too!' the officer went on. 'Dauntless warrior Raghavrao, valiant Achalojirao and fearless Yashvantrao may also step forward to receive their rewards!'

The three young men stepped forward too, their chests perceptibly swelling with pride, and came and stood next to Lakhojirao. Three sardars—Safdar Khan, Farhaad Khan and Moti Khan—moved towards them with slow steps and austere faces, each carrying a golden tray holding some expensive item covered with silk kerchiefs. The well-wishers of Lakhojirao were thrilled at this honour being bestowed upon the entire Jadhav clan, but Noorani Begum's face had turned red behind the flimsy curtains.

Burhan Nizamshah cast an appraising glance at Lakhojirao's well-exercised body and said in a honeyed voice tinged with sarcasm, 'Lakhojirao, it's quite impossible for me to find a more valiant soldier, a more respected and venerable comrade than you anywhere in this world.'

'I'm grateful, my liege!'

'But if a person like you, for whatever reason, goes and joins the Mughal Padshah in the field of battle, what will be our fate then?'

This direct assault flustered the old man. He looked behind to see hundreds of eyes staring curiously at him, which deeply hurt his self-esteem. He said in a voice choked with emotion, 'Huzoor, this can never happen!'

'But what if it happens to be true?'

'Impossible, huzoor! How can the past be overlooked? This body of mine has faithfully served not one or two, but seven consecutive Nizamshahs across forty unbroken years! How can the stigma of betrayal ever be applied to me?'

The Nizamshah signalled with his eyes to four of his closest servants. Mellifluous notes of pipes accompanied the announcement in the durbar, 'The sons and grandson of Raja Lakhojirao of Sindkhed: brave-hearts Raghavrao, Achalojirao and Yashvantrao may now be presented with the royal trophies!'

The mild smile playing upon the visage of Nizamshah brought the temperature in the durbar down substantially. Lakhoji signalled with his eyes to his bewildered boys, which suggested that they should take it in their stride and not get upset. This was quite the norm in durbar dealings.

The three sardaars stepped forward with the trays balanced in their arms, and went down on their knees before the three princes. Lakhoji was deeply gratified at the thought that the Nizam would soon invest his three heroes with robes of honour and raise them to the rank of sardaars. He knew very well that other than Shahaji Bhosale, he alone had the power to change the direction of the wind in the four kingdoms of the Deccan.

But the rhythm of the music suddenly changed. From an auspicious melody it suddenly switched to the drum-beats of war. At the same time was heard the raucous voice of the Nizam himself as he screeched, 'Execute!' At that command, the three sardaars threw the silk coverings off the trays to reveal short, stubby but extremely sharp swords that had lain concealed underneath. They picked up the swords, flashed them in the air, and brought them down upon the necks of the Jadhav boys as they stood bowing respectfully before the Nizam. The heads separated in one fell blow and went rolling towards the sandalwood dais. The bodies crumpled where they had stood, blood gushing from the severed necks.

Lakhoji froze. He couldn't cry, he couldn't scream, he couldn't move his limbs. As he began losing balance, a few arms from behind steadied him. Blood was still bubbling out, unchecked, from the severed heads of his sons and grandson. Something then snapped inside him. Letting out a hysterical cry of 'Reyyy Nijaamaaa!!!', he pulled his sword out and leapt towards the dais. This was the moment for which the Nizam's four servants had been alerted. They had quietly taken position on four sides of the old warrior. And now they converged on him, weapons drawn, and lashed at him ferociously. Despite knowing that resistance was hopeless, Lakhoji let his warrior instincts take over and swung his sword savagely at his assailants. But the contest was starkly uneven and the stabs and slashes kept mounting till Lakhoji finally collapsed shredded and bleeding, but breathing still. A few breaths laboriously drawn, eyes spitting fire as they turned towards the vilely smirking Nizam and finally hardening to glass. Lakhoji had breathed his last.

~oOo~

It was twilight, and the horses were galloping through bushes throbbing with the sound of crickets. Jijau in the lead was cutting through the cold evening air, with her friends struggling to keep pace with her. Daulatabad was not at all far from Verul, and her father and brothers had assured her that they would come straight over to the Ghruneshwar temple after they had finished with their durbar engagements. She had waited at the temple till it had started turning dark, and had finally turned her horse homewards, her mind beset with a thousand doubts.

As it turned darker, the clip-clop of the horses' hooves and the rasping of their froth-laced breath had begun to hit the ears more sharply. One of the friends was not liking this adventure at all. 'Why did you have to be so obstinate, Jiu?' she cribbed, easing alongside her. 'Your mother was right in suggesting that we all visit the temple together, but you and your stubbornness!'

'Yes, we did get stranded there,' said another, 'but those poor priests at the temple and the villagers who had assembled at Verul, how eagerly they had been waiting for the arrival of Lakhojikaka! Even as the sun had begun to set!'

'But then, girls, what could be the reason for Aabasaheb not arriving?' groaned Jijau and rapped the horse hard to release her anxiety.

All in all, it had been a bad day for Jijau. As she had been setting off from the Paranda fort, Shahaji had assured her that whatever the pressure of work, he would catch up with her. In a worst-case scenario, he would get into the Ghruneshwar sanctorum even as the prayers were being performed. But this hadn't happened either. Neither of them had turned up, neither the father nor the husband.

They had now crossed the valley and could see the flames of the torches burning in the cavities of the thick outer walls of the Daulatabad fort. Silhouettes of soldiers on sentry duty could also be discerned. Contiguous to the outer walls of the fort was the township of Nizamabad, lit up here and there with torches and big hurricane lanterns. The area around the tank, however, was clothed in pitch darkness.

As she neared her camp, the strange sight in front made Jijau's heart lurch violently. Could her people have brought down the tents, rolled up the cloth walls and moved away? But how was that possible without keeping her informed?

Jijau reached the camp and jumped off her horse, sick with anxiety. It looked devastated. The cloth walls had vanished, allowing the night wind free passage. The light of the few tiny earthen lamps showed the tent-poles uprooted, snapped rope-ends dancing in the wind, and people scattered everywhere as if felled by a dread disease. Some lay shrunk into a ball, some others just stretched out, disconsolate, all shivering in the cold. They seemed to have lost the strength to stand up on their feet. Who could have brought the entire camp down as if with a stone-roller? Was it an accident or a deliberately inflicted mischief?

Jijau rushed into the open tent, desperately trying to call out to her mother, but she could not find her voice. As she dashed forward, she stumbled on something that lay in her path. She looked down to realise that it was a rumpled human body. In the dim orange light of a lamp, she saw that it was headless. When she recognised the clothes, a tight knot sprang in her stomach and chest that made breathing difficult. A little further down was the head, lying like a coconut fallen off a tree. She ran up to it, turned it round to see the face, and let out a heart-rending scream, 'Yashvantrao! My brother!! How!!! How!!!!'

Distraught with grief, she looked up to see a shattered old woman sitting limp, leaning against the post of the tent in front. 'Aaisaheb!' she screeched as she leapt forward, 'What's happened here? What calamity is this?' As she was about to gather her limp mother in her arms, her eyes slipped downwards to her lap in which lay the mangled body of her father. She lost spirit and sat heavily on the ground, unable to take her bulging eyes away from the gory sight. She slowly raised her hands to her head, held it tight, and started rocking slowly, whimpering as she rocked. The rocking and whimpering intensified as the enormity of the disaster began sinking in. The hands that lay lifeless there, those were the hands that would ruffle the hair of tiny Jiu as she slept in his lap! That mountain of a man, her father, how could he have got rubbed out just like that?

Now Jijau's gaze travelled out into the darkness outside the tent, and there she saw forms emerging from the blackness of the night—servants, relatives, water-carriers, cooks, stepping tentatively forward, shivering as they neared her. The thought that immediately struck Jijau was that they were shell-shocked, terrified, lost; they were looking up to her to lead them out of this valley of death.

Pantaji Gopinath gathered his courage and pushed himself forward. As Jijau stood up, he gathered her in his arms and said, 'Get hold of yourself, Taisaheb. You are our hope! You are the hope of all of Maharashtra!'

'Pantaji kaka, whose villainy is this?'

'It's the Nizam's doing.'

'But why? What did he have against my great father? Why did he go to this ultimate extreme?'

'The Nizam had been fed some false reports—that Lakhojirao was on the verge of shifting allegiance back to the Delhi empire.'

'People blabber all the time, but should that have led to this? A man who spent over half a century in the interest of the Sultan's glory, did he deserve to be delivered this satanic reward?'

A bustle began outside when Jijau's uncle Jagdeorao and brother Bahadurrao Jadhavrao arrived with a bunch of others. They had hurriedly arranged for some bullock carts to clear out of this camp at the earliest, and had begun dismantling and rolling up in right earnest.

This utterly unexpected, dastardly blow had set Jijau fuming. The more she thought about it, the more she lost control of herself. She couldn't stomach the thought of just sitting on her hands and crying over the perfidy of the Nizamshah. Then, a look of decision descended in her blazing eyes. She went up to a sword hanging by a post, pulled it out of its sheath and strode out of the tent. Despite being in a state of shock, Girijabai signalled to Pantaji to go see what her inflamed girl was up to. Jijau leapt on to the horse standing outside, slapped its back and shot off into the darkness in the direction of the fort. 'Wait, pori!' Pantaji screamed after her and set off in chase.

She hadn't gone very far when the sound of the hoof-beats of a dozen or so horses struck her ears. The first thought that crossed her mind was that it could be the enemy coming after her. She pulled the reins of her horse and tightened the loose end of her saree round her waist. But the leading horse that emerged out of the darkness was an animal she knew very well. It was Shahaji heading towards the Jadhav camp.

Word about the tragic event at the durbar had obviously reached his ears, which was why he blocked the passage of Jijau's horse. When she tried to dodge him and somehow squeeze her way forward, Shahaji jumped down from his horse, took hold of her horse's reins with one hand and held Jijau's wrist with the other. 'Don't, Raje,' she yelled, 'don't you try stopping me!'

'Wait Jiu, where are you off to?'

'To drink the blood of my enemy!'

It was with the greatest difficulty that Shahaji managed to have her dismount. He then put his arms tightly round her and began to reason with her. 'You have to get a hold on yourself, Jiu! Calm down! You have a baby in your womb, Jiu, and that too in a delicate state!'

The mention of her state of pregnancy sent a shiver up and down her spine. She shuddered visibly as she applied massive effort and brought her runaway rage under control. She held Shahaji by his shirt-front, pulled him towards herself and spat out, 'All right, Raje, I have this *dohale*, the wish of a pregnant woman, that I want you to fulfil.'

'What is your *dohale*?'

'I want ash to eat.'

'Ash? What ash?'

'Look up there in the distance, that glittering capital of Daulatabad that belongs to the Nizam! Go right now and burn it to ashes! It's the hot ash of that flaming durbar that I want to eat! Please, Raje! Satiate my desire!'

2

THE FLAMING BATTLEFIELD
OF BHATWADI

Shahajiraje and Jijausaheb had galloped off that very night to Paranda, with six or seven hundred horses riding front and back. The ruthless killing of Lakhojiraja and their family had shaken their life to its very foundation. The couple had been living through the strangest of times—sitting atop the highest peak of success one moment and wallowing in the pit of defeat and despair the next.

As they were cutting their way through the cold, biting darkness, the five years of strife and storm they had encountered stood before their eyes …

1624

Whenever the horses of the ambitious Mughals had to gallop southwards, they had to cross the Nizamshahi province that fell on their way; and whenever the people of Bijapur had to move north, they too had to cross the same patch of land—the Nizamshahi land. It wasn't a patch by any definition, though. Starting from Rajapur in Konkan, moving up through Kolaba towards Thane and Kalyan, it held on to the Mahuli line and crossed the Sahyadri. It then took the Balaghat mountain range into its fold and moved towards Hyderabad-Bhaganagar. This was the region across which the Nizamshahi kingdom held its dominion.

The Mughal emperor had lately begun talking quite dismissively of the Nizamshahi rule, stating that the Sultanate would collapse within a matter of days. It was true that the Nizamshahi fortunes had been on the decline for the past few years. Its champion Chand Bibi—who, clad merely in her coat-of-mail, had had the dare-devilry to take on a cellar full of dynamite—was no more there to tend to the affairs of the Sultanate. But for all that, the Sultanate still had the services of its standard-bearer in old Malik Ambar who was moving heaven and earth to keep the significance of the Nizamshahi kingdom alive.

After all the various campaigns and invasions and battles, one thing had become eminently clear to both Delhi and Bijapur—they both had one single, powerful adversary, and that was Nizamshah. If the two of them could come together and drown that Sultanate into the Narmada, all the problems related to the Deccan would drown with it.

It was evening time at the Daulatabad fort, and torches and lamps were being set alight when a messenger came running in with frightening news: 'Huzoor, it's treachery, it's treachery!'

'Why? What happened?'

'Forgive my impudence, Lord, but the news is bad Jahangir, the emperor of Hindustan, has dispatched an army of eighty thousand in this direction. It is clearly his intention to swallow up Daulatabad.'

A senior official, who was also the Sultan's relative, took forward the messenger's theme and said, 'The imperial army is marching with such strength and spirit that we may well get blown away like dry autumnal leaves.'

The emperor leading this expedition, at the head of such a mighty force, was no different from an elephant's foot landing on the jugular. There was prosperity everywhere in the state. The treasury was brimming with gems and precious stones, the armoury and arsenal were loaded, and the granary was overflowing. But an imperial invasion was like a gigantic tidal wave. If the Nizamshahi boat happened to get caught in the current, even the Almighty would find it impossible to pull it out of this misfortune.

Nizam Padshah dispatched a soldier for Malik Ambar to be called over immediately. The soldier returned with the information that Malik Baba had already been alerted by his spies, very early that morning, of the imminence of a battle flaring up; accordingly, the old man was engaged in organising a battle plan. The furrows that had formed on the sultan's face dissolved immediately. Sporting a happy smile on his face, he set off for the front rooftop of the palace. Noticing his wives peeping from behind velvet curtains, he waved out to them to follow him, and four beautiful women trotted out excitedly. The group reached the telescope that had been placed on a raised platform at the front end of the rooftop. They turned the instrument downwards and peeped through the eye-piece at the foot of the fort deep down below.

The wide-open space down there was lit up by hundreds upon hundreds of torches and flambeaus. As Nizamshah sharpened the focus, he saw hundreds of fully armed cavalrymen gathering. Bullock carts carrying cannons were being lined up on a side, while boxes of gunpowder were being loaded on other bullock carts. Looking at the orderly and well-drilled manner in which the work was progressing, it appeared that the Nizamshahi army was forever in a state of readiness to counter any invasion. As the sultan saw his wives' faces light up in glee, he himself bloomed as he said, 'Good, no cause for worry.'

'Why do you say that, huzoor?' asked the senior-most wife.

'Till as long as we have Malik Ambar and that Maratha Shahaji in our camp, why should we entertain any fear?'

The earlier soldier came hurrying over to the terrace. Raising his right fist to his heart and bowing in deference, he delivered the message, 'Huzoor, Shahajiraje's younger brother Shareefji waits outside.' The Nizam nodded.

A Maratha in his mid-twenties stood just inside the range of the amber lamps burning in the parlour. A tunic flaring at the waist, the loose trousers of a chieftain, sporting the rest of the paraphernalia of a soldier like sword and shield, the young man cut an impressive figure. His body language proclaimed his irrepressible spirit and his heroism and courage even from a distance. The Nizam looked towards him with great pride. This younger brother of Shahaji was a renowned archer. People said that nobody in Hindustan could hold a candle to him in the use of javelins and arrows when astride his favourite horse, Dilpaak. 'Yes, Shareefjiraje,' the Nizam addressed him warmly. 'All well? Any cause for worry?'

'Nothing at all, huzoor. Our army will march out of the Khadki camp tomorrow at dawn. Our two army chiefs have some grand strategies worked out.'

'What are those?'

'They have made a decent estimation of where the armies of Mulla Mohammad of Bijapur and of the Emperor of Delhi are most likely to assemble. We have our plans ready for the manner in which we will conduct our assault.'

This was by no means enough to drive Nizamshah's worries away. It was four days since he had heard of the imminent invasion, and preparations for countering the onslaught had begun immediately; but the Delhi army was reported to be eighty-thousand strong and that would be further bolstered by the twenty thousand soldiers of Bijapur, giving the enemy a combined strength of over a hundred thousand. Standing up against this gargantuan force with just about forty thousand soldiers would be a huge challenge. It was in a worried voice that the Sultan queried, 'So, what do you think, son? Do you think we have a decent chance of success?'

'Absolutely, huzoor,' Shareefji responded with enthusiasm. 'Malik Baba instructed me to carry this message to you: he asked me to tell you that you should sleep without a worry in the world. Even if the enemy counts its strength in hundreds of thousands, when valiants like Malik Ambar and the young Maratha Shahaji Bhosale have planted their feet firmly in the battleground, why should you worry at all?'

Nizamshah let out a hearty laugh. He had complete confidence and trust in his two army chiefs. Malik Ambar, of course, brought with him a lifetime of warfare experience. He was seventy-eight years of age, but neither his physical courage nor his zest for the battlefield had waned the tiniest whit. Shahaji, twenty-nine years of age, possessed a handsome, well-built, muscular body. Nizamshah, therefore, felt quite secure placing his weight on these two strong shoulders. His anxiety, however, had nowhere near disappeared. After all, the invaders were no fly-by-night brigands! What was threatening to descend on his land was the tornado of the Mughal army from the one side and the Adilshahi forces from the other.

Nizamshah had this other little curiosity that he thought he would satisfy. 'Tell me this, son, our army is really double-headed, meaning that there are two generals who plan the battle strategy.'

'Yes, huzoor, certainly.'

'But once the regiments have taken position on the battlefield, who among the two issues the final order?'

'I beg your pardon, huzoor?'

'Is it Malik Baba or Shahaji?'

The question flustered Shareefji a little bit. He paused for a while and then began chuckling softly to himself. 'Forgive me, Jahaan-panaah,' he said, 'your question is an equally big riddle for me.'

'Why to you?'

'Because, huzoor, when the battle truly warms up, it completely intoxicates both of them. The fever of battle that shines through their faces makes it impossible to decide whose strategy it is. It looks to me that the final decision seems to have come from a single heart and a single mind.'

The army was on the march and the heavily-built Malik Ambar swayed softly in his royal howdah atop a mountainous Assamese elephant. Giving him company sat Shahajiraje. As the commander-in-chief's seat, the howdah was built of sandalwood and its canopy carried a silver-plated steel roof. From the velvet-lined ceiling hung tassels woven of gold, silver and silk threads. The seating area was covered with thick brocade. For protection against a shower, silk curtains had been gathered and tied to the posts that held the roof, ready for opening up any time the need arose. As the elephant rolled on regally, the gold bells hanging by its neck made a pleasant tinkle. A few other elephants were trailing behind with cannons mounted on their backs.

The team of the brothers Shahaji and Shareefji was as beloved of the Maratha army as Rama and Lakshmana of the Ramayana.

Babaji Bhosale, the nobleman of Verul, had two sons: Maloji and Vithoji. When Maloji had remained childless for quite a long while, his deeply religious wife Deepabai had visited the shrine of the Muslim holy man Shah Shareef at Ahmadnagar. She had taken the vow that in the event of a son being born to her through his intercession, she would name the boy after the holy man. When the boys did arrive, the couple remembered their word and named the elder boy Shahaji and the younger one Shareefji.

Whenever Shahaji was seated in his own canopy, his brother Shareefji would avoid sitting alongside him to the extent possible. Instead of going swinging on elephant-back, he much preferred to go galloping on his fierce and zippy horse Dilpaak.

The animals were moving at a fair pace. Malik Baba would frequently toss an admiring gaze at Shahaji. Originally hailing from the Oromia region of Abyssinia in East Africa, now known as Ethiopia, Malik Baba was sold into slavery at an early age. Black, shiny skin, of medium height and stocky build, he had spread round the waist with age. A lifetime spent in hard labour and vigorous physical exercise had made him strong as a bull. He was known for his unshakeable determination. As he sat in the canopy, his face merged with the darkness of the night. The dim light of the tiny lamp placed in a corner of the howdah, however, picked the glitter of his eyes with amazing clarity.

The night wind had turned cold. For a long while, Malik Baba sat lost in his own thoughts. He was caught in the memories of his childhood. How many events, how many countries and those countless seashores! That dark lad stuffed into a coconut sack by the pirates and smuggled out of Africa! Just a few empty, faceless circles in place of parents! Those slave markets of Arabia! The caravans of camels caparisoned in velvet! The jewellery souks and sweetmeat marts! Then, the many months long journey to India, the lemon tree in front of Baba Shareef's shrine at Ahmadnagar.

Malik Baba reached out for Shahaji's hand and held it in his rough black hand as he spoke in an emotion-laden voice, 'How do I say it, son? I, a Habshi slave, three times I was bought and sold in the four years before I reached Ahmadnagar! I was just a kid then, and the inhuman treatment to which we kids were subjected! Like dogs in the houses of notables! And just so that we didn't create trouble in their harems after reaching adolescence, we were castrated! Like bullocks are! I can only call it the grace of Allah that I found an extremely kindhearted owner in Qazi Hussain. That was the only thing that helped me preserve my manhood.'

'What a life you have seen Baba!'

'Without a doubt! It is nearly impossible for a slave to break the chains on his feet and emerge free. But again, I ran into a benefactor, Chengiz Khan's wife, who showered mountain-sized favours on me.'

'Who was this Chengiz Khan?'

'Oh, he was a minister in the Nizamshahi court. He bought me in the slave market along with crates of dates. When he passed away, his wife freed me for all time from the curse of slavery.'

The army marched on, across rivers, mountains and jungles. During the early morning hours, they would take a break along the bank of some expansive river and rest their weary bones for a few hours. The caretaker staff was instructed accordingly.

The jingling of the bells round the elephant necks created an entrancing ambience all around. The horses trotted along and yet made a decent pace. The thousands of hooves created their own different drumbeats, changing with the changing structure of the soil. When Shahaji reminded Malik Ambar that the enemies' force was more than twice as large as theirs, the old man laughed and said, 'Don't you worry, son. It was just once that I was beaten by the Mughals in the battle of Roshanbagh. Otherwise, right from the time of Akbar down to this Jahangir getting into old age, we haven't ever allowed the Mughal forces to stretch their legs here. Each time that they wanted to chew up the Nizamshah of Ahmadnagar, they had to leave with a few teeth lost.'

He turned silent for a little while and then resumed. 'If you ever go to the markets of Delhi or Agra and make casual enquiries about me, you will hear the most bizarre stories ever told.'

'What kind, Baba?'

'In the opinion of the people there, I'm a black habshi from Africa and I deal in black magic. I have held every Nizamshah firmly within my grasp, quite like one of those domesticated pigeons.'

'This is horrible!'

'I am a voodoo man that controls the dark forces of the nether world, I have the African spirits under my command and make use of dolls. On the quiet, I also make human sacrifices to my African tribal gods.'

'Unbelievable that people can be so dumb and superstitious!'

'The outcome has been that my enemies have made at least forty efforts to eliminate me, either through heinous, cowardly attacks or through the use of poison. But Allah be praised, I have succeeded in destroying the armies of the Delhi emperor even when they have come in rolling like the sea.'

'Waah, Malik Baba, yours really has been one life of courage and strength!'

'It wasn't one man's courage, boy! How could I have managed it alone? I had ten thousand horsemen of my slave regiment riding with me! But the soldiers who really brought Akbar's army to dire straits were your Maratha horsemen and their intrepid horses. These persevering men and animals from the rocky, mountainous regions of the Deccan—I created steel walls out of them for facing the onslaught of the emperor's army.'

'Baba, it's you who created a brand-new battle strategy in the Deccan!'

'Yes, son. The first thing I realised was that such power-drunk armies should not be allowed a moment of peaceful sleep. They should be subjected to unexpected, violent raids. Their food supply should be destroyed. They should be reduced to a state of despair.'

'Hmmm, I get it now. They should never get to know how the Deccanis came, how they fought and how they disappeared. Clean out the battlefield even before they have rubbed the sleep off their eyes. The hit-and-run kind of skirmish, yes?'

'Yes, son, and this is the strategy we shall have to adopt here too.'

'That's right, Baba. Aggressive raids, supple yet powerful, vehement yet lightning-fast. We've to show the enemy the subterfuge of our soil, yes? Waah, Baba!' Thrilled at picturing it all to himself, Shahaji went on, 'My head has lit up bright as a burning torch. This battle strategy of suddenly raiding the enemy and thrashing it hard, let's call it guerilla warfare.'

'Excellent!' Malik Baba responded delightedly. 'You are a poet too, Shahaji, a magician with words!'

They began animatedly discussing the implementation of the strategies of guerilla warfare. Shahaji said, 'Malik Baba, I've always felt this very strongly, that a man lame in one foot can still manage to move around on a crutch, but when a person is lamed in the mind, for how long can he offer resistance?'

This time spent with Malik Baba had given him the opportunity to exercise his own mind. Here was a man who had spent upwards of sixty years on the battlefield, and there was a lot that he had learnt from him.

After some time, Shahaji said, 'Malik Baba, I am haunted by this one dream: When will the flag of self-rule flutter in the Maratha sky?'

'Subhan-allah! Such far-sighted imaginings at this tender age!'

'Honestly, Baba, it fills me with disgust, that we Marathas should be the donkeys to bear other people's load, or the bullocks for pulling other people's cannons! For how long can this go on?'

Malik Baba could well understand the storm raging inside Shahaji, his exasperation at the injustice of it all, his disquietude. He reached out to take Shahaji's palm in his own and said, 'I can understand your anger and resentment.'

People who have travelled to many coasts and harbours, tasted the water of many a river, people who have rubbed shoulders and shared a smoke with world travellers, sailors and officers of distant lands, such footloose savants manage to gather many kinds of knowledge and skills in the process: sculpting, veterinary expertise, knowledge of medicines, culinary arts and so forth. Some take to astrology in a big way.

Malik Baba opened Shahaji's palm and began to study it in the dim light of the lamp. Shahaji laughed out loud and asked, 'So what do the lines on my palm reveal?'

'Singularly fortunate!'

'Who? Me?'

'Of course you! But many times more fortunate than you will be your son! He shall grow into the defender of his soil, and benefactor of his country, of his religion and of the poor multitudes! He shall be a god among human beings and a Rajyogi among gods. I can say this with absolute confidence.'

·ବଓଏ·

A good distance had been covered and much of the night had rolled past. Baba's elephant was rolling on at an even pace. It was dark, and it was just the old man's white pupils that shone on the upper part of his pitch-black face, wide awake like the eyes of a watchman guarding the door. 'Look, Shahaji,' he said, 'I have to forewarn you with this intelligence I've gathered. The Mughals of Delhi and Adilshah of Bijapur are readying to use the contemptible weapon of causing schism in our ranks.'

'What are you saying?'

'Their beastly game-plan is to buy over an important general in our army and undermine our strength through him.'

'Hey Shambho! So, who do you think may have swallowed their bait?'

'Oh, it could be anybody. It could be somebody on whom you have lavished all your love and care. It could even be Shareefji!'

'How can you even think of such a thing? That's absolutely impossible. Your worry in that direction is absolutely baseless.'

'Well, son, life has taught me many a bitter lesson. The damage that a ring of well-entrenched cannons can inflict on the walls of a fort is nothing compared to the havoc that an insignificant relative can cause from the inside.'

The time had come for Shahaji to shift to his own canopy that was trailing right behind. His tired body needed a little stretching out. Malik Baba's elephant was pulled to a stop, Shahaji took the ladder down and went and sat in his own canopy. Some of his lackeys climbed up the elephant, arranged for his bed and hopped off to return to their own horses and ponies. There was a loud call of 'Dadasaheb!' from below. Shahaji looked over to the right and found Shareefji's horse Dilpaak riding alongside his elephant. 'Dada,' called out Shareefji, 'have a little bit of fruit while you are still awake.'

'Yes, I will, don't worry.'

Once he had assured himself that his brother was settled in comfortably, Shareefji nudged his horse forward. He'd proceeded a little distance when seven horses sped up from behind and distributed themselves on either of Shareefji. These were the seven strapping young sons of Vithoji Bhosale, first cousins of Shahaji and Shareefji. They had all set off for this battle with great fervor. The sturdy, broad-boned Kathiawadi horse under Nagoji Bhosale looked quite drained, and that was no surprise looking at the man's size. His friends called him 'baby elephant'. The stress on the poor animal would be such that a groom travelled with him with some replacement horses.

First Maloji Bhosale and then his younger brother, Vithoji, had both enjoyed the privilege of Malik Baba's company and patronage in the Nizamshahi regime. When Maloji had fallen on the battlefield of Indapur, Vithoji had taken charge of running his brother's household.

These ten boys of the house—two of Maloji and eight of Vithoji—strong, tall, big-built, valiant and handsome, they looked like a small unit of an army. With the passing away of Sambhaji Bhosale, they were now reduced to nine.

The brothers were broad-shouldered and deep-chested. When these nine valiants moved around the Nizamshahi lands, they did so with the grace of lion cubs. They went out for rides and hunts together. Armed with swords, battle-axes and bows and arrows, they moved around with a swagger in their steps. There had been many efforts at sowing discord among them, but none had met with even an iota of success.

Only lately had they lived down an episode that had tested their bonds of brotherhood. As often, a big programme of some kind had been organized at the Nizam Saheb's palace in the Daulatabad fort. After the programme was over, the Nizam had felicitated the assembled Maratha sardaars with robes of honour. As the grandly bedecked horses and caparisoned elephants of the sardaars began to ease their way out of the crowd from inside the main gate, Khandagale's elephant lost its temper.

The royal festival had brought hundreds of eager onlookers inside the fort walls. As the foul-tempered elephant began swinging its massive trunk wildly, whole crowds began stampeding. Its powerful trunk was as large as the branch of a tree and would down ten to twelve people at one swing, setting up screams of agony. The more the people screamed and ran, the more the animal's frenzy mounted. The dumb animal did not know in which direction to run and began dashing wildly, as if it had gone blind, crushing people under its powerful legs like so many insects.

People ran in all directions screaming 'Control the elephant! Control the animal!' Jijau's brother and Lakhojirao's son Dattaji Jadhav happened to be there at that moment. He pulled his horse to a halt. Looking at the terrified state of the people around, he turned his horse's head around and charged at the mad elephant. The horse lifted its forelegs to place them against the animal's back. The elephant turned round.

Dattaji jumped off his horse and stood facing the elephant with his sword unsheathed. In a state of high excitement, Dattaji lifted his sword and unleashed a few powerful blows on the elephant's trunk. The force of the sharp blade was such that chunks of the trunk got sliced away and the animal sat back on its hind leg in unbearable agony.

The gory scene had attracted the attention of the turbulent crowd, and they now began to close in in large numbers. The stampede was now getting out of hand. Looking at the turmoil everywhere, Shahaji's cousin and Kheloji's younger brother Sambhaji Bhosale ran forward. He reached up to Dattaji and advised him to cool down a bit. An already fired-up Dattaji took it as an affront and turned his sword at Sambhaji. While the wounded animal lay to one side, Sambhaji and Dattaji began grappling with each other. When the Jadhav and Bhosale youngsters, who were streaming out of the fort, saw what was happening, they turned round and joined in the skirmish. An unprecedented face-off began between the Bhosales and the Jadhavs, swords clanging and both parties getting at each other in all seriousness.

Suddenly the blade of a sword found Dattaji's neck and severed the head from the body like the slicing of a wet stem of wood. While this was happening, Lakhojirao's elephant had moved out of the fort gates. When news reached Lakhojirao that the Bhosale boys had killed his son, the old man was beside himself with grief and anger. He leapt off the elephant, mounted a horse and galoped back into the fort like a bullet racing to its mark.

He saw in front his dear Jijau's husband Shahaji Bhosale swinging his sword mightily in support of his cousins and causing considerable bloodshed among the Jadhavs. Numb with grief and the thirst for revenge, Lakhojirao lost his head and launched a fierce attack upon his son-in-law, not caring whether he lived or died. He swung his sword hard on Shahaji's head that penetrated the young man's headgear. Blood spurted out as Shahaji fell off his horse unconscious and collapsed on hitting the ground.

Lakhojirao's bloodthirsty eyes were now searching for Sambhaji Bhosale. As soon as he spotted him on the other side, he spurred his horse in that direction and immediately got into a scuffle with the boy. Sambhaji's tunic was shredded and his turban toppled off his head. The moment the old man saw his opportunity, he collected all the strength he had and brought his sword down on the young man's head. Sambhaji's skull burst like a watermelon. The impact of the weapon was so heavy and the penetration so deep that the blood that spurted went straight to the old man's face and into his eyes. He wiped the blood and glared around with literally bloodshot eyes.

The entire episode had been triggered by an elephant belonging to a third party, and it brought such catastrophic tragedy upon two renowned Maratha families. In the final count, what had the valiants of both houses gained by thus going berserk upon each other? What banner of heroism had they hoisted? On the contrary, they had both finished off the day with mourning their irreparable losses on the cremation grounds.

Similar internal dissensions and flames of hatred had also brought about the downfall of the ancient Devgiri of the Yadavs and transformed it into the Daulatabad of Muslim rule. Three hundred years had gone by since the Yadav banner had been ripped off the brow of this invincible fort.

As they moved towards a new battlefield, Shahaji, sitting in his canopy, moved with a heavy heart. He would encounter his father-in-law now pitted against him in the Mughal army in the battle that was soon to begin. His three sons would very likely be standing alongside, fully armed. Conflict was imminent.

When he had bid goodbye to Jijau in the afternoon, he had done so with a deeply troubled mind, thinking of her state at the thought of her father and her husband confronting each other on the battlefield. As she had swirled the auspicious lamp round his face while bidding him goodbye, she had said nothing, but her distraught eyes had revealed it all to him. What else would the prayer be that she had sent up to the gods but this: 'Oh! Lord of the Worlds, please protect the turban on my father's head, but at the same time let not the plume on my husband's crown wither either, oh Lord!'

The nine cousins were riding along rapidly on their horses with a merry gait. Shareefji had four or five watermelons in the bag strapped to Dilpaak's saddle. As he rode, he pulled them out one by one and tossed them in the direction of his cousins. The youngsters caught them as they rode, smashed them open with their fists and distributed the pieces around.

The Mughals to the north and Adilshah to the south—these were the two immediate neighbours of the Nizam. Both the neighbours had been dreaming for a hundred years now of swallowing up that piece of sweetmeat lying between them. The major obstacle in the fulfillment of their dream was the unshakeable presence of Malik Ambar. Both neighbours had come with the determination of finishing him off in this battle.

As they moved towards the battlefield, Shahaji thought of the long-ago conflagration that had raged on the battlefield of Indapur. That was the first time he had stepped into a theatre of war. He was eight years of age then. His father Maloji had fallen victim to the enemy cannon, and his pyre had been lit just where he had fallen. With little Shahaji sitting in his lap, Vithoji sat crying inconsolably at the passing away of his elder brother. The widow Deepabai had decided to immolate herself with her husband and was circumambulating the burning pyre. Bangles on wrists, kunku on her brow, she would travel up to heaven on the flames that carried her husband's mortal remains.

The Brahmins were chanting their mantras and Deepabai was all braced up to leap into the fire. Suddenly the chanting increased in volume, accompanied by a deafening beat of the drums. As Deepabai moved forward to meet her destiny, little Shahaji ran and threw his arms round her legs and said, 'Why are you doing this, Matoshri? Take a look at your little Shareef there! He needs the warmth of your lap.' It was a scene to melt a heart of stone. Brother-in-law Vithojiraje could not hold himself back. Spreading his scarf out in the manner of a mendicant, he implored piteously, 'Please listen, Vahini Saheb, please don't do this! Dada's passing away has already brought a big wall down. If my mother-like vahini also goes away, the Bhosale waada will disintegrate for sure! Please listen to us!'

The mother's insides churned. She turned round, spread her arms out and gathering her two sons, pulled them close to her chest. From that moment on, Shareefji had remained the very beat of Shahaji's heart. Whenever those stormy, painful days of his childhood came to mind, Shahaji's throat would choke with emotion.

Around midnight when the Nizamshahi army was moving towards Ahmadnagar, Emperor Jahangir's forces were also marching barely ten miles away. Mahabat Khan had loaded Mughal captains like Lashkar Khan, Bahadur Khan, Jalal Khan and Khanjir Khan with plenty of replenishments at Burhanpur. Bahadur Khan had sworn before Jahangir that he would bring that demon named Malik Ambar alive, strapped on the back of a buffalo like a water bag, and present him before the Emperor.

The spies were perpetually on the move, disregarding all obstacles: the darkness of the night, rivers and defiles, thorns and brambles. They kept feeding priceless information on the position of the enemy—their strength, movement and immediate state. On the basis of this intelligence, Malik Baba and Shahaji were making estimations of where the Mughal and the Adilshahi forces were most likely to rendezvous.

As the darkness of the night began to clear and visibility improved, they could see the turrets of the township in front, its arches and the walls encircling it. The rainy season was still on its way out, and the cold and moisture in the jungles were still quite evident. It appeared that there had been recent rains in and around Ahmadnagar, the paths were still slushy. Animals were finding it difficul to find proper foothold and their speed had slackened.

Though morning had arrived, the sky was thick with clouds. Three camel riders came hurrying in from the front. They brought the news that both the Mughal and the Adilshahi armies would roll in by afternoon.

On the way, they ran into the bed of a smallish river called Kalu. The sight of water sent both men and animals crazy. After days and nights of unceasing travel, their bodies were aching in every joint. The moment they espied water, the elephants lifted their trunks and trumpeted loudly in glee. They made a beeline for the water and simply went and sat down in it. The army officials let them stay there and frolic for well over a couple of hours.

Breakfast time got over. Drums and trumpets were sounded for resuming the march. The elephants and horses were loath to move out of the water and had to be beaten with sticks before they started climbing out to the other bank. They had to pitch camp there. On the yonder side, they could see a huge natural lake. This place lying between the river and the lake seemed to be an excellent spot for the camp, and a number of cavalrymen began dismounting and unloading their horses. Just then came a loud cry from the camping officials: 'Not here! Not here! Further ahead!'

They crossed the lake and kept moving forward and up till they hit plain ground on a plateau, where they were finally told to dismount. The tents of the fauji bajaar—the market that accompanied the army—had already been erected. Lunch was consumed under the open sky, after which the tents of the chiefs were put up.

It was late afternoon when lines of enemy units came into sight, climbing down the slope like an army of ants. The calculation of Malik Baba and Shahaji was that this was where the nut-cracker move would happen. From the one side would arrive the Mughal forces and from the other side would be the Adilshahi army, thus trapping the Nizamshahi men between them.

The smart enemy was rolling down the hillside and heading straight for the comfort and security of the spot the Nizamshahis had been instructed not to occupy just a few hours ago. Within a short time, they began taking possession of the space that lay between the big lake and the river. A few disgruntled horsemen rushed to the temporary conference tent that had been erected, and one of them shouted at Malik Baba and Shahajiraje, 'Come and have a look, princes, see what blunder you have committed.'

'That priceless spot is being swallowed up whole by the enemy! Once those sons of the devil take the lake under their control, our animals will die of thirst!' said a second.

'Quite true, princes!' croaked a third. 'That little river is not likely to survive for more than a fortnight or so!'

Shahaji lifted his head and looked towards Malik Baba who seemed to be deeply absorbed in some other task. Shahaji turned towards the horsemen and said in a commanding voice, 'Get back to your tents without bother. Don't get agitated. We'll see what to do.' The horsemen had no choice but to put their heads down and walk out of the tent.

The secret had now come out into the open that the Nizamshahi forces were less than half of the Emperor's army. The outcome was that the Mughal and Adilshahi men had established their dominance on the battlefield from Day 1.

It was close to eleven at night. Two servants arrived from the general's tent to call Shareefji. During the conversation in the tent, matters flared up for no apparent reason. A loud altercation began between the Nizamshahi soldiers and the Maratha warriors. Voices were raised and abuses began to be exchanged. Word of the fracas reached the general's tent and Malik Baba and Shahaji came to see what the matter was. Malik Baba began pleading with Shareefji with folded hands, but Shareefji refused to bring down the pitch of his voice. Shahaji then suddenly flared up and shouted, 'Do you think that the battlefield is a water tank of the Holi festival?'

When Shareefji was handed down this admonition from his elder brother, he looked at him with flaming eyes and cried, 'I've had enough, Dada. Keep your battle talk to yourself. How could you be so enamoured of this worthless Nizam as to insult me in this manner? I am moving out with my men forthwith!'

'Where are you going, son?' Malik Baba butted in.

'I'll go wherever I want to, what's it got to do with you, Ambar miyaan? You are at the root of this quarrel! You have set the fuse alight!'

Shareefji's face was a sight to see, aflame with grief, anger and humiliation. He was in no state to listen to any word of persuasion. He sent for his horse, leapt upon its back and rode off, a number of his young soldiers after him. Even before they knew it, the head count of soldiers deserting the army in the middle of the night had climbed to over three thousand. When Malik Baba and Shahaji realized the extent of the defection, their faces turned distraught. Such naked display of discord should never have occurred. An atmosphere of misery and deep uneasiness spread everywhere. It was a terrible thing to have happened. Shahaji and Malik Baba were consumed with the worry that there were bound to be enemy spies among the crowd that had gathered to see the spat.

Their worry was not the tiniest bit misplaced. Word of the infighting did reach the Mughal camp, and it delighted them so much that they celebrated it with a feast and went to sleep in a joyous state.

A shower had come and gone during the night. But when the day dawned, it was as if a huge hole had been blown in the Mughal unit. They just couldn't fathom how the clouds of the sky above could have come right up to their tents and exploded. They could see elephant-sized waves come roaring into their camp. Water in every tent, water up to their noses, and nobody could fathom from where this deluge had descended. Cries of 'Ya Allah' and 'Save, oh Khuda' were getting drowned in the surge of the water as men and animals were being swept away in the current. It was with the greatest difficulty that they managed to stay afloat with each other's help.

It was after a long time that the mystery of the flash flood became apparent. It was those Maratha rascals that had blown open the lake at their head. They had crept out in the darkness of the night and dug massive breaches in the embankment with whatever implements they had with them. Their Shareefji Bhosale had hoodwinked the enemy by faking a fall-out with his brother's army and led this midnight venture.

Mulla Mohammad had taken a rude jolt. He sat on his knees in front of his tent, begging for Allah's mercy. Wet and shivering with cold, Lashkar Khan cried in a plaintive tone, 'Mulla Saheb, what calamity is this? What exactly happened?'

'Huzoor, I wouldn't have minded if a few thousand soldiers had drowned in this deluge, but this flood has destroyed the grains, the gunpowder and the animal fodder that we had stacked up for the next fifteen days!'

'What affliction is this, Allah?'

'How do I say it—even before the war has begun, our plans and hopes have started getting washed away!'

The day dawned, but the enemy forces had still not managed to find the time to settle down to the cold morning wind. That was when the Nizamshahi men lit the wicks of their cannons installed on the top of the hill. The vales of Bhatwadi began booming with cannon-fire. Pandemonium reigned in the Mughal-Adilshahi camp: the riders were there but the horses had scattered; the camel-back zamburak guns were all ready to be mounted, but the deluge had sent the camels scampering in all directions; cannons were there, but the gunpowder boxes were not! The chief of the Adilshahi army, Mulla Mohammad, however, was a tenacious old soldier, not easily flustered. Braving the cannon-fire, he brought together his captains and got them to regroup the men and move them three miles behind, and save as much of the food and fodder as they could.

Mulla Mohammad had not yet lost his bearings. His faith in the Mughal cannons was still intact. Besides, there was his unit of three hundred massive mountain elephants that had romped over many a battlefield stretching from Kabul-Kandahar to deep in the south. His immediate concern was to bring order back into his army and restore the morale of his men as early as he could, and he got busy doing just that.

The Bhatwadi battlefield had tasted blood and flesh, and it continued to pulsate at a high beat. Adilshah of Bijapur and the Delhi emperor Jahangir wanted to gain a lot out of this battle. For one, they had to snap the spine of the Nizamshahi Sultanate. For another, they had to pluck out the thorn called Malik Ambar; he was the person who had brought the Nizamshah these days of glory. This black upstart, comes from somewhere, fights his way up to the position of the wazeer and strings the buntings of glory on the Sultanate; this person had to be wiped out once and for all.

Since the agreement was that the expenditure for the entire campaign would be borne by the Adilshah treasury, the Mughal captains that had arrived from the north were in no tearing hurry. The main fighting force of eighty thousand men, however, was of the Mughals, making it difficult for Mulla Mohammad to respond with some bold moves. At the same time, the young among the Maratha forces like Shareefji had begun to turn restless at the prolongation of the war. Matters reached a pass where Shareefji could hold himself no more. He marched up to his brother and declared, 'Enough of waiting, Dada. Let the battle begin!'

'Cool down, Shareef, cool down. Let's trust the dangerously scheming mind of Malik Baba. He may look like he's relaxing from the outside, but one just can't say what chemicals are brewing in his innards.'

'But how long, Dada, and to what extent can we trust the old fogey's systems?'

'Think about this, Shareefji: why are all these big captains of the Emperor's army and the Adilshahi forces sitting quiet in their tents across from here? Why have they not been able to build up their courage? Why aren't they igniting the sparks of war?'

'Stop worrying, boys; you won't have to wait for too long,' came the voice of Malik Baba from behind. The other assembled officials straightened up and welcomed the old man. He looked around with a sense of pride at the gathering: 'You people of the Maratha race, born and brought up in the mountains and valleys of the Sahyadri range, with the ability to run faster than a deer and swoop down like an eagle from the mountain rocks, you are valiant fighters. I am extremely impatient to put your qualities to use in the battlefield.'

The Bhosale brothers assembled there—Shareefji, Mambaji, Sarfoji and others—got a whiff of something extraordinary fizzing inside the old man's heart.

Shareefji was so full of naive energy that he found it impossible to stay put at a place for any length of time. He would gather his small unit and go scouting round the enemy camp at all odd hours of day and night. He had heard a lot about the elephant regiment that the Mughals had brought with them, and the news had made him irrepressibly curious. This curiosity took him and his unit atop a hillock, and there, in the hollow basin of the yonder valley, partially concealed by a fold of the land, he saw the massive creatures. The awestruck Marathas saw some three hundred of those dark hulks frolicking around in the golden light of the setting sun, greedily gobbling up the tender banyan leaves that their mahouts fed them, delighting in the plentiful supply of their favourite munch.

The chief of the elephant regiment was a captain named Manchehar. Tall and thin like a drumstick, he had joined the emperor's elephant stable at Agra as a very young boy and had virtually grown up in their company. Taking care of their health, getting them battle-primed by feeding them marijuana and other psychotropic herbs, maneuvering them on the battlefield, in these and all other matters related to pachyderms, Manchehar was a virtuoso. He had brought over and bred in his regiment animals of the best stock from Assam, Burma and even the Malabar region of the south.

Emperor Jahangir had dispatched Lashkar Khan south with the admonition that he should not step back into the Agra durbar without having first chopped off the head of that old coot Malik Ambar. But the manner in which Malik Ambar had kept the Mughal and Bijapuri forces hanging in a state of agitated suspension, the ease with which he had destroyed their supply of food and fodder, both Lashkar Khan and Mulla Mohammad had been left distraught and panting for breath.

The delay in the commencement of battle had made the enemy restless. One morning arrived the information that Shahaji was all ready to launch an offensive and that triggered a frenetic activity. Kettle-drums were beaten and cymbals struck. A violent clash followed. Malik Ambar surveyed the scene with his falcon eyes, missing nothing. Shahaji, clad in coat of mail and a steel helmet, had ridden into the enemy ranks with great resolve. He cut a valiant figure astride his galloping horse, with the red flag fluttering in the breeze alongside him.

Shareefji, astride his horse Dilpaak, was like a man possessed, raining arrows at the enemy with unerring marksmanship. When his missiles penetrated the arms, thighs, or backs of enemy soldiers, the afflicted men's neighbours would feel the sensation of their own limbs going limp. They lay on the ground, twisting and turning in agony. In another patch were the cousins Shahaji and Kheloji, taking a terrible account of enemy troops.

War cries of Har har Mahadev and Allah-o-Akbar rent the air as the cannons boomed to roast men and animals wherever the fireballs fell. The battle that had begun at noon gained momentum. The smoke and dust that covered the sky dimmed the brightness of the afternoon sun.

It was now late afternoon, but the soldiers of the Nizamshahi and the Marathi battalions were showing no signs of weariness; on the contrary, they were turning bolder as the battle progressed. Lashkar Khan then decided to change strategy. He fed the three hundred elephants of Manchehar into the battlefield, primed with sufficient marijuana to give them a strong high, rendering them uncaring of the fire and the cannonade and the mayhem reigning around them. On one of the elephants sat Lashkar Khan along with Mulla Mohammad, both egging their men on and screaming 'Kill! Smash!! Destroy!!!' at the top of their lungs. As they stood dancing on the howdah, a cannonball flew in with the Mulla's name written on it, carrying his head off and leaving the rest of him lying in a pool of blood. It twitched for a little while and then turned still.

Lashkar Khan was shook at the sudden death of the Adilshahi head of army, but he still retained the alertness to see that his elephants were being mowed down everywhere by the Nizam's cannons. He immediately dispatched his runners to Manchehar and ordered him to turn the elephants back and take them away to a secure place. The reserve cavalry was once again brought back into the battlefield, but the Adilshahi army could not withstand the bold and furious assault of Malik and Shahaji. Winning the battle, however, was essential. Lashkar Khan had begun to froth blood and spittle.

The day clearly belonged to the nine Bhosale brothers. They were fighting at their awe-inspiring best and laying waste everything that belonged to the enemy. The battlefield was steadily getting overladen with the smashed, mutilated, headless, limbless bodies of soldiers, horses, elephants and camels. As the sun dipped further to the west, the Nizamshahi and Maratha forces rapidly marched towards a sensational victory over forces that were well over twice their number.

At Manchehar's end, three hundred elephants had been safely herded out of the battlefield in the northward direction in the fading light! The earth reverberated below their stampeding legs and the bells round their necks clanged wildly.

Amidst the hullabaloo and the bedlam of the battle, the senior generals gathered around Malik Ambar in a makeshift tent to plan their knockout punch. 'Let's immediately send an intrepid young soldier who can crush this big battalion of the enemy's elephants,' Malik Baba told the assembled men. 'Well, now, who volunteers to run into that gorge right away?'

'Nobody else is going for this sacred assignment,' screamed the battle-drunk Shareefji. 'I've already assigned this challenge to myself!'

'You, Shareef? You?' queried Shahaji, thunderstruck.

'What is it, Dada?' asked Shareefji, a cloud descending on his brow. 'What is it? Are you afraid for me? Does your trust in me falter? Or you have doubts about my competence? Even if I am young, I deserve this opportunity for proving my mettle in a daring adventure as this, Dada!'

Shahaji looked at Shareefji's strong, lean image from head to foot. He had never before seen his darling brother so bathed in the spirit of dauntless resolution. He was dazzled at the boy's keenness to embrace the battlefield as his beloved. Holding him back in this state would be downright sinful. He said, 'Shareef, you are a tiger cub. Go take the battlefield in your arms. But, my brother, calamities don't seek permission before arriving.'

'Why do you say this, Dadasaheb?'

'Please take Hambeer Chauhan and our Kheloji with you,' he said as he blessed him.

As Shareefji was leaving, he turned round and glanced at his brother's face. The look in his eyes rattled Shahaji. His eyes carried the pain of a deer that had been pierced with a spear.

Targeting the enemy's entire herd of elephants for capture was carrying audacity to its limits, and the two Maratha chieftains knew it. The very recklessness of the adventure gave them a rush of blood. Bending into the wind and exhorting their stallions to gather speed, they leapt across streams and ditches in pursuit of their prey.

When Manchehar realised that a band of Maratha horsemen was giving him hot chase, he was astounded at their spunk. Or was it foolhardiness? Manchehar was a past master at manipulating his brawny animals in all circumstances and turning the table upon the enemy. Every time he found a shelter in the fold of a stream, he would line up his animals shoulder to shoulder and create a wall, from behind which he would let loose a barrage of arrows and spears. This he did twice as he withdrew, but he could not succeed in shaking off the hyper-charged pursuers.

Stung by the murderous assault launched by Shareefji, Hambeer Chauhan and Kheloji, Manchehar finally lost his cool. He had created the elephant wall for the third time, but he decided to step out of its security. He got into the howdah atop an elephant along with a few companions and turned the elephant round to confront the Marathas that had latched on to their heels. The howdah suddenly became a launch pad for arrows and spears.

When Shareefji saw the enemy sticking his chest out with such valour, he was impressed—impressed to the point of cranking his own fearlessness up by quite a few notches. He spurred Dilpaak to race up to the elephant; once he had come alongside, he leapt and managed to pull himself up and over into the howdah. Red hot with battle fever, the two heroes fell upon each other, swinging their swords with amazing skill and energy. Shareefji then found his opportunity and managed to get a grip on Manchehar's head. He was about to give it the fatal twist when arrows came flying in from the darkness behind the elephants and pierced his broad back and shoulders. Shareefji winced but didn't let his grip loosen. Out of the same darkness then came a heavy, sharp-tipped spear and buried itself deep into Shareefji's ribs. The man was thrown back with the impact of the weapon and toppled off the elephant's back on to the ground, bleeding profusely. A bunch of enemy soldiers sprang out from behind the row of elephants to behead the fallen man, but the alert Hambeer Chauhan raced in and secured the hero's blood-soaked body before it could be subjected to any indignity.

Early next morning, the pall-bearers lowered the litter before Shahaji. Temples throbbing, the veins swelling out on his brow, jaw clenched tight, Shahaji slowly reached out to the red sheet and uncovered the face. All his strength and fortitude, all the steely determination that he had gathered collapsed at the sight of that beloved face: eyes closed, blood congealed in the soft downy beard. Images of their early childhood flitted past his mind's eye: the open spaces at Verul, the *surpaaramba* they played running up and down trees, the visits to the Ghruneshwar temple complex, the frolicking on the riverbank. All his resolve proved inadequate to withstand the pressure of the bellow that began in the pit of his stomach and emerged in a loud cry: 'Shareefji!!! My little brother!!! My boy!!!!'

Shareefji's horse Dilpaak had not tarried in chasing its master to the world of the dead. Within moments of helping its master take the leap into Manchehar's howdah, it had taken a hit in the neck from a ball of fire shot from a zamburak and died instantly. Shareefji's men had brought the carcass of the horse swinging upside down on a pole and laid it beside its master's body. The soldier and his faithful steed were cremated together that evening.

·~≈·

A large number of senior Mughal and Bijapuri captains had been put into chains and incarcerated in a stable under a strong guard. Here were some who had bragged of destroying Malik Ambar and Shahaji stem and root; now, when they were paraded for inspection, legs tied by a sturdy rope in a series with other prisoners of war, Malik Ambar allowed himself an indulgent smile. Suddenly, there was a cry from the Maratha soldiers, 'Look there! There! That's Manchehar!'

Clapped in iron rods and chains, Manchehar was brought to stand before the two Nizamshahi generals. When Shahaji rested his eyes on his brother's killer, his face turned hard. Horsemen and foot-soldiers chanted in unison, 'Behead the killer of Shareefji!' Kheloji placed a sharp

Khorasani sword in Shahaji's hand and roared, "Go, Shahaji, send this man to hell!'"

Eyes laced with blood, brow bathed in perspiration, Shahaji looked at the prisoner from head to foot. When Death stands in front with wide open jaws, the bravest of men find their limbs turning frosty. Manchehar was no exception. Sinking to his knees, he beat his breast and cried, 'Mercy, oh King! Mercy!!'

'No mercy!' screamed the crowd. 'Chop off the dog's head!'

Seeing Shahaji lift his sword and freeze, Kheloji once again shouted, 'Come on, Shahaji! One swing at the neck!'

Shahaji lowered his arm and smiled wanly. 'Forget it, Kheloji,' he mumbled. 'Killing a person who has sought shelter will do nothing to further the glory of us Marathas! Let him live!'

⁓ ~ ⁓

A victory of this order against the Mughals was unprecedented! Their versatile army had never been handed such a comprehensive battering. Considering that they also had the Adilshahi forces as partners in the enterprise, the defeat was all the more humiliating. Jahangir, the emperor of Hindustan, was implacably displeased.

While on the one side Jahangir's strength and power were declining with age, on the other side, his third son Prince Khurram had gone in open revolt against his father, thus keeping him staked to the banks of the Ganga and the Yamuna. It was for the first time ever that the Nizamshahi forces had brought the mighty Delhi empire to its knees and Daulatabad was celebrating it in the style of Eid and Diwali combined.

The city of Daulatabad was eager for the public felicitation of the victorious army and its generals. Burhan Nizamshah, intoxicated with the joy of victory, had ordered for a special durbar to be held immediately.

Jijabai felt justly proud at the stellar role that her husband had played in the resounding victory. Anticipating the honour that would be bestowed upon him, she had accompanied the wives of other chieftains to the beautifully decorated Hall of Mirrors. The big chieftains sat in the front row, waiting for the arrival of the Nizamshah. In the second row sat

Kheloji's brothers Nagoji, Maloji and Kakkaji and quite a few others, all dressed in their finest costumes of silk and velvet.

Horns and trumpets were blown under the arch of the silver-plated alcove outside. A wave of servitors, court officials and guards came rolling in, followed by the sixty-five-year-old Burhan Nizamshah. At a respectable distance of a few feet walked the heavy-built minister Malik Ambar. Excitement at the durbar became noticeably sharper. Shahaji, who was chatting with people near the third row, moved forward to occupy an empty seat in front. At exactly the same time, Kheloji Bhosale, who had entered the durbar with the Nizam's retinue, went for the same seat and lowered himself into it. When Shahaji threw a surprised eye at Nizamshah, he noticed that the big man was not even looking at him; on the contrary, he was respectfully signaling to Kheloji to occupy the seat. The durbar was about to begin; left with no choice, Shahaji located an empty seat in the third row and went and sat in it.

As the programme proceeded, trails of sweat began travelling down Shahaji's broad back. Malik Baba had begun with praising the bravery of the Muslim battalions in the battle. Next, he applauded the chivalry of the Maratha horsemen and infantry 'under the leadership of Kheloji Bhosale'. He acknowledged the sacrifice of Shareefji, even if it was in a single line, and as he concluded, he just about made a passing reference to Shahaji.

A strange wind was blowing through the durbar that day. It became obvious to anybody with sense that the entire charade had been deliberately played out with the intention of embarrassing Shahaji. Stung to the quick, the proud Maratha got up from his seat and began walking out of the durbar with long, angry steps. Not one of those present had either the courtesy or the courage to persuade him back. Nothing different was to be expected from the durbar of toadies and jesters anyway, whose religion it was to go with the flow.

Very early next morning, the slighted Shahaji's retinue was all packed and ready to leave for their palace at Paranda. Jijau, sitting in the howdah with her husband, looked distraught.

'I staked my life in this battle against the Delhi emperor,' fumed Shahaji, 'destroyed his army, plundered three hundred of his elephants, lost a brother like Shareefji in this wretched Nizam's cause, and what did I get as reward, Jijau?'

'Don't take it so hard, Raje! But clearly, this disregard shown towards you, combined with the felicitation of your cousins, was a deliberate effort at humiliating you.'

'I shall have to teach these foolish rulers that they cannot get away with thus rebuffing me.'

'Let go, Raje! Where's the point in casting pearls before swine?'

Shahaji was, however, not merely mortified—he was enraged. The hard-hearted, bone-headed attitude of the Nizamshahi administration had disgusted him beyond measure, disgusted to the point that he was in no mood to see or talk to anybody. He cloistered himself in his palace at the Paranda fort.

One morning, Mambaji Bhosale came visiting him, deep regret and guilt etched on his face. Almost as if begging mercy from his cousin, Mambaji pleaded, 'Dada, from here on I want to stay with you. Move with you wherever you go, right from the palace gates to the cremation grounds.'

'When you have such a stalwart as Kheloji for brother, why should you want to stay with me?'

'I too understand the fear and resentment that this would have excited in certain quarters!' chipped in Jijau. 'If the ten Pandavas of the Bhosale household were to move together, they would win every single Mahabharat! That's the fear that has driven some to this conspiracy of driving a wedge between them!'

'You have taken the words out of my lips, vahini.'

It was after Shahaji and Mambaji had lunched together that Shahaji felt the pain in his heart subsiding.

With just about forty thousand soldiers at their disposal, the duo had brought to its knees the hundred-thousand strong army of the Mughal-Adilshahi combined. The choice of the battleground, the lightning raids during all odd hours of day and night, the disruption of the enemy's supply lines and optimum utilisation of the local conditions—all these factors put together had made guerilla warfare and the names of its originators Malik Baba and Shahaji the subject of admiration far and wide.

It was grossly unfortunate, therefore, that the person who had been so centrally instrumental in bringing about this sensational victory had had to suffer the ignominy of being so pointedly ignored. What had hurt Shahaji far more was that Malik Ambar, who occupied the most important position in the Nizamshahi durbar, should have done nothing about it.

Two days later, a letter arrived directly from Malik Baba, which Shahaji immediately pulled out of its silken bag and began reading:

My dear Shahaji,

You should have been felicitated with much fanfare during the royal celebrations organised at the durbar last week. The manner in which you were ignored and disregarded has caused great pain to my heart. As a father figure to you, I don't know what else I can do now other than advise you to exercise patience. Strange are the ways of the world, strange are the ways of destiny.

The illustrious Mughal emperor Akbar had once sent a secret message to me, advising that I was wasting my talent in the service of a tiny state. He had gone to the extent of baiting me with the offer of the post of a minister in his durbar. But that was the time when a woman of Chand Bibi's calibre, dressed in her coat of mail, stood in defence of the Ahmadnagar fort right in front of the ammunition dump.

Like a latter-day Raziya Sultana, the young widow had sped from Bijapur, where she had been wed, to save her father's realm from being swallowed up by the mighty Mughal Empire. How could I have turned treacherous to her and to the soil of this land? And what were my rewards for this loyalty? At least forty attempts have been made on my life.

I am as unhappy as you are with the present state of affairs. The Nizamshahi of today is no longer as it was in earlier times. Whenever I sit and think of a valiant person like you, I desire that your radiance turns brighter with every passing day. Let your bhagwan and my Allah protect you from all hurdles in your march towards greater glory.

What more can I write?

Your uncle,
Malik Ambar

Malik Ambar's letter did wonders at lifting the spirits of both Shahaji and Jijau.

The next afternoon a message was delivered: Bismillah Saheb, the eminent jeweller of Sholapur had been waiting anxiously since morning in the hope of an audience with Shahaji. Accompanying him was a trader from Bijapur.

The two were invited in. Of medium height, dressed in the best quality clothes, they appeared to be experienced gentlemen of noble bearing. Looking with frank admiration at Shahaji, Bismillah spoke: 'In the manner of a connoisseur falling in love with a blood-red ruby and buzzing round it like a honey-bee, there is a certain person that has been buzzing around you for a long while.'

'Wah! Well said, Miyan!' responded Shahaji with a laugh. 'Here I have spilt my blood on the battlefield without anybody caring a hoot, and here you say that there is someone who is marking circuits round me?'

'There are some pedigreed aesthetes, sir, who look beyond the ups and downs of life and hold an unswerving eye on a diamond of the best quality.'

'Who could this connoisseur be for whom you have been lavishing such fanciful metaphors?'

'A person who has established a township called Navaraspur for the best artists and intellectuals of the world. He is as stout-hearted as you are and as skilled in swordsmanship.'

'Could you be talking of Ibrahim Adilshah?'

'Perfectly right, sir.'

'How can that be? Gentlemen, I believe you have come to the wrong address. I am the Shahaji that sent thousands of Bijapuri soldiers to the doors of death in the battle of Bhatwadi. With my hands not yet cleaned of the blood of his men, Ibrahim Shah certainly couldn't so have lost his mind to want to welcome a bitter enemy like me.'

'We have come to the right address, sir. He certainly is obsessed with the desire of possessing you.'

'But the losses suffered at Bhatwadi?'

'The prince is more concerned about organising his future than about calculating losses of the past. Tomorrow there will be other invaders bent upon razing Bijapur to the ground. Before that happens, we need a strong-spined warrior like you to become the commander-in-chief of the Bijapur army.'

This unexpected, nay, inconceivable invitation stunned Shahaji. His eyes began to glow. As he turned his head towards the inner courtyard, he noticed that Jijau stood leaning against the wall. From the joy and excitement that flashed from her eyes, it was clear that she had been listening to the conversation.

3

THE COMMANDER-IN-CHIEF OF BIJAPUR

1625

The crafty, swollen-headed chieftains of Bidar had been harassing Bijapur to the point of exasperation. It was with the intention of bringing down their conceit that Chand Bibi, as the regent, had invited Maratha chieftains over to Bijapur in 1595. Seen against this background, this latest invitation to Shahaji gained considerable gravity. The opportunity of holding the reins of the army as the commander-in-chief of a huge kingdom like Adilshahi Bijapur was a great stroke of fortune. Having struck this fortune even before he had touched thirty years of age was a matter of great joy to Shahaji.

An old retainer of the royal household named Mograbai came running to the Raja that day and said, 'It's a wonderfully auspicious occasion for you to set off for Bijapur, but if you propose to take Baisaheb also with you, I don't know how you will manage!'

'Why, what's happened, Mogu Akka?'

'Shouldn't you ensure that there are enough amla and tamarind trees in that foreign land?'

'What are you hinting at, Mogu Akka?' Shahaji's eyes sparkled as he shot the question.

'Well, if there aren't, we'll need to carry the stuff from here, that's what. You'll not only be the head of an army, but also a father soon. Our waada will soon have a prince's cradle rocking.'

Shahaji's face lit up like a lamp. He slipped a gold bracelet off his wrist and placed it in Mogubai's hands. Following the indignity in the durbar, first the offer from Bijapur and now this wonderful news had lifted Shahaji's spirit sky-high. Within an hour, camel-riders were dispatched to the Sindkhed palace with the glad tidings, and before three days were out, Jijau's mother Girijabai arrived at Paranda to claim her mother's right.

'The honour of this delivery always belongs to the girl's parental house,' she announced and began gathering the paraphernalia for moving Jijau to Sindkhed. Shahaji would set off for Bijapur on the same day.

Sleep was difficult to come by on the eve of their departure. 'I've heard quite a lot about your Bijapur,' murmured Jijau. 'Many refer to it as the heaven of the south. The silk cloth factories there, the traders from many foreign lands, the prosperity and the comforts of the city, all of that's going to be great fun for you!'

'But with you not there, it'll be like a flute that has lost its notes.'

'*Ishh*! Are you really going to miss me so much?'

'A person may be a big king, he may have great chieftains and ministers and armies hovering around him, he may live in palaces and in the utmost luxury—but how does that make any difference? He may spend his day on the battlefield or in the durbar, but what about the nights? Without you around, the very walls want to collapse on me; the silk clothes set my body on fire!'

'Well, then, get a companion for yourself to provide the love you need!'

'What are you saying, my queen?'

'For quite some time now, I've wanted you to get another wife.'

'What nonsense are you talking?'

'What's nonsensical about it? This second wife will be a younger sister to me!'

Power is desirable only when its graph is on the rise, when life is truly full of prosperity and good fortune.

Sultan Ibrahim Saheb stood at the pinnacle of Adilshahi history. The enthusiasm and honour with which he invited Shahaji to occupy the post of the commander-in-chief of his army was unprecedented—never before had a non-Muslim, more particularly a Hindu chieftain, graced the seat of the chief of the army in a Muslim administration. Through his courageous leadership during the Sultanate's wars, Shahaji too measured up to the trust that the Sultan had placed in him. Under the leadership of Commander-in-chief Shahaji, the cavalry and infantry were raised to peak efficiency.

On the one side, Shahaji, with his valour, loyalty and strength of arms, had left a deep impression on Ibrahim Adilshah; on the other, a sensitive, wise and popular ruler like Adilshah had responded in equal measure by offering unstinting support and patronage to Shahaji. The result was the elevation and strengthening of the seat of the commander-in-chief of the Bijapur army. Within two years, Shahaji had raided innumerable cities and fiefdoms of the Karnataka–Tamil regions, bringing in loot that required to be transported on camel and elephant backs to fill up the Bijapur treasury.

The enmity between Bijapur and Malik Ambar continued as before; the Nizamshahi forces were relentless in their raids into Bijapur lands. Shahaji took personal charge of the army posted in that region and let the enemy taste the wrath of his flashing sword every now and then. It wasn't that he was always successful. Once he was badly cornered in Salpe Ghat when the Nizamshahi forces had attacked from the direction of Phaltan and caused Shahaji to retreat.

That battle had brought Shahaji very close to Sardaar Sambhaji Mohite, who had shown exemplary bravery in the conflict there. Shahaji would often visit the Mohite waada in Bijapur where he made the acquaintance of Sambhaji's sister Tukabai and decided to marry her. He invited Jijau to be present on the auspicious occasion, to which Jijau responded, 'Good, that you have found a person who shall fill your heart and your palace with happiness. I am much too occupied here with the upbringing of our son Sambhaji. I have with me here your memories and the principalities of Pune and Supe.'

The agony of being so far away from his motherland and from his clan was a source of constant pain to Shahaji. The regret of not being present to celebrate the arrival of his son would stay with him for a lifetime. Meanwhile, an interesting piece of information fell on his ears: Burhan

Nizamshah was so delighted with the arrival of the son and heir of Shahaji that he had dispatched a load of gifts to Jijabai as she lay convalescing in her mother's house. The people of the royal household had been as surprised as the population of Sindkhed when a beautifully decorated elephant had arrived at the palace gates. The selection of clothes and jewellery stacked in trunks and baskets suggested to Jijabai that the Begum Saheb herself had played an important role here

On 12 September 1627, as Shahaji was finishing his third year of service to Bijapur, the wise Ibrahim Adilshah II passed away and the winds blowing in the kingdom began turning rapidly noxious. When a public-spirited king disappears from the scene, meaner elements suddenly find the space they had been denied for long. Power loses all sense of shame. It abandons public weal and dances naked in the service of charlatans and crooks. Narrow sectarian politics and religious bigotry find their teeth and talons turning sharper.

There had been other disruptions in other parts of Hindustan within a span of barely fifteen months. Malik Ambar had shed his corporeal frame on 14 May 1626 at the ripe age of eighty; this was followed by the death of the Mughal emperor Jahangir and the ascension of Prince Khurram to the throne under the title of Shah Jahan.

The demise of Ibrahim Adilshah had created turmoil in the capital city of Bijapur. Political power by its very nature recognises neither morality nor compassion. An important ritual needs to be performed even before the dead monarch is lowered into his coffin, which is the placing of the crown on the head of his successor. A heartless, hard-nosed world demands this observance before the hearse leaves for consigning the royal remains to the elements.

As the funeral procession moved through the royal streets of Bijapur, one of the main pall-bearers in the front row was Daulat Khan. While he wore all outward signs of extreme mourning, he was finding it difficult to proclaim openly to the world that the blood that ran through his veins was the same as Ibrahim's. His mother was a highly talented person and the Sultan's closest friend. One of Daulat Khan's deepest regrets was that his mother had not used the wiles that other attractive women employed, of tying the man to her apron strings. If only she had used those skills to good effect, he would have been wearing the crown of Bijapur on his head! Such were the thoughts storming through his head as he led the mourners down the streets towards the graveyard.

The large, beautifully carved blackwood coffin was supported on shoulders, with strings of precious pearls and jewels hanging on all sides. It was quite likely that such brazen display of wealth was not to Daulat Khan's liking. Accompanying the royal funeral cortège were lords and barons, princes and chieftains, rich traders and landlords, and guests from the neighbouring lands. Along with them walked important Maratha chieftains like Shahajiraje Bhosale, Nimbalkar and Ghatge to offer their last homage to the departed king. Ibrahim Adilshah's reign had allowed ample opportunities to Maratha, Telanga and Malabari warriors to display their valour alongside the Muslims. Among them, the Marathas were in the lead, and among the Maratha captains, the name of Shahaji had acquired almost mythical proportions.

Alongside the pall-bearer Daulat Khan walked a tall and scholarly looking Brahmin. Ash lines were drawn across his brow, in the middle of which he sported a perpendicular red mark. The garland of rudraksh beads round his neck and a stole with gold-embroidered borders over his shoulder made him stand out in this Muslim funeral procession. He looked sprightly and walked with a light step. He displayed his closeness to Daulat Khan even in the incongruous atmosphere of a sombre funeral march, going to the extent of mopping the beads of perspiration every time they sprang on Daulat Khan's forehead.

The procession had reached the burial ground at Joharpur. As the coffin was lifted with the support of twirled sheets of cloth passed from below the box and lowered into the grave, the incantation of Koranic verses picked up tempo. Even as the sobs and groans turned into loud howls, there were some who looked with dismay at the expensive garlands of gems with which the box was covered. As the earth began being tossed all over the box now resting in the pit, the Brahmin's stomach churned and his heart bled. 'If only they had been handed over to a deserving Brahmin like me!'

The tradition is to take a purifying bath when one returns from the burning ghat or the burial ground, but this facility may not always become available to even as elevated a personage as a king. For ensuring a pain-free and crisis-free future, certain issues need settling that may often require a bloodbath.

The new sultan, Mohammad, was a mere lad of fifteen, but that is the ordinary person's way of perceiving age. When the posterior rests on a throne of power, however, a strange kind of euphoria begins coursing through the person thus arrived at authority. The magic of this inebriation is quite beyond comprehension. Hard policies need implementation, which may well involve playing with human lives. It was under the thrall of this intoxication that his feet, instead of turning towards his grand palace Saat Manzil, took him in the direction of another pleasure palace close by on an assignment that brooked no delay. Giving him company were just a handful of his closest associates.

Screened by luxuriant flowering trees, this glistering palace carried an aspect of profanity today. The flunkeys and the eunuchs gathered there leaked their wickedness into the air, which was sharply aggravated by the presence of an extremely handsome boy trussed up cruelly to a wooden chair. Up until the previous evening, he was the darling of every citizen of Bijapur. He was Prince Darvesh, the elder son of Ibrahim Adilshah's senior wife. At the time of the arrival of this heir to Saat Manzil, all of Bijapur had remained lit up for a full fortnight, every single night being marked by royal feasts and the distribution of baskets full of sweetmeats. But what is fortune if not fickle! When it turned vicious for the young prince, there was no holding it back.

In a way, Prince Darvesh was really paying for the curse of his mother's ambitions. Before her husband had died, the queen had got into a sordid intrigue for ensuring the succession of her son to the throne of Bijapur, even if it exposed the life of the king to serious risk. The plot had been laid bare and the queen had been beheaded at the king's command. Prince Darvesh had got away with his life because he had been found innocent. Despite his mother's unseemly hurry, Prince Darvesh was seen as the front-runner for the throne of Bijapur.

But as the old Sultan Ibrahim Shah had breathed his last the previous afternoon, he had pronounced the name of Mohammad as his successor. That single statement had brought Prince Darvesh's world crashing round his ears. At the crack of dawn the next day, a bunch of eunuchs had lifted the young boy out of his bed and carried him away in his nightclothes from Saat Manzil to wait for further action. Besides tying his hands and feet to the chair, the persecutors had wrapped his head in a fisherman's net so tightly that he could hardly wiggle his chin.

When the footsteps of Mohammad and his coterie rang on the tiles, Darvesh let out a loud cry. As soon as Mohammad came and stood before him, he wailed piteously, 'Please, Bhaijan, I do not want the throne, I do not care for anything all. I am ready to set off instantly for a pilgrimage to Makkah-Madeena. Please, please have mercy on me!'

Two of the blacksmith's boys were ready and waiting. When they had heard the approaching steps of the king's retinue, they had placed iron skewers on embers for heating. Now as they pulled them out with their wooden handles with the spikes blazing red, Darvesh trembled in every muscle and let out a terrified cry: 'Please, Bhaijan, mercy!!'

'Don't you worry, bhai, I am not going to kill you. We are not playing Mughal politics here to take each other's lives. Just a little discomfort, and that's it!'

Mohammad held the red-hot spikes by their wooden handles and moved forward. When Darvesh saw the weapons closing in on him, he wetted his trousers. While Mohammad too had advanced with great pluck, when he looked into Darvesh's beautiful, terror-stricken eyes up-close, his courage failed him. He had known Darvesh to be a good-natured, kindhearted person; he was also convinced of his innocence. How could he then thrust those skewers into those pleading, soulful eyes?

When Daulat Khan saw Mohammad developing cold feet, he roared from behind, 'You cannot run a kingdom on such lily-livered sympathies, my Sultan!'

The scholarly Brahmin shouldered himself forward, took over the skewers without uttering a word and, without a fuss, planted the blazing ends into the bulging pupils of the unfortunate prince. A deafening scream, the hiss of hot iron meeting liquid substance, smoke and steam, and the sharp smell of burning flesh, and the horrendous deed was over and done with.

Daulat Khan and the other chieftains present looked in awe at Murari Pandit, the Brahmin who had shamed these battle-hardened warriors with such felicity. The new Adilshah's faith in Daulat Khan and his associates became unassailable. The three Brahmins whom Ibrahim Shah had appointed to high posts in the Bijapuri durbar on account of their wisdom and intelligence were dismissed forthwith. All other Hindus occupying administrative and clerical posts in the court were also removed. In the eyes of the new Adilshahi dispensation, including Daulat Khan, the only Brahmin worth venerating and cultivating was Pandit Murari Jagdeorao, a person who could turn dross to gold.

The durbar of the new Sultan assembled the very next day, during which Mohammadshah honoured Daulat Khan with the robe of the prime minister of Bijapur. To celebrate this happy occasion, the prime minister latched on to his sovereign's ears. Mohammadshah then immediately declared the appointment of Pandit Murari Jagdeorao as the chancellor of the treasury and also conferred upon Daulat Khan the new title of 'Khawaas Khan'.

Prime Minister Khawaas Khan was returning to his haveli atop a caparisoned elephant, with his friend Pandit Murari Jagdeo seated beside him. While accepting the flowers tossed at him by the fawning crowds on the road, Khawaas Khan mumbled into the pandit's ears, 'I want the horoscopes of my three wives and their children to be prepared by you, understand?' This delighted the pandit no end. He surveyed the palaces on either side of the road and the flights of masonry stairs leading up to them. Those were the very stairs, Murari remembered, where barely two years ago he would stretch himself out half-starved, shivering in the nights because he had no blanket to keep himself warm.

·ೂಲೊ·

When Shahaji met his cousin in the evening at the haveli, he asked, 'Mamba, the unusual character we met at the graveyard this afternoon, the new chancellor to the new prime minister, who is he?'

'Murari Jagdeo.'

'Have we ever met him before this?'

'Oh yes, he had made his appearance at Daulatabad about four or five years ago as a down and out tramp. A meddlesome busybody then, he hardly knew from where his next meal would come. And look at him now! Spends his time with the mightiest and the noblest, and he has become quite adept at enjoying legs, whether of the poultry kind or of pretty young girls.'

'Nice fun, this!'

'His spirit of enterprise, however, needs to be appreciated. Imagine, just three years back he sold lumps of tar to credulous Daulatabad courtiers and threw baits of jungle herbs to lure barren women into his trap. That's the Murari Jagdeo we have here.'

Light then suddenly dawned upon Shahaji and he kept staring at Mambaji for a long while.

Mohammed Adilshah was just about fifteen or sixteen years of age. Very soon, some of the most orthodox Islamists had gathered around him. As the commander-in-chief of the army, Shahaji had to requisition large amounts of money for meeting the expenditure of the army. With the new administration in place, both Prime Minister Khawaas Khan and his chancellor Murari Jagdeo sat upon the cash box like the fabled cobras guarding the wealth of the realm.

As time went on, the entire Bijapur administration and particularly Daulat Khan allowed Murari Jagdeo to walk all over them. Disgusted with the man's behaviour, Shahaji informed Mohammadshah in clear terms, 'My men shall not go any more to rub their noses at your Muraripant's door. You must understand that I can do justice to my post of commander-in-chief only if I am regularly supplied with the funds I need.'

The atmosphere at Bijapur began changing rapidly. The hardcore Islamists in the Bijapur durbar found that they had a willing listener in the new Sultan. 'Your highness, you have the responsibility of bringing the Sultanate back to Islamic ways. Your late father Ibrahim Shah caused grievous harm to our religion during his reign with his shameful acts.'

'What are you talking about?'

'For one, he had been so totally obsessed with wanting to become a great singer. He would himself sing all those blasphemous songs in a loud voice. He had gone to the extent of installing and praying before the image of the Hindu goddess Sarasvati in his endeavor to master the art of classical singing.'

'Ya Allah! That was heresy of the most profane kind! We shall have to change all that.'

Mohammadshah now began carefully examining the activities of Shahajiraje, who was the favourite of his father's times. He also announced in the court, 'We shall shut down Navaraspur, which was established exclusively for encouraging Hindu arts like singing and dancing.'

Murari Pandit possessed may skills like astrology, black magic, wrestling and fencing. But the skill at which he was a past master was sycophancy and extreme obedience. If asked to jump two feet, he would be keen to jump four. Shahaji found his spirits suffocating in this new dispensation. News now reached him of Shah Jahan wanting to annex Daulatabad to the Mughal Empire, particularly after the obstacle called Malik Ambar had disappeared. Word also reached him that Daulatabad was sharply feeling the absence of a general like Shahaji.

As the atmosphere in the Bijapur durbar turned more and more asphyxiating, the pull of the motherland turned proportionately stronger for Shahaji.

4

THE RESOLVE FOR SOVEREIGNTY

1630

The heinous slaughter of Lakhojirao Jadhavrao and his sons had sent shock waves all through India.

How difficult it is for a mother to nurture a foetus in the womb, to take care of it! And in her delicate state, to what extent would destiny want to test her?

A foetus of less than three months in her womb and a father, huge as a tree, lying lifeless before her! Alongside him lay her two younger brothers and a nephew. The Sanskrit scholar in Shahajiraje was finding it difficult to imagine how the tears emerging from her lacerated heart would have found the way to her eyes and flowed down her cheeks at the sight of her dear ones so mercilessly slaughtered.

It was a long ride from Devgiri and bringing the pregnant Jijausaheb with care and concern such a long distance had been an ordeal for him. Shahaji had taken a solitary break and reached the palace at Paranda the previous night after a brisk ride.

The entire sequence of events of the last five years had gone rushing through Shahajiraje's mind's eyes during that travel—the blazing battlefield of Bhatwadi, the unexpected passing away of brother Shareefji who was dearer to him than life, the golden gate of the overlordship of the Bijapur army that was opened for him by the wise ruler Ibrahim Adilshah, the backsliding that happened during the mad reign of Mohammad Adilshah, the passing away of Malik Ambar in the interim, the return to the service of Nizamshah, the unrelenting conflict with the Mughals and finally the senility that overtook Burhan Nizamshah—his brutal assassination of Lakhojirao and the annihilation of Jijau's entire family.

Shahaji was in a state of extreme physical exhaustion. All through the night, it had been movement, movement and movement—sometimes on horseback and sometimes in the palanquin. For Jijabai too, sitting in the palanquin with her legs folded up in this advanced state of pregnancy had been agonising. When her cramps became unbearable, she would go horseback for some time. The pits and stones that lay on the bypaths made even the horseride difficult.

But the event that had triggered this journey had been so horrific that the discomforts along the way were nothing in comparison. Before dawn had broken, the retinue entered the Paranda fort through the main gate. The torches on the ramparts were still aflame. The massive rampart walls were thick enough to accommodate cannons in many of its alcoves.

Jijabai opened her eyes in the private chamber. It was time for a light early morning breakfast. The sun rays were streaming in through the eastern windows. The hubbub from the soldiers gathering on three sides at the foot of the palace could easily be heard: the neighing of horses, the instructions of the captains, the calls of the grooms, the yells for the arrangement of fodder for feeding the animals.

Jijabai was about to turn on her side when she felt the touch of a soft little hand on her face. She instantly took that hand in hers and kissed it softly. Five-year-old Sambhaji had been waiting at her pillow for his mother to wake up. Jijabai pulled him into the bed and took him into her embrace. The child could feel her breathing gathering pace.

'Did you come very late in the night, Aausaheb?'

'Yes, my child.'

Jijabai ran a loving hand over the child's head, kissed him a few times and held him tight. The eyes of mother and child were heavy with unshed tears. The news of the heartless killing of his mother's father, two brothers and another kin would undoubtedly have reached his ears, and at five he was old enough to understand its tragic import.

The physician Daaji Shastri arrived. He touched her hot forehead and felt her pulse, after which he gave her a greenish concoction to drink. As he handed over the rest of the medicines to Gomajipant Pansambal, he addressed Shahaji, 'Raje, it is difficult even to visualise the kind of lightning that has fallen upon your in-laws' house.'

'An unimaginably dastardly act ... but what can anybody do in the presence of fate?'

'We perfectly understand the enormity of the jolt you have suffered, but after all that, how can you ever take your eyes off this other responsibility of yours?'

'What are you talking about, Shastri?'

'Whatever the state of your other affairs, the queen is carrying. It becomes the prime duty of us all to take care of the child in her womb.'

The Raja gave instructions for things to be put in order. Jijabai rose from her bed with the greatest difficulty. A few maids had been assigned to help her move around. They began walking towards the inner verandah, with Shahaji trailing them through the passage. As Jijabai turned round to look at him with disconsolate eyes, Shahaji said, 'May no one ever be visited by such a despicable level of treachery!'

'Raje, the very thought of this fiend Burhan Nizamshah sets me on fire. What breed can such a loathsome creature belong to? Wasn't it on account of this man, this fiend, that you had dragged upon yourself the combined might of the Mughals and the Bijapuris at Bhatwadi? Turned your blood to water?'

'Yes, this is the wretch for whom my Shareefji laid waste his life. He is the beast for whom we suffered this everlasting loss!'

'When the innocent faces of my three young kinsmen flash before my mind's eye, I begin to quake. The parents' house is a sanctuary of peace and for any woman, a fountain of love. It is this heaven that this blackguard has obliterated forever. A sinner like this Nizam shall meet his end in a similar sludge of blood and gore, that's for sure!'

'Without a doubt, Jijau! A treachery of this order I shall never be able to forget.'

'But what does one do about it?'

'As of now, just this, Jiu, that from here on, I shall never accept employment in the service of this perfidious Nizamshah.'

The Raja walked into the meeting hall to find that his senior advisors, Pantaji Gopinath, Gomaji Pansambal and the administrator Naropant Deekshit, had already assembled. Naropant informed the king, 'Please don't worry, sir. If you peep out of the window, you will notice both the squares below are choc-a-bloc with horsemen.'

'Such alacrity!'

'Raje, your circumstance is so unusual that the wind itself would have carried the news to the soldiers.'

'That's quite true, Raje. Your troupe would hardly have reached here by dawn when horsemen came riding in at your heels, and even as we watched, they've swelled to well over five thousand. You just have to pass the order. Just peep out, the men and animals are all twitching for action.'

'Every one of the horsemen has a little bundle tied round their waste, with victuals enough to last for two or three days.'

The king was overcome at the state of readiness of his people. He went round among his assembled chiefs like Gomaji, Naropant and Jaisinghrao, placing an affectionate hand upon their shoulders as he passed them.

Jijabai quickly took her bath and finished her morning chores. The Brahmins had noticed the bustle around the house; accordingly, they abridged the prayers and wound up the rituals snappily. It had never happened before that the twelve Jyotirlingas lined up in the king's temple had not been paid due obeisance.

Burhanshah should at least have kept in mind the relationship between Shahaji and Lakhojirao. After all, Shahaji occupied the seat of the subedar, the highest administrative post in Burhanshah's Sultanate.

As Shahaji sat with his chieftains worrying about the future, Jijabai walked in. 'Your lordship should take everything he sees around him into account. Patience is the need of the moment.'

'The entire sky has crashed around my head, Jiu!'

'It's during such times that a man's wisdom abandons him, they say.'

'There's no stepping back from here!' said Shahaji in an impassioned voice, locking his eyes into Jijabai's. 'You remember the sharp questions you would throw at me whenever you drew your rangoli maps of Hindustan? The armies of every single Padshah ran on the strength of Maratha horses and Maavali men, you'd say, but was there a patch of land that the Marathas could really call their own? Well, in the name of Shambhu Mahadev, I have decided to provide an answer to your soul-searching question. I have resolved to draw out the boundary of a Maratha kingdom with the tip of my sword and colour it with my blood.'

The stirring words coming from their king set the blood of his audience on fire. Some of them were so galvanised that they broke into hurrahs of Har har Mahadev! and *Jaijai Shambhudev!* Then followed cries of 'Hail King Shahajiraje!'

Within moments, a miracle began to take shape in and around the imposing and extensive fort of Paranda. The king's horsemen burst across like honeybees exploding out of their hives and began ransacking the precincts of the citadel. The Nizam's officials were bewildered. If the subedar of the Nizamshah had gone on a rampage with his men, who could stand up to him in opposition? The first things they emptied out were the contents of the treasury: gold, silver, precious stones and expensive clothing. Then they raided the armoury and carried away boxes of gunpowder, guns, swords and spears and denuded the warehouses of all the tent material that lay there. Twelve hundred bullocks and over five hundred mules and pack-horses were lined up and loaded with the plunder slung across their backs in sacks. As this caravan began moving out towards the main gate, a few of Shahaji's lieutenants rode up to him and asked, 'In which direction do we move?'

'What a question to ask? Exactly thirty years ago, a jagir[2] was gifted to my father Malojibaba under the stamp and seal of Malik Ambar and the Nizamshah. That's the direction you take.'

'Towards Pune, then?'

'That's right. We have our ancestral houses in this town on the banks of the Mula-Mutha, and that's where we shall meet.'

'We obey.'

'And yes, please tell my friends there that after a campaign around the province, we are reaching there at their tail to hoist the flag of our own independent country.'

By the afternoon, the king had set the animals with the pillaged merchandise on their way and brought matters in order for his own departure. His entire personality was glowing with the incandescence of

---

[2] A type of feudal land grant in the Indian subcontinent during the Islamic rule, starting in the early 13th century, wherein the powers to govern and collect tax from an estate was granted to an appointee of the state. The tenants were considered to be in the servitude of the jagirdar.

the pursuit that was now driving him. Jijabai couldn't take her eyes off her husband, held in a hypnotic hold by the remarkable animal magnetism that exuded from his every pore. She was riding beside him as he moved out with his minister and his chieftains towards the main gate. As they were riding out of the gate, Shahaji pulled the reins of his horse, rather unexpectedly, and stood still.

'What is it, Raje?' asked Jijabai softly. 'Could you have forgotten something?'

'Yes, something beyond all value, something greater than the best of our jewels. Come, let's give it at least one last look.'

He turned his horse round and trotted over excitedly to the other side of the large park in front. On a circular estrade stood a massive cannon. Made out of eight metals mixed in lead, it looked like a well-built, particularly healthy elephant calf.

Shahaji got off the horse and walked deferentially towards the venerable weapon. 'You shall not cast your eyes on another cannon of this kind across the length and breadth of Hindustan,' he whispered to Jijabai.

'This is so transparently the weapon of Ranchandi, the Goddess of War!'

'It has the strength to roast an entire province without pausing for breath. No wonder it's named Muluk Maidan, the queen of the battlefield.'

The king signalled to a smart young man who instantly stepped forward and eased himself into the mouth of the cave, squeezing his body into it like an agile cat. Shahaji turned round with pride and said, 'See the enormous jaw of our Ranchandi? This eternal symbol of Maratha pride was cast in a foundry in Ahmadnagar.' Another young soldier stepped forward and took measurement of the cannon to show that it was nine arms long and had a circumference of nine hands too.

Shahaji cracked an auspicious coconut over the barrel of the gun to record his reverence, and then walked towards his horse. Jijabai eased herself alongside him and remarked, 'This tigress of the battlefield has quite stirred you up, Raje! Have you fallen in love with it, or what?'

'Not merely that. I've put our campaign for establishing our kingdom in order, I propose to come back here. I shall then have this priceless heritage taken in procession all the way to Pune.'

Shahaji's regiments then stormed out of Paranda, not bothering with the usual pattern of breaking their journey into stages, destroying the Nizamshahi posts, ransacking towns and laying waste the forts that fell in their way. The news of their ferocious campaign spread everywhere like wildfire. The sentiment everywhere was that the Nizam should never have committed the outrage of assassinating Lakhojirao when he had no rhyme or reason for doing so. On his way, Shahaji looted the huge market at Sangamner and ransacked the manors of the Nizamshahi nobles for good measure. On his way out of the town, however, he stopped at the ancient temple of Lord Shankar and had holy water poured over the idols inside.

Climbing over the Baleshwar mountain range under the grueling sun had been a tiring exercise for Shahaji's troops. Finding a decently wooded grove of blueberry trees, the men hastily erected a tent for the royal couple to stretch their tired limbs. Jijabai slipped into a quick siesta, but the king's eyelids, despite being heavy with sleep, refused to close. It was in this state of drowsiness that Shahaji set off on a trip to the snow-covered land of Mount Kailash. And then, when he was not expecting it at all, Lord Shankar came and stood before his bewildered eyes. Lord Shiva himself had taken material form before him.

Every aspect of the great god stood distinctly before his vision: the mighty Ganga flowing between those matted locks, that slim crescent outlined against the knot of hair on the head, that cobra—blue-green for having sucked the poison out of the world—wound around His neck like a necklace. The matted-haired God sat on His tiger-skin holding many a weapon in His multiple hands. He was the Giver of boons, the Giver of strength and potency, the Granter of courage, the primal, greatest Ascetic of all! Here He was right in front of the king's eyes, in the company of His celestial consort Parvati! The king was thrilled to high heaven. But more thrills followed. Shivashankar placed His divine hand upon Shahaji's head and pronounced with great affection, 'Child, misfortunes come upon one's life like rain-clouds and disappear in the same manner. You must resolve never to lose heart nor to stray away from the path you have chosen. My blessings on your head a hundred thousand times over. Your Bhosale lineage shall very soon achieve unimagined greatness. Your second son shall be arriving soon, and he shall be the master of great virtues and a man of great valour. He shall prove to be the scourge of all the evil forces on earth.'

The Divine pronouncements exhilarated the king beyond imagination. Bending his head low with gratitude, he pleaded, 'Oh God of Gods, what care should I exercise while bringing up this child?'

'Let this blessed child stay with you only during his younger days. But do not imprison him in the luxuries of the royal palace beyond that. Let him drink of the winds and storms of the wide-open world. Let him singe in the hot blasts that dry the sap of plants and trees. Remember this, child: only when steel softens in the blazing furnace of the blacksmith can it be hammered into the desired shape of a beautiful statue.'

Shahaji woke up with a start. When Jijabai, lying next to him, noticed his elated demeanor, the wanton glitter in his eyes and the exuberant confusion on his face, she giggled softly and said, 'All right, now, confess and be done with it. Tell me about the god who visited you in your dream.'

Shahaji turned in stupefaction towards his wife and gazed and gazed. He then slowly took her hands in his and murmured, 'Yes, Jiu, that ineffable Power informed me that the child who will soon be born to us will be the pinnacle of virtuous deeds and the friend of all humanity.'

Shahaji's dispatch riders had moved ahead of him; as a consequence, his friends in Junnar, Narayangaon, Udapur and other villages on the way were all preparing to meet him. Shahaji and Jijabai remembered the tradition of the Bhosale family of service to Lord Shiva. Babaji and Vithoji had restored the dilapidated temple of Ghruneshvar. Malojibaba had built a big lake in Haibatpur in the Mann province, thus removing the shortage of water that the place would face during the annual Mahadev festival. Only recently, while he was in the service of the Adilshahi Sultanate, Shahaji had renamed Haibatpur as Shikhar Shingnapur and had expanded the lake there into a much bigger water body.

The blessings of Shankar, the Lord of Mount Kailash, that rested on the house of Bhosales, the stories related with them and their memories churned him up. 'Jiu,' he said in a thick voice, 'how does one repay the debts of gratitude of this benefactor? Once I have set things in order at Pune, please remind me of one thing.'

'What thing is that?'

'Of making a visit to the village of Yavat near Pune.'

'Why?'

'To pay a holy visit to Bhuleshvar. It is the place where Ma Parvati had assumed the form of Uma and captivated Bhagwan Shankar through her divine dance.'

'Oh, the Bhosales had reached there too!'

'Yes. My father Malojibaba would cross the Ghodnadi and regularly visit the Mahadev of Shikhar Shingnapur via the mountain pass of Kedgaon. Once, as he was sitting quite exhausted, Bhagwan Shankar appeared before him and said, 'I am sitting on the path in the incarnation of Bhuleshvar. Take a little rest on the steps there too before you proceed further.' Since then, it has become a tradition with our family to take a holy sighting of Bhuleshvar Shiva.'

Shahaji had a large number of friends in the settlements around Narayangaon and Junnar. The glad tidings had begun to reach them that it was no longer an empty appendage; the '-raje' of Shahajiraje now stood for what it really meant—a king. That was why, once the entourage crossed the ghats, massive crowds had assembled to felicitate them on the public grounds of every one of the villages on the way like Belhe and Mhalunge. The women would swirl lamps round their heads and pour water on the horses' hooves. Even the animals were given an application of turmeric and kumkum paste as a mark of respect. Pieces of bhaakari were swirled around their heads and thrown into the lanes to cast away the evil eye. There was one single prayer that rang in the air: 'Lord! Bring success to our king!'

As Shahaji's horses reached the river Kukadi near Narayangaon, Vijayrao, the fort-keeper of the Shivneri fort, came thundering down with his horsemen, a cloud of dust trailing behind. He was especially happy with the way events were developing. Shahaji's son Sambhaji rode cockily by his side. Vijayrao gifted robes of honour to Shahaji and then to Sambhaji too. The decision of Sambhaji marrying Vijayrao's daughter had already been taken.

In due course, the horses left Khedmanchar behind, and the whiff of the Maaval valley hit the nostrils of the troops, throwing Shahaji into a turmoil of nostalgic memories. This was the land near Pune and Supe that the Nizam had gifted to Malojiraja in the year 1600. Where was the region of Verul-Daulatabad, and where this land in the environs of Pune? Even earlier, when he roamed his native land—the land of Maaval, the valleys of Indrayani, Neera, Gunjavani, Pavna, Aambi, Mula and Mutha—he would exult. This land, its holy rivers, shrines and temples, the wind that blew here, and these rows of mountains that stood as sentinels around it, the thought that this holy earth of Maaval was his own filled him with ecstasy.

Earlier, land was assessed on the basis of whatever was under the plough. But Malik Baba had brought in a modern, fault-free standard of measurement. Malik Baba was the first big Islamic official in these provinces to get the black mother carefully measured, gather the land tax according to the quality of the soil and come running at the cry of the poor man during times of famine. One of Malik Baba's closest friends was Malojiraje. It was while touring in their company as a young boy that Shahaji had trodden upon the Maaval soil. He counted some of the finest young boys from these villages as his friends and wrestling companions.

Shahaji had, at different points in time, served the Nizamshahi Sultanate, the Adilshahi Sultanate and also the Mughals. Wherever he was, he had found employment for the young boys of Maaval according to their skills and abilities. The strapping, well-built ones joined the cavalry; the weaker ones were fitted in as water-carriers. Some others found work as foot-soldiers, and yet others were given government loans for animal husbandry for providing the army with bullocks. All these energetic young Maavali men had been delivered Shahaji's message by fast-moving couriers.

Shahaji ran his eyes over this massive gathering of excited Maavali youth assembled in the square now. Lifting his arms towards them, he said, 'Friends, the land is ours, the ploughs are ours, it is we who bear the yoke of slavery on our necks and slog on the farms. But as soon as the crop is ready for harvesting, in comes some sultan or a padshah as the owner and seats himself on the dyke. We are left with the bare stalks, while the golden grain is carried away to fill the padshah's cellars. To swell his treasury. Brothers, how many more generations do we expend for pulling these ploughs of slavery?'

'Well said, Raje, truly said!' These were groans emerging from years of exploitation that fell upon Shahaji's ears.

'Listen, you son of Maloji, you just give us the call!' roared an old man from the Bhose valley as he patted his grey whiskers. 'We shall lay down our lives for the fulfillment of your dream. If our villages are destroyed, we will carry our children and live in the wilderness of the mountains, but give battle to the enemy. Don't you worry on that count.'

An oath was sworn for the creation of their own state. This year, the rains had given the Maaval region a complete miss. It was the month of Aashaad and water was already in short supply. Hence it was decided that the next meeting would happen when circumstances improved.

In the bedroom that evening, as they were turning in, Shahajiraje remarked to Jijabai sarcastically, 'What does one say about this extraordinary munificence of the emperor and the Nizamshahi? These Islamic rulers grant to us the provinces of Pune and Supe, and they believe that they have emptied barrels full of gold over our heads.'

'I haven't quite understood you.'

'This is something that needs understanding. Both of these provinces are really a permanent headache for these rulers because they lie at the borders of their kingdoms. You cross Indapur and Ujani and you are into Adilshahi territory. Cross the river Ghodnadi there and it's Nizamshahi land! There, on the other side you cross Khedmanchar, and from Junnar onwards are the Mughal provinces! What all this means on the ground is that these lands are converted into jagirs and tied round our necks. On the one hand, it passes as an act of benevolence and on the other, it keeps us busy fighting numerous enemies. Their borders stand protected against each other too!'

There was admiration in Jijabai's eyes as she heard her husband lay out the intricacies of Deccan politics. 'But we are not awfully concerned, because we have Queen Jijabai as our partner in this enterprise. That is our greatest strength. Thank you for keeping the flame of revolt alive in our hearts. That is what will give us the courage to fight on and bring our mission to fruition.'

'What's so special there?'

'What's not special there? Our Jijau is the mother figure of Maaval, a menace for the Muslim marauders. It's on account of the assurances given by all of you that we have inaugurated the campaign for a new, independent land of the Marathas. And then, we have the blessings of the Mahadev of Ghruneshvar, Bhuleshvar and Shingnapur. What more can we desire?'

5

THE PLOUGH OF THE DONKEY

The situation in the Bijapuri durbar was worrisome and confusing. Young Mohammad Adilshah rested his pale eyes on the entire court. He then looked towards his minister and asked, 'What is the real news regarding this Shahaji? What disruption has he been causing in and around Pune?'

'That man has really crossed the limits, huzoor,' began Khawaas Khan. 'He has established himself in a palace called Malhar in a neighbourhood of Pune. He's been supplying money to the soldiers for getting new stables ready and has been lending money to the farmers too. He's also laid the foundation of a new fort named Daulatmangal close by. He's been dreaming of establishing his own capital there.'

'Capital?'

'His insanity has been increasing by leaps and bounds. A number of young lads from Deshmukh and Deshpande families from the Baara Maaval region have been gathering around him. The carpentry and blacksmithy workshops in and around Pune are all busy forging sharp weapons like swords and spears. Huzoor, his demeanor is not at all the kind that sits well on an ordinary chieftain.'

'So?'

'How do I say it, *zill-e-subhani*? This Shahaji wants to become a shahenshah of the Marathas!'

While this discussion was in progress, the sound of a loud giggle came to be heard. All the assembled chieftains looked around angrily to see who this stupid person could be. As all eyes rested on Murari Pandit, the culprit continued to laugh and said reassuringly, 'Why should this Shahaji be getting up to such childish pranks? And why should this durbar be wasting its time on it?'

'Don't you find it worrisome?'

'Not at all! The fact is that we Marathi people—whether we are Brahmins, or of the Maratha caste, or of any of the numerous castes or sub-castes—what does history tell us? That we take birth with the exclusive purpose of serving some padshah or sultan somewhere or the other.'

'The matter is not as simple as Murari Pandit makes it out to be. If a person like Shahaji, who has served as the commander-in-chief here, should turn to rebellion, it's going to be the ruin of us.'

'It's better to pluck the plant of rebellion out before it takes root,' said Mohammadshah, irritably. 'Tell us who should be sent to Pune to uproot this Shahaji.'

'I shall be honoured to go, huzoor.'

'Wonderful! Randullah Saheb shall bring victory to this mission.'

'Randullah Saheb is a valorous soldier, without a doubt,' broke in Khawaas Khan with some insistence, 'but Murari Pandit may also be sent with him.'

On hearing the proposal, Murari Pandit responded, 'What can I do, huzoor? It seems I carry the blessings of the god of fire on my head. If ever somebody has to be uprooted, destroyed, annihilated, my brain runs faster than a horse does. There's nothing sillier than these Margatthas dreaming of becoming kings. Why don't they learn to be happy minding their horses? Or, they should work like donkeys to fill their bellies. Why should they fill their heads with impossible dreams of becoming kings?'

'Well said, Pandit.'

'Thank you, my lord. Now that you have placed this responsibility upon me,' declared Murari Pandit in open court, 'I shall do such terrible magic that not merely the township of Pune, but a good seventy to eighty villages around it shall be brought to utter ruin. The farms shall become so pestilential that no crops shall grow in them; the roots of the trees will get chewed up by white ants; women will turn barren and move from door to door in their insanity; soil, fruit, flower, womb, they shall all forget how to bear seeds.'

All of the Baara Maaval region, meaning Twelve Maaval, the region of the twelve river basins, including the jagirs of Pune and Supe, had been distressed by the twin menaces of drought and the sultan's men.

The sky, it appeared, had been playing a joke this year. White clouds would drift in and then just scatter and die. Every one of the monsoon months had gone dry. A shower or two was all that the entire rainy season could account for. Nobody remembered having seen the beds of rivers Mula and Mutha as dry as they had now turned. The entire world had gone dry. When even human beings were scouring across miles and miles of the countryside in search of a potful of drinking water, the state of the animals was piteous beyond imagination. They either began collapsing in their barns and stables or wandered through waterless jungles and valleys till their legs could hold them up no more.

The other peril was that of the sultan.

Shahaji had his spies like Bhimraya in the Bijapur court, who would keep him informed of the developments there.

The heat of the natural crisis as well as the pressure mounted by the sultan began to oppress Shahaji. The family deity of the Bhosales was Shankar. It had been a long-standing tradition with them to pay their obeisance to the Lord at his Bhuleshvar court in Daulatmangal. Shahaji had now decided that once his kingdom had taken a firm footing, he would establish his capital city in Daulatmangal and control the region of Pune and its surrounding areas from there.

There were a hundred concerns and anxieties that had descended upon the king at the same time. The child inside Jijabai's womb had now grown substantially, causing frequent bouts of vomiting and thus making it imperative for them to move to Shivneri at the earliest. It was also time that the king's eldest son Sambhaji tied the nuptial knot. Jayanti, the daughter of Vijayrao, the fort-keeper of Shivneri, had already been chosen to be the prince's bride. With the intention of driving away the crises that were crowding in from all directions, the king had begun the *abhishek*, the ritual of giving a holy bath to the statue of Bhuleshwar that day.

The priests busied themselves with elaborate preparations for the ritual to ensure that the entire ceremony went off without a hitch. Just as the final elements of the puja were being performed, three horsemen were espied galloping into the lower gates of the fort. As they came nearer, the king recognised them as the accomplished spies of Bhimraya's team.

Pilajipant Deshpande served the tired horsemen with some jaggery syrup and consecrated sweets from the puja. Shahaji was so curious for the news these men had brought that he did not bother to change out of the ceremonial clothes and called them aside. When they had all gathered behind the temple, he asked with a smile, 'So, how goes the Sultanate? What's the size of the crisis?'

'It's big trouble, Raje. Most of all, the campaign has been handed over to Randullah and Murari Pandit. An army of at least ten to twelve thousand will set off from there in a couple of days. Also, a lot of poison has been spread all around there with regard to Your Highness.'

'Oh Jagdamba! Since we have planted the stake of our new kingdom, some big men there would have lined up an explosive list of complaints!'

'It's not merely this, Raje. Along with this revolt, they say that Shahajiraje proposes to mount an assault with his army on the Adilshahi kingdom.'

'On the Adilshahi kingdom?'

'Yes, Raje. This news has raised a storm in all of Bijapur. You are on the verge of sending a big army to launch an attack on the Meraj fort; and at the same time, your soldiers have started off to pillage the city of Athani.'

Shahaji laughed loudly at hearing these exaggerated reports. 'We shall certainly raise the flag of revolt for the future of our land; but from where could you have dug up these entertaining stories regarding Meraj and Athani?'

'Raje, this is not hearsay. There are roughly drawn out maps of both these places circulating in the palaces and manors of Bijapur, showing exactly how and from where you propose to launch your attacks.'

'It's truly astounding, this poison-spreading ability of our enemy!'

'Nothing astounding there,' broke in Jijabai from behind. 'Your noxious rat Murari Pandit has risen to a high rank there, hasn't he? How that venomous animal is going to nibble and bite, who can say?'

A detailed discussion took place with the spies right there. It seemed certain that the assailing forces would reach Supe and Pune in the next four days. From Bijapur to Pandharpur and from Pandharpur to Indapur-Supe—it wasn't a long haul anyway. It was, therefore, necessary to take some quick steps. Besides, keeping Jijabai anywhere in the vicinity of Pune would be altogether too risky.

A decision had to be taken quickly and acted upon immediately. Shahaji had great faith in the intelligence and wisdom of Jijabai. Taking her aside, he let out a deep sigh and said, 'Jiu, I believe I have competence enough to measure up to all my other responsibilities, but what's to be done regarding the confinement of the princess of Sindkhed? In such a delicate situation as this, I don't want to be away from you even for a moment.'

'In which direction do we ride, then?' asked an anxious Jijabai. 'The enemy's cavalry will be here in a couple of days' time.'

'Yes, that's quite true. Something needs to be done, that's for sure.' For the first time ever, there was a tremor of a faraway fear in Shahaji's voice.

'How does the Shivneri fort strike your lordship?'

Shahaji's eyes sparkled at the suggestion. Grabbing at it with both hands, he said, 'All right, then, let's start packing. We'll cross the river Bhima close by and move towards Shivneri along the Ghodnadi route. It's an absolutely priceless suggestion, Jiu.'

'Well, we're already committed to strengthening our bonds with Vishwasrao's family through our Shambhuraya's marriage. It also happens to be our Shareefji's in-laws' village.'

'Yes, his wife Durga lives with her father there. The fort is invincible and surrounded by thick forests on all sides, gruelling to penetrate. That makes it perfectly safe for you and the baby. Let's head there, then.'

Shahaji dispatched Pilaji Deshpande and Gomaji in the direction of his palace, Malhar, in Pune. His mind was whirring with strategies for blocking and giving fight to the Bijapur forces at Indapur very soon.

It was fortuitous that a number of palanquins and litters had arrived on account of the *abhishek* ceremony. It would have been hazardous for Jijabai to travel on horseback in her present state. With her earlier four pregnancies having resulted in miscarriage, the royal physician had advised her to exercise extreme caution. The raja had therefore decided that he would accompany Jiu to the Shivneri fort, settle her down, and then turn round immediately and return to his mission in Pune.

As they travelled past desolate farms and waterless rivers, Shahaji was flabbergasted. He simply couldn't believe that this was the same state highway along which he had travelled from Sangamner to Pune just a little over three months ago. He remembered the enthusiastic villagers, the people who had assembled in hundreds to welcome their new king. All of that had vanished! Wiped out! Whatever disappeared was because of the near total absence of rains. The ugly scene that met his eyes was that of dispirited nature and barren farmlands, as if *bhaakari* had been left to roast on the fire for too long and allowed to turn into coal and ash.

The last few months had experienced nothing but the scorching sun and a flaming sky, with not a trace of rain anywhere. The helpless farmers had seen their crops wither before their eyes and die. The soil had broken into huge, deep-running cracks. Milch animals had gone dry.

It was a custom among villages in the Maaval region for strapping village youth to maintain a small stable. Brothers and cousins would come together and set off to work as soldiers in the armies of this king or that. They would set off on their soldiering around the time of Dussehra and return to their families just before the monsoons were due to arrive, with their salaries and whatever plunder they had gathered. The present year, however, was a nightmare. When water was not available for their horses, fodder was a far cry. The starving animals turned weak and came down with diseases. The stables started emptying out and villages looked ravaged. Pilaji Deshpande would tell Shahaji about those desperate times, 'Raje, there in Solapur towards Hyderabad, starvation has created a reign of terror. People are slaughtering their bullocks to feed their children. They are even eating horse-meat there!'

'What unfortunate times have arrived!'

'At our village near Sangamner,' said another, 'people had set out to burn down the butcher's house. He was reported to be selling dog flesh, passing it as goat's meat.'

'Raje, to douse the fire of the stomach, people have forgotten all sense of shame or sympathy. There are places where the men of the house have turned into demons. I've heard stories of people hardening their hearts and slaughtering kids to keep starvation away.'

'Really! People are facing a calamity of mountainous proportions. Exactly 152 years ago, in the year 1478, a similar famine called Durgadevi's famine had swept across the land. That was the period when our saint Damajipant was an official in the court of the king of Bidar. He had got the state granaries opened to bring succour to the people devastated by the famine.'

Shahaji was distressed by the scenes of misery that he saw as he moved along the road. The people had been nauseated by the battles and expeditions of recent times. He felt revolted at the thought that not a single king or sultan ever bothered to rush to the aid of his hard-pressed subjects. Jijabai sat peeping out of the tiny window of her palanquin: the dried-up rivers, just sand and more sand as far as the eyes could reach, the thirst-ridden subjects with their coconut shell cups wherever there was a tiny spring. Some people were digging out the moist looking roots they could find close to riverbeds. They would pound them to powder for their next meal. Human beings had been reduced to mere bags of skin and bones. Even their eyes had begun to look like wells gone dry.

Many villages on the way had been abandoned, with people having moved on in search of food and water. The tiny earth-and-stone huts sported locks on their front doors. Some particularly concerned hut-owners had even laid branches of thorny bushes across their entrances. Entire villages had turned empty of people. It was only in a rare compound or two that some unfortunate family could be spotted.

On the way, they ran into a settlement of half a dozen huts at the other end of a devastated village. There was this stone-and-earth hut in front. The barn behind it was bereft of animals. An old woman sat on a log of wood, her body shrunken. When she noticed horses and palanquins and litters come riding up the dust-laden road, she opened her eyes and ran towards the advancing party. When Jijabai's palanquin-bearers stopped at her instruction, the old woman closed in and begged, 'Give me something to eat, please. Have pity on this old woman.' At a sign from Jijabai, the subedar accompanying her placed a bundle of food items into the old woman's hands, causing her wrinkled face to break into a huge smile. She carried the bundle away as if it were a pot of gold.

Another old farmhand materialised and stood before Shahaji's horse. Folding his wizened hands, he said in a trembling voice, 'Sarkar, please can you part with that pasodi, the rug that you carry? I shall be grateful.'

'Why just the rug, dada?' chimed Jijabai from her palanquin. 'Ask for a few days' worth of grains. Ask for something expensive.'

'No, child. For this poor, homeless old farmer, your rug will be a bigger gift than the sky up there.' With tears in his eyes, the old man went on, 'I swear by Ma Amba, it's been such a terrible time that there isn't a patch of cloth left to put on one's back. There isn't a rag left at home for my two young daughters and my two daughters-in-law to put on. They cannot step out of the house during the day, so they have to wait for nightfall to go out for meeting the compulsions of the body. The males have gone to distant parts in search of food. I spend the entire day at the doorstep. The women stay confined inside for having no clothes. This rug of yours will do good. Four pieces for the four of them, and they'll be able to cover their shame.

A sob escaped Jijabai. She handed over the rug to the old man and added to it a few of her personal items of clothings.

The caravan of palanquins, litters and horsemen was making rapid progress. It was important to reach Shivneri before it turned dark. The sight of the destitution of her people had seared Jijau's heart. She couldn't staunch the tears that flowed from her eyes. Ceaselessly went her prayers to Goddess Bhavani: Oh, mother of the world, when will you bring relief to my people from the twin calamities of the famine and the sultan?

In the dim light of the dawn, two horsemen arrived from Pune, bringing bad news with them. Shahaji had fallen into deep anxiety. He didn't know how to break this jolting information to Jijabai. He managed to gather courage and blurted out, 'Jiu, all our happiness has been snatched away. Three Bijapuri chieftains have descended together on our land. That Murari Jagdeo has been dancing naked in Pune like a monkey gone rabid. He has set the city on fire.'

'*Ago bai!*'

'The wretches have brought with them an army of ten to twelve thousand soldiers. The first thing they did was to burn down the arches. They blew up the bastions and burnt down our courts. They've also torched the village of Bhigwan. The populace of the villages on the way has run away with their cattle and are hiding in the neighbouring forests.

The invading army has been setting alight the villages on the way as it advances towards Baramati and Supe.

Shahaji's face had turned a sight to see. A contrary wind had begun to blow in the valley below Shivneri fort. Black clouds had assembled, as if in fear, behind the mountains that lay before their eyes. His disquietude, the rapidly changing expressions on his face and his clenching and unclenching fist were telling their own story. In an effort to unbottle him, Jijabai urged him, 'Please tell me exactly what has happened.'

'Jiu, our Punwadi! Our Pune, dear!'

'What's happened to Pune?'

'Those scoundrels have subjected our beautiful Pune to the donkey's plough, literally donkey's plough.'

'What are you saying?'

'Some ten to twelve thousand horsemen came riding under that half-witted Murari's flag, their eyes burning with the flame of vengeance and their hands carrying live torches. Those demons brought with them gangs of masons, blacksmiths and labourers, and demolished the walls round Punwadi. They then went on to demolish our grand palaces Malhar and Mhalsa, razed those beautiful buildings to the ground.'

'*Bai ga!*' Jijau stuffed the end of her saree into her mouth to suppress her sobs.

'Jiu, those two paved wells inside our compound, wells that couldn't be emptied by teams of elephant-buckets, those blackguards have filled the wells up with earth, they have run stray cattle across the rose garden that my mother had nurtured with such care!'

Jijabai couldn't hold back her tears. It was as if a dream picture had blown up inside her head and the splinters had buried themselves in her skull, such was the agony she suffered.

'The miscreants then entered the residential localities and set the houses of the poor inhabitants on fire. They not only destroyed the manors of our court functionaries but also burnt down the roofs of temples. The statues and masks of our gods were reduced to dust. Besides, they set alight the crops and houses of around fifty villages around our jagir. This Murari Jagdeo is nothing less than the illegitimate progeny of a donkey. He has carried destruction to its limits.'

'But where did this villain come from?'

'He sent harrows into the burnt-out farms. He yoked donkeys instead of bullocks to the ploughshares. A good sixty to seventy villages around Pune saw the strange sight of donkeys pulling the ploughs. This wicked malefactor Murari has performed these heinous deeds to fill terror in the hearts of the poor farmers. He planted a huge stake in the farm of a peasant and hung a garland of torn footwear on top. He tied broken cowries, old, worn-out brooms and even rotten lemons to it.'

'But why would he want to do these insane things?'

'To instill terror deep into the bones of these simple farmers and ordinary peasants.'

As Shahaji was explaining his understanding of the horrific events, he was surrounded by his relatives and women of the royal household. Even the serving maids were standing behind doors and giving ear to him.

'But Raje, what would be the reason behind unleashing such mindless destruction?'

'To cause conflagration, burn down crops and blow cremation-ground horns to advertise that nobody should stay any further in this blighted land. Nothing but desolation will grow in these lands. Cattle will die and women will turn barren.'

A discussion began in the verandah. Abaji Tukdev, an administrator in Shahaji's court, came up with his opinion, 'Look at the various forms and strategies that the rascals have been putting to use: Of the campaign heads dispatched from Bijapur, one is a Muslim, Randullah Khan; the second is the Maratha Ravraya; and the third is this Brahmin Murari Jagdeo. But the kind of poison that this Brahmin carries in his head, I doubt if even God Yama carries such venom in his.'

'But what soil has this demon emerged from?' asked Jijabai.

'This snake comes from a village called Dhom near Wai. He's a *Dashagranthi* Brahmin. He's said to have visited Kashi and learnt the Vedas. That makes him a master of the holy books as well as of warfare.'

'Raje, it looks like this man has both destruction and rancour sticking to his skin.'

'Quite true, Ranisaheb. This riddle about the human species I have not been able to resolve: how it looks, how it behaves, how it lives! Strange!'

'Panditji, there is this mountain of Bhuleshwar on way to Indapur. Shahajiraje and Jijau had organised a huge puja there a few days back.'

'What kind of puja?'

'It has to be a supplication for something really big. Besides, huge stones from the region of Jejuri are also being carried on donkeys for the construction of a new fort.'

'Oh, I see! Bhu-lesh-war! Which brings Shiva in again. I've not been able to resolve this riddle regarding the Lord of Kailash.'

'What's that?'

'Abandoning the rest of the world to their fate, why does Bhagwan Shankar get excited so often about ensuring the welfare of these Bhosales?'

The news regarding the construction of the new fort had quite rattled Murari Jagdeo. He got into intricate discussions with his almanac expert as also with his crystal-gazers and voodoo men. Murari Pandit had been riven by doubts. It was quite some time ago that he had begun to suspect that there was certainly some black art behind the rising fortune of Shahaji Bhosale. He threw this question at one of his favourite disciples. 'Ghanshyama, boy, test these things against the touchstone of your intellect and see if you can crack them.'

'What things, Gurudev?' asked Ghanshyam, pulling his monkey cap further down his ears.

'You donkey, you! Take the example of Bhatwadi. The Nizam and he had such a tiny little army, and yet they shredded hundreds of thousands of the enemy army to bits!'

'And yet, that fool of an Adilshah received his tormentor with such honour!'

'Not just honour! He had taken him in a procession around Bijapur and made him a general, that is the commander-in-chief of his forces!'

'What can be more shameful, Gurudev? You offer a diamond-studded nose-ring to the one who has chopped your own nose! That was really going too far!'

Murari Jagdeo and his forces should have been on their way to Bijapur the previous day along with Randullah Khan. As decreed by Mohammad Adilshah and his senior Bijapuri officials Khawaas Khan and Mustafa Khan, the precincts of Pune had been wrecked altogether. Following instructions, donkey ploughs had also been run. All assigned work had been duly performed.

Randullah had taken not a whit of interest in burning Pune to the ground or destroying the lands in and around it. On the contrary, he had got dancers and courtesans called over to his camp and spent all his time in riotous celebrations with them.

Randullah Saheb had been quite insistent that Murari should return with them, but Murari had had his way and stayed behind with a small army of two thousand troops. He set off the next day in the direction of Indapur. He had reached the village Yavat by afternoon, and there he caught sight of the mountain of Bhuleshvar. He turned his elephant's head in the direction of the mountain and decided that he would stay there. When he ran up to the hillock and saw the ancient Hemantpanthi Shiva temple, the champaka trees and the bel trees so dear to Lord Shiva, he was quite overcome. He got together his sorcerer and black-magic disciples and said, 'If a person like Shahaji is willing to discard the rest of the world and dreams of building his capital here, the place is bound to be sacred and beneficial.'

The army was compelled to strike camp around Yavat. The next day morning, Murari called over his political advisers and other officials and announced to his deputy Rayarao, 'We shall not lose control of this religious spot anymore. From here on, this sacred place shall be my own capital town. Get busy, all of you, and make preparations for completing the half-built fort here. Call over all your artisans, masons and workers.'

A seasoned soldier like Rayarao stared at Murali Pandit open-mouthed. Irritated, Murari snapped at him, 'Why are you ogling at me like an idiot? Go on, get busy. We have to make the capital city here.'

'For whom, Panditji?'

'For me, you moron! Keep this in mind. Murari Jagdeo has become king here. Not just king, but king of kings.'

Murari identified an etched rock as the sacred place for his throne and got the puja started. He placed his footwear on top of the stone, and his sorcerer disciples began mouthing incantations in a language that nobody could understand. Rayarao and the other officials stood looking dumbly at the footwear placed on the rock.

The beautiful make of that footwear had for long been the topic of discussion among the soldiers. Murari had called a special cobbler over from Hubli to Bijapur to create that unique footwear. Its leather had been made of an otter's skin that was found either in the river or deep in the jungles. It was no wonder it elicited great gossip in the army as a footwear that was as expensive as half the cost of an elephant.

Rayarao and all the others were stunned by Murari's whimsical behaviour, but Murari himself was in no mood to care. He established his camp there and announced that he was formally starting the administrative work of his state with immediate effect. He even dispatched a letter of this announcement to Bijapur.

He ordered his officials to begin preparing for a grand coronation ceremony for himself, assigning to himself the grand title of Dharmaavataaro Raajaadhiraaj Maharaj Rajarshi Pandit Murari Jagdeo Prabhu: Saarvabhaum Pratinidhi, which in simple language would translate to 'the Incarnation of Dharma, King of Kings, the Greatest of Monarchs, Outstanding Scholar, God Himself, the Ruler of the Universe'.

A few sensible men along with Rayarao came forward and tried to make sense with him. 'Panditji, you are an extremely close friend of Khawaas Khan, but sir, but this enterprise of getting yourself coronated is going a bit too far.'

'Silence! And mind your language, all of you! I am the King of Kings.'

'Forgive us, Panditji, for our trivial doubt.'

'All right, ask.'

'With the Musalmans having their own big Adilshahi at Bijapur, why would they want to make you king?'

'Rayarao, you are a fool of the first water.'

'Watch it, Panditji,' Rayarao warned him. 'This kind of intransigence can be punishable by death in that Islamic kingdom.'

'Ignorant fool! What conception can you have of the power of my intelligence? There shall be a miracle within the next four or five days.'

'What kind?'

'Your Mohammad Adilshah and his beautiful Badi Begum shall themselves come and visit us here.'

'Why?'

'To offer their respects to me during my coronation. To request my blessings on them.'

There was deep unrest among the Bijapuri soldiers. There was no doubt that Murari Pandit was losing his mental balance, but who could dispense wisdom to power? The Bijapuri captains got into the nearby villages and hammered the Deshmukhs, Deshpandes and Patils into accompanying them to the Bhuleshvar hillock. They were all compelled to bow before the new king.

Two days went by. A chieftain named Dalvi left for Konkan on durbar-assigned work. Worries in the kitchen mounted. The famine had hit the region so hard that despite the flaunting of gold coins, there was no food of any kind to be had; no fodder for the animals either. But who was going to tell this to the monkey who rode on Khawaas Khan's shoulders?

On the fourth day, King of Kings, the great *Maharajadhiraj* Murari Pandit Prabhu got out of bed late. He walked out of the tent into a hot day. Murari felt a sudden churn in the stomach. He rubbed his eyes in disbelief and looked around fearfully. A bare sixty or seventy of his immediate servants and their horses were all that he could see. The rest of the army had decamped for Bijapur some time in the early hours of the morning.

Maharajadhiraj Pandit Murari Jagdeo could do nothing but look helplessly around him.

6

TEARS ON THE BANK OF KUKADI

1630

Even if the entire sky were to collapse on his head, Shahaji was determined not to hold himself back. The one single anxiety that was bugging him was for those Maaval valiants waiting for him. There was one maverick that had sprung up today in the shape of that Murari Pandit. Tomorrow there would be another psychotic to deal with. It was best to grapple with them right now.

Shahaji finished his bath at the crack of dawn and offered fresh flowers to the idol of Lord Shankar. His companions were already mounted and ready near Hathi Darwaza, the Elephant Gate, of the fort. They all set off at a gallop and crossed the Lendhi stream. This area had seen many strange upheavals. Who knew how many political giants lay buried in the ancient graveyard nearby? The horses were moving straight as arrows in the darkness of the dawn, and the only sound that could be heard was their snorting and the clatter of their hooves.

When the sun had moved up in the sky, the horses arrived at the bank of the river Kukadi. What had been only vague patches began to acquire a clearer form. There was a decent flow along one side of the river and the perspiring horses dipped their tongues into the flow to slake their thirst. Shahaji espied a bunch of horsemen on the other side of the river.

One of the horsemen on the other side let out a loud call to which Pilaji Deshpande immediately responded. When the figures on the other side became more distinct, Shahaji was quite overcome at recognising them. The very friends from Maaval whom Shahaji had set out to meet had sent their young boys or relatives to meet him. There were a few senior men in the mix too. Konde Deshmukh, Paigude, Pasalkar, Maral Deshmukh, Shilimkar, Gayakwad, Marne—so many young warriors from the best houses of Maaval had come running for a meet with their king.

The seniors in this crowd of youngsters were Pasalkar Baba and Prabhu Deshpande. They gathered around the king in the dense blueberry grove alongside the riverbank. The Maaval lads had brought with them a few reins and saddle equipment as samples. As the king was examining them with some curiosity, the agony that the old men had carried bottled inside them burst out. 'Raje,' they cried, 'the preparations we had got into were massive in scale. Your dream of a Maharashtra, a separate, independent kingdom of the Marathas had set the entire region of the Twelve Maavals—all the twelve mountain ranges—on fire. The last three or four months, none of us could sleep well on account of it—neither the young nor the old. Young men from every single village had tied scarves round their waists and rushed out. The armies we had created in every village were like mountains of steel.'

When their voices choked with emotion, the young men took up, 'What a lot of faith you would have placed on us young men of Maaval!'

'But what could we do, Raje? Catastrophe struck. Like an arrow penetrating the rib cage, the famine pierced our hearts and bled the life out of us.'

'Yes, Raje, and we don't have the strength left in our bodies to pull that murderous arrow out. Sheer starvation has turned our animals to dust and men into monkeys.'

'Raje, drought and diseases have emptied our huge stables. To prevent the disease from spreading across the village, the carcasses were dragged out of the villages by teams of bull-buffalos.'

'How fervently we had desired to go galloping across the country with your banner fluttering in our hands, Raje! Take a look at these reins and these saddles! The women and children of our farmers' household hold them to their chests and cry, that's the only use these pieces have seen!'

'If this horrible famine had not swallowed up our animals, and along with them our resolve, a new chapter in history would have started on this Maaval soil.'

The Raja had known about it all along, but this interaction with the victims brought home to him the enormity of the holocaust. There had been a few villages on the banks of the Mula and the Mutha around Pune that had managed to raise a half-decent harvest; but they had then been visited by this fell disease called Murari Pandit whose army had devastated farms and villages more effectively than a swarm of locusts could. As for the villages in the mountain belt, the severe drought had taken charge of breaking their backs. Women and children of lately prosperous houses roamed the jungles in search of food and water. The region of Pune had never witnessed a dual calamity of this scale.

Neither Shahaji nor his brave associates from the Maaval valley could hold back the copious tears that flowed down their eyes. Kukadi Mai's eyes had turned wet too at this heart-rending sight.

It happens occasionally that the servants of the household come up with priceless suggestions. Narmadabai came up with one that afternoon. 'Rani saheb, we are well aware of the disaster that's struck your parental house, but even so, your mother is waiting for you there at Sindkhed.'

'Yes, but how did you get to know all this?'

'Ain't I your shadow, then?' she retorted. 'These huge mountains reaching up to the sky, the deep gorges and gullies here, and these roaring winds! How could you think of bringing up your little prince in this kind of a climate? Sindkhed is any day better!'

'We are not going anywhere, we've firmly decided on that.'

'But in these mountainous—'

'Understand this, Narmadey, we don't propose to raise a parrot here, or a bird of that kind. We shall give birth to an eagle. And you know, don't you, that an eagle's eyrie is located on top of a mountain cliff! We want our prince to be nurtured in these wild places, to clash with winds and storms.'

Jijau had been a tough person from the day she was born. As a child she was better known as Jija the tigress. Now, as she was resident in Vijayrao's palace in Shivneri with a seven-month foetus inside her, she would often set off with her sister-in-law Durga Devi or with her little daughter-in-law Jayanti. The moment she stepped out of the palace, the heaviness of her body would vanish. She had made friends with the ancient tamarind, peepul and champa trees inside the fort complex. If ever she felt out of breath as she walked, she would sit down on a log under a tree till her calves had recovered their strength. She was sure to make at least two trips to the ancient Shivai Devi temple on the other side every day.

Monsoon had departed and winter had settled in. The night wind had begun to bite sharp. It would travel across the hills and valleys before descending upon the fort to settle there. Braziers would be kept burning to ensure that the mother-to-be was kept sufficiently warm. Vijairao's wife and Sambhaji's child bride Jayanti's mother, Sarsa Devi, would personally take care of all of Jijau's needs, ranging from meals to the smallest item of cosmetics.

The ancient caves of the Buddha's times and the shelters where the Bhikshus would sit for their prayers stood witness to the antiquity of the fort. The stone images of Maruti and Ganpati, weathered smooth by sun and rain, told of the rule of the Yadavs of Devgiri sometime in the past. Later, the Nizamshahi regime had been inaugurated from this fort. It was from this ancient fort that surveillance would be kept on the trade route that began from the faraway seacoast and climbed the mountains of the Konkan range to move towards Naneghat. Conquering this spot was as difficult a job as could be imagined. As soon as one crossed over the Lendi stream below the fort, one encountered the five massive gates just past Somatwadi. The gates were made from old teak and studded with sharp, beak-shaped, fist-sized spikes, thus ruling out the tactic of the assaulting forces using elephants to bring the gates down.

It was on account of the invincibility of the fort and his faith in the fort-keeper Vijayrao Vishwasrao that Shahaji had made arrangement for resolving the difficult issue of Jijabai's confinement.

Vigorous campaigns, spirited sallies and counter-sallies, political manoeuvres, and ceaseless alarums and excursions—this had become the prescription for living life. Death would always be a fellow-traveller during such times of ferment. But for all the uncertainty and turmoil, it wouldn't do to delay the banns beyond a certain point. Elder son Sambhaji was eight years old now, and as per the convention of those times, he was quite of age to be got married. Accordingly, the marriage celebrations of the young prince with Jayanti Devi, the daughter of Vijayrao, were held in the fort around Diwali time. The people present at the fort for the occasion were not many, but the gala event was celebrated with great fanfare. The past few months had brought much pain and misery to Shahaji and Jijabai; they were grateful that Vijayrao had stood with them during these difficult times.

The challenge of administering a kingdom wouldn't allow any rest or respite. The day after Sambhaji's marriage, Shahaji took his horses out of the private gate below the fort. The emperor Shah Jahan's forces had reached Nashik and Dhule, and there was work to be done.

The wedding celebrations had allowed a good eight or ten days of much-needed distraction, with Vijayrao's family playing the generous hosts. As sinking ships exude a reek that causes mice to jump off the vessel, among humans too, difficult times send their earliest messages to the near and dear ones who scurry away faster than mice can. That was the kind of period that was rolling past.

The slaughter of Jijau's father and brothers at the hands of that foolish, disoriented Burhanshah; that unprecedented and beautiful dream of creating one's own kingdom destroyed by a famine; the donkey's plough that the clever but iniquitous Murari Jagdeo ran over Pune; the burning down of the capital even before the state had arrived; it was a series of unending tragedies and calamities.

However valorous a person may be, when the termites of worry start burrowing into the body, they get deep into the bones and render the body hollow. On her way to the Shivai temple or back, Jijau would often sit on the parapet of one of the stone tanks close by. These tanks had been made for storing ghee, which would be used to massage the bodies of injured soldiers to help them recover from their ailments. As she sat on the parapet, she would send her gaze skimming over the hills and valleys that surrounded the spot, and mull over the misfortunes dogging her life. Sita Mai of the Ramayana had had to suffer through a similar exile, but at least she had the benefit of having Lord Rama by her side. Also, she wasn't weighed down by worries for the future because the throne at Ayodhya was safe and secure, even if far away. What did Jijabai have here in her exile to offer her solace? The independent state that had been brought to birth with such hopes had been throttled to death by destiny. The capital city had been ravaged, their own palace had been razed to the ground.

In this moment of her loneliness, she didn't even have the company of her eight-year-old son Shambhu. The boy had tossed off the trappings of wedding the previous evening, and ridden away with his father the very next day. There had been protests, of course, and even Jijabai had put in a weak plea, but Shahaji had been quite firm. 'As fish's babies cannot survive out of the sea, the sons of valorous men need battles and campaigns to keep breathing.'

The constitution of a woman turns delicate during pregnancy. She gets emotionally high-strung too. The company of her husband can be immensely gratifying during such times. But with urgent campaigns to attend to, Shahaji couldn't find the time to indulge Jijabai. He had, however, done all that he could by appointing some of his best men to ensure her well-being. Balkrishna Hanumante, Shamrao Nilkanth and Raghunath Ballal were some of his ablest officials. Seniors like Gomajibaba Pansambal would patrol the residence night and day as if they were security guards.

But what about the crises that kept springing up on a daily basis? True, Jijabai had a lion for a husband, but destiny too had been weaving circles like a venomous snake, choking the breath out! What about that?

Vijayrao had a personal armoury in a corner of the palace. It was choc-a-bloc full of weapons like spears, swords and shields. One morning, Jijabai walked into the armoury and pulled out two swords from the wooden stand in which they rested. She then got her maid Yamuna to accompany her to the wall on the rear side of the palace, the wall that overlooked the valley on the Konkan side.

Sarsa Devi was busy in the temple when the sound of clanking swords drifting in from the rear wall startled her. She peeped out inquiringly and was met by a bizarre sight. There was Jijabai, coming down spiritedly at Yamuna, while the poor maid was fending with extreme caution, conscious of the delicate state of her mistress, terrified at the thought of causing her any damage.

'What's going on here, Jijausaheb?' Sarsa Devi asked.

'I was getting awfully bored just sitting here and doing nothing.'

'*Aga bai*! But these war games in your condition?'

'I just don't know what I should be doing. At least I can keep myself distracted, Akka Saheb. The little prince inside and his movements don't let me rest anyway. Just thought I'd brush up my skills a little bit.'

Sarsa Devi laughed heartily, took Jijabai by the hand, and the two walked back into the palace.

Little Jayanti had drawn beautiful rangolis round the dining board on the floor. Jijau had taken a biggish plank for herself and sat herself down cautiously with her legs folded under her. It was in this cramped state that she took her meals. Sarsa Devi finished her meals, folded her hands at the plate and heaved herself up. Widening her eyes at Jijabai, she laughed and said, 'See how the body turns stiff sitting on the plank? How could you have even thought of fooling around with a sword?'

'How do I describe this muddled state of my body, vahini? Sometimes I feel like roaming around atop an elephant; at other times, I want to get on a tiger's back and hold it by its ears; I want to sit on a glittering yellow throne of gold, or turn into a peacock and go gallivanting in the blue sky.'

'Most entertaining, these cravings of yours!'

'I sometimes want to build huge temples and distribute charity with an open hand. I want to found a new religion!'

'Oh goodness! A new religion altogether?'

'Yes, the religion of humanity! A religion as vast as a huge river that accommodates into its span all the countless streams that flow into it! A refuge for all the dispossessed and the downtrodden!'

Jijabai's voice suddenly became thick. 'How many injuries can one take in a single lifetime, vahini? The body seems to have got used to it all now. Unrelenting hassles, anxieties, exiles and uprootings—these words seem to have been created only to give us company.'

Jijau's eyes turned wet involuntarily. As Sarsa Devi stared at her nonplussed, Jijabai continued in an embarrassed tone, 'Sorry, Akka Saheb, what you see are not tears; they are liquid fire that seem to be oozing out of every pore of my body. Here's my husband who has helped cover the roofs of four kings with tiles of gold. And have we got a palace of our own? At least a decent hall? If the wife of this dauntless warrior is today compelled to find shelter in someone else's wayside fort, how's it different from a bird looking for alien nests to deliver its young one?'

'Why should you consider us as aliens, JIjausaheb?'

'No, no, please don't misunderstand me, we are truly beholden to you. What do I say? It seems that our injuries have become our gods!'

Vijayrao Vishwasrao had left strict instructions regarding his royal guest: she should never want for anything, however trivial. Maids and bondsmen, officials and clerks, all of them were in perpetual movement to ensure that the confinement went off smoothly. Durga Devi and Jayanti were in attendance round the clock.

Shahaji had gathered a big reputation across all of southern India. As a result, word hadn't taken time to spread that his wife was in confinement in Shivneri. The women of the fort had plunged themselves enthusiastically into the task of doing up the room assigned for the childbirth. The walls were given a coating of lime and beautiful pictures of peacocks and other birds were painted on them. The doors were strung with garlands of colourful beads and glasses, with a few pearls thrown in for good effect.

As the day of the blessed event came closer, women of all the important families of important townships like Junnar, Udapur and Narayangaon began gathering in the fort; some among them had years of experience in midwifery. The best physicians of the region had been housed in the yonder palace, ready with their herbs and potions. A large number of working-class women from the valley—milkmaids, fisherwomen, herdswomen and others belonging to various jungle tribes—began climbing the fort even before it was light, bringing with them fresh milk, butter extracted from cow's milk and baskets upon baskets of jungle fruits. They would all gather around the pregnant queen and gaze at her admiringly.

There would be old women too among these visitors, old but sturdy. They would join up with the girls and move up the chain gates with baskets and trays balanced on their heads. With the dawn just beginning to disperse its golden rays, these women would hold the chain with one hand and the burden on their head with the other as they negotiated the climb. They had to use their toes too in this acrobatic exercise to get some purchase on the rock. Jijabai never failed to be dumbfounded at the devotion of these women towards her, to say nothing of their athleticism.

She would regularly call over Gomaji Baba and distribute fistfuls of money among these hardworking women.

A number of the old crones gathered there would sit talking about tales of their younger days. When Akbar the Great had travelled all the way from Delhi to wipe out the Nizamshahi rule at Ahmadnagar, Sultana Chand Bibi had brought the little Nizamshahi prince over to Shivneri for refuge. The old women would get into long descriptions of the dignity with which Chand Bibi conducted herself in the fort and the popularity she had gained among the people there. Ironically, it was one of her own servants, a Khoja of her Ahmadnagar court who had played foul by her. He had spread the false rumour that she had joined enemy forces. This had so enraged a few in the crowd that they had slaughtered the courageous woman who had travelled all the distance only to safeguard the interest of her parental kingdom of Ahmadnagar. Her own subjects, however, held her in such great affection that they refused to believe the story of her death. They continued to believe that Chand Bibi was hiding in the Shivneri-Junnar region, waiting for the opportunity to strike back.

The carpenters of nearby Ambegaon were renowned for their skill. One Changdev came over and took in hand the fabrication of a beautifully carved cradle for the little one. When Shivappa, the goldsmith of Junnar, heard of this, he too arrived with his helpers to weave some of his own art into the woodwork. It was barely three or four years earlier that the present emperor of Hindustan, Shah Jahan had been staying incognito in Junnar along with his young princes Dara, Shuja and Aurangzeb. Shivappa would proudly proclaim that he had made intricately designed gircles, necklaces and rings for the princes.

·ೊ೩ಲಿ೨·

A huge imperial army had laid camp on the open grounds of Chandanpuri. The tent of Asaf Khan, the subedar of the Mughals, was astir with activity. Some sixty to seventy elephants and a large number of stables to accommodate some 15,000 horses were spread around the camp.

A huge canopy had been erected in front of the main tent to welcome Shahaji into the service of the Mughal Empire, where Asaf Khan had welcomed him with great fanfare. Shahaji had spent the previous evening near a hillock in Chandwad. He had got up at the crack of dawn and paid a visit to the ancient temple of Goddess Renuka Devi. While seeking her blessing, he had beseeched, 'Oh Mother of the world! The kinds of abuses that the human body has to suffer, a goddess as mighty as you never has to confront. Give me a powerful blessing, Mother, a blessing potent enough to bring to an end the cycle of misfortunes that has been dogging your devotee.'

Three other senior Mughal chieftains were present for this important function besides Asaf Khan. Asaf Khan had received Shahaji's request for this opportunity to serve under the Mughal banner quite a long time ago, but knowing that this matter lay well outside his purview, he had dispatched it to Agra by camel-post for the consideration of the emperor himself. Considering Shahaji's stature, his reputation, and most importantly his volatile temperament, nobody had been sure whether Shah Jahan would accept the him in his service.

However, the response that had arrived from Shah Jahan had blown away the minds of the Mughal officials. It was as if the emperor had emptied camel-loads of joy upon the supplicant's head. The *firman* that he had issued not only appointed Shahaji a chieftain of five thousand horses, but he had also appointed three of Shahaji's cousins—Maloji, Mambaji and Kheloji—as chieftains of three thousand horses. The emperor had gone still further and had appointed nine-year-old Sambhaji as chieftain of a thousand horses. The generosity of Shah Jahan had stunned Shahaji too.

An extremely expensive box had arrived from Agra as a special gift from Emperor Shah Jahan to Shahajiraje. Asif Khan was overcome as he presented the jewel-studded box to Shahaji. Wiping tears of joy from his eyes, he said, 'Shahajiraje, I've not met a more fortunate person than you. Have you any idea what this box contains?' So saying, he pulled out of the box an extravagantly costly *choga*, a velvet gown with buttons made of rare emerald, the very gown that Shah Jahan had donned when he had first ascended the Mughal throne. Instead of giving the gown to one of his sons, he had sent it over to Shahaji to express his regard for him.

As they continued talking, Asaf Khan gently placed his arm on Shahaji's shoulder and took him to a side. 'Raja Saheb,' he said, when they were alone, 'you may safely assume that you are the favourite of all your gods and goddesses. The pace at which the winds are blowing, the day may not be too far when you may be appointed the subedar of the Mughal Empire for all of the Deccan.'

'The subedari of the Deccan?' Shahaji was stunned.

'Absolutely, Raja saheb, the subedari of the entire Deccan dominions of the Mughal Empire, a post that the emperor of Hindustan keeps reserved only for his favourite prince, a post that no non-Muslim person can even dream of, not even his gods and goddesses!'

Jijabai swaddled infant Shivba in a velvet wrap. She had gone to the Shivai temple along with Durga Devi and a few of her serving maids to pay her obeisance to the goddess. It was on the goddess's name that she had named her little one Shivaji. On her return journey, she sat for a long time under a huge old tree close to Ambarkhana. Memories of her parental home, particularly of Lakhoji, had come flooding back to her. How the old man would have loved to take his grandchild in his lap!

Meanwhile, in the Chandanpuri camp, Shahaji received instructions from the emperor to go after the rebellious Darya Khan. Like a true professional, Shahaji got into his stride and wiped out both Darya Khan and his army. That done, he began fretting for a trip to Shivneri.

He reached the fort late on the night of the fifth moon. No one can tell whether the vales and hills of those parts got advance information of the king's arrival. Jijabai had lately got into the habit of retiring early. Once the evening bath with warm water was done with and the little prince was fed his medicines and diluted cow-milk, Jijabai would apply a spot of black on the infant's fair cheek and broad forehead. She would then wrap up his ears, draw away the influence of any evil-eye with salt and mustard and put him into his cradle. The soft rattle of the gold chain and the tinkle of the tiny bells made the infant's eyelids heavy, and he would soon be fast asleep.

That particular evening, however, the infant prince refused to go to sleep. Eyes wide open, he stared with curiosity at the colourful wooden birds and parrots rocking on the upper beam of the cradle. For variety, he would jingle the bells on the braces round his wrists and ankles to entertain himself. Jijabai complained with mock irritation, 'What's wrong with this kid, Narmadey? Could this blockhead have got a whiff of his father's arrival?'

As if on cue, the sound of neighing horses was heard from below and Jijabai's left eyelid throbbed. She broke out involuntarily, '*Aga bai*! It looks like the king's party has arrived!'

The king walked in and stood drinking in the sight of the frisky kid in the cradle. His poet's heart was thrilled at the sight of the fair, cuddlesome bundle of energy. 'Jiu,' he mumbled, 'on a full-moon night a few days back, it was so difficult to sight the milky white moon, the sky was so full of dark, thick clouds. How often I searched for our *Chanda Mama* behind those dark layers!'

'So, could you locate him finally?'

'How could I? He had quietly sneaked out of the sky and sought refuge in your lap, hadn't he?'

It was a night of unbridled joy for Shahaji. He distributed gifts to the servants with a free hand and presented the expensive silk clothes he had specially brought along to Vijayrao, Sarsa Devi, Durga Devi and Jayanti. The court workers and the grooms and footmen were also loaded with clothes. The real fun arrived when a rivalry sprang up between Sambhaji and Shahaji, both of them competing to hold the little one in their arms. To add to the entertainment, the babe-in-arms seemed to be enjoying it thoroughly too.

It was very late in the night when Jijau and Shahaji went to bed. Shahaji couldn't keep the pride out of his voice when he said, 'Jiu, that emperor Shah Jahan seems to have fallen so much in love with me that he may make me the subedar of the Deccan. Why, if I were to stretch myself out a little bit, who knows, he might gift the jagir of Kabul and Kandahar to me!'

'*Ago bai*!' Jijabai turned serious in the middle of a laugh, 'what should I make of this?'

'You think this is a trivial gift?' asked Shahaji, looking deep into her eyes.

'No, Raje, most certainly not,' came Jijabai's riposte, like sparks flying off swords clashing against each other. 'The two of us have so well digested this poison called life that we shall never ever compromise with our mission. You and I have taken birth only to fight for the dignity of our soil.'

·ೞಲ·

The hundred-and-thirty-year-old Nizamshahi rule had finally come to an end. The Adilshahi regime had helped the Mughal Empire in realising its very old dream of drowning the Nizamshahi kingdom out of existence, and now, finally, the belt that lay between Delhi and Bijapur had been ripped away.

Powerful chieftains had established their own suzerainty over the territories under them. Rehan Khan had taken the Solapur fort and the surrounding areas under his control; fort-keeper Vijayrao Vishwasrao had made the Shivneri fort his own; towards Cheul, Nizampur and Roha, the Siddhis Saba and Saif Khan had gained ascendance, while Siddhi Ambar had gained control of the Janjira fort near Dandrajpuri. Not one of them, however, had the mettle or the vigour to claim suzerainty over the former Sultanate of Ahmadnagar. It was against this background that conversation began in the Pemgiri fort between chieftain Pilajipant Prabhu Deshpande and Jijabai.

Looking Shahaji in the eye, she said, 'Raje, it's a number of years now since you have been nursing this dream of "Maharashtra". Realise it now by becoming the Padshah yourself.'

'Jiu, I don't think circumstances are ripe enough for that.'

'Raje, I believe that you certainly must collect yourself and take the leap,' said Pilaji Deshpande.

Noticing that Shahaji was in the grip of an uncharacteristic state of hesitation and diffidence, Jijabai got up and walked up to him with firm steps. As she stood towering over him, she flashed the lightning of her gaze at him as she declaimed, 'Raje, you are recognised all over Hindustan as Shahajiraje Bhosale. The very Ibrahim Adilshah whose forces you had vanquished considered himself privileged to appoint you the commander-in-chief of his own army. The emperor of Delhi considers it his greatest gain to count you among his friends. If a lion-hearted, valorous soldier such as you allows his weapon to remain unsheathed, how can one look askance at the rabbits scurrying around the town?'

For a long time, Shahajiraje sat turning things over in his head, letting out deep sighs after every little while. The muscles of his face then hardened, his shoulders turned taut and his eyes lit up. 'Yes,' he said, rising to his feet, 'what you two have been saying makes eminent sense. True manhood lies not in bursting crackers in somebody else's pavilion, but in setting alight the cannon fuse on one's own bastions.'

This beam of a new opportunity streaming out of a crack in the surrounding gloom suddenly lit up the Shahaji's imagination. The map of his land began to sketch itself out on his mind's wall-slate. Speaking with impressive gravity, he said, 'Although Delhi controls Daulatabad, we still hold the territory from Nashik, Tryambak, Sangamner and Junnar right up to Konkan down there. The jagirs of Pune and Supe belong to us by right and by decree. So, if we can join the dots from all four directions, what's the harm in playing a new hand? Come along, then, let's see what destiny has in store for us.'

Nothing could have thrilled Jijabai and all the others more.

Then began the sittings, the detailed discussions and the outlining of strategies. Important functionaries like Mambaji Bhosale and Sarjerao Ghatge began gathering around. After the evening meeting was over, Mambaji Bhosale came over to Shahaji's bedroom to bid him goodbye. Looking deeply uncomfortable, he mumbled, 'Dada, why do you want to light sparks that may burn your own clothes?'

'Meaning?'

'Forgive me, Dada, for speaking candidly. I don't think we Marathas are naturally cut out for becoming independent kings or trying to establish their own kingdoms.'

'Quite obvious from your behaviour, otherwise such cowardly and inauspicious words would never have escaped your lips. Is there anything other than this that you have to say?'

'Why would the Muslim chieftains want to help us in this enterprise?'

'Look, Mamba, for the past twenty years, I have been traversing across the Bijapur Sultanate, the Daulatabad palaces and the lands of the Mughals lying in the entire area stretching from Burhanpur to Mandu-Sagar. Every one of the chieftains in these three main power structures, who are big names today, have been my friends since the time they were searching for their feet. We've ridden together, we've eaten together, we've sung and danced together. I know it's stupid to be blowing your own trumpet, but if you look closely, all of these Muslim chieftains know well about the vigour of my sword. But they are a great deal more wary of our intellectual strength and our enterprise.'

As Shahaji was going after Mambaji hammer and tongs, Jijabai walked in from the yonder hall. The flustered Mambaji turned towards her and appealed, 'Vahini, Dada here is no Shah, no Khan and no Ambar either. How's he going to survive as a king amongst this crowd of Muslim chieftains?'

Jijabai heard him out and responded with a laugh, 'Why are you worrying, Bhauji? For how long can a person live in fear? You need to come together, all of you, and summon your daring and courage. Even the slightest excuse is enough for you all to bend over backwards before the alien, so much so that your character has suffered a decline. Let some never-before deeds of valour roll out of your combined swords!'

·~ঔ৹·

One evening, as they lay together on their eiderdown mattress, Badi Begum rolled into Mohammad Sultan and grumbled, 'This has to be brought to a halt, my lord. However expensive the footwear, even if made of otter-skin, it can never be carried on the head, can it?'

'What's the matter, Begum? Could you be talking of that Murari Pandit?'

'Absolutely!' came her candid response. 'I've never liked that man's behaviour, or even his character.'

Under the indulgence of his mentor Khawaas Khan, Murari Pandit had gone on waxing in power and influence these last four years. While nobody had doubted his sharpness of mind, his whimsical activities had put fright into the hearts of all around him. Mohammadshah had himself received complaints about his eccentric behaviour. Even otherwise, the arrogance of a Brahmin pundit couldn't have gone down well with the Muslim warlords of Bijapur. But he happened to be the favourite lapdog of the Wazeer Khawaas Khan, and discretion had demanded that lips stayed zipped.

When the Mughals had laid siege to the fort of Daulatabad, Fateh Khan had been the de facto head of the Nizam Sultanate. His own Nizamshahi soldiers inside the fort and Adilshah's forces that had rushed to their aid had been giving bitter battle to the besieging army, but crisis had developed with regard to the supply of food grains.

Khawaas Khan called Murari Jagdeo over one morning to his palace and sounded him, 'Our men and animals are in dire straits there in Daulatabad. With food running out, they are in a hellhole.'

'Khan Saheb, please tell me what I can do. You just have to say the word.'

'Our forces caught inside the fort are collapsing with hunger.'

'Just say the word, huzoor, tell me how I can be of use.'

'Look, all of us chieftains and the Sultan himself have gathered rice, wheat, and a whole lot of other commodities from our regions, and we've done that in a mere two days.'

'So, then, let's go galloping that way immediately!'

'That's just what I've been saying. The earlier we reach there, the more men and animals that can be saved. The enterprise is full of hazards, and that's why I've deliberately chosen you for the job.'

'Most certainly, huzoor! Leave everything else to me.'

Murari Jagdeo set off full-belt with his merchandise of food and other provisions, stopping on the way only for catering to the needs of the horses and camels.

Murari Jagdeo saw Ambarkot around the outer part of the Daulatabad fort. Beyond the barrier, the battle was in full swing. The booms of the cannons resonated in the sky while the air was thick with dust. The screams and shouts of men and animals fell steadily on the ears. Murari's associate shouted into his ear, 'Once the provisions reach inside and Fateh Khan drives away the Mughals swarming around him, he shall hand the fort over to us, as has been agreed.'

Murari suddenly felt a heady sensation crackle inside him. The wiseacre residing in him suddenly came awake. He lifted his hands high in the air and roared, 'What nonsense! How can that cunning fox ever be trusted? Isn't he the monster who killed his own benefactor, the Nizam?'

That was when an official of Fateh Khan, who had sneaked out of a secret door in the fort, presented himself before Murari. The Bijapur as well as the Daulatabad soldiers, as well as animals, were collapsing where they stood from starvation, he reported, and begged Murari to waste no time in reaching succour to them. At that, Murari flared up and said, 'Tell your foolish Fateh Khan to first hand over charge of the fort.'

There were two reasons why Emperor Shah Jahan had returned for the second time to the Deccan: to get that rebel Shahaji into a straitjacket and to conquer the fort of Daulatabad. Absolutely determined to win Daulatabad by any means possible, he had dispatched his chieftain Khan-e-Khanaan to the battle-front. The impassioned Mughal soldiers under Khan-e-Khanaan's banner had created a circle of fire around the bastions of Daulatabad. They had dug huge trenches outside along the walls of both Mahakot and Ambarkot.

Fateh Khan and his Bijapur associate Khairiyat Khan had been giving a tough battle from the ramparts of the fort. The Mughals, on the other hand, were equally determined to capture the fort, and towards this effort, they had readied a good sixty or seventy swinging ladders for use at the same time. Ropes were being used to string up ladders five-persons tall, and these were being placed against the walls. The Mughal braves were staking their lives in an effort to go tripping up over the fortification and into the fort. Fateh Khan's soldiers on the other side were doing all they could to defeat this assault. They would hack at the ladders and toss the Mughal soldiers clambering over them into the air. The big and small cannons, meanwhile, had been booming away. The consequence of this bitter clash was that soldiers from both sides were getting killed or seriously crippled.

The Mughals were successful in stringing up a dozen or so ladders on one patch of the fortification. Dodging the fires, they managed to scale the Ambarkot wall, which was about forty feet in height and a massive thirty feet in width. The Mughal officers looked incredulously at the thick, invincible walls, and stared at each other in wonder. 'Ya Allah, was this Ambar a man or a monster?' they exclaimed. 'We haven't seen such colossal walls even in our dreams!'

Fateh Khan's emissaries once again made a beeline to Murari and tried to bring him round. 'All the other formalities can be handled at a later time,' they pleaded, 'but our hungry and thirsty soldiers first need food!' Murari Pandit, however, remained unmoved by all their pitiful entreaties.'

On the one hand, there was no food, on the other, the fired-up Mughals were straining forward to get a bite at them. The situation inside the fort was turning more and more desperate by the minute and slipping out of control. The sight of this man-made catastrophe was turning Fateh Khan insane. As he looked out of a secret window towards the foot of the fort, he could see the Mughal soldiers emptying sacks of gunpowder into every hole and crack of the fort walls. The future looked dark when a message from a Mughal chieftain was handed over to him. 'Why are you so determined to destroy your precious lives?' it read. 'Surrender. Allah and the emperor are generous. We shall immediately give food to your soldiers and forty thousand gold coins to you. We shall load you with presents.'

The harried Fateh Khan sent one last desperate message to Murari Pandit, 'I am willing to roll at your feet, if you so desire, but first dispatch food. If supplies don't arrive immediately, we shall be compelled to go and embrace the Mughals.' But this despairing, anguished message too left the conceited Murari Pandit unmoved. Instead of relief, he sent back the arrogant message, 'Send the keys to the fort immediately. If you fail to do so, I shall chop your head and toss it over the fort wall.'

The fire that burns in an empty stomach is far more devastating than gunpowder stuffed in a cannon. The starving soldiers espied the ladders going down the fortification walls and saw this as their only opportunity. They were too crazed with hunger to bother about friend and foe. Between two and three hundred famished warriors shimmied down the ladders and presented themselves in the Mughal camp. 'Please give us some food first,' they begged. 'After that you may blow us up with cannon fire.' The shrewd Khan-e-Khaanan had the unfortunates served food. He was too shrewd a warrior to miss this opportunity of getting converts.

Fateh Khan, meanwhile, waited and waited for the relief promised from Bijapur to arrive, but he was waiting in vain. He wiped his tears. Now he was staring at the yawning jaws of death. As a first act of precaution, he dispatched the women and children towards the rear end of the fort and secured them in the dark dungeons there.

As Murari retired for the night in his tent outside the besieged fort, he complimented himself on the manner in which he had ground Fateh Khan under his heels. It was at dawn that he was jolted out of his sleep by ear-drum shattering explosions. The thunder-claps were so enormous that the horses tied in the stables sprang up on all fours and elephants began trumpeting in panic. Murari himself was thrown out of his bed at the shock. Collecting himself up with difficulty, he swallowed a couple of times, and peeped out of the window of the cloth wall of his tent. What met his eyes sent him staggering once again. The huge explosion had blown open a massive mouth in the forbidding fort walls. A fifteen-feet-long hole stood gaping there now.

Fateh Khan had gathered all the men that he had been left with and surrendered to the Mughals. He had handed over the keys of the fort to Khan-e-Khanaan.

When morning came, the main gate of the Daulatabad fort was opened. Inside could be seen teams of bullocks yoked to frames on wheels. The world outside had had no idea of the dance of death that starvation had danced inside in the past three days. The frames were piled thick with bodies of men and animals as if stacked with crops harvested from the farms. The stench of putrid flesh that hung in the air was so thick that it could be cut with a knife. The human corpses alone counted to well over three thousand. The line of the bullock-teams with their trailing frames loaded with their ghoulish merchandise was unending.

As Murari stood behind his tent flap watching the horrific sight, handkerchief to his nose, he asked one of his minions, 'I haven't made a mistake somewhere, have I?'

7

IN THE KINGDOM OF PEMGIRI

1632–35

The one topic that was discussed in the Bijapur court every single day was that once the Mughal horses decided to set off from their post in Burhanpur, there would be no one left to stop them from reaching the forecourt of the Bijapur palace.

Akbar, Jahangir, and now Shah Jahan too! It had been the dream of every single emperor at Delhi to make the lands of Jinji and Rameshwar, right up to Madurai, reverberate with the hoof-beat of their horses. There had always been a faction in the Bijapur court that had supported the existence of the Nizamshahi Sultanate. Not because it had any particular affection for Daulatabad; they had regarded its presence as a useful obstacle for keeping a check on the ambitions of the Mughals.

As soon as the Nizamshah's kingdom had been razed to the ground, the Mughal demon had emerged from the dust-cloud and made clear its intention of swallowing up the Adilshahi kingdom next. Its army had begun mounting simultaneous raids upon a number of posts like Paranda, Dharur and Beed. Consternation ruled rampant among the planners and strategists that sat around Mohammad Adilshah on how this onslaught could be checked. That was when news reached them of Shahaji making preparations at Nashik and Sangamner for hoisting the flag of his own new kingdom.

As circumstances begin to change, the utility of even such a destructive element as fire becomes evident. A discussion led by the Sultan was in progress, with senior wife Badi Begum Saheba, Mustafa Khan, Randullah Khan and many other exalted functionaries in attendance. Prime Minister Khawaas Khan, who had read the direction of the winds well, came up with the suggestion, 'Shahaji has been an old associate of ours. If our aim is to blacken the faces of those red-faced devils of Delhi, we need the services of a valorous warrior like him.'

The Bijapur court finally arrived at its decision: the Mughal advance had to be blocked at any cost. One good way for doing so was to make friends with Shahajiraje, and the best way to go about it was to offer every possible support to his effort at creating his own kingdom. The decision was unanimous.

Shahaji, on his part, had begun to strive in right earnest towards the realisation of his dream. There was this ancient fort of Pemgiri near the Baleshwar mountain that lay in the Sahyadri range quite close to Sangamner. It looked old enough to belong to the time of the Mauryas, maybe going as far back as the age of the Buddha. A number of tanks and ponds belonging to the Satavahana period could be seen scattered all over the place. Despite the fact that it had lost usage in recent times, it was quite a well-located place, with Khandesh, Daulatabad and the Kalyan port beyond the mountains on the one side and the Pune region on the other. When Shahaji and Jijabai had first set eyes on the ruins of the ancient mansions and the empty stables attached to them, they had appeared to be ghost-infested places. Pickets of the Nizamshahi guards and soldiers from the Mughal territories on the other side would often gather in one of the deserted verandahs and while away time playing cards.

Jijabai arrived with a barely three-year-old Shivba to settle in this deserted fort at Pemgiri. As always, she had a regiment of five thousand horses with her. A few chieftains like Pilajipant Deshpande, Sarjerao Ghatge, Mane and Kale came along, and made arrangements for themselves by fixing out some of the crumbling mansions. With Jijabai now in residence, a number of other people from the neighbouring villages, young and old, came over to work in the durbar or at the mansion. Footfalls increased rapidly, all kinds of activities began and the place sprang to life. What had been a barren landscape transformed itself in a few days into a vibrant fort.

Hopes revived in the king's heart. He sent a message to friends like Khawaas Khan in the Bijapur court as also to Adilshah himself, stating, 'There were eighty-four forts in the Nizamshahi Sultanate. The Mughals have managed to snatch away one Daulatabad fort—true, but that's no reason for mouths to run dry. There's the old capital of Junnar with its administrative traditions and culture still intact. We have courageous men, huge mountains and impenetrable valleys and gorges for company. I am convinced that we shall erect a new kingdom here.'

Shahaji began gathering his forces. The first thing he did was to dispatch letters to his closest friends and relatives. To his son's father-in-law Vijayrao he wrote, 'You and I are doubly related. I have no doubt that the prospect of a richly caparisoned royal elephant rocking and rolling at the doorstep of your relative can only cause you joy. This enterprise that I've undertaken will one day make your daughter a Bhosale queen. I request that you turn your horse's head towards Pemgadh without delay.'

Pemgadh was not too far away from Junnar or Shivneri; when two days passed since the messages were dispatched and no horses were noticed kicking up the dust on way to the fort, Shahaji felt anxious and disappointed. Noticing the furrows on her husband's brow, Jijabai came up to him and said softly, 'I know you are upset at this lack of response from our relation-by-marriage at Shivneri. But should you take it so much to heart? Great if he comes along, and not much lost if he doesn't.'

'Rani Saheb?'

'Look, this is an old disease that rests in the soil of our country.'

'Disease?'

'Of course! Any joyous occasion happening in a relative's house or a neighbour's house and jealousy takes over. One has to take this as a given and just keep moving on!'

Hectic preparations were in progress at Pemgadh. The fort was so ancient that the buildings had begun to crumble with the steady assault of the elements across countless years. The old wooden pillars of the palace had been hollowed by termites. The ponds and tanks used for storing water had silted up, and tenacious wild shrubs had sent roots into the joints between the masonry stones. Shahaji and Jijabai worked relentlessly to repair the ravages wrought by time.

Not everyone of Shahaji's immediate relatives could gather enough audacity, though. His first cousin Kheloji Bhosale had the reputation of a lion-hearted daredevil, but he hadn't come visiting for a long time now. This had never happened before. Whether it was the Adilshahi court or the Mughal camp at Chandanpuri, Shahaji had made it a matter of prestige to ensure that Kheloji was accorded the same honour and military rank as himself.

This indifference coming from his close cousin so stirred Shahaji that he had the younger brothers of Kheloji called over to his palace. Addressing the younger cousins Mambaji and Maloji, he said, 'Boys, don't you think this is deeply painful? The clarion calls of Maloji Raja and Vithojibaba of Verul had reverberated in all four directions. Never before have we allowed distance to creep into our mutual love and affection.

Maloji said, 'How can we ever forget our past, Dada? When your father Maloji fell martyr in the battlefield, it was our father Vithojibaba who brought us all up together under the warmth of his wing. It was in remembrance of his elder brother that he named me Maloji. How can such blood relations be forgotten?'

'Arey, remember the episode of Khandagale's elephant? And a hundred others? The extent to which we ten brothers had gone for our family pride! Why is Khelojirao's horse running in all kinds of random directions now?' asked Shahaji.

Two camel-riders arrived at Pemgadh the next day. They had travelled day and night from Bijapur to deliver the letter of Khawaas Khan, the wazeer of Mohammadshah. The letter made interesting reading:

In the service of your lordship Shivajiraje,
   Fort Pemgadh, somewhere in the region of Sangamner.
   I send this letter drafted expressly by Baloba Pagnis, the head clerk in the durbar of our chief administrator, Murari Jagdeorao.
   We here at Bijapur have received with great excitement and satisfaction the news that you have taken in hand the enterprise of raising a new kingdom. Ten years or so ago, you graced the post of commander-in-chief at Bijapur, during which period I, Khawaas Khan, and all others like Randullah Saheb and Mustafa Khan were mere boys. At that time, we had the singular good fortune to work under your tutelage and to gather invaluable experience during the

campaigns against Kerala and Rameshwar in the Deccan. Therefore, when a preceptor of your eminence now stands at the cusp of becoming a king, it is quite natural that disciples like us, should feel deeply contented.

Shahajiraje, there is a reason for my addressing you on this topic. Your genuinely valiant cousin Kheloji Bhosale has been camping outside our durbar for the past few days. He has been asking for an independent military command and had an audience with the Sultan saheb yesterday. Although he hasn't said so openly, he doesn't seem to care the tiniest whit for your efforts at kingship.

Therefore, if time and circumstances permit, you should by all means become the king of the Marathas; but meanwhile, you need to exercise great caution and move with discretion. As an immediate convenience, you may want to hunt out a boy belonging to the Nizamshah's lineage and place him on the throne. No matter who occupies the throne, the treasury and the army shall remain firmly in your grip. What more advice can be given to a person as well versed in statesmanship as in the art of war as you are?

I await your response.

Khawaas Khan, Wazeer-e-Azam
Sultanate of Adilshah

The next few nights were spent in anxiety. Both Shahaji and Jijabai had virtually forgotten what sleep meant. They spent most nights turning from one side to the other.

It was during one of these sleep-deprived tossings and turnings that Shahaji said, 'What's the point, Jiu, of merely carrying courage in the heart and strength in the wrist? All this effervescence of ambition will need to be bottled for the present. Circumstances do not allow for indulgences of this kind.'

'So, what do we do, Raje?'

'What our well-wishers have been suggesting all along—strategising. Locating a boy from the Nizamshah's lineage and placing him on the throne.'

The search began the next day, but as it happened, it didn't have to go on for very long. There was this old fort called Jivdhan near Naneghat, at the very edge of the Sahyadri range. This is where the tall peaks of the Sahyadri chain disappear, where, from below the sharp, broken cliff of the fort, the Konkan region begins. A lonely fort set in a difficult terrain. When it's raining heavily, one can hear, night and day, a cascade falling with a roar down the cliff; when it's winter, the thick clouds of fog refuse to dissipate; and during the cruel summer months, water becomes so scarce that, leave alone men and animals, even the birds move away in search of kinder lands. No more punishing spot could be found for placing the most inveterate criminals in confinement. That was where, in solitary confinement, was placed an unfortunate young prince, paying for the crime of being born into the Nizamshahi fold. He had obviously been perceived by a more ambitious claimant as an obstacle, and had therefore been dumped into this hellhole as a royal prisoner.

Shahaji immediately dispatched a squad towards Jivdhan under the leadership of Pilajipant.

When, after crossing hills and forests, Pilajirao's team reached the foot of Jivdhan, they became the first bunch of human beings, after three years, to set foot on the land that lay around the penitentiary, not counting, of course, the men who kept guard on the prisoners. The young prince Murtaza and his mother were so delighted at the sight that they began to literally shriek and dance with joy.

Till as long as the Nizamshahi Sultanate was in place, a regular food allowance would be sent from Daulatabad for the royal prisoners at Jivdhan; but once the Sultanate was overthrown and the capital taken over by the Mughals, the captives had sunk below the line of visibility, as had their keepers. The allowance vanished, the salaries of the guards stopped too. Starvation resulted, leaving the Begum with no choice but to hand over her gold ornaments for hocking to raise money for survival.

The mother and son duo made quite a striking sight in the Pemgadh palace. Begum Saheba was tall, slim and very fair. The perpetual semi-darkness of the cell had turned her skin white as a lizard's underside. Their royal silk and satin clothing had turned dull and flimsy with frequent washing.

Murtaza was just eleven years old then. The sudden confinement had brought his education to a grinding halt. The news that her son would be anointed the next Sultan was something straight out of a dream for the mother. Responding to Shahaji's proposal, she quite ingenuously insisted, 'Raja Saheb, make me a Sultana or a Demona, I don't care, but first please retrieve all my ornaments from the pawnbroker at Kalyan.'

It took no time for the news to spread that Shahaji had opted to become a kingmaker instead of going for kingship. This would take practical shape only after the enthronement of young Murtaza and the formal reading of the *khutba* in his name. It had always been Shahaji's nature to subject himself to extreme physical labour and to keep his administrative and military officials similarly engaged. Thus, while on the one side a major recruitment drive was on along with the regular military exercises, on the other side raiding parties, fifteen-hundred strong, were entering into Konkan and plundering the harbours of the foreigners. Revenue too had begun to be forcibly collected in all the areas that lay between Nashik and Pune.

Meanwhile, Kheloji Bhosale had had his ambition fulfilled too: he had persuaded Adilshah to grant him a big mansab[3] near Nashik and had begun to mount vigorous campaigns on the Mughal provinces on behalf of his new master.

With just a few days to go for the coronation ceremony, the fort was in the grip of hectic activity. One day Jijabai asked Shahaji, 'Is the Adilshahi sultan really going to be present in person for the coronation, as he had promised?'

'Well, not in person now,' Shahaji laughed, 'but one of his big chieftains will certainly arrive with his retinue to mark his attendance.'

A few days later, Pilajipant said, 'Raje, the news is that a very powerful chieftain of the Mughal forces at Daulatabad, a person named Iradat Khan, has set off for Pemgadh.'

'Why? The coronation is still ten days away!'

Shahaji wasn't the only person to have been perplexed by this question. The administrative office was more preoccupied with preparing for the

---

[3] Comes from Mansabdari system. Mansabdar was a military title used during the reign of the Maratha Empire, the Mughal Empire and the Deccan Sultanates. The mansabdar had to maintain an army with cavalrymen and animals.

coronation than with matters of running the state. The matter of fitting out a royal wardrobe for Prince Murtaza was being handled on a war footing, with artisans from Konkan, Kalyan and even Nashik on the yonder side participating. The goldsmiths of Junnar, Nashik and Sangamner were in perpetual orbit round Begum Saheba. The dowager Sultana-to-be was in very high spirits these days. She was soaking in the experience of a world whose doors had opened up for her, thanks to Shahajiraje.

Iradat Khan's contingent arrived at Pemgadh earlier than expected and made a beeline for the administrative hall. After a quick embrace with Shahaji, the chieftain made a sign to his accompanying official, who stepped forward with a gold tray. He whisked off the embroidered silk cloth with a flourish to reveal a cylindrical roll that contained the royal *firman*.

Softly laughing to himself, Shahaji proffered the stem of the hookah to Iradat Khan and said, 'Why don't we have a completely open discussion here? What does the Mughal emperor expect from us in return for all his favours?'

'So be it, huzoor. Rajaji, this lump called the Nizamshahi Sultanate that had been sticking in the Mughal throat for generations, it's only lately that this lump has got dissolved. Why, then, would you want to start the turmoil of creating another Nizamshahi? Why would you want to earn the emperor's displeasure?'

'Khan Saheb, I suppose you would grant us the right to shape our own future by seating a king of our choice on the throne and hoisting our own flag!'

'Raja Saheb, over and over again you have been rejecting the gift of friendship that the emperor has been offering to you. The consequences of this move can be quite bad, Raja Saheb.'

This raised Shahaji's hackles. Making an effort to hold his temper, he said, 'Don't you think, Khan Saheb, that you are issuing threats to me in my own palace?'

Iradat Khan's eyes turned moist as he said, 'It's likely, huzoor, that you would have forgotten, but the previous time round, Shah Jahan Saheb had sent you as gift the immensely expensive gown that he had worn at the time of his ascension to the throne. The symbolic value of that gown is so high that princes have been known to kill each other for its possession. I am sorry that I have not been able to change your heart, and I leave with a sense of shame at having failed in my mission.' A disappointed Iradat Khan left for the guest house.

As Shahaji was about to sit for his meal, Mambaji arrived, and Jijabai had another *paat-paani*[4] placed upon the floor. Among all of Kheloji's brothers, Mambaji was the closest to Shahaji. When the meal was over and Shahaji went and sat on the swing, chewing some sliced pieces of areca-nut, Mambaji began, 'Dada, you've got two sons Sambhaji and Shivba as your responsibility. Forget the rest of us, but you need to worry about their future.'

'What are you talking about, bhavoji?' asked Jijabai.

'Vahini Saheb, by age I am more like a son to you than a brother-in-law, but look at what the emperor has offered: a mansab of 22,000 for Sambhaji and the subedari of the Deccan of which even the gods would be envious. My question is, why should a person commit the sin of turning the Goddess of Wealth back when she has come walking to your doorstep all the way from Delhi? How many more years are you going to expend combating utterly unwanted trials and tribulations?'

'We want to see the sun rising on our own independent kingdom,' responded Shahaji, his face glowing with a strange radiance. At the same time, feeling a little bad for his cousin, he said, 'Mambaji, why are you so beguiled by the emperor?'

'So, what do you think the Mughal emperor of Delhi is? Some goldsmith of the souks of Sangamner for kicking around?'

'Look, Bhavoji, we have no interest left in working any further under this sultan or that emperor. When you set after a mission, you don't sit calculating profit and loss. We are satisfied with what we have.'

'Arey wah! What bricks of gold have you got stored in your treasury? When you had to go for confinement with this Shivba here, in whose house did you take shelter? In the house of your son's father-in-law! In Shivneri! In the land of the Mughals! What wild, indigestible ambitions have you been holding on to? And what has been the result? Those palatial structures in Pune have been razed to the ground.'

---

[4] A wooden dining plank for sitting and eating on the floor.

Shahaji received Mambaji's red-hot words with equanimity. His eyes, however, were fixed on how Jijabai was taking it. She too had decided to be indulgent of the well-intentioned barrage that her favourite brother-in-law had let loose. 'Tell me, bhavoji,' she asked calmly, 'is it a sin to want to establish a kingdom for the welfare of the poor and the dispossessed?'

'Vahini, just the thought of challenging such mighty forces fills me with fear!'

'Fear of what? Failure? Death? Why should one fear it at all, bhavoji? What's the ultimate fate of this five-arm long human body? A potful of ashes, no? But those who die fighting for the welfare of the poorest of the poor, the fragrance of glory that emanates from them, like from sandalwood—this fragrance stays on for ages and ages.'

'Bhai, these Margatthyas should stay with the job of ploughing the field and do some good farming,' Saif Khan, the Nizam chieftain groused with his friends. 'At the most, they may buy cows and sit milking them! But now, suddenly, they want to go against their grain and let this bug of kingship climb to their heads!'

The township of Nizampur had sprung up lately at the lower end of the Tamhani ghat where the Nizamshahi Sultanate maintained a big elephant nursery. It housed well over three hundred elephants, which were put to use whenever a war flared up anywhere between Cheul on the Konkan coast right up to Rajapur, the entire stretch of land that fell under the control of Saif Khan. Now, after the fall of the Sultanate, Wazeer Khawaas Khan had issued a decree from Bijapur that all the chieftains should hasten to Pemgadh, swear their allegiance to the new sultan Murtaza and pay their respect to Shahaji.

The region of Pemgadh, Sangamner was in the grip of commotion, and Khawaas Khan had dispatched Murari Pandit at the head of a ten-thousand strong army towards Pemgadh. Saif Khan, however, had not been the least bit appreciative of these exciting developments. The very thought of bowing before a non-Muslim person, particularly a Maratha chieftain like Shahaji, was anathema to him. But earning the displeasure of Bijapur was not a pleasant thought either; therefore, willy-nilly, he had prepared documents surrendering the land stretching from Konkan to Jawahar to the suzerainty of the new kingdom, and dispatched it to Pemgadh.

The game of destiny continued to play itself out in the life of Shahaji and Jijabai: joys and sorrows, sun and rain. A large number of Maratha chieftains, senior administrators, noblemen and barons had come to meet Shahaji; a large number of them had given assurances of presenting themselves at the appropriate time; but the people in whom he had imposed the greatest faith—people like his friend and relation-by-marriage Vijayrao—refused to stir from their comfortable seats or even to get into some kind of conversation. This discord displayed by his intimates hurt him considerably.

One morning, after he had finished worshipping the twelve Jyotirlingas, Shahaji was struck by a thought. He immediately got a squad ready of his most trusted men and dispatched them to Junnar under the leadership of Pilajipant.

Junnar had a number of huge palaces belonging to the Mughal and Nizamshahi grandees, and some of them were lying deserted. Shahaji had instructed the squad to get into the empty palaces and dig up the basements and cellars. The next evening Sarjerao Ghatge came running back with the great news: in the cellar next to the palace in which Shah Jahan had lived while in Junnar, they had unearthed a big treasure of precious stones and gold.

The news delighted Shahaji. In his mission of creating a new kingdom, he had been feeling strapped for cash, and this secret wealth was just what he needed. 'See?' he told an equally delighted Jijabai. 'Just goes to show that we shouldn't get bowed down by circumstances. The gods seem to be signalling that some great good is marked out for this land at the hands of the Bhosales.

The date for the coronation was coming closer. The thought that a new Nizamshahi—in reality the reign of Shahajiraje—was soon to begin had caused the excitement in the villages and farms to mount with every passing day.

After having drunk in and digested the politics of the Deccan, Shahaji was determined that no calamity would now make him withdraw from his mission. He was also determined that his administration would be inclusive of all castes and creeds, and had accordingly begun to take conscious steps towards that end. Acceding to the request of some of his Muslim friends, he dispatched a large fund from his treasury for the upkeep of the shrine of a Muslim saint near Nashik. There were a host of other things that needed his personal and immediate attention.

The day on which the ten-thousand-strong army of Bijapur entered Pemgadh, hundreds of local soldiers as also court officials felt their hearts swell with pride. They were now reassured that Shahajiraje's dream of establishing his Maratha kingdom would soon be realised. All the important chieftains, like Sarjerao Ghatge, Mohite, Gayakwad, Mahadik and Kale, joined their king in welcoming their Bijapuri guests. When Murari Pandit crossed the arch of the main gate along with his attendant officials to enter into the fort of Pemgadh, he was delighted with the arrangements there. Shahaji noticed something quite peculiar happening around Murari Pandit: a young Muslim boy was running alongside the Brahmin with an arm-long Persian mirror in his hands. Murari would keep looking into the mirror after every little while.

After the long journey, Murari Pandit was considerably tired, but he relished the meat of the wild rabbits that was served to him. As he sat in the very first row for his meals, Shahaji's attention was drawn towards the man's appearance. The otherwise fair and handsome Murari's face was covered with white patches of leucoderma. The skin below the ears and on the throat had now started turning black. It was on account of this affliction, obviously, that he had got into the habit of observing himself in the mirror every now and then.

In official terms, Murari Jagdeo had arrived for the coronation as the representative of the Adilshahi Sultanate; hence it had become obligatory for Shahaji's administration to offer the courtesy due to him, to house him in a palace appropriate to his status and look after his comfort.

Jijabai casually asked Shahaji, 'Does this honoured guest have any memory of the destruction he had wrought in Pune not very long ago?'

Shahaji responded with a laugh, 'Not a word has he spoken about that. In any case, what can we do now? Are we left with any choice but to worship this scorpion that sits on God's image?'

The coronation ceremony of eleven-year-old Murtaza Nizamshah went off like a dream. Khadki, Bhaganagar, Solapur, Jamkhandi, Mandu, Burhanpur, Surat, Paranda, Ausa, Beed, Bidar, Kandhar, Cheul, Jawhar—there was an endless list of towns and principalities from where princes, grandees, soldiers and landlords arrived in their hundreds, but the event was made memorable by the Begum Saheba, the queen-mother. She had called over the best-known jewellers and goldsmiths from Kalyan, Sangamner, Khadki and from as far away as Burhanpur too. Her passion for buying gold had become the topic of discussion everywhere and a cause for worry in some quarters. 'This woman,' exclaimed Jijabai to Durga Devi, 'how many more sacks of gold is she going to buy? Is she buying for this one single life or for the next seven ones too?'

While some conversation was in progress that day inside Murari Pandit's palace between him and Shahaji, a number of children were playing out in the courtyard. Suddenly, the children's commotion took on a higher pitch, and voices could be heard shouting at each other. Eleven-year-old Sambhaji rushed inside, with three-and-a-half-year-old Shivba following at his heels. Shahaji noticed that Sambhaji carried in his hands an extremely expensive brocade robe. Shivba carried a sharp, short blade, with which, it appeared, he had punched a number of holes in that piece of clothing and rendered it quite useless for wearing.

Shahaji pulled the boy close and seated him in his lap. He then looked around with pride at the assembled company and said with a laugh, 'Could you people have forgotten? When Shivba was born, a noted astrologer had sworn by the horoscope that this son of mine would grow so powerful that he would extinguish the flaming torch of the emperor of Delhi. This little event of today only foretells what is due to arrive.'

※

Despite the fact that the coronation at Pemgadh had passed off successfully, there were those who believed that this experiment of Shahajiraje would flop. But Shahaji was a competent administrator, and he now had under his control upwards of sixty forts spread across Balaghat, Baglan and Konkan—some of them small, but some others of considerable size and strength.

Kheloji Bhosale and his brothers Parsoji, Maloji, Mambaji and Nagoji had earlier been in the employment of the Mughals, but with political circumstances having changed and the winds blowing differently, they had shifted their allegiance back to the Adilshahi Sultanate.

One day Shahaji returned to his palace in a highly agitated state. 'Rani Saheb,' he told his wife, 'please do something about this brother-in-law of yours. Get this Kheloji under control. Talk to Gaurabai, maybe, or a time may soon arrive when there'll be nothing left to do except count the stars in the sky.'

'Has he been up to some serious mischief?'

'Very serious mischief! He's been so thrilled with being back with Bijapur that he's made it a passion to mount bold raids on Mughal properties. Scattered everywhere from Burhanpur to Nashik are these Mughal posts, stations and camps, and this man has been driving them to despair. Kheloji and his brothers have gone on a mission of plunder, destruction, and in some places, they have even begun slaughtering Mughal soldiers.'

'*Bai ga!*'

'One of these days it may well cost him his life!'

As per the Adilshahi political sources, Murari Jagdeo had extended his stay in the new capital. He had continued with religious regularity his fetish of peering into the Persian mirror like a coy young girl. Shahaji couldn't hold himself from remarking one day, 'For how long will you continue to bother yourself with these white patches, Panditji?'

'It isn't the patches that bother me much these days, but my beautiful skin has started turning black like over-ripe taro roots. What should I do for that? These black patches all over have started frightening me now.'

'But you have been a wise, knowledgeable, saintly—.'

'Oh, please cut out all those lies about wisdom and knowledge. At all odd hours of day and night I hear those piteous shrieks, those blood-curdling wails! I have no choice but to confess—that conflagration at Daulatabad, those thousands who died of thirst and hunger inside the fort! Their curse has come down upon me, I'm sure.'

'Try to put it behind. Time will set matters right.'

'Yes, but how many sins? At how many places? Indapur, Supe, Pune! I drove cattle into standing crops, I set fire to houses, I devastated temples!

The agonised cries of countless people and my own conceit and arrogance have brought me to this state.'

'What arrogance?'

'The arrogance of power! Once power arrives, pimps and prostitutes do not need any invitation for a visit. Some grandees had brought young girls over from Goa! Tender young kids from Portugal! Who can say which of those mischievous girls stung me in one of those Bijapur orgies and ruined my beautiful complexion?'

Shahaji understood the terror that had gripped Murari's heart and instructed Pilajipant, 'See if you can find someone who has a remedy for our royal guest's ailment.'

Within a few days, the Raja had an answer to his query. Close to the confluence of the Bhima and the Indrayani in the Pabal region lived this ascetic named Rudranath, whose herbs and rituals could bring about a major cure in skin ailments. Murari Jagdeo was delighted at this news. At around the same time, a message arrived from Khawaas Khan, asking him to return to Bijapur at his quickest. Preparations for his return began. He was to leave half of his ten-thousand-strong army behind in Pemgadh.

Shahaji accompanied Murari up to the Pabal province. Quite near the confluence was this village named Nagargaon where the ascetic Rudranath lived with his herb-dispensing disciples. Arrangements were also made for oblation by fire. For breaking the invisible circles of black magic that had been woven round Murari, a special fire was lit at the bank of the confluence into which red pepper would be tossed. The man would break into violent bouts of coughing and his eyes would stream when he was made to inhale those fumes.

Murari continued with his daily oblations around the fire, prayers and immersions in the confluence for a holy dip five times a day. Finally, the day of the dark night of the month of Bhaadrapad arrived, the day of the solar eclipse, 23 September 1633 by the English calendar. Yogi Rudranath was an awfully hassled man that day. In his last-ditch effort at getting rid of his ailments, Murari Jagdeo had made preparations on a grand scale. As per the instructions of the Yogi, a *tula-daan* had been organised, charity through the *tula* or the weighing scale, in which twenty-one kinds of gifts were to be given as charity to the poor, mendicants and holy men who would gather for the occasion. They would include the gift of cows, gold, horses and an elephant. News of this unprecedented event had spread around fifty villages in the vicinity, which had resulted in hordes of poor beggars, mendicants, ascetics and hermits gathering at the confluence near Nagargaon, giving the event the dimension of a carnival.

It was obviously Shahaji who had made arrangements for the gifts to be distributed on behalf of Murari Jagdeo. Rudranath was distributing the gifts as they were taken off the weighing scales. Twenty weighings had been finished and distributed, and now it was the turn of the elephant to be given away. When Shahaji pointed at the animal to be gifted, everyone, including Rudranath, broke into a laugh. Which poor person could an elephant be gifted to? It was obvious that no recipient of this gift would have the wherewithal to look after a creature so expensive to maintain! After some consultation, it was decided that in lieu of the elephant, Murari—in effect, Shahaji—would give wealth equal to the weight of the elephant. The solution, however, had raised a far heavier problem—how would the elephant be weighed? A small village like Nagargao had no scale that could measure the weight of an elephant!

Murari Pandit went up to Shahaji and said, 'Raje, you are the master—not only of the sword, but of the intellect! You alone can tell us how this problem of weighing the elephant can be resolved.'

As he stood at the embankment of the confluence, Shahaji laughed and cast a glance at the spread of the river in front. Noticing a boat on the other side, he sent one of his servants to have it rowed across. He now had some sturdy planks laid out in the boat and got his men to ease the elephant on to the boat. He drew attention of those present to the level to which the river water had risen against the embankment and had the level marked out. This done, the elephant was brought off the boat and logs of wood were placed into it till the water rose again up to the mark. These logs of wood were then used as weight to measure the wealth that would be distributed in lieu of the elephant. The camp that had come up at the confluence was brought down a couple of days later. Murari Pandit left for Bijapur along with Saif Khan, and Shahaji departed in the direction of Pemgadh. On account of the grand charitable event of the *tula-daan* that was organised in Nagargaon, the village came to be known as Tulapur from then on.

8

HERE SHAHAJI, THERE SHAH JAHAN

One evening, finally, the calamity descended. It didn't take time for the news to spread across Pemgadh and reach the palace. The jolt of the news was such that Jijabai felt dizzy and immediately sat down on the edge of the terrace. The misfortune had struck not any particular individual, but the prestige and good name of the entire Maratha community. If what they had understood was true, it was nothing short of the roof collapsing on one's head.

Sitabai, Pilaji Deshpande's wife, rushed to Jijabai, asking after the news. Sitting next to her, Sitabai asked in a whisper, 'Auji, this Khelojirao is our lordship's first cousin, isn't he?'

'Yes, he is.'

'Which means, of course, that Gaurabai is your sister-in-law! How could the wretched Muslims dare to so much as touch a woman of such a high lineage?'

The lovely evening wind began to feel like a summer blast, compounding the confusion in her mind. By a stroke of misfortune, Shahaji, too, was not in residence. He had left with his squad that very morning for some important work, and there was no saying whether he would return in the next two days or eight.

Sensations of thirst and hunger vanished. All that remained in the head was the image of the young, happy face of her good-natured sister-in-law. Jijabai and Gaurabai had always got along very well. After Shivba's birth, she had come over to Shivneri and spent a few days with her. She was a loving, thoroughly home-bound person. Beautiful to look at and virtuous of nature. Why would God want to visit misfortunes upon her?

Jijau sent for Naropant Deekshit and instructed him to send messengers in all directions so that the king could be called back at the earliest. It was frightening to even listen to the story. How could this happen to the relative of a formidable Maratha chieftain, the daughter-in-law of Vithoji Bhosale of Verul and the wife of Khelojiraja? She had entered into the Godavari near Nashik for a holy dip, and a bunch of Mughal soldiers came raiding and abducted her by force?

More information came to light the next morning. This dastardly act had been committed under the direction of the biggest Mughal chieftain in the Deccan: Sardaar Mahabat Khan. The act was far too abominable to sit well with the prestige of a senior wazeer of the Mughal Empire.

The entire day slipped away in anger and outrage and in the relentless wait for the return of the Shahaji.

It was on the third day that the neighing of horses was heard outside the palace gate. Jijabai rushed out and met Shahaji on the doorstep. She roared in fury, 'Raje, why didn't you come crashing down on that diabolical Mahabat Khan? Why didn't you chop off his sinful hands? Gaurabai is our sister-in-law, after all!'

'Jiu, please understand the whole situation. There's nothing as shameful in the event as you have imagined it to be, at least not yet.'

'Are you saying that—'

'Look, it's nothing like the horror stories that have been circulating among the people. It's true that she's been abducted, but she's been placed in confinement in an inn close to Chandwad. Fortunately, the Mughal officials have used a little bit of their head, it seems. They have brought over a few ladies from some reputed families of the nearby village to stay with our sister-in-law.'

Jijabai let out a huge sigh of relief. Shahaji went on, 'Mahabat Khan has written a carefully worded letter to Khelojiraja, saying that they have abducted his "royal clothing". They have not so much as touched the "clothing", but have kept it with great care and honour. He writes that if Kheloji wants to see the face of his virtuous wife again, he should dispatch four lakh rupees immediately. For the past so many days, he has driven sleep out of the eyes of the Mughals because of his daring raids, and if he doesn't compensate by paying the penalty levied upon him, sleep shall abandon him forever. He has threatened that the honour of his chaste wife could be sullied too.'

When Shahaji gave her the details of the worrisome message, Jijabai turned red with anger. 'With such a terrible crisis hanging over our sister-in-law's head, instead of racing ahead and pulling the crisis out by its roots, how could you think of turning your horse towards Pemgadh?'

'Well, if the person whose honour is at stake doesn't seem agitated, how does one rush to help?'

'What does that mean?'

'How do I explain this to you, Jijau? We had actually set out to confront that Mahabat Khan and chop him to pieces, but we received a message on the way from Khelojirao, asking us not to act in haste.'

'*Aga bai!*'

'So, now, what do I do? The fact is that I have never been able to make sense of Kheloji's illogical tendencies. On top of it, the matter is sensitive, therefore I thought I should take you along if I have to go there.'

'Yes, and a good thing too.'

Shahaji's horses left at the crack of dawn. Kheloji and his brothers had made camp at this inn near Nashik on the road to Burhanpur along the Godavari. They'd heard that Mahabat Khan was lodged somewhere between Tryambakgadh and Dindori.

As soon as Shahaji and Jijabai entered, Kheloji and his five or six brothers gathered around them. The recent episode seemed to have broken the spirit of the entire family. The twirl of Kheloji's cocky moustache seemed to have gone limp and his face was tense with worry-lines. His love for his wife and the closeness they enjoyed were common knowledge. No wonder, then, that the recent episode had shaken him. He cut a sorry figure as he sat on the rug on the floor of the inn, his knees gathered against his chest. Shahaji took his hand in his and said, 'Look, Kheloji, however audacious this Mahabat Khan fancies himself to be, he's no Porus nor Alexander. Come on, get up. Let us Bhosale brothers join forces and teach that sinner the lesson of a lifetime.'

'What are you suggesting?' asked Kheloji in a dry voice.

'Let's beat our war-drums and raid that man's camp. Let's tie that bastard to our horse's legs and drag him around the town.'

The passionate words of Shahaji stirred Kheloji's brothers and they turned an expectant gaze towards their eldest brother. Continuing with his theme, Shahaji went on, 'Kheloji, you just give us the nod. Our swords will do the rest.'

Kheloji remained pregnantly silent—not so much as a squeak out of him. Both Jijabai and Shahaji were mystified by the man's coldness. The only other way of salvaging respect was by paying a ransom of four hundred thousand rupees, and that would be a mountain-sized fund to raise! How many of his mansions, how much of his property Kheloji would have to blow away in the marketplace? The thought sent Shahaji's head reeling. He assured Kheloji, however, that he would be glad to help in raising the money.

But Kheloji's response continued to be cold. In fact, it had begun to appear that he hadn't liked Shahaji's arrival at all. Here was Shahaji, at the cusp of re-establishing the Adilshahi Sultanate at Pemgadh, with a massive army in his possession; and yet he was being restrained from teaching a lesson to a tyrannical chieftain who had dared to sully the family reputation! This mystifying response hurt Shahaji immensely. As he began walking out with Jijabai in despair, all that Kheloji could utter in a lack-lustre voice was, 'Dada and Vahini, thank you for the concern you have shown for us. Problems have a habit of coming and going, but I believe we have the competence to handle them. Please don't take these matters too much to heart.'

'I want the branches snipped right now, before this wild story called "Shahajiraja" spreads out too much,' Emperor Shah Jahan declared to his aides in the court of the Daulatabad fort.

'Jahaan-panaah, please forget about this Shahaji altogether. He is nothing more than a commonplace person.'

'Khan Saheb,' retorted the emperor in exasperation, 'for the last four years we have maintained an army of two hundred thousand soldiers in the Nasik[5] and Baglan areas under the stewardship of mighty generals like

---
[5] While the Marathas called the province 'Nashik', Muslim rulers preferred to call it 'Nasik'.

Iradat Khan, Asaf Khan, Asad Khan, and now Mahabat Khan, but what has been the outcome?'

In attendance that day were stalwarts like Khan Durran, Khan Zamaan and Shah Jahan's brother-in-law Shaista Khan. The emperor's favourite queen Mumtaz Mahal had passed away on 7 July 1631 at a young age, leaving him utterly distraught. Since he was stationed in Burhanpur, he had kept the queen's body preserved in a coffin in the graveyard of the city.

Shah Jahan had a few other wives too, but Mumtaz had been as close to him as the clothing on his back. Her intelligence and her mature advice in matters relating to the running of the empire had contributed critically to his efficiency. That was why her passing away during her fourteenth confinement had left the emperor bereft and agitated. The grief was so overpowering that he would sit lamenting her loss for days on end. As he proceeded with her coffin to Agra, with dreams of building an immortal memorial for her, he had no space in his mind for matters administrative. There were two rebels, however, whom he could not get out of his head: one was his general Khan Jahan Lodi, and the other was Shahaji.

Four monsoons and four summers slipped by, during which considerable change had come about. Shah Jahan's forces had uprooted and destroyed Lodi and his armies. After reaching Agra, he had been getting steady dispatches from his father-in-law, Asad Khan: despite the honours bestowed upon Shahaji and his cousins, Shahaji had been duplicitous and gone on to co-opt the support of the Adilshahi Sultanate, and established a brand-new administration at Pemgadh. During the early days, the emperor had dismissed this act as a childish prank that would peter out in a few weeks' time. But three years had now rolled by, during which Shahaji had run an excellent administration and built up a strong army. This news of the rebel moving from strength to strength had become a source of great annoyance to him.

On the one side was the Adilshahi of Bijapur, which wasn't as subservient as its status demanded, and on the other was this renegade Shahaji that had been spreading like a mountain; no wonder, then, that the emperor was fuming. The work of building the Taj Mahal on the bank of the Yamuna for his beloved queen had got into stride. He had also appointed Mahabat Khan to beat Adilshah and Shahaji into submission, but success had by and large been eluding them. For the empire to be peaceful in the north, it was imperative that the conflagration lit up by Shahaji in the south be doused; imperative enough for Shah Jahan to take matters into his own hands. Accordingly, he had travelled down the Baglan-Nashik highway to ensconce himself in Daulatabad.

'Shame on this life!' he snapped. 'The emperor of Hindustan has to travel to as far down as the Deccan, for the second time at that, to settle matters with a mere Maratha chieftain! Twice!'

'Lordship, the man is decidedly valiant. Could we have fallen short of winning his heart over?'

'This is nonsense!' he barked, turning red. 'What have we not done towards increasing his honour and prestige? Iradat Khan went to the extent of gifting a mansab of twenty-thousand to his boy who is barely knee-high. We had also expressed our readiness to gift him whatever sized mansab he himself desired. In his very first meet with him, our wazeer had given him a grant of two lakh hons towards building up his army; money that he had not even asked for, remember? After having received such kindness from us, why does this ingrate continue to whip up trouble for us?'

'Huzoor!'

'There had been just two worries that had kept sleep away from our eyes in our Agra palace.'

'Aalam-panaah?' queried Mahabat Khan.

'One was that invincible fort of Daulatabad, and the other, this bounder Shahaji. By the grace of Allah, we have managed to penetrate the fort, but this thorn in the side still remains: Shahaji Bhonsla.'

A minute or two of silence, a deep sigh, and Shah Jahan went on, 'I simply don't understand what this man wants! We had shown our willingness to grant him the ultimate gift—a gift that no Deccan Hindu would ever dream of—the subedari of the entire region! But even that has been rejected!'

The disappointment of the emperor caused immense anxiety among the sardaars gathered there.

With his statement on political realignment, Shah Jahan had given the free-flowing conference a new turn. The senior soldiers and administrators gathered around had sensed the mood of their emperor and were consequently letting their tongues go free. Smart and handsome,

Turkish-looking Asaf Khan broke in. 'Badshah salaamat, if I have your permission, I can happily go any time to Shahaji with the message of your friendship and the offer of the subedari of the Deccan. I am sure I shall return successful.'

The proposal went down well with everyone present, and a number of them heaved a sigh of relief. Shah Jahan's eyes travelled to Mahabat Khan who looked not merely grave but positively distraught. Shah Jahan asked, 'Mahabat Saheb, what is the matter?'

'Your lordship, I have already made strenuous efforts in this direction even before your exalted company touched Burhanpur. I had dispatched my special couriers with this exact message of friendship to Pemgadh.'

'Well? What happened?'

'Failure.'

'Arey, what does that mad Maratha want, after all?' Shah Jahan almost screeched.

'Jahaan-panaah, he's possessed with the idea of building his own kingdom—a kingdom for the Marathas. Shahaji's over-riding ambition is not to be just a king, but the king of the Marathas.'

'Well, that brings our efforts to an end, then. Even the emperor of Hindustan has no remedy for this kind of madness.'

With the intention of castrating the Adilshahi forces along with Shahaji, he laid out a three-fold snare. Accordingly, he selected three of his best young generals for this enterprise: Khan Durraan, Khan Zamaan and his brother-in-law Shaista Khan. Khan Durraan was put at the head of a twenty-thousand-strong army, and his assignment was to attack the areas that included Kandhar and Nanded and capture the formidable forts of Ausa and Udgiri. A similar twenty thousand were to march under the banner of Khan Zamaan. They were instructed to first capture Ahmadnagar, and then, after taking over the Bhosale jagir of Chambhargonda, they should either move towards Bijapur via Ashti or, if the need arose, they should turn round and descend into the region of Konkan. Shaista Khan was put in charge of an extremely powerful cavalry of eight thousand horsemen, and told to assault the regions and forts where Shahaji held the maximum sway, namely Tryambak, Nashik, Sangamner, Junnar, Shivneri, Galna, and Jivdhan, and finally descend into Konkan via Mahuli.

The conference got over when the emperor rose for his afternoon prayer. As he was leaving the palace, he looked around at all present and declared, 'Whatever happens, we shall not leave behind Agra-Jamuna to descend into the Deccan for the third time on account of these Marathas. This renegade named Shahaji Bhosale has to be rubbed out for all time.'

※

All the top chieftains of the Bijapur durbar had gathered around Badi Begum. Ankush Khan stepped forward to voice the opinion of everybody present. 'Forgive us, Begum Saheba,' he began, 'but our durbar seems to have slipped into the control of a certain sorcerous, rabble-rousing hypocrite.'

'Ah, you seem to be talking about that Murari Pandit,' laughed Begum Saheba, 'but the matter doesn't appear troublesome to us at all.'

'But Begum Saheba, we have just one question for you: if it had been somebody else because of whose folly three thousand of our famished and thirsty soldiers had died during the Daulatabad catastrophe, would you have allowed that sardaar the gift of life? Even if he had been a Muslim sardaar?'

'On the contrary, you would certainly have got the man buried alive in the fortress walls of Bijapur!'

'How could he have dared to do what he did, despite being a non-Muslim?'

The sheer number of grievances against Khawaas Khan and Murari Pandit was shocking. Looking at the tense faces that surrounded her, she softened and assured them, 'All right, we shall take action.' After a few moments of thought, she threw a counter-question at them, 'How about coming up with a suggestion or two? What do you think we should do with Pandit?'

'We believe that the great scholar should be sent to his holy Kashi, so that he can gain further scholarship.'

This out-of-the box idea brought a smile to the queen's lips. As they were setting out, she advised them to meet Khawaas Khan on the way. Khawaas Khan ran his eyes over the long list of complaints and said, 'So you want to send our Pandit away to Kashi, all right. Where do you think I should go? Makkah-Madeena?'

The wazeer's churlish response did not go down well with the supplicants. The chieftains decided that they would wait for the return of their senior mentor Mustafa Khan Jamkhandi from his Belgaum tour and then give their effort another shot.

One evening, the news spread around the city that Sardaar Mustafa Khan had been arrested by the Belgaum faujdars[6]. A court official of Mustafa Khan's seniority could not possibly have been arrested without the seal and signature of the sultan himself; Begum Saheba was quite sure that a royal order was bound to have been issued to that effect. But when she went in to enquire, she found that no prior permission had been sought for Mustafa Khan's arrest; in fact, it came to light that the sultan was not even aware of it. Trembling with anger, she shot a question at the sultan himself, 'Is this our Sultanate or somebody else's?'

The atmosphere had suddenly taken an explosive and fearful turn. The bugles were blown, and the court was called to order. Even women, who ordinarily avoided visiting the durbar, had gathered in large numbers. As had been Khawaas Khan's habit, he arrived at the court a minute or so before the cries of the heralds. Although every single eye was locked upon him, he walked with nonchalance; the redness of his eyes, however, as well as his puffed-up face was giving the game away.

The court came into session. At a signal from the sultan, Shahamat Khan looked straight at Khawaas Khan and posed the question: 'Wazeer Saheb, why is your chief administrative officer Pandit Murari Jagdeo not to be seen anywhere today?'

'He has left for some important work, your lordship,' Khawaas Khan responded to the sultan after a respectful bow. His body language was as dignified as ever.

'What work has he gone for?' queried the sultan directly.

'He's left for Yetagiri.'

'What was important work was this durbar that has been called today. And why did he have to take his troop of soldiers along?'

---

[6] Police authorities

'Huzoor, he has gone to arrest Imam Khan with a force of ten thousand soldiers.'

'Ten thousand? Against one of our own?'

'Lordship, this Imam Khan of Yetagiri has been disobeying our orders; and you are aware, huzoor, that disrespect for the wazeer is equal to disrespect for you, huzoor.'

'But ten thousand with Murari?'

'It doesn't matter, lordship! The prestige of the Sultanate is as high as the sky itself.'

At a signal from the sultan, Shahamat Khan stepped forward with a few documents. He then called over five political administrators and clerks, and asked them in a grave voice, 'Look carefully and tell the durbar whose signature this is.'

'It belongs to Wazeer Khawaas Khan Saheb,' they replied in unison.

The sultan's cold gaze scanned the durbar, from one end to the other. As he tried to speak, his voice choked. He let out a deep sigh and began, 'This document was on its way to the emperor of Delhi, but our inspector of posts intercepted it on the way along with its couriers. I request the durbar to hear out the glorious words that have emanated from the pen of our dignified wazeer. Read, Shahamat Khan!'

Lord of Hindustan,
The reason why I dare to bother the supreme sovereign of Delhi is this: all the grandees and chieftains in our Adilshahi court here are embroiled in their own petty politics. The sultan is mad, and his courtiers drunk with conceit—such is the state here. Huzoor, please deliver us from the vexation of these demons. It's your forces alone that can lay mines under the steel bastions of Bijapur and blow holes in its invincible walls. You simply have to give us the signal by rattling the outer doors, and my loyal followers, like Murari Pandit, will arrange to unchain them from the inside. This Khawaas Khan shall happily arrange to transfer the charge of the treasury and also the armed forces of Bijapur into your hands.

As the explosive matter of this letter was being read out, angry cries of 'traitor', 'defector' and 'snake in the grass' had started rising up from every corner of the hall. Very soon it had grown into a frenzied roar. Despite the murderous glances being thrown at him, Khawaas Khan stood his ground for a little while. For one, he was a very strong person, and for another, he was standing inside a circle of his closest associates. To begin with, therefore, no one had the immediate courage to launch an assault upon him. But as he sensed the grave danger to his life and made his move to escape the durbar hall, a grandee named Kareem Parja lunged at him from behind and wounded his forearm with a dagger. Bleeding profusely, Khawaas Khan rushed down the stairs of the hall to where his groom was waiting with his horse. He suffered another stab of the dagger on his back, but somehow managed to leap upon his horse and galloped through the stones that had begun raining upon him.

Khawaas Khan entered his mansion in a seriously injured state and locked the door from inside. As the noise outside gathered volume, the sweat- and blood-laden man found a corner and went on his knees to pray to Allah. Meanwhile, the multitude that had gathered outside pushed at the gates of his mansion. A large number of those in the throng were captains of the sultan's army. One of them, a chieftain named Siddi Rehan, stepped up, knocked the door of the mansion down, located the cowering Khawaas Khan and beheaded him with a single swing of his sword.

Murari Pandit was in Dharwad when he heard of the assassination. Taking care that the disastrous news did not spread any further, he departed with his forces towards Halyal in the dead of the night.

The news, however, had spread like the wind all across the Adilshahi territory that both Khawaas Khan and Murari Pandit had turned traitors and plotted to give the reins of Bijapur into the hands of Emperor Shah Jahan. Cries of 'betrayer', 'turncoat' and 'renegade' were resonating from every patch of the Sultanate. Murari Pandit had no magic tricks left in his bag to turn the tide of events. With some of his most loyal soldiers quietly deserting him now, Murari was now in a state of despair.

He was apprehended within minutes of entering the precincts at Halyal, and packed off immediately under tight security to Bijapur.

On the strength of his vices as well as virtues, Murari had virtually ruled over Bijapur for the last six years. Whenever he walked into the gates of the city, he would be given a warm welcome. On 22 August 1632, when he had arranged for the cannon *Muluk Maidan* to be pulled from Paranda into the city behind a row of bullocks, he had been felicitated in the manner of having won a great battle. This time, however, as he entered the gates, all that came flying towards him were dung balls and broken slippers.

When he was finally dragged into Sultan Mohammadshah's presence, he looked no different from a jungle cat that tribal hunters occasionally brought in. His face was a terrified red; the hair on his head and face had grown wild. It was a piteous sight for all to see. Yet, in the middle of the purgatory he was in, his hyper-active mind would not let him sit still. Even when at the end of his tether, he had sent a secret envoy to the sultan with a few hundred thousand rupees for appeasement. But his ruse had failed. And now, as he stood bedraggled in the middle of the durbar, all his bluster had finally deserted him. The poisonous atmosphere ranged all around him threatened to swallow him up raw. But the desire to live on had not stopped throbbing in him. The knowledge, however, that there was no hope whatsoever of his coming alive out of this circumstance had sent his bitterness skyrocketing.

Squirming and flexing his inadequate muscles against the ropes that held him down, he began spitting out abuses at the sultan and yapped, 'Maybe you have Sultan Ibrahim as your father, but you are ultimately the progeny of a kept woman, a whore, aren't you?'

That snapped the patience of the courtiers. They leapt upon him with swords and daggers. Somebody caught hold of his jaw and forced it open, while another attacker pulled his tongue out and chopped it off with a blade. He was then dragged out of the hall, bleeding profusely, tied to the back of a stray donkey, and made to do the rounds of the market. Everywhere he went, he was greeted with stones and slippers. A few of the most impassioned ones then literally tore his limbs off his body one by one and tossed them in different directions.

The blood-soaked donkey was granted its boon of life. Some among the crowd threw a few garlands of flowers on its back and kicked it on its rump, sending the dumb animal braying away in no particular direction.

'The farmer was not being able to control the belligerent bullock tied at his door; hence he did what he thought was a very smart thing, by inviting the tiger to settle the matter for him. The tiger, of course, killed the bullock and polished it off in no time. Was he likely then to dutifully turn back to the jungle? Of course not! He then leapt at the farmer's throat!'

This was the delightful allegory with which the Sultan began the conference, setting his courtiers laughing. But when he spoke next, his voice had gone up a few decibels, and there was palpable anger in his voice. 'Just for the sake of wreaking vengeance upon that foolish Nizam, we shouldn't have invited that tiger living on the faraway banks of the Jamuna. Now that it has tasted blood, it wants to leap at the Bijapuri throat!'

'But, Lord,' begged Mustafa Khan, 'what do we do now?'

'Clearly, we should not repeat the same mistake. We should not allow the Deccan to turn weak on any account whatsoever. Which means, of course, that we should stand by Shahaji Bhosale's side on every possible occasion.'

Emperor Shah Jahan had taken the reins of the battle in the Deccan in his own hands. He had stationed himself close to Devgiri and was personally supervising the units that went after Shahaji. Three armies began moving at the same time: Khan Jahan's forces from Solapur, Khan Zamaan's men from Indapur and Khan Durraan's army from Bidar, began moving towards Bijapur. They vanquished the formidable forts of Ausa and Paranda on the plains and ransacked important towns like Sultanpur and Hirapur on the way. And before one could register it, they were barely twenty-five miles from the gates of Bijapur.

The Bijapuri army, on its side, had made massive preparations for a bitter counterattack on the Mughal forces. They had demolished the embankment of the big lake at Shahapur near Bijapur, to ensure that the Mughal elephants and horses went without water. They had gathered the inhabitants of the close-by villages inside the city fortifications and torched the countryside.

Shah Jahan had unlimited resources to lean upon: food and fodder, gunpowder and weapons of war. Stretching from Kabul-Qandahar to Assam at the foothills of the Himalayas, from Bengal to Malwa and further east to Surat and Ahmedabad in Gujarat, lands yielding rich revenues lay under his heels. If ever a region was hit by famine, his administration had the strength to reach immediate succour to them from some other prosperous part. Besides, the strength of the Mughal army across the empire added up to six hundred to seven hundred thousand men. That was why Shah Jahan had handed over to trusted lieutenants the charge of quashing rebellion in some northern parts and the construction work of the Taj Mahal, and had himself come down to the Deccan with the determination of breaking the spine of both Shahaji and Bijapur once and for all.

The Bijapur strategy of cocooning themselves by sowing cannons round their city walls began turning counter-productive. Contrary to expectations, the Mughal army refused to abandon the battlefield and return home. The Bijapuris trapped inside the city walls, on the other hand, began to feel the shortage of food and fodder. Alarm bells began ringing.

The pressure of the huge Mughal army began to be felt all across the south. The emperor had pitched camp in the precincts of Verul-Daulatabad. Neither Sangamner and Pemgadh nor Junnar were too far away from that spot. Shah Jahan was in a position to indulge any whim at short notice. His army could mount an assault on Pemgadh from Daulatabad well within two days. As the days passed by, it appeared that the Mughal forces were straining on the leash to leap at the enemy and swallow it whole.

Even as the world watched, three monsoons had descended on Pemgadh and moved on. Destiny, however, had not been as generous to Shahaji as he would have hoped. He had with him chieftains like Ghatge, Katey, Gayakwad, Kank, Thomre, Chauhan, Mohite, Mahadik, Kharate, Pandhare, Wagh and Ghorpade, and he had well over ten thousand of the finest Maaval horses to run for him. Unfortunately, however, the Muslim Nizam chieftains had not come forward in sufficient numbers to support Murtaza Nizamshah and—by proxy—kingmaker Shahaji.

Jijau too had realised one thing very early on: the water from the Pemgadh tanks was quite difficult to digest. The fort belonged to really ancient times. A number of the ancient buildings there had been repaired for the coronation ceremony, and a few new maads and havelis[7] had been built too. But unhealthy elements had begun to poke themselves out of

---

[7] Manors and mansions

the belly of those ancient walls. There were the horse flies and fleas that were making life miserable for the animals. Also, the fort walls did not enclose much space, making it impossible to house a decently big army inside. The elephant squads and the cavalry, therefore, were required to be stabled in the villages Pemgiri and Nimgaon at the foot of the fort. For water, the animals had to be driven to the banks of the Pravara a little distance away.

As Shahaji started getting sucked into the twists and turns of circumstances, he decided to shift headquarters out of Pemgadh. He moved his court and the Nizamshahi administration to Junnar.

Having Jijabai live life alongside him had been for Shahaji nothing less than experiencing heaven. He himself was amazingly courageous by nature. His personality would remind Jijabai of the span of a big, wide river. When at home, once the day's work was over, he would sleep as peacefully as a hermit. Against this background, it was painful for Jijabai to notice that he had lately turned restless; he didn't sleep well, and there was a tremor in his breath.

It was another such restless night. As he lay tossing and turning, Jijabai placed a concerned hand on his back and whispered, 'Raje, if you as the king allow yourself to be thus eaten up by worries, what's going to happen to women like us?'

When the words fell upon Shahaji's ears, he sat up in bed, looking distraught. 'After all, how much can a single person strive and struggle, Jiu?' he groaned. 'Those twelve gorges of Pune and another twelve of Junnar here, we gained control over the valleys of twenty-four rivers within three years. All across the Sahyadri mountains, there in the region of Baglan, and those regions on the other side of Balaghat, Latur, Beed and Nanded, can you tell me one river basin, one hilltop, where your husband has not galloped his horse in his effort at nation building? Even the trees that line the mountain passes and the jungle tracks recognise me as a friend. If the poor things were to be granted the gift of speech, they too would have narrated to you the melancholic tale of this crazed person named Shahaji.'

An overwrought Jijabai placed her head upon his shoulder and comforted him, 'Raje, you have fought very, very hard. The struggle that you undertook was actually beyond the capacity of humankind.'

'Yes, but what have I gained out of it?'

'Well, you can't say that you have gained nothing! You have given this region three years of ideal administration. You revived the energy of your teacher Ambar Baba and handed over unutilised land for the poor people to farm. You got land transferred in their name. You gave the aboriginals, the herders, the other tribals and the sons of the soil the right to exploit their jungles.'

'So, I did succeed somewhere, you would say?'

'Of course! We have the right to be proud of what you have done! After the reign of the Yadavas ended in this land, surrounded by this gaggle of badshahs, which other Hindu king has stood up on the strength of his own abilities? The boom of your exploits vexed the ears of the emperor of Delhi, causing him to abandon the banks of Yamuna and strike camp in the jungles of Verul-Daulatabad!'

By the definition of a calculating world, Shahaji may not have attained much success in tangible terms; but he did have the satisfaction of sowing the seeds of a new era with his own hands.

The night was late. Shahaji suddenly remembered and exclaimed, 'Rani Saheba, our Shambhuraje does not seem to have returned to the palace yet!'

'What can the boy do? Both our sons are chips off the old block. Shambhu is getting ready on the cavalry ground for tomorrow.'

Just then, a messenger reached right up to the bed chamber door with an urgent message. Shahaji went out hurriedly to receive him. 'There's a lot of activity in the enemy's tents, sarkar! It looks like the Mughal squads are preparing to enter the Sangamner region here and into Chambhargonda on the other side in a day or two.'

Right behind the messenger came Pilajipant, Hanmante and Gomaji Baba for a meet with the king. Looking towards Gomaji Baba, Shahaji rattled, 'Pant, I know it all. The emperor's beloved brother-in-law Shaista Khan is coming with a twenty-thousand-strong army, with the intention of burning down Sangamner and Akole.'

'Do you propose to get into the battlefield yourself?'

'Without a doubt! But this time, we propose to dodge the enemy and descend into Nashik from the side of the Patta fort. That's where we shall decimate the Mughal forces.'

'Then, what about the Sangamner area?'

'The young prince shall handle this area.'

'What? Sambhajiraje?'

'Yes! Why not? He's not a kid anymore! He is all of thirteen now. You shouldn't think that the only thing I did in these past three years was to blow the trumpet for that Nizam's boy. I've also taught our Sambhaji and also little Shivba how to play sport with fire. Pant, the son of an acrobat learns to dance on a rope even before he can tie his loin cloth. Along the same lines, young and valiant Maratha boys, too, should learn the skills of handling sword and shield, shouldn't they? Isn't that their primary duty?'

The palace stayed awake for the remainder of the night. The horses began to neigh at daybreak in front of the palace. Sambhajiraje had finished with his bath at the crack of dawn. He first visited the temple and bowed before the images of Goddess Bhawani and Lord Shiva, and accepted the consecrated piece of sweetmeat from the priest there. Then he placed his head at the feet of his mother and father, who blessed him and held him in their embrace. Shahaji loosened the sash on Sambhaji's waist and tied it all over again. As he stood at the palace door to bid Sambhaji goodbye, another messenger arrived panting, and reached up to the king with Pilajipant's help. 'Speak,' said Shahaji, looking at him. 'What news have you brought?

'Sarkar, Badshah Shah Jahan has put into the battlefield another chieftain by the name of Sayyad Jahaag. He has been trailing Shaista Khan, and after dodging leftwards and rightwards, he proposes to advance towards Pemgadh-Junnar.'

'His forces?'

'He shall be riding at the head of twelve thousand stallions.'

Adolescent Sambhaji leapt on his horse's back. While Jijabai and the maids swirled a flame round him to drive away evil spirits, the place began to resonate with cries of 'Har har Mahadev!' As the young prince was on the point of spurring his horse forward, a loud cry was heard emanating from the palace, 'Dada! Dadasaheb, wait! How can you—?' Eyes still heavy with sleep, five-year-old Shivba came running out of the palace, his little sword in hand. Holding on to his brother's feet, he cried out, 'Dada, how can you go alone, leaving me behind here?'

Shahaji lifted up little Shivba and held him to his chest. Jijabai stepped forward and pulled his cheek playfully, saying, 'Little prince, just grow up a little more, and the battlefield will then be all yours.'

'How can that be, Ausaheb? I too have learnt to use the sword along with Dada here. So, how can he set off alone?'

Shahaji immediately pushed the child towards his brother. Shambhuraja pulled his brother into his embrace, landed a kiss on his cheek and applied the spur to his horse's flank. As the horse galloped away, the proud parents stood looking in its wake, eyes overflowing with pride and with tears, watching Shambhuraja disappear from their sight like a gust of wind.

9

OUR SUN, OUR EARTH, OUR RESOLVE

1634–1635

Sarjerao arrived early in the morning and presented himself before Shahaji. 'News from Daulatabad is not heartening at all,' he reported in a grave voice.

'Sarjerao, this Shah Jahan has not been able to ensnare Shahaji, and that's the reason he's deliberately placed his foot on Mohammadshah's throat. But have some details come to hand?'

'We'll get an update by nightfall. There's one Ganesh Pandit who's a special agent of Adilshah. His camel has set off for a meeting with you, I've heard.'

The camel-rider reached the Junnar gates in the evening. The guards took him under custody and took him to Shahaji's palace. Two days of journey had tired out Ganesh Pandit. He first sat down for a meal of rice and clarified butter before his audience with Shahaji began. Ganeshpant laid the circumstances out before Shahaji. 'Whatever skirmishes and battles had to happen have happened,' he said. 'Now that the dust has settled, a friendly agreement has been drawn up. All its provisions have been decided too.'

'What are the exact contours of the agreement, Ganeshpant?'

'The first important provision is that the Nizamshahi has to be put to rest for good and be divided between the Mughals and the Bijapur Sultanate.'

'What are going to be their boundaries?'

'The river Bhima. Everything on the north will be taken over by the Mughals and all the land to the south will become Adilshah's territory.'

'Any other important clauses?'

Letting out a deep sigh, Pant responded, 'Raje, this entire agreement pivots around two points: one is the division of the Nizamshahi Sultanate and the other is your own future.'

'Ah! The emperor does seem to have taken our matter a little too much to heart.'

'Yes, sarkar, I have seen the entire set of instructions with my own eyes. I remember it word for word: the Bijapur Sultanate has been advised not to take this person named Shahaji in their employment; and if they ever feel like doing so—'

'Yes, go on!'

'—then they should first get you to immediately vacate all the important forts you have taken under your charge: Shivneri, Tryambak, Rajdher, Tringalwadi, Pemgadh and Bhimgadh. After being taken over, these forts should formally be handed over along with the keys to the present Mughal officers.'

The atmosphere of the meeting had heated up considerably. Jijabai, sitting on the other side, had begun to look agitated too. It was tyranny all the way, being perpetrated under the guise of agreement. The blades of that invading saw were going to cut deep into all that Shahaji had been erecting with such labour. All the blood and sweat that he had poured into his enterprise till date was going to be wiped out clean.

The worry lines on Shahaji's forehead deepened; the blaze flashing in his eyes was impossible to conceal either. He banged his fist into the palm of his other hand and roared, 'Who, after all, is this lord emperor of Delhi, and who is this Adilshahi nobody? Whose land is it and who is passing orders on it? What have these rank outsiders to do with the forts that always belonged to our ancestors? I don't care whether it's Shah Jahan or his father Jahangir. Keep this in mind: we shall not let any of these foreign powers so much as to touch the bolts and latches of our forts!'

The tenor of the meeting changed entirely. Shahaji's body began trembling with rage.

Ensconced at Daulatabad, Shah Jahan had begun to ride the backs of the Bijapuri and his own chieftains like the devil incarnate. He had let loose a stream of threatening missives to Mohammadshah too. 'Why the delay? Why is the agreement not being implemented forcefully? If Shahaji's hands have not yet been tied as per the provisions of the agreement, is it then worth the paper on which it has been written? What's holding things up? And who's responsible: you or your chieftains?'

It had become a kind of holy pursuit for the Mughals, dislodging both Shahaji and his Pemgadh experiment from their very roots. They had twice set fire to the native lands of the Bhosales like Pedgaon and Chambhargonda. This outrage, however, had not dissuaded Shahaji from tirelessly riding around his principalities at all times of day and night, instilling courage among his soldiers and subjects. Across an area stretching from Nashik and Junnar to Ahmadnagar, forty thousand of the emperor's men had been at Shahaji's heels.

Shahaji had been fired up with a strong sense of self-esteem. The open stance he had adopted was this: 'The agreement would have tied the hands of the Bijapuris, not mine!' Often, his back would not touch the earth for four days at a stretch. On account of being the capital city, Junnar had been put under immense pressure. The Mughal captain Sayyad Jahag had kept the battle going ceaselessly around the city walls. The flame of vengeance burnt so strong in the emperor that along with his loyal chieftains, he had also pressed Adilshahi warriors like Malik Rehman, Siddi Marjan and Randullah into the battlefield. Those who had been friends not so long ago had now begun to hound Shahaji like enemies.

The town of Junnar had become virtually a bracelet of fire. The Mughals had ringed the sturdy city walls with incendiary bombings. The townsmen caught in the conflagration escaped as swiftly and safely as they could, smuggling out their families and animals into the surrounding countryside whenever there was a lull. Thirteen-year-old Sambhajiraje had taken charge of holding the town against the Mughal onslaught. His own manor had been reduced to rubble by Mughal cannons. The rest of the royal family, including Durgabai and Jayantibai and their maids, had been shifted to the relative security of Shivneri. The young prince was left with no land to lean on; but he had not relaxed the pressure of his thighs on his horse's flanks. He had an army of four thousand fighting under him, and he used his men to mount guerilla raids upon the enemy, cutting off their supplies and looking for every opportunity to harass them.

Ali Wardi Khan had been making endless forays to capture the fort of Shivneri, but his forces had been stalled each time at the Hathi Darwaza[8] and the Parvana Darwaza. The massacre that Sambhaji and his men would wreak upon the enemy was so heavy that the Mughal soldiers had caught a dread of confronting him. The thought of crossing the river Lendi for a night encounter would send shivers down their spines.

Sambhaji's squads would go whizzing around Junnar like Catherine wheels. Thus, without anybody realising it, four months had gone by in this everyday conflict. Summer had gone, but even during the early months of the monsoons, Shahaji and Sambhaji had kept the battle going. Jijabai would ride her horse alongside her husband with equal vigour. Very often would she seat little Shivba in front of her, tying him tight to her stomach. The little prince would sometimes ride behind his father, too, tied securely to his back with a length of cloth.

It was a strange life that the couple was literally riding through, forever on horseback, as they galloped out of one fire into another. To cut losses to his army, the Shah Jahan would mount unanticipated raids on Shahaji. His focus was on apprehending Shahaji alive; but the task seemed impossible—the horsemen hovering around him like sea waves had been riding with him for thirty years. With a minimum of six to seven thousand horsemen always encircling him, Shah Jahan's ambition of catching Shahaji alive was never going to be fulfilled.

That was when destiny dealt Shahaji a cruel blow. A force of three thousand horsemen was travelling to Ahmadnagar in the dead of the night under the charge of Babaji Kate and Adikrao Mahadik. It was raining heavily and the darkness was unrelenting. As was to be expected, they ran into a river in spate, and there was no choice left except to camp on the bank till such time as the waters subsided. They took whatever shelter they could find under the peepul trees and lit their little fires to prepare their meals. Tired after a day's hard ride, the soldiers were busy with their dinners when a force of ten thousand Mughal soldiers surrounded them

---

[8] These forts had specials gates for elephants to pass through.

from all sides. The entire camp of three thousand Maratha soldiers was immediately made to surrender and taken into custody.

Shahaji was in Ranjangaon when he heard this disastrous news the next day. The blow was so unexpected and so distressing to his unyielding nature that the tears froze in his eyes. His voice vanished and even his feet resented carrying the burden of his body. Jijabai persuaded him to accompany her to the ancient Ganesh temple nearby. Shahaji walked into the sanctorum and sat unmoving for close to two hours. Jijau tried to bolster him. 'Raje,' she said, 'this statue of Lord Ganesh was installed by no less a being than Lord Shiva Himself. This, then, is the holy spot that marks the eternal bonding of father and son. You are sure to find a way forward here.' Jijau prayed to Lord Ganesh and got young Shivba to offer a string of five coconuts as oblation.

Shahaji had lost all desire for food, but Shivba turned obstinate too. He chased after his father and compelled him to eat a few morsels. Looking at the endearing efforts that his little son was making at comforting his father and impressed by his cleverness, Shahaji finally began to thaw. Snatching at this opening, Jijau began to reassure her husband, 'Get over it, Raje. We've confronted far worse circumstances to arrive at this point, down a very treacherous road.'

'Jiu, three thousand of my best men are now caught in this vortex of misfortune. It appears to me that darkness has descended everywhere.'

'No, Raje, don't say that. Even as a tiger lies injured on a solitary cliff, it has to continue roaring like a tiger. Our Shahajiraja, too, must thunder like a cloud.'

'But for how long can this go on?'

'If you want to see flowers of independence bloom on these thorny hedges of Fate, you cannot afford to stop. Rise, Raje, rise!'

This remarkable conversation between his parents, and the language of the sword emanating from his mother's mouth, would have touched a chord in little Shivba. He picked up the sword that lay to one side and handed the unsheathed blade to Shahajiraje. Startled at this unexpected gesture, Shahaji was so overcome that he hugged the child passionately and said, 'My child, if something untoward happens to me during this war, for the sake of this land, you should never sheathe this sword again.'

From the next day onwards, Shahaji resumed his struggle with renewed hope and vigour. 'Whether it's Ghruneshwar or Bhuleshwar,' said Jijabai, 'or the Mahadev of Shingnapur, Lord Shiva's blessings have always been with the Bhosale family. Intimations of this truth keep reaching us over and over again.'

'You are right. The shadow of the merciful Lord has always been on us. That's the reason why, since the battle of Bhatwadi, we have adopted the battle cry of Har har Mahadev—Praise be to Lord Shiv Shankara! Let Truth Prevail'—when coming down upon our enemies.'

'At the sanctum of the temple at Ranjangaon yesterday, it was both Lord Shiva's son and our own son who shook you awake again.'

'It's absolutely true, Rani Saheba ... and as I observe little Shivba, every little act of his gives me such reassurance for the future. But these days, I feel as if I am being squeezed from all sides. Destiny, storms and the enemy have descended together upon us.'

'So, should that make us halt, Raje? The struggle we two have been waging all through our lives—should we abandon those dreams?'

'Halting and abandoning our mission cannot even be dreamt about. But looking at the way destiny has unfolded, our policies will have to change; never our aims.'

The rains were fallings unabated. The struggle was showing no sign of slackening either. The news was that Khan Zamaan was on Shahaji's track as he moved between Ahmadnagar and the river Bhima. Sangamner had fallen, Nashik and Dindori, too, had come under Mughal control. Prince Sambhaji had been handling the incendiary conflict in and around Junnar with considerable competence. For the past five days, however, no news had arrived from that direction. The sky was dark with rain clouds. The shadows of adversity were refusing to thin out either.

The emperor had a massive army at his beck and call; in sharp contrast, Shahaji had a force of twelve-thousand cavalry, out of which three thousand had been locked away as prisoners of war. It wasn't the kind of jolt that an already emasculated army could easily absorb. To give the dodge to Khan Zamaan, who was hot on his heels, Shahaji once again moved in the direction of Pune. Fortunately, the Bhima was not as swollen as it could have been. There were barges at hand too. The river even offered them convenient slopes, thus making the crossing a whole lot easier. It was deep in the night that they reached Lohgaon.

The headman of the village as well as the other officials were of course there to welcome Shahaji, but the welcome was made warmer when every hearth got busy preparing dinner for the tired shelter-seekers. It was after many months that the fugitive soldiers gorged themselves on fresh, hot, nutritious food served by the entire village. At the crack of dawn, the army began to enter the river close to the manor at Yerawda. Just then, couriers brought news that provided some relief to Shahaji's heart. Khan Zamaan had halted his chase a few miles in the rear. The Mughal army was on the point of turning in a different direction.

The river here at Yerawda had quite a lot of water; the slope was quite uneven too. Half of Shahaji's force had crossed over. A good three hundred of the animals, horses as well as mules, were carrying the king's luggage, making the crossing a delicate affair. On the other side of the river was a grove of fig trees, with a small clearing in the middle. As Shahaji stood there in the mild drizzle, it looked like something was cooking in his head.

Standing their steeds to one side or holding them with their reins, the young Maavali soldiers gathered to listen to their chief. 'Our Maavali heroes, for the past four years you have tied thorns to your legs and walked with me with blood-spattered legs. The assaults of fate have been so grievous that they have compelled me to take a cruel decision, and I seek your forgiveness for it. From this point on, I shall be able to carry only half my present force along with me. The rest of you will have to wait the monsoons out in your villages, and help your horses regain strength for a new war.'

'No, Raje, no! If destiny has marked us out, we shall die for you. But we shall not desert your company!' A wave of unrest spread through the gathering.

Raising his hand for the assembly to hear him out, Shahaji continued, 'Please calm down. A thousand worries surround us from all sides. Sultan Adilshah has turned helpless. The emperor of Delhi has sworn to destroy us and has suspended the construction of the Taj Mahal halfway to descend to the south. To add to that, the monsoons are not being kind. We do not have the wherewithal to look after a large army. The flood delivered a heavy blow the other day, leading to the arrest of three thousand of our horsemen. With calamities riding into us from every direction, we are left with no alternative but to seek shelter in some secret haven and bide our time.'

The state of their king stunned the men. Half to be left behind? The fear of being a part of that half was a mountain-sized fear, and they were not willing to confront it. Looking at their state of confusion, Shahaji continued, 'My valorous men of Maaval, this temporary withdrawal is not the surrender of our dream. It's not desperation either. We have fought, but never bowed. When we want to leap across a chasm, we take our horses a dozen steps back, throw the reins loose, and then race them up to the edge and fly. It's just for this rainy season that we have to draw back, so that we may take our leap immediately after it. It's unfortunate that the dream of our own kingdom of four years ago was struck by the evil eye of destiny and our enemies. Now, this, our second effort at the Pemgiri kingdom, has resulted in a battle that has brought the emperor of Delhi from Agra to these parts to obstruct our way like an inauspicious black cat. But let me assure you that when we get back to launch our third effort, we shall perform miracles that the world would never have seen before. Meanwhile, I shall not forget your favours for the next seven births.'

His voice turned thick. 'Forgive me, friends, a person dreams dreams and goes and does all he can for their fulfillment, but providence works in its own uncaring manner and throws obstructions impossible to foresee. Absolutely anything can happen. In the event of any untoward development, I want to assure you that my wife Jijabai Saheb shall always be with you to unfurl the flag of independence for our country. Till such time as her sons grow up, she shall keep fighting valorously alongside you.'

The drizzle had stopped and the rumble of the water flowing down the river had become stronger. As his brave soldiers stood weeping, Shahaji carried on instilling faith and courage into them. 'It's a number of years now that for the sake of our independence I've been in conflict with this earth, its thorns and brambles, its rocks and stones. Since the very moment that the idea of Maharashtra took birth, Jijabai Saheb has been my witness and eager participant. Understand this, too, friends, that handing over a sword to a woman is no reason for a man to feel that his manhood has been challenged. The first thing is,' he continued, with a smile playing upon his face, despite the gravity of the situation, 'that it is not considered good form to praise one's own wife. But in case some among you don't know, our Jijabai Saheb here, is the beloved daughter of Jadhavrao of Sindkhed. A number of you may perhaps have seen her skill at horse riding; but her prowess with the sword is something that has left me astounded. That's why I say that our women picking up the sword is no reason for the men to feel insecure. On the contrary, we should strive for glory to come not just to ourselves but to our womenfolk too. During our times of distress, it's our goddesses too—whether Mata Bhavani or Mata Kali or Mata Parvati—that pick up a sword or a trident to fight against adversities. Therefore, if circumstances demand, JIjausaheb is altogether capable of taking our mission forward.

'The second important thing is that there is no reason why you should allow these temporary setbacks to dishearten you. Please be absolutely reassured, friends, that this darkness you see is the darkness before dawn. It's our own cock that shall crow to herald the arrival of a new day; the day that shall mark the beginning of a new life of joy and sovereignty over our own valleys of Maaval here.'

The Kondhana fort was located in the heavy-rainfall belt of the Sahyadri range. Which was why it was always raining cats and dogs there. Geographically, this fort fell in the Pune principality; but the kings of the Deccan, while granting principalities to their chieftains, had kept this fort under their own control. The Kondhana fort, therefore, was at this point under the Adilshahi administration. The clerks and officials of the fort were personal acquaintances of Shahaji; as a result, even while the Mughal and Adilshahi forces were hunting for him, he didn't see any risk in taking shelter in the fort for the time being. Besides, the rains during that time were so heavy that it would have been nearly impossible for any army to come looking for him there.

The agent of the palace at the fort was Dadoji Kond'dev. It was through him that the revenue would be sent to Bijapur. Dadoji enjoyed considerable intimacy with Shahaji because the Bhosales held the traditional authority of patils and deshmukhs[9] over the districts of Hingni, Burdi and Deulgaon, where Dadoji had held the post of accountant for many years. He was over sixty-five years of age, with a stout but strong constitution. He was acerbic, obedient and completely committed to the service of his master. Shahaji, therefore, was favourably disposed towards him. Pansambal Kaka, who had accompanied Jijabai to Shahaji's household after her wedding, and Dadoji were great friends at the fort, and both of them were devoted to little Shivba.

In the process of chasing Shahaji, Khan Zamaan had moved further on after crossing the Salpa ghat[10]. On his way, he had plundered the old but prosperous towns of Kolhapur and Miraj falling in Bijapur territory; the news was that he was now descending towards Raibagh. On getting to know that Shahaji was close by, the petty officials of the nearby villages as well as the senior denizens of the twelve Maavals would come to meet him despite the heavy rains.

The days spent at Kondhana carried the uncomfortable feeling of a calm before the storm. Junnar had slipped away a few days earlier, causing Jijabai great anxiety. Knowing how she would be fretting, Shahaji told her, 'Rani Saheb, please stop worrying about young Shambhuraja. His army has suffered grievous losses, I hear, but he himself is safe.'

But her mother's heart would not let her sit still. 'When?' would be her refrain. 'When am I going to set eyes on my son?'

A secret missive arrived from Randullah Khan one night, which informed that Shah Jahan was convinced that he had the war quite under control. He had, therefore, moved out of his Daulatabad base and shifted to the Mandu fort in Central India, where he intended to wait out the monsoon season. But from there, too, he had kept his knee pressed on Adilshah's throat. 'Conquer the forts under Shahaji's control and hand them over to us immediately; else our elephants, instead of moving north towards Agra, will turn round to Bijapur to settle accounts with you.' The intractable emperor refused to be shaken from his purpose. He had carried his royal guards with him, but left an army of over fifty thousand soldiers in Baglan, Balaghat and in provinces on

---
[9] Patils were village headmen and deshmukhs were the heads of districts.
[10] Mountain range

either side of the Sahyadri. Come hell or high water, Shahaji had to be destroyed at all costs.

News had reached the emperor's camp that Shahaji had sought shelter in the Kondhana fort. Hence, Randullah had thought it prudent to alert Shahaji. 'Rajaji, so far I have managed to stay true to our friendship, but I may soon lose my ability to do so. The emperor refuses to relax his hold on the sultan's throat, and therefore, we may have to raid the fort any day now to arrest you.'

Hard times had latched on to Shahaji with a vengeance. He was compelled to reduce his army by another two thousand men. It was with the greatest difficulty that he had persuaded them to return to their villages and wait for a call from him. With three thousand five hundred horsemen for company, he began descending from the mountains into the Konkan region in the face of rains whip lashing them all the way down. Food and fodder had begun to vanish, but worst of all, little Shivba had begun to keep very unwell. It was for the first time in Shahaji's life that his army had become a difficult load for him to carry.

Half way across, Shahaji sent another fifteen hundred of his horsemen to Prabalgad near Panveli. Braving the incessant torrent and riding through slush and slime, Shahaji and his men stood at last at an elevated point at Danda Rajapuri, from where they could see the sea waves being whipped up by the strong monsoon winds. There in the middle of the raging waters stood the fort of Janjira, submitting itself to the battering of mountainous walls of water from all directions. During these savage monsoons, the irregular soldiery of the Siddi chieftains had also removed themselves from the fort. It would therefore have been foolhardy to move into that stark, desolate, windswept fort at a time like this. Shahaji decided to erect his camp at the hillock nearby.

He then sent word to an old friend of his, Inayat Barabandi, who enjoyed considerable influence in the areas of Cheul and Carlisle. As a well-regarded trader, Inayat moved freely among the officers of the English and Portuguese armies stationed there. While Shahaji waited for the arrival of his friend, Shivba writhed in high fever all through the night.

Jijabai and he sat by their son all night, placing wet cloth on his forehead to bring the temperature down. While Shivba's fever was of great concern, Jijabai was equally worried by the miserable state to which her husband had been reduced. Here was a man who would face the onslaught of booming cannons without blinking an eyelid; to see him so perturbed and discomposed by the ill-health of his son was unnerving.

Shahaji had great expectations from the Portuguese at Cheul. Because of the native and foreign trade that had picked up in recent times, the harbour town of Cheul had made a name for itself. There was a Pune-sized township close by, two forts and a number of bastions. The next day, Inayat Khan came galloping in from Cheul. Shahaji had already called a clerk over the previous evening and got an adequate letter ready. It was imperative in these difficult times to seek out a small escape route. With an army chasing him, the rains reducing him and his men to destitution, and the worrisome state of Shivba's health, Shahaji had already reached his wit's end. Political asylum with the Portuguese under such circumstances would be of great help.

On 26 September 1636, Shahaji handed over to Inayat a petition addressed to Captain Antonio Carneiro de Argao stationed at the Portuguese fort of Cheul:

Dear Captain Saheb,
No man should be visited by days of such perturbation and unending worries as I have been going through. Earlier, when I was serving in the territory of either Nizamshah or Adilshah, I was always sympathetic to Portuguese interests. It's after giving you a gentle reminder of those times that I write this letter to you. When Time and Tide turn hostile, men with constitutions of steel get crushed. I, however, have still not lost courage or hope. For three full years, I ran an excellent administration at Pemgadh in the name of Murtaza Nizamshah. Even now, he and his mother live under our protection in the Trimal fort near Balaghat.

Currently, I have a robust, seven- to eight-thousand strong cavalry under my control; some of them, however, have been sent home to wait out the monsoons. I am sending as an annexure the present strength of my army, along with a list.

The times that we are passing through are difficult; but relying upon the excellent relations we have enjoyed with the Portuguese regime over a long period of time, I request you to stand by me during these testing times, and I seek shelter for our women and children in your coastal fort at Cheul. The bad weather conditions have been adversely affecting the health of our children, about which I am particularly worried. We shall not be remiss in meeting whatever expenditure is incurred for the upkeep of our families. We shall be happy to write over to you the revenue collection of a few of our villages for meeting this expenditure.

We have a small child by the name of Shivaji whose health we are particularly concerned about. I beg for your generosity and request you to open the door of Portuguese hospitality to us during our times of difficulty. A time may come when we may forsake our shadow, but we shall never allow distance to creep into our friendship for the rest of our lives.

Inayat himself carried the letter to Cheul and returned late the next night after an audience with the Portuguese captain. A distressed Shahaji immediately badgered him with anxious questions. 'What happened, Inayat? What did the captain saheb say? Does he know me by name?'

'Who doesn't know you, Raje?' Inayat responded. 'Captain Antonio was particularly solicitous about you. He read your entire letter thrice over, right in my presence. He proposes to pass on your information to Goa by the mail-bag that leaves tomorrow morning.'

'Goa?'

'Yes, he says that this is a political matter of a rather high order, and only his seniors can decide on the policy they need to adopt. He will have to seek advance clearance from the Portuguese governor at Goa before he can take any decision.'

'What's your own assessment? Is there any chance of shelter being offered?'

'It looks difficult, Raje.'

'Why?'

'For one, I don't think the Portuguese are going to move as rapidly as you need them to. For another, one doesn't know to what extent the Portuguese will be willing to invite the wrath of Delhi and Bijapur for your sake.'

Nemesis, it appeared, had decided to shred Shahaji into ribbons.

A disappointed Shahaji abandoned the camp at Danda Rajpuri and met two trader friends near Nagothan. He offloaded the trunks and baskets loaded on fifty horses and mules, and placed them in their temporary custody. The trunks carried Jijabai's expensive silk sarees and Shahaji's royal clothing of the highest quality. Some others were stuffed full with golden lamp stands and silver ornaments. There were gold dishes that had been gifted during weddings in Bijapur, Pune, Sindkhed, Phaltan and a dozen other places. It was deeply distressing for Jijabai to part, even if temporarily, with things that were not only expensive by themselves, but were also associated with cherished memories. Circumstances, however, had left her with no other option.

The journey towards Panveli continued, where it was decided to take shelter in the forts of Muranjan and Prabalgad. Travelling on a road full of slush and stones, they crossed the jungle of Thakarwadi to reach Prabalgad. The fort looked soaking wet with rain and haze. All the other hills around it, including the grand tusk of the Kalavatini and Matheran beyond, lay wrapped in a dense blanket of fog.

The land was dense with trees and bushes of jungle fruits. The ceaseless rains had covered not merely the rocks, but even the tree trunks with thick, green moss. The soldiers who had arrived earlier did try to put things into order. Despite the heavy rainfall, Jijabai found time to offer her prayers to the worn-out statue of Lord Ganesh at the fort and the red lead-coated Hanuman. It was imperative for her to beseech all the gods and goddesses to bring relief to her ailing son.

They continued to experience here the massive rainfall that they had been hoping to leave behind at Konkan. The little prince would stir out of his disturbed sleep, and lie staring out of the fort windows at the wild vegetation that abounded everywhere. Moisture dripped down the walls of the temples and all other structures. The walls were laden with greenish fungus and lichen.

One afternoon, the rain took a small break and the jungle wind began playing among the bushes. As the prince lay peeping out of the window, he suddenly pointed his finger out of the window and called out to his mother, 'Aau, Aau, come over here, quick!'

'What's it, little one? What are you looking at?'

'Look! Look down there and tell me what you see in that green tangle.'

'I don't see anything at all!'

'How's that possible, Aausaheb? Can't you see that red golden light in those bushes?'

Jijabai looked long and carefully through those bushes, but she could see nothing. Her heart then sank. Could the prolonged illness be causing the boy delusions?

On the one side, the rains were refusing to relent, while on the other, Emperor Shah Jahan hadn't tired out either. Sitting far away in his fort at Mandu, he would not allow his Sahyadri and Balaghat soldiers a moment of respite. He kept them hopping all the time.

The Muranjan fort wasn't secure by any means either. A bunch of couriers reached there one midnight and told Shahaji in clear terms, 'Raje, please leave this place as soon as possible.'

'Why? What news have you brought?'

'Yesterday afternoon a big Adilshahi chieftain was seen climbing down the Karjat mountains hurriedly along the Sidee hills. Those wraiths can launch a raid here any time after sunrise.'

Once again, before the sun had begun to peep out, Shahaji and his horsemen started their climb down the fort. Despite an entire team of physicians travelling with them, Shivba's health remained a matter of concern. He had turned so weak that he couldn't sit in a palanquin. Sitting astride a horse was out of the question. Shahaji then seated him on the horse in front, and tied him to his stomach. It could have been the warmth of the father's chest that put him at ease, but the boy slept like he hadn't slept for many nights. The snores emanating from him gave some comfort to Shahaji too.

By the time they reached the Kalyan harbour on the way, it was rapidly turning darker. The Durgadi fort there looked more like a rampart for keeping watch, making a stay up there with an army quite risky. Shahaji was moving stealthily and fast, which ruled out any quartermaster force moving in advance. Since it had turned dark at Durgadi, the boatmen and fishermen had anchored their boats and left. The king's men, therefore, had to go searching for them in the villages nearby.

Shahaji quietly got up and entered into the nearby bushes. When he didn't return for a fairly long time, Jijabai felt suspicious. She handed over the child in her lap to a maid and entered after him. There, behind the cover of a small bush, was the king, shedding copious tears. There was no bigger sin for a king than to shed tears before his soldiers, she knew, and her heart went out to her husband for finding this quiet place for unburdening his chest. She reached up to him and took him in her embrace. They took the blueberry bush in their embrace too. Little droplets of rainwater were rolling off the thick blueberry leaves too, as if the tree had joined in commiserating over the test to which Shahaji and Jijabai were being subjected.

In an effort to lift the spirits of her husband, Jijabai said, 'What encouragement can a mere woman give to a mature, heroic person who has brought half of Hindustan under his heels?'

'Jiu, I have never been so scared in my entire life. This fear cannot be of any divine or temporal power either. It's on account of seven lives of meritorious work that God has given us this pot of gold named Shivaji. The disregard towards his health causes my heart to break into splinters. If truth be told, the king's robe fell off my shoulder quite a long while ago. It's just a distraught father these days who flings his arms in all directions and begs hoarsely, 'God! Please let this gift of gold stay on with me!'

'Stop worrying, Raje. Destiny has brought both of us to the very highest point of inquisition. Our boy Shiva is going to come out of it unscathed. Our life caught in this horrible cataclysm of misfortunes and cycle of highs and lows, our elder son Shambhu fighting there in the jungles and mountains with an army of just four thousand, our little Shivba with his uncertain health—our living, our fighting, our falling and our rising again, could all of this be the source of a divine blessing?'

'Jiu?'

'Over and above that, this dream of the land of Maharashtra, this happy dream of an independent state—it requires great magnitude of mind to be able to even dream such dreams. Whatever I have heard in my mother's house from the mouths of enlightened men, whatever I have digested of their sagacious words, its sum and substance that I as an ignorant woman can say is this: unprecedented dreams such as yours may only perchance fall to a person's lot after hundreds of years have gone by.'

'Yes, Jiu, but they're still dreams for all that! If no earth of reality sticks to them, then what's the difference between such dreams and autumn leaves falling off trees? What sense is left in all these hollow words?'

10

THE CHAINS OF MAHULI AND EXTERNMENT

A full day's ride left the lower regions behind. The village of Shahapur, nestled in the groove of a shallow valley, came into sight. On the left was the huge, long and snaking mountain range of Mahuligad. The fort itself was about three-thousand-arms tall, insurmountable, and surrounded by innumerable cliffs and deep gorges. On the right side of the fort, some of the hills in the range had collapsed, giving the standing cliffs the shape of dragon teeth reaching for the sky. They could also be compared to the bamboo-and-paper minarets carried in a Moharram procession.

It was twilight. The light of the setting sun had turned golden. It was an entrancing sight. The entire landscape was ornamented with innumerable valleys, streams descending straight from the mountain-tops into the folds and curves below and water bodies scattered everywhere. As Shahaji's troops reached the fortifications of Mahuli, they noticed that clusters of soldiers had already made camp near a stream there. When he noticed the ochre flags fluttering amidst them, he instantly knew that the camp could belong to none but his son Sambhaji. He had arrived there that morning from Naneghat after crossing the mountain at Murbad. Both Shahaji and Jijabai were thrilled at meeting their son, who had returned from his first campaign hale and hearty. They ran towards each other and were soon tangled in a triple embrace.

All three realised at the same time that a tiny someone was clinging to their feet. Sambhaji looked down, let out a loud cry of 'Shivba!' and scooped the little one up in his arms. Shivba was feeling a lot better than he had felt for many days. The rough and tumble of the campaign had coated Sambhaji's juvenile face with a layer of hard tan.

The royal family found some flat rocks along the stream and sat down for a little while. The day was fading. The rains had given them a decent respite, too. The men in charge of establishment had moved forward to put things in order at the fort. Shambhuraja asked his father in a soft voice, 'Abasaheb, how do we take our next steps forward?'

'Son, There are tough times ahead; our face-off is with the emperor of Delhi himself.'

When officials of Shahaji's team, Nilkanthpant and Pilajipant, presented themselves before him, he threw a sharp glance at them and said, 'Keep this in mind, we have to climb up to the fort this very night. Also, after having taken charge of the fort, we have to keep the fight with Bijapur and Delhi on for a minimum of six months.'

'But, Raje,' Pilajipant asked hesitantly, 'is the fort-keeper here going to open the gates of the fort so readily?'

'Don't worry, you won't even have to pull your swords out of their sheaths.'

'How is that possible?' queried Jijabai instantly.

'Because the fort-keeper here is none other than my brother Mambaji.'

The fort guards had been doing their rounds at the foot of the fort. Darkness had fallen and flambeaus had been lit. All that could be heard in the silence of the night was the sound of the waterfalls. The guards instantly recognised Shahaji's men and bedlam ensued. The fort was at a considerable height and its access tortuous. Draft animals like donkeys, mules and bullocks carrying the load were nearly dead by the time they reached the top.

When Mambaji so unexpectedly set eyes on Shahaji, Jijabai and young Sambhaji in the dim light of the flambeaus, all his grievances dissolved, and he immediately took his cousin in a tight embrace. By the time they reached the palace at the head of the fort, it was dawn. Mambaji had dispatched his messengers ahead for the preparation and for laying out the meals. When they got up from their meals, the sky had begun to turn brighter. The pall of darkness was being pulled out of the sky to reveal the soft morning greenery of the fort in the monsoon months.

Without bothering to stretch his back, Shahaji leapt back on his horse. With Mambaji riding alongside him, the two cousins set off for a survey of the fort. Mohammad Batga, the founder of the Nizamshahi Sultanate at Ahmadnagar, had spent some time in this ancient, rough-hewn fort at Mahuli that fell in the region of Konkan. It was one of his earliest acquisitions. Its circuit was half a mile long, and its width was just as impressive. In point of fact, it was really three forts clubbed into one, with Bhandargadh in the south and Palasgadh at its northern end. The primordial forest that surrounded it from all sides was so dense as to instill fear and keep out inquisitive intruders. As he rode through its precincts, Shahaji was busy working out his strategy for the immediate future. Looking at the contribution of nature to the security of the fort, he was quite sure now that it could be held for a good seven or eight months, even with a small defending force.

Spies brought news the very next day: Randullah Khan had crossed the creek at Kalyan and was closing in rapidly. In the evening came the other news, that Khan Zamaan was descending Naneghat to move towards Mahuli, and that his horses should be at the ramparts in the next two days.

Within four days, Khan Zamaan brought his Mughal forces from the one side, and Randullah Khan led the Adilshahi men from the other; the two met at the foot of Mahuli fort. Even before the battle gets underway, it is essential for the battleground to be closely examined.

The quartermaster units of the Adilshahi and Mughal forces immediately began circumambulating round the base of the huge fort. Even at their best speed, they took a day and a half to do a single round. The two enemy generals Randullah Khan and Zamaan Khan just kept ogling in wonder at the enormity of the fort in the morning light. Knots formed in their stomachs when they did the simple arithmetic of gauging the spread and the height of the fort. The extent of the fort was so huge that they counted as many as eighty-four streams descending from the top of the fort into the precipices all around it. This meant that if one had to move into the space that lay between two streams, they often had to travel a good distance up and then travel down after doing the crossing. Doing this for eighty-four fast-flowing brooks and freshets was a difficult and dangerous task. It had tested the strength and stamina of both man and horse of both the armies, and brought both down to desperate straits.

As they stood below the fort, Randullah and Zamaan Khan couldn't take their eyes away from the top. Zamaan Khan said, 'Going by the emperor's orders, I am required to scale the fortress without wasting any time, and tie that Shahaji up like a monkey, and carry him away to be presented before him at the Mandu fort.'

'In that case, you must get immediate sanction from the emperor.'

'For what?'

'Your desire seems to be to raid the top of the fort, tie Shahaji up like an animal and drag him down. But to do that, you will have to sprinkle the precipice of the climb with a minimum of twelve thousand heads of your Mughal soldiers. If you can do that, your mission can be accomplished.'

Zamaan Khan turned cold at this advice from the old man.

The two armies together had posted nearly five thousand men around the fort. About the same number of men were left with them for the battle. A large number of small posts had been constructed at lower altitudes. When it was raining, visibility shrank to a few feet, and during the night, the right hand wouldn't know where the left one was.

Shah Jahan was relentless in the pressure he was putting on Zamaan Khan, but he would turn a deaf ear to all of Khan's requests for more men and weapons. With the mountain ranges having stood up to play the shield for Shahajiraje, the two armies were left with no option but to wait and watch. They sat, hoping for a day when the fort would run out of supplies.

Three months passed by. Shahaji had three thousand men and four thousand fighting and draught animals up there on the fort to feed. He knew, of course, that supplies were dwindling fast, and a day would arrive when they would run out. He also knew exactly what the guests down below at the foot of the fort were waiting for. With the supplies now having sunk to dangerous levels, it was after a good three months that he finally gave the nod for a dialogue with the enemy.

The news arrived that the Mughal official Khan Zamaan would come for the first meeting, a proposal Shahaji declined immediately. He sent word that he would like the discussions to begin with the Adilshahi official Randullah Khan. The day arrived when one afternoon Randullah Khan stood in the quadrangle of the palace. One look at each other, and Shahaji and Randullah rushed into an embrace with cries of 'Oh my friend!' 'Oh my brother!', leaving the onlookers utterly stunned and confused. As soon as the talks began, Randullah used the authority of the senior and shot out, 'How long do you propose to live this life?'

'The fault is yours, not ours.'

'How can you say that?'

'Khan Saheb, the land is ours, but the sovereignty is yours! The soldiers who die are ours, but the flag of victory that flutters is yours! This is the misfortune of us sons of the soil, and that's all there is to it.'

In the interim, two of Randullah's lieutenants Kanhoji Jedhe and Dadaji Lohkare came over to meet Shahaji. More or less of the same age as Shahaji, Kanhoji was basically a powerful landlord from Maaval. He had joined Randullah's service when the latter was the subedar of Rahimatpur on the bank of the Krishna, and had risen to the post of prestige that he currently enjoyed in the Bijapur army. On meeting Shahaji, he paid him fulsome compliments by saying, 'So many big, reputed Maratha families have entered into the service of Sultans and emperors; a large number of them would have earned wealth and prestige too, but Shahaji, you are one of a kind.'

'In which case, Kanhoji, let's not limit this appreciation to merely singing paeans in my name!'

'So, then?'

'Tell me, then, what you are willing to do for the welfare of your family, your people, and for the welfare of this Maaval soil?'

'Do this one thing for us, Raje. Get me and this Dadaji here out of Randullah's service and bring us into fold. We shall spend the rest of our lives at your feet.'

A formal tripartite conference began between Khan Zamaan, Randullah Khan and Shahaji. Shah Jahan had not liked Shahaji's experiment with Nizamshahi at Pemgadh. It was with the express purpose of bringing peace on his southern border that he had brought about the destruction of the Nizamshahi Sultanate, blown holes in the fortified walls of Daulatabad. As a matter of fact, the emperor was determined to annihilate the Sultanate root, stalk and leaf, and was demanding possession of Murtaza and his mother, the Begum Saheba, currently in Shahaji's custody. Shahaji agreed in principle to hand his charges over to Delhi, but before that, the emperor would have to meet a few demands of his too. 'Look,' he told his two interlocutors, 'if a meaningful accord has to be reached amongst us, our rights on our ancestral lands have to be given back to us, as had existed before.'

'What rights are those?'

'The land that lies between the rivers Neera and the Bheema, specifically, the principalities of Pune and Supe should return to our possession.'

Both Khan Zamaan and Randullah Khan assured Shahaji that they would persuade their masters to accede to his proposal.

One day, Shahaji invited Khan Zamaan and handed over to him a letter carrying his seal. 'I request you to dispatch this letter to the esteemed emperor Shah Jahan, wherever he may be, as early as possible.'

'Such urgency? What's in it, Raje?'

'After giving deep thought to the matter, I have arrived at the conclusion that considering my age and the circumstances in which I find myself, it will become imperative for me to get into the service of one power or the other; and if that is so, why should I then settle for Adilshah? Why shouldn't I accept the overlordship of the emperor of Delhi?'

'It's a good thought.'

When Randullah Khan met Shahaji a few days later, he urged him not to delay sending his settlement proposal to Bijapur. The passing years had not treated Randullah's health with any noticeable kindness. The strong, sprightly, young giant of yesteryears had morphed into an overweight, heavy-moving slob. 'My friend,' he said to Shahaji, 'there are a few things I wish to see settled before I join my Maker. One of those things is to see a close friend like you shake off his nomadic existence and find stability.'

'Thank you, Khan Saheb, for the friendship you have always extended to me.'

'But, Raja, we carry this grouse against you. We have this proverb in Bijapur, which means: here I am showering all my love on you, but all you care for is your camel!'

'Don't talk in riddles, Khan Saheb, lay it out straight!'

'Well, here I am, straining and sweating to see you properly settled, but you seem to have sold your heart to the Mughals!'

Shahaji managed to get away without answering that charge, and a few days thus drifted by. Shah Jahan, on his side, was keen to get the Deccan issue settled once and for all. The masterplan had been ready with him for well over six months now. He had so sold himself on this settlement that he had instructed his advisors to get the document of this most important achievement of his life etched on a plate of gold.

This confinement at Mahuli had now begun eating into Shahaji's spirit. All that he could see after so many years of struggle was failure and the duplicity of Fate. Despite the renown he had earned all across Hindustan for being the most resolute, the most competent and the canniest of all the chieftains in the Deccan, all that he could see in front was unrelieved darkness. Since his mansion in Pune had been burnt down, he had no roof he could call his own. His elder son Sambhaji had had the valour to bring an accomplished general like Shaista Khan to despair in the battle of Sangamner a few months ago; yet, he too was thrashing about in detention along with his father.

One day, Khan Zamaan came up to the fort in an animated state. His demeanour clearly suggested that he had received the emperor's response to Shahaji's letter. Khan Zamaan handed over a scroll, which Shahaji shook open and began to read immediately. This was what the emperor had written:

> Shahajiraje,
> A person of your distinction, fearlessness and renown has written of your desire to embrace the suzerainty and service of the Mughals. We thank you for resting such faith in us. But we seek your forgiveness in having to turn down your proposal with a great deal of regret. We are aware that becoming a Mughal subedar would undoubtedly bring you great joy. But the fact of the matter is that it is not within the means of this Shah Jahan to offer that post to you, despite his being the emperor. We shall not be able to afford it either.

This forthright letter from the emperor increased Shahaji's worries. It was getting difficult for him to comprehend exactly what these two powers had in mind regarding him.

One such afternoon, Randullah came visiting along with Khan Zamaan, and said excitedly, 'Congratulations, Raja Saheb, things have transpired exactly as you had wanted them to. All that you had asked for has been granted to you. The principalities of Pune and Supe have been turned over to you without any preconditions.'

'Splendid!' gushed Shahaji. It was after a long, long wait that he had heard something pleasant.

'But there is one condition, huzoor,' piped in the Mughal chieftain Khan Zamaan. 'The principalities of Pune and Supe will stay within your family, but in actuality you will not be able to enjoy the privilege of being the jagirdar of these places.'

'What strange things are you talking?'

'Listen, Rajaji, you suffer no loss at all. On the one side, all the land and the wealth here will stay with your clan, while the other benefit is that you will be shifted to Bijapur to occupy the prestigious post of a chieftain in the Adilshahi court.'

The import of this condition placed Shahaji under tremendous stress. The settlement that the Mughals had offered was a magic dagger that would not actually enter the stomach, but would cause grievous wounds all the same. There was no grief of loss, but there was no joy either of having made any gain.

After a little while, Khan Zamaan left for his camp at the foot of the fort, but Randullah Khan dragged his feet and finally turned around to return with his friend to the mansion. When the two sat down for their meals, Jijabai noticed a kind of coldness that stood between them, and her heart missed a few beats.

Randullah Khan was aware of the grief, anger and frustration that were running through his friend's veins. When a handful of food slipped through Shahaji's fingers and fell on the plate, Randullah placed an affectionate hand on his friend's shoulder and said, 'Stop worrying. These Muslim valiants with twisted minds are giving you back your principalities—you should be satisfied.'

'But what about their insistence that I shouldn't be the jagirdar of my own jagirs?'

'So, what difference does it make? God has given you a strong and sturdy jagirdarin like your wife Jijabai, hasn't He?.'

Shahaji was moved by Randullah Khan's confidence in Jijabai. But in the next moment, he asked, 'Randullah miyaan, you are an important chieftain belonging to that camp. You, at least, should be able to tell us the reason behind such an outrageous, diabolical manoeuvre to keep me away from my land!'

'Well, truth be told, Shah Jahan was obsessively fired up. He had told our Adilshah Saheb in clear terms: this irrepressible Maratha named Shahaji had nibbled away seven years off his life, and he would not take his thumbs off Adilshah's jugular if the sultan didn't provide him with the settlement he desired. The sultan was instructed to give Shahaji all the wealth he demanded in and around Pune. But the man himself should be compelled to move to Bijapur; he should be given as big a chieftainship as he desired.'

'But why would he want it so?'

'The emperor's decree was absolutely clear: the sultan should never commit the error of allowing that Margattha Shahaji to stay in the Sahyadri mountains, comfortable behind a rock; because this man's mere presence causes the rocks to melt. Keeping Margatthas like Shahaji in the mountains is no less dangerous than walking into an ammunition store with a naked flame.'

The royal family got busy winding up their stay in the Mahuli fort. Pandemonium reigned among attendants, retainers and all variety of minions—men as well as women. Well before he departed, Shahaji had made all kinds of plans for settling his family in the principality. There was a sprawling mansion in village Khedebehre near Pune, in which arrangements for a temporary stay would be made for Jijau and Shivba. Accordingly, clerks and administrators had been dispatched to bring the place into decent shape. Murari Pandit having reduced the Bhosale palaces Mhalsa and Malhar to dust and ashes, instructions had been issued to Dadoji Kond'dev to start the construction of a new palace in Pune.

When Shahaji entered the inner quad of the Mahuli mansion, Jijabai looked at him and asked, 'Haven't you got back your principalities of Pune and Supe from Adilshah? After having received all that you had demanded, why has the web of disappointment not disappeared from your brow?'

Shahaji responded with a doleful laugh, 'Jiu, when a big tree falls off its cliff, the tree alone can know the agony of being torn off from its roots.'

'Raje!'

'Yes, Rani Saheb, my body has been nourished by the waters of holy rivers like the Bhima, the Kukadi and the Indrayani. The grains of this earth and these rocks are what compose our flesh and blood. So, you can imagine how it would feel when we are pulled out from our roots and sent to be transplanted in some foreign soil.'

Shahaji left, leaving Jijabai startled. In his face, she saw the intensity of the pain that exiles have suffered through times eternal. The articles of the Mahuli settlement had appeared quite simple and straightforward to her till this moment, but the payoff, she could see now, was severe. This assault was like somebody sweet-talking all the while and then suddenly pulling out a machete and chopping off the legs from the knees.

Shahajiraja was bursting with holy anger. 'What kind of god it is who is delivering this justice, Jiu? And what is this judicial system that has passed this verdict? Who is this Islamic emperor of Delhi who fixes it all with this other Bijapuri Adilshah of the Deccan? And places a wicked condition upon this Shahajiraja, who was born a son of this very soil, that he should not stay in this range of the Sahyadri mountains that belonged to his ancestors? And he should pack up his belongings, load them on his back, and walk out of the holy land of his ancestors like a nomad?'

'There is one thing that I had forgotten to ask your lordship: what do we do in the future about our little Shivba?'

'Shambhu is anyway with us. Shivba will stay with you. I had discussions on this issue the other day with Baji Palaskar. The two of you should stay either in Khedebehera or in Pune. You are the only person who can manage our Pune jagirdari with efficiency.'

Despite a choked throat, Jijabai spoke with clarity: 'Look, Raje, if you do not want to take me with you to the Deccan, it is all right. But why do you want to harm my illustrious child—my Shivba? You should take him along with you.' Jijau took Shahaji's hand in hers. The rims of her eyes had turned moist. She let out a deep breath and didn't utter a word. Within a moment she digested the painful storm raging inside her and said, 'In the end, I am an *Arya* woman. Where the husband lives, that's where the wife lives too. Why have our religious books said: where there is Raghav, there is Sita?'

The Raja's breath too seemed to jam, but he said, 'Jiu, do you think that I don't know the tales of the Ramayana? It's not I but the world outside that acknowledges: bunches upon bunches of the fragrant flowers of Sanskrit poetry hang by Shahaji's lips! But Rani Saheb—'

'Yes?'

'Show me another Ramayana where Ravana, the lord of Lanka, comes and sits upon the chest of the citizens of Ayodhya, reads out the decree to them that even after finishing his fourteen-year exile, Rama should not return to Ayodhya? How, how do I just walk out and stay permanently exiled from this Ayodhya of mine, this Sahyadri?'

Shahaji had turned sombre. Jijabai waited for a little while, swallowed her pain, and said, 'Look, our goddesses too refer to their husbands as the master of their life-breath. I must come along with you to Bijapur, because without you, I shall simply suffocate, don't you know?'

'Jiu-rani, this is not the time for us to worry about our breaths. Slavery has gagged the breath of our poor subjects, of everyone including the animals and birds all across Maharashtra. This suffocation is immensely important.' Shahaji looked straight into Jijabai's eyes and asked, 'Jiu, why are you so insistent today?'

'Look, Raje, I don't care at all for living a life of pomp and luxury, but the mother's heart within me cries. If our son Shivba goes with you, he will get the best possible training in the company of the children of the other chieftains. Archery, swordsmanship, horse-riding, he will become adept in a thousand such skills.'

Shahaji laughed out heartily at Jijabai's words and said, 'You are quite right in a way—if Shivba comes to Bijapur, he will live in the company of the princes there, who enjoy the luxury of heaven in their huge glass palaces and roll in their soft, satin beds. He will see for himself their grand stables, their plush comforts, their great savants and scholars, their linguists experts. So, what you say is right: if he graduates from that academy there, our son will become truly great. But what does that mean?'

Jijau didn't know what to say. She was stunned. But Shahaji immediately added, 'If Shivba grows big after consuming the water of Bijapur, what does that mean? Big exactly like his father is big. A powerful chieftain like Bhima, but yoked to another person's cart. That is unacceptable to me. Shivba's initial education should happen here, on the soil of the Sahyadri.

At the most, he can be called over to Bengaluru for his training in arms whenever the need arises.'

The new thoughts that were flowing out of Shahaji's mouth like white-hot lava dazzled Jijausaheb. He said, 'Jiu, there are many pleasure-seeking, self-indulgent princes who have been ruined by the excess of wealth that surrounds them. So, does our Shivba go and add to their number? How do you forget one simple thing, Jiu-rani? It's a place that produces clones of chieftains, in fact, slaves, that will later serve the Sultanate with all their heart and soul, every one of them. This unfortunate wilderness of the Sahyadris has not seen for hundreds of years how an independent, self-reliant king looks. The supreme king of this land must emerge from and grow up in this very land. Our son should grow up in these springs, in this air, roaming around in the slush and mud with its poor, hard-working people. On the fields of the Marathas and the farmers, with the children of the tribal communities living in the forests, in the courtyards of the maangs and mahaars[11], in the playground of nature, coated in the redness of this soil. He should reach up to the sky!'

Jijabai was overwhelmed. Her eyes began to shine with the tears that had collected there. Holding him tight in her embrace, she said passionately, 'Raje, what an amazing dream! The prophet who shows the path to these dreams is as important as the braveheart who realises them.'

'Jiu!'

'Yes, Raje. It wasn't you but the soil of this land that was speaking through you just now. It is the lamentation of the soil that has been crushed for centuries by the hooves of foreign horses. But tell me this, Raje—' she paused. Then, wiping the hot tears streaming down her cheeks, she continued, 'Will this dream-tree of ours bear fruits one day?'

'Why not, Jiu? *Aga*, you have seen the tall trees growing in the valleys and gorges of Maaval, haven't you? When the branches of these trees keep rubbing against each other in the forest wind for a long time, it automatically begins to rain sparks there. Fires erupt. In the same manner, let the flambeau of our mission, in the shape of our Shivba, catch fire, so

---

[11] The two most populous outcastes across Maharashtra. Untouchables.

that the chains of slavery tied to the legs of this Maratha soil are snapped. Let him grow up to the height of the sky in the lap of this soil.'

Having left the Mandu fort, the emperor Shah Jahan's army had begun moving in the direction of Agra. The emperor himself sat in pomp in a canopy resting on gold posts. His attention was nowhere focussed on the thousands of horses, elephants and camels that marched all around him. On his lap lay the *firman* of the Mahuli Pact of 24 *Zil Haj*, 1044 (31 May 1635) carved on a plate of gold in beautifully calligraphed letters. That pact was a gift given to him by the All Powerful Allah. That '*sulookh* shall remain eternal like the indestructible and inanimate wall of Alexander'. Shah Jahan had deliberately got this sentence inserted into the pact. Shah Jahan was looking again and again at the royal seals of the emperor and the sultan etched on the golden letters of the pact as also the palm-impressions of both Shah Jahan and Mohammadshah. His attention would travel again and again to the sixth section of the pact. He had removed Shahaji Bhosale from the Sahyadri mountains and had got him forcibly externed to Bijapur. He had cleverly got the Adilshahi sultan to ensure the firm implementation of this condition. The emperor was basking under the glory of having succeeded in his mission of getting the fire named Shahaji under control and reducing the heat along the Deccan borders of the Mughal Empire.

11

IN BENGALURU—UNDER THE TUTELAGE OF HIS FATHER

1640–1642

'If you had been present at Shivba's marriage, wouldn't I have shone brighter than gold?' Jijau would mutter to herself often. She had also written letters in this faked anger and sent them to Shahajiraja at Bengaluru.

From the very day that the festoons of auspicious leaves had been hung for the house-warming ceremony at Lal Mahal, Jijau had begun to fret about the marriage of her younger son. The image of the fair, chubby, glowing face of Shivba with the baubles of a bridegroom hanging from his forehead began dancing before her eyes. As per the Maratha custom, children were married off at the age of ten or eleven. Accordingly, as soon as Shivaji turned ten, Jijau became enthused about applying turmeric to her darling son's hands.

Jijau's choice fell upon Saibai, the daughter of Mudhoji Nimbalkar of Phaltan. Nine years of age, with a sweet, contented deportment, vivacious eyes, wheat complexion, erect posture, this picture-perfect daughter of Nimbalkar had simply stolen Jijau's heart. Not having had a daughter herself, she had always felt the need for the reverberation of the footsteps of Lakshmi, the goddess of prosperity, in the palace.

The relationship between the Nimbalkars of Phaltan and the Bhosales of Verul went back many years. Shahajiraja's mother Deepabai belonged to this family; she was the sister of Vanangpal Nimbalkar. While the clamour of the auspicious musical instruments was in progress, Jijau had tucked her sari's end into her waist and stood up to officiate this propitious event. In the absence of Shahajiraje, she had taken up this mission on his behalf.

17 April 1640. All of Pune had been decked up for Shivba's wedding. Half of the town had been covered by pandals and welcome arches. A few processions of elephants had already reached Pune from Phaltan. Various neighbourhoods had turned riotous with the arrival of the headmen of the Maaval valleys and the chieftains and captains of the old Nizamshahi Sultanate as guests. Diwali-like joy pervaded the air everywhere. At the time of the marriage, Jijau's expectant eyes would keep searching the gate outside the marriage pavilion. Her husband was surely a tough administrator and an alert general, but for all that, he was a tender-hearted Sanskrit scholar with poetic sensibilities. Jijau, therefore, was sure that he would arrive at the last moment, even as the auspicious rice was being showered on the couple, and feed her with laddoos of joy.

Jijau waited with a palpitating heart, but Shahaji just couldn't make it on account of the pressure of work. He, however, did send his administrator Naropant Deekshit, Deekshit's two sons Raghunathpant and Janardanpant, the poet laureate Jairam Pinde, and a hundred other persons from Bengaluru. They carried with them colourful baskets, gold platters, rolls of silk and trunks full of ornaments.

Along with these gifts, Shahajiraja had also sent a letter for Jijau. She immediately undid the silk string and began reading it right there in the pavilion with a pounding heart:

> Please don't be disappointed, Jiu. It was duty that came in my way. Otherwise I had put myself in readiness to gallop off at the last minute. But because of administrative work of extreme importance, I could not manage to come. However, I am extremely eager to see the face of our new daughter-in-law. Please do not be in any tearing hurry to go to Phaltan as soon as the wedding ceremony is over. Instead, make all the efforts that you can to come over to Bengaluru with Shivba and his wife as early as possible. Shivba's second mother, our son Sambhaji and his wife Jayantidevi, son Vyankojiraja and the entire royal family are even keener than I meet all of you. Therefore, without wasting

IN BENGALURU—UNDER THE TUTELAGE OF HIS FATHER 167

any time, begin packing so that you may multiply our happiness a thousand times.

.ಆಶಿ.

Shahaji stood with his entire family at the gates of Bengaluru to welcome his son Shivba and his new daughter-in-law. A number of citizens of Bengaluru had also joined up to participate in the Raja's joy. Right in front stood a tall, slim, sprightly young man of sixteen or seventeen, whom everyone called by the name of Koyajiraje. He seemed to have taken the lead everywhere and moved around like a tiger.

Alongside were Naropant, Janardanpant, Shayar Ali Khan, the court jester Krishna Bhatt, Tukdev, and a few others. Five caparisoned elephants stood at the city gate, waiting for the arrival of the newly-weds. There was also a guard of honour, a small fleet of caparisoned horses and a few camels also similarly decorated. Ostentatious *pagadees* and *phetas* of cloth twisted round itself and spreading out at the top like a cock's comb, clothes of the finest weave and texture—the enthusiasm among those assembled was boundless.

Shahajiraje and Tukabai swirled lemons and bread pieces over the couple, and threw them away to drive away the evil eye. Everybody was delighted at seeing the mischievous-looking bride: Saibai's expressive, shy, longish, sharp-nosed face, her wheatish forearm covered with green bangles, the hair-parting filled with vermillion, like a red-hot chilli pinned on her head, a wide forehead on which descended an emerald pendant, earrings studded with diamonds and pearls, gold armlets on the upper arms and anklets on her feet.

The little girl seemed to have got buried under all her clothing and ornaments. Tukabai took Saibai in her embrace and showered her with warm kisses. Sharp-nosed and bright-eyed Shivba was looking extremely handsome. The pearls stitched on to his headgear and his jewel-studded necklace glittered in the yellow light of the flambeaus. The newly-weds were made to sit in a gold canopy atop one of the elephants and carried in procession to the palace on the fort.

Although it had now turned dark, the flambeaus and flaming torches had turned night into day. The guard of honour, the musicians playing upon their instruments, the drummers of the southern provinces banging on their drums— the procession passed through the massive main gate of the fort. The decorations made in the alcoves of the ramparts of the fort looked stunning. Shahajiraja's main palace lay inside the fort. The bride and groom were first taken to the ancient Ganesh temple inside the fort to pay their obeisance. Dazzled by the reception being given to him, Shivba whispered to Jijau, 'Masaheb, looking at all this pomp and show, I want to go and become a bridegroom again.'

'You are right, Shivba,' said Shahajiraje with a laugh, 'I had decided quite early that I shall fully compensate for my absence in Pune.'

Before she had reached the outskirts of Bengaluru, Jijausaheb had been a worried woman. Her revered husband had been compulsorily exiled from his country and soil; therefore, worry about his well-being had been stinging her heart. But when she saw the caparisoned animals entering through the main gate of Bengaluru, when she saw the palace in front glittering with decorative lamps, and most of all, when she saw the popularity that Shahajiraje enjoyed among the people and the participation of the citizens of the Deccan in his joy, she was not merely happy but stunned.

As they were entering the temple of Ganesh, Jijau placed a loving hand upon Tukabai's shoulder. A shiver passed through her. These two wives of Shahaji were meeting for the first time. Slim and energetic, Tukabai was a good seven or eight years junior to Jijau. Since the time that Jijau had stepped on the soil of Bengaluru, Tukabai had never left her side. She would address Jijau as *Akka Saheb* or elder sister.

It was very late by the time they reached the palace, and Jijau and Shivba were very tired. Dadoji Kond'dev, who had accompanied them from Pune, had been accommodated in the inn beyond. The three-week journey on horseback from Pune had been exhausting. A number of palanquins had travelled with them too. The fatigue of so many days had got into Shivba's body like a fever. He never knew when he fell asleep. Once in the bedchamber, the Raja asked Jijau in a soft voice, 'Ranisaheb, how do you find our Tukabai?'

Jijau lowered her eyes in abashment. 'Oh, she's great. Till the time I came here, I had been a little worried.'

'Fearing what kind of second wife the husband has placed upon your head?'

'No, nothing of that kind,' Jijau responded with a laugh. 'You have not brought me a co-wife, but my sister from some earlier birth.'

The two of them were meeting each other after a gap of four years, hence they just couldn't decide what to say and how much to say. The warmth that the two felt after such a long separation from each other was of quite another kind. The Raja then hurriedly took updates from Jijabai on the ongoings in the territories of Supe and Pune. Suddenly, Jijau said, a little emotionally, 'Raje, how simple it would have been for me to come here with you, chasing the mirage of happiness!'

'It is entirely because of your sacrifice that the Pune inheritance of the Bhosales is still intact. It has already suffered the humiliation of the donkey plough at the hands of selfish foreign powers. If you hadn't tightened your girdle and stood up courageously, our meritorious city would have turned into a graveyard. Besides, you have also performed the extremely important task of bringing up my dream, Shivba, on the soil of Pune.'

'Yes, he is now eleven.'

'That work itself deserves my gratitude a million times over. Now that you are here, you will see how I turn this lump of gold into a dazzling ornament.'

The king had now told Jijau what he had been wanting to tell her for a long time. On hearing Shahajiraje's words, Jijau could not hold herself back and burst out with: 'Wah, Raje, I have been observing since I crossed the boundary into Bengaluru—your standard of life here, these opulently done up palaces, the massive fort and the beautiful sandalwood palace for your lordship! But beyond all this grandeur, what delighted me most was the love that the people here have for you!'

'Meaning?'

'Meaning that I feel awfully proud. Wherever my king goes, he lives not merely like a king but like an emperor.'

Shahajiraje paused to think for a while, and then said with a smile, 'Jiu, one has to stay forever alert here. The Adilshahi sultans are as weak of ear as they are large hearted. As a result, there is absolutely no saying when the wind and water will change directions and strangulate you.'

Koyaji Raje continued to hover around the three princes till late into the night, looking after their needs, passing orders everywhere. Actually, step-mother Tukabaisaheb, half-brother Vyankoji and elder brother Sambhaji, had all gathered in the evening on the verandah, hoping for a long chat. But sleep had so overpowered Shivba that he couldn't stay awake.

He suddenly woke up at dawn. The fragrance of fresh flowers was floating in through the windows, accompanied by the squawking of peacocks on the greens outside. Just then broke out the words of Pinglya Joshi's song '*Pinglya aalaa re aalaa*', rendered musically to the beat of wooden drums. Shivba pulled aside the silk curtain and was amazed at the splendour that dawn had spread out there: rose-beds, vines tangled everywhere, grape-vines raised on frames—the entire scene visible from the window was soothing to the eyes.

A bunch of Brahmin boys were loafing around the palace, singing in the raga Bhoopali. As the curtain of darkness began to lift, the huge arch of the main gate at a distance began getting visible. On it could now be seen armed soldiers doing their rounds of surveillance. Suddenly the beat of drums was sounded in the porch under the arch, announcing the arrival of a new day. At almost the same moment, the sounds of cymbals, trumpets and conch shells burst out from one of the halls in the palace.

Shivba walked a few paces through a small passage towards the rear. There, he encountered a grand shrine as tall as a man. The prayers had begun there at dawn. The musical instruments had now joined in as accompaniment. Shivba looked around with astonishment. He couldn't work out how his mother Jijau could have joined the prayer at the break of dawn. The priest Vishwanath came forward with the sacred *prasad*, which the prince accepted with reverence.

The beds of Sambhajiraje, Shivba and Vyankoji had been laid out in a large chamber. Sambhaji and Vyankoji were still fast asleep. 'Up, boys, up!' Jijau cried out. 'It's morning now!' A bunch of a dozen or so Brahmins began chanting mantras in the verandah in front of the palace. It was a daily ritual. They were chanting prayers to wish Shahajiraja an auspicious and fruitful day.

Jijau said to Shivaji, 'Go take a ride outside if you feel like it.'

Shivaji smiled. Koyajiraje had arrived at this early hour, and stood waiting. 'Koyaji dada,' Shivba exclaimed, 'this fort looks colossal!'

'Yes, of course! The circumference alone measures a good mile. It has nine huge gates. The walls surrounding it are studded with twenty-six sturdy bastions.'

The rays of the morning sun had started running excitedly into the massive palace. Shivba set off with Koyajiraje for a round of the fort. Koyaji was telling him excitedly, 'When your father came over here from the fort of Mahuli, he was presented with this fort and the province around it to govern.'

'So, basically, this fort belongs to Adilshah, doesn't it?'

'No, no, this land belonged to a powerful Hindu king named Kempe Gowda. But the father and son team of Randullah Khan and Rustam-e-Zamaan laid siege to it. A three-thousand-strong Adilshahi army faced a stand-off of six months before they managed subdue it. There was a lot of bloodshed.'

'Really?'

'Yes. As soon as the fort fell, Adilshah Mohammadshah Saheb handed it over to Shahajiraja, almost as a sacred offering on a banana leaf.'

'Truly amazing!' Shivba exclaimed. Running his eyes over the massive walls that encircled the fort, the huge gates and the palace, he said, 'But had the other Bijapur chieftains acquiesced to this transfer?'

'Of course not! They fought tooth and nail against it. The poor men were utterly shocked at this handover to a Hindu chieftain from a foreign land. Chieftains like Mustafa Khan and Afzal Khan even went and complained to Adilshah, 'You must test out this non-believer Shahajiraja before you hand over this fort to him.'

'Ah! Then?'

'Mohammadshah said that there was no need for that. He said that his father Sultan Ibrahim Saheb had already tested him out thirteen years earlier, and Shahajiraje had passed with flying colours as a well-wisher of Bijapur.'

'It really is astonishing that my father, who is from Maaval, should be seen as a Bijapuri chieftain here.'

'Nothing astonishing here, Shivba. The subjects of this land, the courtiers and Sultan Mohammadshah Saheb himself address your father as "Maharaj Saab" or "Raja Saab".'

'Even in correspondence?'

'What do I tell you, Shivba? Whenever Sultan Mohammadshah Saheb writes to Shahajiraje, he always mentions that he is a pillar of his Sultanate, he is its foundation. It's not as if he makes these remarks when he is writing to the Raja alone. Even when he writes to others, when he has to give reference, he always introduces Raja Shahaji as somebody who is like a son to him, a pillar of his Sultanate.'

'Wah, wah!'

'Shivba, if you move around Bengaluru and Bijapur, at every step of the way you will see how the people hold your father in awe!'

When Koyaji and Shivba returned to the palace, they heard the sound of musical instruments emerging from the massive hall on the other side. The sound of horns, trumpets, tambourines and drums flared up suddenly. Jijau hurried out and said, 'Our Lordship is stepping out, it seems.' That was when Shahajiraje emerged from a passage, dressed in sparkling white clothes and with a golden stole thrown across his shoulder. The assembled retinue of slaves, servants, Brahmins and musicians bent low and saluted him with reverence.

The royal physician quickly stepped forward and held his wrist to check his pulse. Two dark-skinned, boorish, bare-chested Deccani Brahmins wearing bright-coloured turbans stepped up in their white *dhotars*. One carried a shallow golden bowl filled with clarified butter in his hands, and the other carried a similar silver bowl. The Raja looked at his reflection in the clarified butter in the bowl. He then picked up Shivba in his arms. Seeing his own face in the silver bowl, the young prince laughed.

The soft, velvety lawns in front of the palace were soon left behind. What Shivaji saw in front now was a huge ground measuring a good ten to twelve acres. All around the ground rang the bells hanging from the necks of elephants. A few camels too roamed around the periphery, swinging their legs like the branches of trees. The sound of battlefield music rang out, a big cloud of dust gathered under the arch of the Mysore Gate, and a number of units of cavalrymen began racing in.

Arrangements had been made in front for seating the royal family. Shahajiraja sat along with his three sons, both the daughters-in-law and Jijau, while a few officials sat alongside them. Shivba did not need to be told that all of these exercises were the routine maneuvres and drills of the army. As soon as the horns were blown, units of fifty horses would enter the ground. The horses would first take a round at great speed, and the horsemen would then get ready for their battlefield drills. Horses would run into each other, and swords would clash. The soldiers would let out loud battle-cries and joust into each other with passion, taking adequate care that they were not causing hurt to each other.

Shahajiraje swept a proud eye at his warriors, and said to his princes, 'Do you recognise these brave lads?'

'Raje,' said Jijau, 'most of these boys look like boys from our Maaval valleys!'

'Ours?' quizzed Shivba.

'Yes, Baalraje[12], I have about ten thousand horsemen in my own personal army. Out of those, a good seven or eight thousand braves are from our own soil because they automatically bring with them the sturdiness and the tenacity of our land. Our army is our toughest weapon. They are like the trident that rests in the hands of Kali Mata.'

'And all of these drills?'

'When there is no campaign going on, we have them do these rehearsals for at least five days in a week. A sword cannot retain its sharpness unless it is rubbed against a file. In the same manner, these drills are necessary to keep the spirits in the bodies of these brave men alive.'

A kind of competition of valour, courage and manliness was in progress on the ground. Bullock carts followed in the wake of the horses. Bullocks were used for pulling the big and small cannons, boxes of dynamite and the stone-missiles used in the cannons. A sharp tournament began between bullock carts of all sizes. The bullocks could not accommodate the artificiality of the drill, and a number of them would get wounded on account of being charged up. Around the same time, on the nearer side of the ground, four-hands-tall hurdles made of logs had been erected. The horses would come racing from a long distance and leap over these hurdles.

.ॐ.

'Wake up, sons, the dawn has broken, princes!' Shahaji's voice would resonate in the bedchamber like the rumble of a lion in the valleys. Shivba

---

[12] Marathi for prince

would be the only one awake before the call came. Koyajiraje would often beat Shahaji to it and be ready by his side with all his morning ablutions over. It was a mystery as to when he slept and when he woke up. At the king's call, Sambhajiraje, Vyankojibaba and Shivba would spring out of their beds and get ready for training.

They would walk briskly towards the gymnasium. There would be a spring in Shahaji's step as he walked with his princes. He would look like the experienced king of the jungle, walking with his cubs with great panache. The scene would stir Jijau's heart as few things could. Whenever there was no collective drill with elephants and horses, Shahajiraje would sweat it out vigorously in the gym with his princes. His purpose was to ensure that his princes received scientific training in the art of war. They had to be readied to break out of any conflagration with confidence and courage. They had to be given the strength to face any obstacle and stand against it without flinching.

He would teach them how to put horses, camels and elephants to the best possible use on the battlefield, and alert them to the mischiefs that the animals could play. The princes would be made to climb a saddleless, bare-backed horse and learn to control it with the pressure of their thighs on its flanks. 'The most important thing is to sit firmly on the horse. Once you have learnt to sit comfortably and with confidence, you can easily leap up to the sky astride it.'

Sometimes, a few excited bullocks would be released from the cattle-pen, with no ropes round their necks nor through their nostrils. These aggressive animals would be released on slimy ground. Shahaji would show the princes how to gain control over a wayward bullock, first with the shaft of a javelin and then with a simple bamboo cane. He would show them how horses were fed with some opium-like herbs to make them wild, and how one could jump upon their backs with well-timed leaps. When the king's sixty-year-old body went shooting like a spear and tamed a frisky animal, the princes would stand and watch with awe and envy.

An agitated elephant had once been released on the field, and Shahaji deliberately assigned the job of subjugating it to Shivraya and Koyajiraje. A wonderful contest ensued between the two to bring the mountain-like Malabari elephant under control.

Sometimes stout ropes would be thrown down the multiple bastions of the massive Bengaluru fort, and the boys would be trained to rapidly shimmy up the ropes like snakes in a chase, holding the ropes with their hands and their toes. At other times, they would be taken to one of the dense jungles around Bengaluru for an expedition. They would be told to climb up massive banyan and peepul trees and bring down beehives.

Early in the morning, they would join their father in physical exercises: a thousand sit-ups and push-ups and yogic exercises like the 'surya-namaskar'. Shahaji had had the good fortune, during his youth, of receiving strength training from Malik Ambar. Later, with age, Malik Baba had let his body go to seed and become flabby like a shapeless bullock. Remembering those times, Shahajiraje would admonish his princes, 'If your ambition is to clash with extraordinary enemies and conquer difficult battlefields, as a warrior you should be careful with your food habits. You must keep your body in top shape and gain the agility of a deer, force of an elephant and energy of a horse.'

As they watched the display of the horses, Shahaji told his sons, 'Boys, the battle of Bhatwadi turned out to be a great teacher for us. This battle changed the strategies and the weaponry of engagement. It taught our warriors the importance of always being on the alert.'

Shahajiraje turned emotional at the thought of Bhatwadi. He took this opportunity to express his desire of raising a pedestal at Bhatwadi as a memorial for his brother Shareefji. He told the princes, 'Keep this equation close to your heart: There can be no battle without regular drill, and there can be no state without battle.'

While the field exercises were in progress, the kitchen servants hurried in. They laid out tables under the mango trees there, European style, so that the king and his family could take their refreshments while watching the show. A bullock's horn had pierced the stomach of another bullock in the head-to-head clash, leaving the injured animal writhing in agony. A unit of royal physicians had rushed to offer treatment. Looking in that direction, Shahajiraje said, 'When it is raining cannon-balls on the battlefield, one has to throw one's horses across the fires lit by the enemy. The game of war needs to be played with immense courage and fervour.'

When Vyankoji turned his face away in despair at watching men and animals getting injured, Shahajiraje said in a stern voice, 'The king's duty is of utmost importance. It will never do for a fisherman's son to sicken at the smell of fish; the farmer's son should worship the aroma of the soil; in the same manner, a prince should desire more and more the smell of blood and fire.'

'Abasaheb, this kind of grandeur and destiny cannot possibly belong to any Maratha, for sure, nor could it have fallen to the share of any Muslim chieftain of Karnataka,' said Shivba.

'Son, destiny is nothing but a golden mongoose that keeps running away from man. Only on the strength of his hard work can a man leap at the mongoose and catch it by its mane.'

Shahajiraje turned to Jijau and asked, 'I neither come from these parts nor do I belong to the Islamic faith of the rulers. Why, then, do the emperor and the sultan both want so much to have none but Shahajiraje?'

Shivba had been observing his father's discipline, his army, his principles and policies. Reaching into the essence of all these things, he responded lucidly, 'Even if the other chieftains carry brocaded and velvety clothes on their back, I think that Shahajiraje is the only person who moves around wearing the armour of fire on his body.'

Tukabai was startled hearing Shivba speak so maturely, and Jijau looked extremely pleased.

Shahaji said, 'What Shivba says is absolutely true. These Muslim rulers are no relatives of mine. But as a mark of my professional duty, I always keep my men and my animals in a state of readiness. It is on account of my battle-alertness that Adilshah Saheb feels satisfied with me.

Shivaji's days in Bengaluru were rolling along. His biggest gain was that he was getting to live close to a valorous father, who was so deeply concerned about the welfare of his subjects. Also, he was learning horse-riding skills in the company of his half-brother Koyaji Dada. Koyaji was accomplished in wrestling, *daandpatta*, javelin throw and all such skills. He was senior to Shivaji by at least six years. The Koyaji who leapt like a tiger on the practice grounds in the mornings, looked utterly different from the Koyaji of the evening durbars. He was accomplished in Sanskrit and linguistics.

IN BENGALURU—UNDER THE TUTELAGE OF HIS FATHER 177

Within the first week of their arrival in Bengaluru the powerful chieftain Randullah Khan invited the royal family to his manor. A large number of people in Karnataka knew of the open secret that Randullah Khan was Shahajiraje's bosom friend. Randullah Khan had spent some years in Rahimatpur on the bank of the Krishna as the governor of the province. He had given the town the beautiful name of Rahimatpur after his own name. There was a town named Haibatpur in the Adilshahi region of Maandesh. It had a vibrant temple of Lord Shankar. Shahaji had had a large lake built in the town, and brought pressure upon Adilshah to have its name changed to Shikhar Shingnapur.

Every time the memory of his stay in Rahimatpur resurfaced, Randullah would turn nostalgic. He would refer to the province as heaven. Randullah's son Rustam-e-Zamaan the Second was also present at the feast hosted for Shahaji's family. In fact, Adilshah had conferred the title of Rustam-e-Zamaan on Randullah himself, and that was the name the son had picked too. Young Rustam-e-Zamaan was of the same age as Shivaji; as a result, they became very close during the Bengaluru sojourn.

From the perspective of the Bhosale family, this stay at Bengaluru proved beneficial in bringing the three brothers—Sambhaji, Shivaji and Vyankoji—together. Sambhaji was about seven years elder to Shivaji and Vyankoji. The three princes got along very well in the palace. Vyankoji and Shivaji were the same age. Sambhaji would look after his two younger brothers in the spirit of an affectionate father figure. Besides, the command of two thousand horses had brought on his mien a gravity that looked quite endearing.

Jijau paid careful attention to Shivaji's maturing age. Whether it was the cavalry or the cannon factory or their manufacture, Shivaji would be particularly attentive towards everything. He would also visit the smithy and the blacksmith's lane. In the company of Koyaji, he had also seen different kinds of elephants in the elephant camps; he had got himself acquainted with diseases that struck elephants and horses. One day Shahaji called over from Bijapur a warrior named Siddhi Ambar who belonged to the community of slaves. It was said that nobody could match him in his command on horses. When Shivaji gained a teacher like Siddhi Ambar, he simply lost himself in horses. He would go galloping day and night. A little bit of rest, and he would immediately return to practising swordsmanship and javelin-throw on horseback.

Everybody was sitting one evening for an after-dinner chat. Remarking on the obsession that Shivaji had with horses, Shahaji said, 'My prince, when I see your fascination for horses, I am reminded of Shareefji.' The memory of the passing away of Maloji on the battlefield of Indapur, Shahaji's taking over the role of a father for Shareefji and his sudden and tragic death in the battle of Bhatwadi overwhelmed Shahajiraja. Jijau too remembered Shareefji's gold-hilted sword. Jijabai had had the sword sharpened on a whetstone at Shivneri and given it to Shivaji.

After doing the rounds of the elephant camps, the armoury and other places, the princes would make their way to the durbar. Shivaji showed extraordinary interest in court matters too. Even before Shahaji entered the court, a number of jagirdars, princes and ambassadors from other lands would have arrived. There would be a large gathering of learned men, scholars, poets and healers. The court administrator Naropant Deekshit would be in a flutter before the Raja arrived.

The arrival of Shahajiraja to the renowned 'Navagazi Durbar', the Court of the Nine Passions, was like the magnificence that Pauranic kings and emperors were reputed to enjoy. One could stare at the glitter in the Navagazi meeting hall for hours. The roof was covered with attractive paintings of fish and tortoises. The carpets laid out on the floor were thick and soft. An awning was carried over the Raja's head. Men and women slaves stood on either sides, waving fluffy hand-held fans called chowries; at the centre of it, Shahajiraje, swaggering in with his hand on the bejeweled hilt of his sword was a sight for the gods. The poets, the learned men, the scholars stood up and bowed low to offer their salutations. He strode past the obsequious courtiers towards the throne that had lion-skin laid on its armrests.

Seating arrangements for the princes had been made at one corner of the king's podium. Koyaji sat next to Sambhaji, Vyankoji and Shivaji. Koyaji was quite a popular personage at the court. Most of the assembled scholars seemed to like him. Koyaji asked, 'So, Shivba, how do you find our Abasaheb's durbar?'

'What can I say?' Shivaji responded, overwrought. 'Someone from the Maaval soil of the Sahyadri comes to such a faraway place, and avails himself of this royal splendour—this can only be a distant dream for anyone.'

Koyaji would keep crossing over every once in a while to the row of the scholars to check if they needed something. This Navagazi Durbar had eighty-nine poets and scholars who knew numerous languages and had been exposed to numerous cultures. They were paid monthly salaries from the government exchequer.

The Bijapur court had hordes of Urdu, Arabic and Hindi poets, while the Bengaluru Navagazi of Shahajiraje had an assembly of all Deccan language experts. The major assembly was of scholars who had come from the land of Maharashtra. Poets from northern India like Jadurai, Durg Thakur, Dwarkadas and Sham Gussai, would breathe life into conclaves. A number of scholarly poets like Vishwanath Bhatt Dhokekar, Tukdeo, Shesh Pandit, Vireshwar Vaidya, Jayaram Pinde, and Janardan Pandit would bring in the Marathi flavour. The taste of Kannada poetry would be brought in by Subuddhirao and Trimal Vyankat Naik. The court jester, Krishna Bhatt, would have the gathering in splits with his satirical songs. Ali Khan Saheb was a master of eight languages. He was as proficient in Sanskrit as he was in Urdu.

Vyankoji gave Shivaji a pleasant surprise. Till this visit to Navagaz, Shivaji had thought of his brother as a chatterbox. But here, in the durbar, when he saw his command over Sanskrit and Prakrit and the lines he had committed to memory, he was astounded. Sometimes Shahaji would get into the spirit of *shabd-maadhurya*[13]. He would then throw Sanskrit riddles at the assembled scholars; searching for the answers would make them break into a sweat.

Shahajiraje extended patronage to many poets and learned men. He would often give them gifts of Arab and Turkish horses. Once he had been so delighted with a poet that he had gifted him an elephant.

Shivaji would often go visiting the towns and villages around Bengaluru that fell within Shahajiraje's principality. There, he would hear the subjects singing praises of his father and his many great deeds, and feel justly proud. Adilshah had given Shahaji the Bengaluru jagir, which was worth five hundred thousand hons. Since the city walls during Kempe Gowda's

---

[13] Playing with the lilt of words

times were made of earth and stone, they had begun to collapse at a number of places. Shahaji took up the gargantuan task of bringing them in good repair. He also gave personal attention to the growing of new gardens and laying flower beds around the lakes. The Raja's impressive personality, his large-heartedness, aesthetic sense, knowledge of many languages and inexhaustible, overflowing enthusiasm—all of these virtues made him extremely popular with the soldiers, farmers, court employees, as well as the citizens of Bengaluru.

About ten months had rolled by since Shivaji's arrival and the beginning of his strenuous training. During this period, Dadoji Kond'dev had made a visit to Bijapur with the revenue collections, deposited the money in the government treasury, and returned to Pune. At dinner one evening, Shahaji said, 'I suspect that our princes may not have the opportunity to stay longer at Bengaluru.'

'Why, what happened?' Jijau asked anxiously.

Shahaji, however, let out a hearty laugh, and said, 'No, no, nothing worrisome, but news has reached Bijapur of you people coming to Bengaluru a good eight to ten months ago.'

.ॐ.

In Bijapur, the living arrangements for the royal family were made at a place called Mehmaanpura near the Taj-bawadi. It had a line of mansions, each one of which faced a vast water body. Although it was called a 'bawadi', which means a well, the reservoir was huge enough to supply drinking water to the entire city of Bijapur, besides supporting the big military encampment there. The beautiful flowerbeds that were laid out everywhere, the cool breeze blowing in from the lake, the air heavy with the perfume of flowers—it was an extremely beautiful locality. Sultan Ibrahim Adilshah had got this reservoir constructed to commemorate his wife, Begum Taj Sultana.

A big personage had come visiting Shahajiraje at his huge mansion, and he stood waiting at the entrance. He wore a long, loose, red tunic, his hair rolled down over his shoulders, and his long beard reached down to his chest. His two disciples stood on either side of him. One of them handed over to him an earthen pipe loaded with marijuana. He had a mysterious aura. Introducing his sons to the visitor, Shahajiraje said, 'Meet our great ascetic Gaurikanchan Baba. His wandering stretches from the Himalayas right down to Rameswaram.'

Gaurikanchan had some urgent work with the Raja. The Raja got up and took him along to the rear verandah where they discussed their business. Gaurikanchan took leave of the king and rode off along with his disciples.

Once in Bijapur, Shivaji was eager to have a look at the mighty city. Since Randullah Khan's main palace was right there in Bijapur, Shahajiraje immediately called over his son Rustam-e-Zamaan. Shivaji took this opportunity and set off immediately for a spin around the city. Shivaji turned goggle-eyed at seeing Bijapur's prosperity and splendour. He was dumbstruck. Nowhere else, and never before, had he seen such twenty-five-foot-tall and fifteen-foot-wide walls that surrounded the main fort. On top of these walls and going round the fort, was a series of over a hundred formidable, impenetrable bastions. Also, going right round the wall was a moat with clear flowing water. The moat was so deep that elephants were often taken there for a wash. One entered the fort through ten gates with massive arches.

Rustam-e-Zamaan took Shivaji atop a huge bastion. Shivaji saw with unbelieving eyes a nine-arm-long, invincible cannon made of five metals. The mouth of the cannon looked frighteningly like a tiger's wide-open jaws. The circumference of the mouth itself was nine arms long. As he examined the powerful weapon, he involuntarily cried out, 'The Muluk Maidan cannon!'

'Wonderful, Shivaji! Your power of observation is one among a million. How did you remember it?'

'Rustamji, this cannon was the tigress of our fort at Paranda. It was regarded as the symbol of our manhood. But your Murari Jagdeo performed the miracle of dragging it all this distance.'

'Yes. This unwieldy cannon had to be dragged across so many rivers and mountains. People say that it brought to grief six or seven hundred bullocks and a number of elephants. They were ruined.'

On hearing of those memories, Shivaji's face turned red as a carrot. He was fuming with anger. Biting his lip, he muttered, 'What could that educated idiot called Murari have gained by dragging this symbol of our valour so far? What prize did he carry away in his tattered sack after all his crafty maneuvres? Even the scavengers of carrion had refused to carry his unclaimed corpse away from the lanes of Bijapur, they say.'

This city not only had massive buildings like the Gol Gumbaz and Jama Masjid, but also a spread of huge palaces and manors belonging to the Adilshahi chieftains. Extensive gardens, beautiful lakes, arches of flowering vines, such were the attractions of this enchanting city. It was clear that the Adilshahi sultans had given a lot of importance to the security of the city. The area where the Sultan's palace and court and other important buildings were located had another moat going around it. Buildings like the Anand Mahal, Gagan Mahal, Saat Manzil, as also a number of mosques and shrines, were also given special care.

'This is the world-famous Gol Gumbaz!' Shivaji just kept ogling at the magnificent building. This couldn't be the work of a couple of years. It would clearly have taken fifteen to seventeen years, and turned thousands of artisans and labourers old in the middle of their youth. As Shivaji lost himself in admiring the building, Rustam-e-Zamaan said, 'My father Randullah Saheb always says that your father Shahaji Maharaj has an immense contribution in the construction of this building.'

'Really, Rustamji?'

'Absolutely. Shahaji Maharaj had made his army travel long distances, to places like Rameshwar, Tanjore, Madurai, Jinji, to plunder the wealth that went into the making of this heavenly structure.'

'Wah!'

'My father says, leave alone the doors and walls of this building, even the massive elephants and horses of Bijapur cannot ever forget the debt they owe to Raja Shahaji.'

There were a few Hindu temples inside the walls of the central fort. Shahaji had himself taken the initiative and constructed a Dutta temple there. Shivaji was quite amused at finding a Brahmin alley too in Bijapur. As per Shahaji's advice, Ibrahim Shah had founded a new township called Navaraspur, next to Bijapur, for the promotion and contemplation of music, languages and art. The Bijapuris who had annihilated the Vijaynagar empire in the battle of Rakshas-tagadi, had had brought over to Bijapur a prodigious amount of plunder of gold and precious stones on the backs of thousands of bullocks. The town was now prospering. They also had trade relations with faraway China. Raw material was brought over from there to run factories in Bijapur for the manufacture of silk. Shivaji, Sambhaji and Vyankoji visited those factories too.

One day, while Shahajiraje was having breakfast with his sons on the small lawn in front of his mansion, Randullah Khan arrived. While talking to Shahaji, Randullah Khan studied young Shivaji from head to toe and said, 'It's a great opportunity. Send in a request.'

'For what?'

'Your elder son has already received a command of two thousand horses. Get after Adilshah now and insist on a command of nothing less than seven thousand horses.'

Shahajiraje made no comments on Randullah's advice, but Jijau shot up from behind and said, 'Why should we talk of these mansabs? My Shivba does not have the temperament of serving under someone.'

Jijau looked at her son with great pride. Picking up the thread from her, Shahajiraje said, 'He has been born with the disposition of Lord Hanuman, of wanting to swallow up the entire sun.'

Everybody within earshot felt that she and Shahajiraje had uttered something stupendous, hot, like a spark of fire. Randullah was taken aback. He kept glancing towards Jijau, as if fearing that he had committed a terrible blunder. After a while, he departed.

A delegation of Europeans arrived in the mansion next to where Shahaji had been housed. There were a number of big traders in it, particularly from Holland and Portugal. Jijabai went up to Shivaji and said, 'These are highly experienced people who have come from very faraway lands. Go interact with him, forge a friendship. Understand the world.'

Shahaji was very curious about these white foreigners. Their long, animal-skin hats, tapering on one side, and with multi-hued feathers stuck on top of them; boots that reached up to their knees; their coats—their apparel, in comparison to the clothes of the Hindustani people, looked colourful and attracted attention at once. The delegation had with them a pair of Brahmins, who knew the Dutch and Portuguese languages very well. Hence, they functioned excellently as interlocutors in any durbar or government office.

The *firangi* group lived in the neighbouring bungalow for many days, and from them, Shivaji went on gaining loads of information about Europe. When they had become thick, one of the Europeans gifted Shivaji with a map that showed the European continent and India. He also showed Shivaji pictures of lightweight, swiftly deployable cannons made from new forging techniques. There were pictures of the 'ghorab', the 'tarandi' and many other kinds of ships too. Shivaji asked the guests, 'When will ships of this kind be built in India?'

'But they are already being built! The Portuguese have opened factories in Goa to make them.'

'Absolutely amazing!' said a stunned Shivaji.

'This is not all,' said the *firangi* guest. 'The Dutch have recently built a fortress in Konkan on the coast at Vengurla. That is where they have begun imports and exports.'

One day Shivaji went to Jijau and said, 'Aausaheb, you were right. One cannot understand the enemy's weaknesses without entering into their camp. If you have to cross a river, you must wet your feet.'

'What are you trying to say?'

'This Adilshahi Sultanate that extends its dominion right up to the bank of the Narmada on the one hand, and on the other hand, brings raw silk from faraway China for its own silk industry here—my desire to understand its secret as also its power has become a matter of honour.'

Jijau smiled softly at seeing Shivaji's interest and enthusiasm.

The day on which they were to go to the Bijapuri durbar was a proud and crucial day for Shivba. Very early in the morning, Sambhaji called him to his room and, placing an affectionate hand on his shoulder, said, 'The Adilshahi durbar is a veritable nerve centre of unbridled power and authority. The decorum, and the *bartaav*, as it is called in the language of this durbar—that is, one's conduct—holds a lot of significance.'

'Yes, Dada.'

When the three princes were setting off for the durbar, both JIjausaheb and Tukabai performed the ritual of neutralizing the evil eye. Shivaji touched the ground before the two women with his forehead, to take their blessings. Jijau was anxious, about this day and about Shivaji's future.

The princes made their way along the water course of the lake in the garden and by the side of the dancing fountains in the direction of

Saat Manzil, in whose basement the royal durbar was assembled. When Shivaji entered the durbar palace, he was awestruck by the grandeur in all directions—the multi-coloured chandeliers hanging from the roof, the glittering, brocaded clothing of the courtiers. More than two hundred noblemen and grandees were standing humbly in front of the Adilshahi throne. The aroma of sandalwood hung heavy in the air.

The golden throne was right up there in front. That was when the call of the herald sounded: 'Alert! Alert! With respect, with due regard and concern! The refuge of the world! The sun of the Deccan! Sultan Mohammad Adilshah is making his arrival!' Drums and trumpets began to be played. Adilshah sat on his throne. His eyes fell on Shahaji, who stood right in front. Shahaji bowed and made his respectful salutation. Adilshah looked at Shahaji with great warmth and contentment. His gaze then shifted towards young Shivaji, who was standing next to his father. He asked in an imperious tone, 'So, is this your son?'

'Yes, he is, your highness.'

'Very nice. He looks like a spirited boy!' said Adilshah in chaste Marathi. That was when Shivaji remembered that his father, Ibrahim Adilshah, had been a scholar of the Marathi language.

Adilshah let his eyes rest on Shivaji for a few moments. The grandees standing next to him whispered, 'Make your salutations to the Sultan Saheb, son!' Shahajiraja too whispered urgently, 'Son, make your salutation!' But Shivaji stood, rigid as ever. Randullah then quickly stepped in and picked up another subject for discussion, smartly turning Adilshah's attention in another direction.

On the other side of the transparent, diaphanous curtain sat the ladies of the royal household. At the head of the group sat a queen with a longish face and a sharp, long nose. Shivaji had the sensation that she was watching him with her sharp blue eyes.

The work of the durbar got over in an hour, and the hall began to empty out. Adilshah left immediately. A movement was seen on the other side of the curtain. A servitor ran out and informed Shahaji that Badi Begum desired to see him. Shahaji took Shivaji with him. The Begum Saheba gave Shahajiraje instructions regarding some work in Bengaluru. Shahajiraje realised that the queen's eyes were fixed on Shivaji. Pointing her henna-tinted and bejeweled finger at the boy, she said, 'So, this is your prince!'

'Yes, yes, Begum Saheba,' stammered the Shahaji and admonished Shivaji, 'Raje, make your salutation!'

Shivaji pretended to be totally confused and just stood unmoving. Seeing that, the Begum lifted a brow above her blue eyes and hissed, 'The arrogant boy who doesn't know how to make *salaams* to the Sultan-e-Azam, why will he care for me?'

12

TRAINING FOR THE MISSION

Shivaji returned from the durbar to the mansion to find that Jijau was sitting on a swing in the garden. It was quite clear that Vyankoji had fed something into her ears.

Shivaji was amused. Vyankoji, being the frisky person that he was, would surely have blabbered something to her. As he entered, he heard Jijau's loud call, 'Come, son, come. You seem to have set the durbar alight today, I hear. Shivba's confusion increased. Was there anger in his mother's voice or was it amusement?

Vyankoji butted in. 'Aausaheb, why should a person show such stiffness?'

'So, what exactly happened in the durbar, son?

'This Shivba neither bowed before the Sultan nor did he greet the Begum Saheba.'

The women of the manor also came out at the same time, accompanied by a few slave girls. Saibai had got wind that her husband had committed some kind of offence in the durbar. She was a bit nervous.

'Matoshri, all I have to say is that Sultan Salaamat is the ultimate repository of power here! One does have to care at least a little bit about his fancies!'

'Impossible! Impossible!' said Shivaji in the manner of a rebellious poet opening his heart out before a superior court. 'Where's the need for servitude? I haven't taken birth to become the frilly border of some emperor or sultan's pavilion!'

The change in Shivaji's disposition and his sudden spirited vociferation left everybody stunned. Saibai heaved a sigh of relief. Just then, Tukabai's two brothers Sambhaji and Dharoji Mohite arrived. Immediately after them, a Maratha sardaar named Raje Shirkey also walked in.

It was now a big assembly of the Bhosales. Soon it split into two groups: the seniors forming one, and the youngsters another. It didn't take much time for games, songs, fun-filled chatter and songs and poetry to fill the air.

Shahajiraje came home a little late. He sounded delighted as he said, 'Do you have any idea what a wonderful day it was at the durbar today? Our Sultan Saheb has decreed a most gratifying *firman* on me today.'

'Gratifying *firman*?' quizzed the assembled relatives.

'Yes, absolutely! He said that he couldn't manage to attend Shivba's wedding in Pune and missed out on the opportunity of seeing the rituals that are performed at our weddings. He has decreed, therefore, that Shivba should get married all over again here in Bijapur.'

The two families of the Bhosales and the Mohites were so delighted at this news that they broke into an applause. 'So be it! Splendid!'

'But shouldn't we first take the sanction of Shivba's wife?' somebody asked. 'Where's she gone?'

There was another burst of laughter. Polygamy was quite the norm in that society, but Shivba blushed, nevertheless. The decision for a second marriage was made, and alongside it began the search for a new bride. That was when the attention of some veered to the verandah where Saibai was sitting on a swing with her friend Saguna. They were busy chatting. 'Look, look! Won't they make a pretty pair as co-wives?'

Once more there was a loud roar of guffaws. Raje Shirke, who was present among the crowd, came forward and held Shahajiraje's hand. 'Raja Saheb,' he said, 'that girl sitting with Saibai is my jewel of a daughter, all right?'

'So, then Shirke Mama, what's your opinion, then?' queried a few together.

'I'd come hopping on one leg to tie the silken knot with the Bhosales,' Shirke responded, and everybody endorsed the statement with thunderous clapping.

Sultan Mohammad Adilshah arrived in person to the wedding pavilion and stayed on for quite a long time. Badi Begum Saheba was to come as well to bless the couple, but she suddenly took ill. All the eleven Maratha sardaars of Bijapur came over with their families and spent the four days of festivities completely absorbed in the joyous event. The entire Brahmin colony of Bijapur had also turned up for the occasion.

The evening on which the decision of the marriage had been taken, Shivba had been quite upset. Looking at his agitated face, Jijausaheb had asked, 'Anything the matter, prince?'

'Matoshri,' he griped, 'I do not agree with this tradition of tying the wedding knot with a score of women.'

Jijau turned still for a moment, but soon she began talking in a persuasive tone, 'Prince, as we live through our lives performing our duty towards our Kshatriya caste, we encounter new battles and invasions every day. The path across we are required to walk is not merely slippery, but it is actually carvedn on the point of a sharp sword. The manly hand that grips the sword and wields it with valour in the theatre of war, there's no saying whether it will return hale and hearty to its palace. The macabre sport of diseases and disabilities keeps playing out all the time, too.'

'That's absolutely true, Aausaheb.'

'Keeping in mind this life of strife, teetering between life and death, that waits for the future king, this building of bonds among kinsmen and relatives can be of great advantage. Look at what has been happening on the banks of the Yamuna. Those Mughal emperors right from Akbar to Jahangir, and all the way down, who consider themselves supreme, they haven't won all their wealth and prosperity only on the strength of their swords. They have also created friends and relatives through the mechanism of marriage and thus spread their network of power everywhere. Therefore, after carefully examining, the demands of time and circumstance, there is nothing wrong in a king going for multiple marriages for the sake of a brighter future.'

Shahajiraje once returned very late in the night. It had been the Raja's routine to dismount and sweep inside the manor like a breeze. This time, too, he breezed in, but his face looked very downcast. The two wives, Jijau and Tukabai, exchanged glances. He looked in the direction of Jijau who set about laying out his dinner, and said, 'I'm not hungry today. A little bit of milk will do.' Then he immediately made for the bedchamber.

Jijabai soft-footed her way to the bedchamber. She had to find out why Shahaji looked so upset. She saw him stretched out on the bed. He looked exhausted.

Tukabai walked in too. Shivaji and others followed. Shahaji handed over the bejeweled turban on his head to a minion, and as soon as he was sure that the minion was out of earshot, he let out a sob.

'What is the matter, Raje?' Jijabai asked in a tense voice.

'My brother Khelojirao is gone. A terrible thing has happened.'

'Gone? At this age?' asked Tukabai.

'*Bai ga!* How could this have happened?' cried Jijabai.

'Gone means he was carried out to the beat of the public crier's drum outside a village near Daulatabad and hanged. It was a public hanging.'

'*Bai ga!! Arey re!!*'

'This deed was not done by any local hoodlum!' Shahaji could barely get the words out of his choked throat.

'So, then, who?'

'This was done at the command of Aurangzeb, the son of the Delhi emperor, Shah Jahan—'

'But Aba,' asked Shivaji in an incensed voice, 'what was the offence that my uncle could have committed?'

'What can one do, son! In a way, the real fault is not even that Aurangya's. It was your uncle Kheloji himself that invited this misfortune upon himself. Disappointment had already sent him round the bend. The four lakhs he had paid as ransom to Mahtab Khan to get his wife Gaurabai released, that was no small amount. Even earlier, he had abandoned the Mughals and joined up with Adilshah. On top of that happened the unfortunate abduction. After the fall of Nizamshah, the Bijapuris became friends with the Mughals. The Delhi administration then brought pressure to bear upon Adilshah and took away Kheloji's chieftainship too. Finally, he was left with neither this nor that. He was finished, poor man.'

'On top of that, he was an extremely obstinate person too,' said Tukabai.

'We tried hard to reason with him. This was life, I had told him, black clouds do gather, but they drift away too! But he refused to listen to us. While I went on climbing the ladder of success, he kept tumbling in the slippery alley of regression. In that state of desperation, he raised a gang, and like a bunch of village hoodlums, he went from village to village raiding the houses of moneylenders.'

'It's so painful to hear of a Bhosale heir coming to such a sad pass,' said Jijabai.

'Complaints were made about his robberies, plunders and highway holdups. The fact is that Aurangzeb had warned him of strict action, but his delinquency refused to stop. Finally, Aurangzeb put a captain named Malik Hussain on his trail, and Kheloji was caught with all the goods from his last robbery. A rope was then slipped round his neck, he was dragged to the precincts of the village and hanged publicly by a tree.'

Shahaji said in a grief-laden voice, 'My heart breaks to pieces when I hear of the blood of a renowned Maratha having been spilt so meaninglessly. Such a miserable death should not have been administered to one of Vithoji Bhosale's sons.'

One morning, Shahajiraje's family left Bijapur with an escort of six hundred cavalrymen and foot-soldiers. The route to Bengaluru was arduous, requiring them to cross the rivers Krishna, Ghatprabha, Malprabha and Tungbhadra and a number of dales and hills.

They came upon the basin of the Krishna on the first day. As they were plodding through the sand rising on the yonder bank, they saw four elephants, covered in mirror-work caparisons, standing on a hillock. This had been arranged by administrator Naropant and Koyaji to make the travel comfortable for the royal family. Inside of Bijapur, nobody had the privilege, and therefore the permission, to travel on a howdah atop an elephant-back. It had been dinned into the minds of the people that this was a magnificence created by Allah exclusively for the use of the Adilshahi sultans, and this protocol was strictly observed.

When Koyaji met his father, Shahaji discerned the concern and confusion clouding the young man's face. Shahajiraje took him to one side and asked, 'Baalraje, I had asked you to meet me at the Ballalrayan fort, so why this early—'

'An urgent message reached me, so I couldn't hold myself back. Couldn't sleep for the last two nights—'

'What could be so urgent?'

'The royal family could be in some serious danger.'

'What are you saying?'

'Somebody has paid a lot of money to one of these herders' gangs to launch an attack on your family.'

'This happens all the time. There is no cure for envy and jealousy, is there?' Turning a little sombre then, Shahaji continued, 'All right, we'll see. Meanwhile, keep your serial guard posted around us all the time.'

'That's the reason why I have come running all this distance, Aba.'

Shahajiraja had always been aware that his rising power in the army as also in the Adilshahi administration overall had caused great heartburn and jealousy in some quarters. That was why he had not attracted undue attention by using an elephant while in the capital city.

For the journey ahead, Koyaji had ensured the strictest possible guard round the clock. After a few days of travel, they came upon the Charmadi ghat. The near vertical slopes of the ghat left even the horses and elephants out of breath. They must have put behind half of the ghat route when the sound of horses' hooves was heard coming from the bushes on top, putting the armed security guards riding in front of and behind the royal family on alert. They held their breaths as tight as they held their weapons.

The person who emerged from the bushes was the Shahaji's loyal chief of stables, Siddhi Ambar, along with his cavalry of a hundred battle-hardened horses. Half of those cavalrymen were native Marathas of the Maaval region. The remaining half were dark-skinned Deccanis and tall, well-built Malabaris. Shivaji was delighted to see Siddhi Ambar because he had been his much-loved horse-riding trainer.

Shahaji stayed at the Ballalrayan fort for a night's rest. After so many days of strenuous travel, they all slept soundly. However, he woke his three princes up before dawn and commanded Vyankoji and Shivaji to take a different route from that point on. Nobody knew what plan he had in mind. The royal ladies, Tukabai, Saibai, Sagunabai and Jijau, were confused.

The forest belt of Ballalrayan had a large number of valleys and streams. The forest wind made a whistling sound as it blew, and the branches of trees knocked into each other and made clacking noises, waking Shivaji from his sleep. He came out to the front terrace of the palace inside the fort, and saw in front the flaming flambeaus of the night guards. Koyaji's horse was moving slowly forward from behind, with Koyaji himself looking around with extreme alertness.

Shivaji was impressed with Koyaji. In fact, he was quite a riddle to Shivaji. Except for his dusky complexion, he looked exactly like Shahaji. Both of them were so like each other, and so close too. Also, looking at the respect he commanded everywhere, Shivaji had begun to entertain doubts. His height, his broad chest … he was a spitting image of Shahajiraje.

As he turned round from the terrace to return to the palace, he saw his mother standing in the verandah with a shawl wrapped around herself. She too would have heard the sounds and woken up. She looked at Shivaji with a little bit of concern, and asked, 'Were you unable to sleep, son?'

'Aausaheb, may I ask you a question?'

'Yes, of course.'

'A person works so hard for your husband, and with such loyalty?'

'Stop. Don't say another word.'

'But—'

'Look, he is your father's adopted son; therefore, your brother. He is spotless of heart and sweet by temperament. Come along, now. You must not speak any more on this subject, and I must not tell you anything more either.'

The confusion in Shivaji's mind dissolved. On realising that it was Shahajiraje's blood that ran through the arteries of such an excellent person like Koyaji made his chest swell with pride.

The sky had just turned a shade lighter. Keeping in mind a few days of travel ahead, the servants had separated the luggage of the two princes from the rest of the caravan's. Their personal servants would also be travelling with them. Horses began neighing in front of the palace. When they saw Siddhi Ambar's and Koyaji's army units standing in readiness up there in the square, the entire royal family mentally prepared itself for a new journey ahead. The interesting thing was that in front of the squad were Baba Gaurikanchan and five or six of his disciples, sitting atop their horses. Shahaji's daughters-in-law Jayantibai, Saibai and Sagunabai were clueless. However hard they tried, they couldn't fathom in which direction their husbands were going, and on what secret mission.

As soon as Shahajiraje appeared, Gaurikanchan not only bowed in respect, but also stepped up eagerly and bent low to touch the king's feet. In front were Gaurikanchan, Siddhi Ambar, Koyaji, Shivaji and Vyankoji, and behind them was the tail of a hundred and fifty horsemen and servants. In a little while, the entire troupe disappeared from sight into the greenery in the far distance.

When Shahajiraje came into the hall, he saw Tukabai, Jijabai and the three daughters-in-law standing there in utter confusion. Both Jijabai and Tukabai began bombarding him with questions: 'What's this strange thing happening here? That blighter Ambar arrives with his fresh unit of horses; today this Baba Gaurikanchan suddenly materialises in the forest from nowhere! At least let the mothers who have borne these boys be told a little bit about what's going on! Where have our princes gone, and on what enterprise?'

When he heard the grievances of his two wives, Shahajiraje laughed heartily and said, 'Oh, yes, of course, you must forgive me, you two. I forgot to do the introductions because of all the hurry and scurry. That Gaurikanchan is no ascetic or monk. He is an officer of our intelligence network.'

'So, then, what does that make him?'

'He is Bhimrai, the head of our espionage department. Baba Kanchan is that too. He is a Brahmin from the nearby territory of Jinji, extremely sharp, valourous and, of course, loyal.'

'But where is this army cluster headed towards? On what mission?'

'Before our princes Vyankoji and Shivaji enter into the administration of a kingdom tomorrow, it's extremely important that they taste the waters of a dozen or so provinces. That's the responsibility I have placed upon the shoulders of our Bhimrai and Koyaji. They will first go to Hassan and Mysore. Then they will undertake a journey twisting this way and that, and cover Tanjavoor, Jinji, Trichinapally, Madurai and Kanyakumari; and if possible—either on their way now or during their return journey—

do a round of our Balapur and Kolhar jagirs too. The Tamil region, the Malabar province, the big rivers and mountains there, the pilgrimage towns, the big and small jagirs that fall on the way—this is going to be a five- or six-month-long sojourn for sure.'

When the two queens and their daughters-in-law heard the itinerary, they looked at Shahajiraje with eyes bulging out. The Shahaji decided to rib his two queens and said, '*Arrey!* Come back to your senses! You seem to fear that your two birds have flown away for good!'

At this jibe, everyone burst into laughter.

'Raje, it's now two years since we left Bengaluru. How much longer do we stay here?'

'Well, Jijau, if you ask me, I am perfectly happy here.'

'Why?'

'I had this dream of imparting to our brilliant son Shivaji rigorous training in outdoor and intellectual activities, and I feel delighted that I have mostly done that.'

The residents of the Bengaluru palace began feverishly preparing for the journey to Pune. The packing had begun in right earnest. In the private chambers, discussions were always on regarding future plans and missions. Finally, Shahajiraje opened his heart up to his family and said, 'I have with me our son Sambhaji to help me look after Karnataka.'

'What, then, will happen to Vyankoji?' asked Tukabai instantly.

'Vyankoba will have to wait for a little while.'

'The cuckoo calls; the harsh cawing of the crow continues all the time; but can eagle-chicks find satisfaction in simply flying over the fencings on the farms? Their dharma lies in flying over the tops of high mountains, building their nests on ways that lead up to the sky.'

'Ah! Now I've made sense of your lordship's metaphorical language.'

'You read minds, Jiu.'

'Oh, come on!'

'Now you may take this king of eagles named Shivaji to your Maaval. He has now acquired the strength to fly up to the highest peak.'

They had to depart for Pune at the earliest, and there was a mad bustle in the palace to pack up forgotten last-minute items. In the previous few months, the three princes Shivaji, Vyankoji and Sambhaji had cast a spell over the scholars of the Bengaluru durbar and developed close friendship with them. Therefore, the scholars and noblemen had decided to invite the three princes over to the court and felicitate them before Shivaji turned his horse in the direction of Pune. This was an invitation that could not be turned down.

While starting off the proceedings of the durbar, Shahaji said, 'What gifts does a king give to his princes? Elephants, horses or camels decorated with leaves of gold? Or a province? Or palaces or trunks overflowing with jewellery? My prince, from the perspective of this materialistic world, I have never been able to give you any kind of wealth, and everybody knows this fact.'

The queen mother, Jijabai, and the other ladies of the royal household, sitting to the king's right behind diaphanous curtains, and all the assembled poets, scholars and the grandees were perplexed. What, exactly, did Shahajiraja want to say? Shahaji went on, 'The wealth of our jagirs in Pune and Supe is not something we have earned by the sweat of our brow.'

Turning rather emotional, he took a pause, got a hold on his feelings, and then continued, 'There would have been many empires in this world before me, many emperors, many potentates, who had gathered immeasurable wealth. They would have passed on to their heirs enormous wealth, boundless lands and, perhaps, mines of diamonds and gold. I, however, as a thoughtful father, have decided to gift to our Shivaji only a small gift. This is such an extraordinary gift, that by holding it in reverence, he will, of course, bring fame to the Bhosale family; but even beyond that, he will bring deliverance to the poor, destitute denizens of these mountain ranges, the Twelve Maavals, who have been ground to dust by centuries of slavery. This gift will help him clear the way for a just swarajya. I am so overwrought by the potential that this gift carries that I find it difficult to find adequate words for it. Therefore, I shall let son Koyaji elaborate on it further.'

Koyaji stood up and paused for a while to gather his breath, and then began, 'A little while ago, our dearest Abasaheb, that is Shahajiraje, confessed that he had given Shivaji nothing in the form of wealth and property. I can call it only our great good fortune that we have been blessed with this god-sent opportunity to witness the presentation of the priceless bequeathal that Abasaheb wants to make to Shivajiba in this durbar.'

Koyaji looked to his right, where a few men stood with a gold platter in their hands. At a signal from him, they came forward. Koyaji lifted from the platter something that had been wrapped in silken cloth and handed it over to Shahajiraja. At a signal from the Raja, Shivaji nimbly stepped up. Shahajiraje unwrapped from the silk cloth a dazzlingly bright gold plate and handed it over to Shivaji. Shivaji lifted the plate high so that everybody present could see it. On that bright gold plate were etched some words.

Shivaji made his obeisance to all the seniors assembled in the durbar. He then placed his forehead at the feet of Jijabai and Tukabai, and went back to his seat. Koyaji began to speak in an impassioned voice, 'Our revered father Shahajiraje had been searching for a subject that would form the core of Shivaji's future goals, policies and dreams. A number of these scholars responded, a lot of wordplay happened; but he didn't like any of the responses. Finally, it was the poet that rests inside Shahajiraje himself that broke into petals of words and spread them about before Shahajiraje. Those incomparably beautiful, divine words have now been embedded in my memory, too:

Pratipachchandra rekhev vardhishnu vishvavandita
Shahsunoh shivassyaisha mudrabhadraaya rajate

'Ladies and gentlemen, the royal maxim that our Abasaheb has himself composed for his son means this: as the moon begins to wax in the sky from its first night onwards, so should the renown, the authority, the greatness of Shivraya, son of Shahaji, grow phase by phase. May it be a prayer for the entire world. May it go on waxing forever in order to make the lives of the common people good and fruitful.'

At the end of the celebration, the courtiers gathered there as well as the scholars insisted that Shivaji express his thoughts. Shivaji stood up with all humility to address the gathering. Holding the gold plate close to his heart, he said with gratitude, 'What a beautiful and matchless gift has come my way from my great father! I take this opportunity to give my beloved Abasaheb this pledge: I shall read this royal maxim over and over again to gain inspiration from it. In a way, the beautiful words engraved on this gold plate will always keep a sharp watch on me, and ensure that whatever I do is as expected by your mandate.

'When sculptors or painters with extraordinary talents create a work of art, when a painter creates the picture of a peacock on a wall, legend holds that he blows such life into the bird that a day arrives when the peacock hops off the wall and goes dancing down the royal streets. There are lores of great singers who have sung the Deepak raga with such virtuosity and passion that the lamps all across the town lit up by the music so created. It is this intensity and passion that has helped my revered father prepare this royal seal. With this durbar as witness, I declare that one day this Shivaji shall not fall short of bringing to life the inner notes of this royal seal and string the buntings of his deeds all across the wide sky. This seal that our dear father has gifted to me shall become a lifeline for the poor, the needy and the destitute.'

As Shahajiraje paced around the palace, questions related to Pune were crowding in his head. It was important to look after the Pune jagir, to repair the destruction wrought by the asinine acts of Murari Jagdeo, and to breathe new life into the debilitated spirit of the subjects. It was important to awaken a new consciousness on the banks of the Mula-Mutha. Speaking on this topic to JIjausaheb, he said, 'Shivaji will now have to take the reins of the country into his hands. He will have to begin the task of Pune's reconstruction immediately. I am taking my next steps forward, keeping in mind the demands of that mission. I have decided to send a few but extremely capable administrators and servitors along with you.'

'Your wish is my command.'

'Our Dadaji Kond'dev is an industrious chieftain. He already possesses the subedari of the Kondhana fort given to him by Adilshah. He has also proved his excellence in handling the accounts of the native towns and villages of the Bhosales. On the strength of all his accomplishments, he shall be the chief administrator of Lal Mahal at Pune. I will also send some other gems from our court here along with him.'

'Your choice is bound to be appropriate.'

'Our Siddhi Hilaal, a Habshi slave by birth, a Musalman by faith, is an extremely sincere person. Shivaji has learnt much from him as his student in horse-riding. There would be a cavalry of a thousand horses under this Siddhi Hilaal. What do you say, Shivba?'

'Very well, Abasaheb.'

In the same sitting, Shahajiraje announced, 'As the Peshva of the administrative office, Shamrao Nilkanth will look after office work. As the minister of finance, Balkrishnapant will take care of the intricate arithmetic. Sonopant will be useful to Shivba as the administrative secretary or notary. Raghunath Ballal will be the paymaster; he'll look after the hassle of salary disbursement. Besides, people like Narayanpant will always be available for clerical work.'

He had decided to accompany his family for a few days to bid them goodbye. Shivaji's elder brothers Sambhaji Raje and Vyankoji, of the same age, and step-mother Tukabai would travel with their retinue up to the bank of the Tungabhadra. Koyaji was racing his horse in lockstep with Siddhi Hilaal. His heart was heavy at the thought of having to soon part with Shivba.

It was quite late by the time they touched the inn at the bank of the Tungabhadra. After the royal family had finished with their dinner, they sat down for a discussion.

The three princes had seated themselves on mattresses. In front of them sat Shahajiraje, leaning against a bolster. His position in the family was like that of a huge banyan tree sheltering all the branches and roots hanging down from it from winds and storms.

Adopting an intimate tone, the Raja said, 'There has been one question that has been bothering all of you for some time, hasn't it? You have been wondering why I haven't spoken clearly on a certain matter, haven't you?'

'That's true,' replied Jijabai. 'It's happened a number of times.'

'Ranisaheb, often it becomes necessary in life to absorb the punches and keep one's lips sealed. The network of our enemy's spies is so cruel and strong that it had become imperative for me to ensure that word of my future plans didn't get out.'

Going by Shahajiraje's statement, they had now crossed over to the other side of the danger line; he now considered it important to talk to his sons about things that would be important guidelines for the future. He asked his sons just one question, 'Tell me, whether it is these five sultans of the Deccan or the emperor of Delhi, what gifts and awards can they give to us Marathas or the other chieftains and jagirdars from other lands?'

'Gems and jewels? Gold coins?'

'Brocaded clothes and high-quality dresses?'

'Jewel-embedded swords?'

'Ah, I'll tell you, expensive Arabian or Persian horses—'

Most of them came up with their lists of things as per their imagination and intelligence.

'Well, now tell me, what is that one thing that these Islamic rulers will never be able to give?'

Nobody had an answer to this riddle. The Raja then looked towards Shivaji, who had been quiet until now. 'Yes, Shivba, what do you think?'

'Forts!'

The answer jolted everyone. It was so perfectly aimed that they felt as if the seat atop an elephant had collapsed, and they had come tumbling down. Shahajiraje was delighted with Shivba's answer. Looking at the others, Shahaji said, 'If you think a little deeply, you will realise that a fort is something that is impossible to lay hands on. If it ever comes to that, these Muslim rulers wouldn't mind plucking their eyes out of their heads and putting them in your hands in exchange for one. If you bargained harder, they would chop their knees with an axe and hand them over to you. As for their forts, they would never let you come anywhere near them.'

'Wah! Very rightly said, Abasaheb!'

'The reason? For thousands of years, a fort has been the very centrepiece of a king's power and his control over his territory.'

Shahaji lost himself in the vision of the past for a few moments. Then, in a charged voice, he said, 'Shall I tell you the great pain that rests in my heart? When I had first announced the establishment of self-rule, *swarajya*, how great it would have been if I'd had a strong fort like Mahuli or Rayari under my control? I would have fulfilled the dream of my very own Maharashtra years ago! On the strength of these strong forts,

I would have been able to keep with me a force of hundreds of thousands of soldiers!'

'Our land of Maaval is full of such invincible forts!'

'That's what I've been telling you, Shivba. Forts are going to be the key to your success in the future.'

This was a night that father and son would have wanted to be unending. The morning would soon dawn that would pluck the dear ones apart. Sleep had disappeared from a number of eyes.

Dawn began to break. The voices of the quarter-master staff and the calls of the boatmen began reaching them from the river.

The king hurriedly looked around. From his high vantage point on the raised bank, he could now see the activities below on the water. Several rafts and boats could be seen anchored to the bank. Koyaji and Bhimrai, the chief of the spy unit, were personally keeping it under surveillance. The boatmen had already done a few rounds at dawn across the Tungabhadra river. Koyaji had got three hundred horses across as cargo. Although it was still pitch dark on the other bank, Shahaji realised that his horsemen were inside there; this he guessed from the way the flambeaus would light up for a little while in the yonder bushes and then be extinguished when the need for them was over.

Koyaji and Bhimrai presented themselves before the Raja to inform him that all preparations had been made. Bending low in salutation, Koyaji said, 'Three hundred horsemen have been carried across to the other bank. I have also personally confirmed that all the boats and rafts are in good shape.'

As they were in the process of crossing the river, nature had slowly withdrawn the black sheet of darkness from over the surface of the water. Reflections of the blue sky and the puffs of white clouds overhead had begun descending into the water. Suddenly, the subdued whistles of wild birds and a few soft whispers came floating across from the trees on the other bank. As the Raja's boats began moving towards the other bank, the rows of trees submerged in the darkness came closer. Just then came the sounds of hissing and tapping, and a shower of arrows came swishing from the trees on the other bank to fall upon the convoy of boats. An arrow found its mark in the forearm of a boatman who was standing with his barge-pole, and he let out a loud shriek of 'Ah! I'm dead!' The Raja pulled out his sword and stood up.

This daring attack from the front spread confusion in the royal family. 'Who's that?' shouted Koyaji and Bhimrai, 'Thrash them!' And so saying, they leapt into the water. Sambhaji, Shivaji and Vyankoji were also on the point of leaping after them when the Raja signaled to them to stop. Just then, they began to hear swords clashing. Cries of 'Kill! Slash!' came from the other bank. The Raja gestured to his sons and to the rest of the family to lie down on the boat because a few arrows were still flying in from the other side.

Another scream of 'Kill! Smash!' erupted from the bushes on the other side, followed immediately by the painful shriek of people getting mortally wounded. The commotion in the yonder bushes ceased. Shahajiraja had full confidence in Koyaji's and Bhimrai's abilities. He was hugely surprised that anybody should have dared to launch this raid on his adequately armed caravan. Amidst all the confusion that reigned, the royal boat ran into the silt on the bank. Sambhaji and his men immediately got off the boat. The guards and servants in the next boat jumped out too, making it easy for the womenfolk to be taken across all the silt and slush.

The sun was now nice and bright. Shahajiraje had still not been able to recover from the shock. A few months back, he had once run into Koyaji in the jungle, on his way back from Bijapur to Bengaluru, where the boy had voiced his suspicion of such a mischief being imminent. The corpses of four of the assailants lay on the mount on the other bank. Koyaji's squad had attacked them with such violence that their blood-soaked faces had been battered beyond recognition. Koyaji and Bhimrai had then immediately set off in hot pursuit of the remaining assailants.

The trees on either side of the track were festooned with freshly chopped heads. Separated from the bodies with swords and hatchets, the macabre heads were tied to the branches by their long hair. Blood was still dripping from the hacked necks. The king examined the hideous, black heads carefully. They looked like brigands from the jungles of the south. The custom in Karnataka for such brigandry was decapitation.

In a little while arrived Koyaji's squad, wearing the contentment of victory on their faces for having wiped out the gang. Seated on his horse, Shahaji asked, 'Who were they, Koya?'

'A bunch of rascals from Chikmaglur close by here.'

Light meals were taken in a mango orchard. Placing his hands on Saibai and Sagunabai to give them his blessings, Shahaji said, 'Ranisaheb, take good care of these girls of mine in the Pune palace, please.'

Jijau didn't say anything. Shivaji took Koyaji and his other brothers in a tight embrace. He then bowed and placed his head at Tukabai and Shahajiraje's feet. The king took Shivaji in an affectionate embrace. The others jumped on their horses while Sai and Saguna got into their palanquins.

Jijau went on her knees before Shahajiraje and took his blessings. She stepped a couple of steps forward and immediately turned round. She told her husband in a hoarse voice, 'Your lordship need have no worries. I am carrying our Shivaji to the Maratha land of Maaval. At this point, I can only promise your lordship that I will sculpt our Shivaji into such a radiant, living piece of art that ten of Shah Jahan's Taj Mahals will look pale in his glorious presence.'

13

ASSAULT AGAINST SLAVERY

There are certain days in man's life, certain moments that carry a foil of gold, the aroma of sandalwood.

When Shivraya had first returned to Pune from Bengaluru-Bijapur in 1643, even before he had climbed up the steps of Lal Mahal, he had been strongly conscious of a divine visitation. It was as if the Shivba that had returned was a different person from the Shivba who visited Karnataka two years earlier.

On the very first morning after returning to Lal Mahal, Jijausaheb called Shivraya to the palace shrine and gave him a handful of fresh jasmine flowers. 'Shivba,' she said, 'I'm quite sure you would have felt this too, but this tour of yours to the south has been the best thing to happen to all of us.'

'Without a doubt, Matoshri! The kind of knowledge I attained there could not have been gathered even after travelling thousands of miles through dense forests or by sailing across the seven seas. The profound benefits of what I learnt in Bengaluru is magnificent and divine, and it will prove to be critically advantageous to us in the future.'

'And your father's memories?'

'How can you ask this, Ma Saheb? Is there a need at all to ask such a question? The twenty-odd months that I spent there were spent in the uninterrupted company of a prophet, an angel. I have a father as tall as a mountain, who gave seven years of sleepless nights to Emperor Shah Jahan, and a mother as deep as an ocean, who faced the storms of life-threatening crises in order to keep the boat of my life afloat. With the blessings of you both, I shall challenge Destiny and show how the peaks of the Himalayas are really dwarfs in comparison to the valour and the renunciation of the Sahyadris!'

A new kind of ardour had taken charge of his mind and body. When stormy winds begin to blow, they uproot and drag with them the vegetation on either side. Looking at the fervour with which Shivba was driving himself, his friends from Maaval were charged up, too. It was as if Shivba had tied wheels to his legs and would go roaming the countryside night and day. The Pune of those times was a big and prosperous township, but a doomsday merchant named Murari Jagdev had brought it to rack and ruin. The strong fort walls had been brought down; the big mansions had been razed to the ground; the flourishing town on the banks of the Mula-Mutha had been laid to waste. There was a village called Malikpur next to Hadapsar. It had come into being when, during the time of Malik Ambar, a number of his chieftains and workmen had created a large settlement there. With the passing of time, the name of this little township had morphed into Malkapur.

Upon newly arriving in Pune, Jijau had established a court in Lal Mahal to deliver justice to her subjects and put a salve on the physical and emotional wounds of the hard-working people.

It had become imperative to rebuild the shattered self-confidence of the farmers and peasants. Foxes and wolves roamed the fields unchecked. Dadojipant instituted cash rewards for the hunting down of wolves. The ploughing of the fields with donkeys had brought down a bigger curse upon the minds of the farmers than upon the land. To lift the morale of the farmers, Jijausaheb came up with a brilliant remedy: she got the goldsmith to fashion a gold ploughshare. When the people saw this gold plough turning the earth, the dread that had settled in their bones evaporated. The jinx had been broken and people's faith in their land had been restored.

Good days returned for the gods, too. The temple walls began to be erected. The farms around the settlement began to be furrowed; the newly sprung green on the fields brought to life a new vibrancy in the hearts of men.

Even before the sun was out, the open sand-beds along the riverbank began reverberating with the drumming of horses' hooves. This was Siddhi

Hilaal's thousand-horse cavalry getting ready for its day's exercise under his leadership. Shivba was always there, participating in steeplechases and horse racing. His circle of friends, among the youngsters from the mountain ranges of the Twelve Maavals, was steadily expanding. Young boys from farming families would take turns sleeping in the porches or galleries of Lal Mahal so that they could go to the riverbank in Shivba's company. Brahmin boys too would tuck up their dhotis to get atop the horses. Shivba had great affinity for mahars, mangs, chamars, fisherfolk, nomads and all such tribes. It was this affinity that provided the youngsters of these communities with the opportunity to hone their horse-riding skills.

Earlier, all that the boys of these parts had been familiar with were the mules of the Bhima banks and the local horses that people kept for sport. But, now they were riding strong, broad-backed, high-spirited Arab, Turkish and Kathiawadi animals. Even otherwise, carrying the courage and passion in their blood for riding a tiger, these boys from Maaval loved sweating it out on the backs of these horses fed on royal fodder.

For the four years before he had gone to Bengaluru, Shivba's beat had been limited to Pune and Khedebehara on the other side of the Katraj lake. A colony called Shivapur had slowly grown inside the area. Konde Deshmukh had some mango orchards there and Shivba too had some alongside his. Shivaji was still a boy when he had left for Bengaluru, but when he returned to Pune in his thirteenth year, it was as if he had sprouted the wings of an eagle. He had crossed the confines of the Mula-Mutha banks and Khedebehara. Shivba's horse now galloped to every nook and corner of the Twelve Maavals in the company of his friends.

.ೊಲೆ.

Shivba and his friends had decided not to go into the mountains and vales that day. Some sixty or seventy of them were riding through the streets and alleys of Pune. In due course, they got to the riverbank. During summertime, the bank would turn quite dry, allowing people to use it as a marketplace. People from the nearby valleys would gather in large numbers to buy and sell.

Shivba's squad was moving forward. The market was filled up with big and small articles put out for sale. Hundreds of bullocks and an equal number of buffaloes, horses and goats chaperoned by turbaned villagers were crowding the place. The younger kids in their petticoats and tunics were creating as much noise and chatter as the goats and poultry around them.

On one side of the bank was a grove of ancient banyan and peepul trees. When Shivba's eyes descended from the canopy of leaves and branches, what he saw below made him pull his reins instantly. They all froze and stared. There were a number of very young boys and girls lined up for sale under the tree like earthen pots. They were all painfully thin, tangle-haired, frightened-looking children belonging to the poorest of households. When Shivba's eyes drifted further down towards their legs, a knot formed in his stomach: as cattle are tied to stakes to prevent them from running away, so were the legs of these little children tied to one another.

Barely had the despicable sight registered with him when he looked to the right and saw a still more horrifying picture: a number of young girls and women from poor families had been made to sit in the market as items for sale. They belonged to all strata of society: some were from the hill tribes, some others came from the peasant class. There were dusky-skinned women from Deccan farms and fair Hyderabadi girls from Muslim families. There were blond, white-skinned Christian girls, too, from Cheul-Wasai and Goa who had been brought over for sale.

Shivba turned to a companion and asked in a hoarse voice, 'Chintoba, what's going on here?'

'This is what is called the flesh market.'

'What's that?'

'Cattle are sold in the cattle market. Here they sell boys and girls. It happens every day.'

The sight jolted Shivba. His attention then drifted to the Persian and Turani traders minding their merchandise with silver-handled whips in their hands. Over-fed, obese bodies, henna-tinted beards, curled-up, Islamic caps on heads, ankle-long green tunics over flaring trousers, they were going around hawking their goods among the customers crawling around the flesh market, 'Yours for the asking, brothers! Fresh stock straight from Bhaganagar! Five beautiful damsels for five hons!'[14]

'Use them at home! Use them in the shop! Use them for gifting in marriages! Special discounts for bulk purchases!'

'Use them in your kitchen! Use them in your bed! Fully matured goods! Fresh stock! Just arrived!'

The sight brought Shivba's blood to a boil. The lust-driven, unsavoury rogues that had gathered around the slave-girls were pawing them all over without any restraint whatsoever: kneading their shoulders, fondling their waists and pinching their buttocks.

Not being able to contain himself any further, Shivba spurred his horse forward and swung his horse-riding cane on the backs of the traders in front. His other companions also rode into the market and began belabouring the traders. Assaulted thus, some of the traders thrust their hands inside their tunics and pulled out sharp knives to mount a counterattack. But the boys riding with Shivba were tough Maaval youngsters who could not be scared away. They got after the traders with a vengeance and began hammering them with gusto.

When the customers, brokers and traders in the neighbouring market saw the rumpus, they came running in. A large number of them recognised Shivba as the son of Jijau. The jagir belonged to him; he was the master. Once the identity of the young horsemen became known, the traders began to back off. Shivba's companions got off their horses and hacked off the ropes tied to the ankles of the slaves. Some of these hostages had been kidnapped from their homes; some had been sold as slaves; and some had been off-loaded by step-parents. After the immediate joy of having rid themselves of their bonds, some began worrying about how they would survive. 'Where will we get our next meal from?' some were heard wondering.

Shivraya and his companions herded these newly freed hordes to Lal Mahal. Jijausaheb was bemused at seeing this ragged procession trooping into the courtyard of the waada. Shivba had not yet cooled down. When his comrades threw some of the arrested traders before his horse, he flared up, 'What kinds of demons are you? After taking birth as human beings, how can you sell other human beings into slavery?'

---

[14] The currency of those times.

'Huzoor, we are people with families too, and this is our profession!'

'Keep this in mind now! I shall not tolerate this flesh market in my jagir from this moment onwards!'

Even after berating the merchants, Shivba could not stop feeling revolted by this vile trade. How was it at all possible that flesh-and-blood boys and girls could be sold like cattle? He called over his clerks and began taking them to task: 'This kind of flesh market should never be seen again in Pune! It should be banned by law!'

Some of his officials tried to bring him round by telling him that slave-trade was an old practice that happened everywhere—Kabul, Kandahar, Peshawar, Dhaka; in fact, across the world. Even if it were outlawed in their own jagir, the slave-traders of the world would remain outside their control.

That was no reason, however, for Shivba to desist from firmly applying this law within his own province. He enforced such a heavy penalty upon the offenders that very soon this unrestrained sale and purchase of human beings almost vanished.

In the beginning, when Shivba's young army entered a hill-top habitation of herdsmen or the hamlet of the aboriginal tribes, the young and old of that settlement would scamper away and take refuge in the nearby jungles, from where they would peep out in fear. But when they noticed the smile that played upon young Shivba's pleasant visage and the trust-seeking twinkle in his eyes, they began gathering courage. From then on, it didn't take much time for the Twelve Maaval to embrace Shahajiraje and Jijau's boy wholeheartedly.

Once a whirlwind gets into a bamboo grove, it creates a merry mess before it retreats. A similar whirlwind had got into Shivba's head that would not let him sit in peace. The slavery of these destitute, oppressed, down-trodden, guileless people of the forest should be brought to an end—this servitude and serfdom of the poor, of vulnerable womankind, of the meek and the timid who were being sold in the slave market—or the *randi bazaar* as it was called in local parlance—for peanuts! The state to which the community had been reduced by the petty landlords could not go unchecked. The fleecing of the poor by the high priests of religion had to be ended. And the barbaric army of the tyrannical Muslim rulers that descended at will like locusts had to be stopped in its tracks.

As they were returning from Karnataka, Shahajiraje had said a simple thing that Shivba had found very important because of its implications: 'These Muslim rulers would part with their elephants and horses, nay, even the pupils of their eyes if the need arrived, but under no circumstance would they surrender their forts. Forts are the ultimate locus of their power.' Whenever he remembered these words, he would tell Jijausaheb, 'As Abasaheb has said, all the forts of our province should be under our control. We must do whatever we can—raid, attack, wage battles—but capture the forts for ourselves. Forts are the key to prosperity.'

Whenever Shivba went riding through the wilds of the Sahyadri, his probing eyes would linger on the forts that stood on the shoulders of its valleys and hills. How big was each one of the forts? How resilient and strong were their walls and main gates? What exactly was the status of the ordnance lying in the arsenals and the grains in the warehouses? How many forts had turned rickety? How many of the dilapidated forts could be strengthened with the repair of walls and masonry work? An extraordinary fervour propelled Shivba day and night to travel like lightning through the mountain ranges.

Jijau exercised complete sway over Lal Mahal. It didn't take long for people to realise that the cases of physically crippled people, hapless women, in fact, of all the weak and powerless, were heard with great dispatch and alacrity in the portico of this mother-figure. An important principle was being enforced here: delaying the delivery of justice was not a sign of power but a violation of rights. Quick delivery of justice was a meritorious act. Jijau would herself sit in judgment. Both Dadoji Kond'dev and Kazi Abdullah had their separate courts to ensure quick disposal of cases. If the petitioners were not satisfied with the judgment, they had the right to go on appeal, which would then be heard by Jijau herself.

After attentive listening, acute observation and sufficient study, Shivba too became adept at handling the balance of justice. Very often, when touring the Maaval, he and his associates would carry their mobile court with them. They would sit on the outskirts of a village or under the canopied shade of a mango tree and hear out people's pleas. The subjects were delighted at this availability of justice at their doorstep.

Young and old, the denizens of the gulches and ravines of Maaval began to develop a sense of pride in their king, Shivbai. His open temperament and behaviour that included all in their embrace, the contentment that people felt upon meeting him as one of their own; his humility, the attractive smile that played upon his soft, innocent face, won the hearts of all. This prince sat with his poor subjects on their earth-and-dung-coated floors under their single-sloped roofs and behind grass walls, and ate their raggi bread and onion with them. His broad brow sometimes sported ashtagandha powder, and at other times, a crescent moon. His personality was like a magnet to young and old alike.

⁓ঞ⁓

'Prince, learn a little bit to stay behind in the palace! Every little while you are out on your rounds of the ravines and defiles of the Maaval region!'

'Well, Aausaheb, if I must be completely honest, this red soil of Maaval has an irresistible pull on me. I have friends there who stake their lives for me, like Kondaji and Yesaji Kank, our Suryabhan Kakade, Baaji Jedhe, Bhikaji Chor, that Tryambak Sonedev, that Daadji of Narasprabhu Gupte, and then Chimnaji, and those boys of Mudgal Deshpande—Narayan and Balaji, all of them are my friends. The parents of every one of them have grown up in abject poverty, sweating it out on the fields; they have had limitless faith in fair play and humanity, though. Those experienced, mature, loving elders in their houses! What do I say, Aausaheb? The attraction that a barn full of calves has for a cow, that's the passion that gets into me for gallivanting around the Twelve Maavals.'

'*Aho*, but, Shivba, what special stuff do you see there?'

'How do I say it, Matoshri, and how much? The blue sky that stretches over the head of the Maaval region teaches me to leap high. The cows and calves, the sheep and lambs that roam free on the cliffs and crevasses teach me agility and sturdiness. The dense trees growing there remind me of meditating savants and saints sitting lost in their thoughts on the bank of the Ganga. These thick forests give me the direction to reach right up to the root of any branch of knowledge. The tall mountain peaks there, the tortuous mountain sides, the armies of red ants climbing up the boles and branches, those salamander lizards that teach one to keep moving up impossible stone walls with determination! Truth be told, Aausaheb, the entire wilderness is so steeped in the magic of mindfulness that it is always teaching me the lesson of tenacity, resilience and struggle.'

Actually, the land of Maaval was not alien to Shivba. In earlier times, it was a part of the Nizamshahi kingdom up to the river Neera. His grandfather Maloji Raja was the first to have received the jagirs of Pune and Supe. Now, it was Dadoji Kond'dev who continued with the land revenue system of Malik Baba.

Shahajiraje's life was a story of many ups and downs. He had seen the durbars of the Mughals, the Nizamshahis and the Bijapuris. But he had never forgotten his native Maaval. He had found employment for many Maaval youths, given them holdings. He had appointed them as officials like Deshmukhs, Deshpandes, Patils and Kulkarnis in the revenue department. That was the reason why Shivba thought of the Deshmukhs and Deshpandes as a part of his larger family. That was also why he always received a very warm response every time he called on them. There was always whole-hearted support for all his plans and policies.

However, not all the senior men were ready to march to the same beat. Some of them did create hindrances. Krishnaji Bandal of the Hirdas Maaval valley crossed the line. Shivba was standing once at Shivpur along with his friends when they saw a bunch of injured horses come running in from the adjacent jungle. Shivba not only recognised these animals, but also knew them as belonging to Dadoji Kond'dev's stable. The tails of these animals had been chopped off. This act of cruelty was an audacious expression of Krishnaji Bandal's malice towards Shivaji. This act of deliberate instigation caused tempers to rise in Lal Mahal. Shivba was livid with anger.

Instructions arrived from Aausaheb, and a few wheels turned the next day. Dadojipant met Kanhobaji in the Shivpur market. Kanhoji called over Krishnaji Bandal and peace was established for the time being. However, his feudal arrogance refused to dissipate. He was again summoned to Purandar and made to see reason. When he refused to mend his ways, he was put into a sack and thrashed. Finally, his arms and legs were chopped off. That was when the fever of impudence finally left him. After the delivery of such exemplary punishment, no Deshmukh or Deshpande dared to repeat such acts.

One day a grave voice spoke out like the voice of destiny, 'Babaji Bhikaji Gujar, you are the Patil of Ranjhegaon, Khedebehra, and you have committed an offence. You have committed the sin of outraging the modesty of a poor, helpless woman who was resident in her father's house with her children. We have personally examined the application of the complaint, the reports of witnesses and other pieces of evidence related to the case. The investigations made on the complaint have established your guilt. The charge made against a government official like you of having misbehaved with a powerless woman in a despicable manner has been proved beyond doubt. Babaji, son of Bhikaji Gujar Patil, as a punishment for the crime committed by you, I hereby pronounce the sentence that your limbs be chopped off your body immediately.'

The pronouncement had the sharpness of doom about it. The immediate implementation of this unprecedented sentence—those limbs hacked off the body of the perpetrator like the claws of a crab and the helpless, limbless body lying writhing in a pool of blood. The gory scene was enough to make a numbing impact on everyone around.

The shock waves created by the punishment meted out by that small court did not remain limited to the Twelve Maavals. Within two days its echo had reached every nook and corner, shaken every leaf on every tree across the hills and dales, like a gust of wind. Such an unprecedented variety of justice could now be delivered!

The word spread across regions near and far that a mere boy-king like Shivba had passed such a strong, revolutionary judgment. He had blown the trumpet of justice for helpless women in a male-dominated system.

Otherwise, what value did an uneducated, rustic, defenceless peasant woman have in the account book of society? How many dispossessed women had been trampled underfoot by tyrannical men, generation after generation like lumps of earth being broken by bullocks in a rice field! No braveheart had yet been born who would apply the brakes on such unrestrained activities through the court of law.

What occurred that day had neither been seen nor heard of before. With that one single judgment, the prince named Shivba had gained for himself the title of 'Shivraya'—Shiva the king. The destitute and the working class were thrilled beyond words at having found a savior. It was after countless years that the scream of unfortunate womanhood had pierced through the stone walls of the tyrannical Sultanshahi system.

Ordinarily, the pronouncement of such a dreadful judgment would have caused another woman to collapse on the spot with terror. But here, as the words of the judgment had begun falling on Jijau's ears, her face had turned harder and more resolute. All the other clerks and officials and Shivba's associates assembled there had turned to stone. When Shivraya climbed down the steps of the court and began walking towards his palace, he wondered what had given him the conviction to pass such a sentence.

Shivraya then began remembering those ceaseless discussions with his mother. That marriage procession of a grandee on a Bijapur road and the wedding gift given to the bride by her father as dowry. Trays loaded with gems and precious stones in a horse-pulled chariot in the lead, and the retinue of slaves bringing the rear—a thousand or so men and women, about seven hundred of whom were destitute women, ranging from eleven to twenty-five years of age. A number of them had fair, pretty, Persian or Turani faces. There were quite a few Deccanis, Brahmins, Muslims and some Bengalis too. Nobody knew anything of their names, origins, caste and creed. There was no reason to know anything either. For working at home, for working in the garden, pulling water, grinding the corn, their hard-working bodies would be of great use. If somebody also wanted to make use of their young bodies in the bed, it would not be a legal offence. The reason? These poor souls, these slaves, had no right to live their lives as human beings.

Randi bazaars were held everywhere in this cultured, civilised world for supplying the rich and powerful with young girls to feast upon.

Whenever a battle was won, merchants, traders and customers would be thrilled at the expectation of new 'stock' coming into the market. This merchandise would be in great demand during weddings in the houses of the big and mighty. Hundreds of such slaves would be presented as dowry for the bride to take to her groom's house. Nobody had any concern or sentiment at all for the girls and boys so gifted. They were traded in exactly the same manner as goats and poultry were counted out. This entire enterprise had the recognition and sanction of the government.

Emperor Jahangir had himself sold off a few hundred thousand girls as slaves to the king of Prussia.

The present Delhi emperor, Shah Jahan, had turned disconsolate at the loss of his beloved wife Mumtaz. He had only lately got a mausoleum constructed, that would serve as an eternal memorial to his love for her. Yet, his harem was overflowing with hundreds of beautiful young girls picked up from poor households. Not content with that, he never kept male guards when he stayed at his palace in Agra Fort. To make sure that he encountered only beautiful faces, he had given arms training to young Tartar girls and appointed them as guards. Seeing these tall, strong and attractively built Tartar girls everywhere that his eyes fell was the greatest pastime of the great emperor.

Shivraya would speak with Jijausaheb on a wide variety of topics. One of the subjects they often discussed was the slave market and the state to which slaves were reduced. He once said, 'Aausaheb, whether it is the Nizamshahi or the Mughal Empire, women seem to matter even less than sheep and goats in these Muslim kingdoms; they could as well be termites.'

'Hold on, Shivba. There is no reason to be proud of Hindutva in regard to this,' Jijau replied. ' Even today there is this Hindu king named Vijay Raghav who rules over a kingdom called Jinji in the south. How many women, do you think, has this great man married with gods and Brahmins as witnesses? Take a guess.'

'Twenty-five or thirty, I am sure.'

'*Aho*, this Vijayrao has married over five hundred women in a proper, legal manner. This wretched man, drunk with the conceit of power and wealth, what does he think of young girls? Straw heaped atop a loft?'

Vishwasrao Dighe, a childhood friend of Shivraya, met with him one morning on the steps of Lal Mahal. He began singing his praises. 'Shivraya, have you any idea of the riot you have caused in all directions by pronouncing a sentence upon that wicked Patil of Ranjha and by immediately putting that sentence into effect?'

'Riot? What do you mean?'

Tender-hearted Dighe began giving him a brief account of all that had occurred in a soft, low voice, 'Kings of great lineage, emperors, priests, Brahmins, censors, powerful magnates, even traders and touts with money in their waistbands consider it a mark of valour to assault young women. After all, who is there to listen to their calls of distress? However much they ring the gongs and bells, the god sitting inside the sanctum sanctorum cannot be roused from his sleep. On the contrary, he pulls a band over his eyes and sits quiet as a mouse. But the kind of sensation and joy that has been created by this episode of Ranjhekar Patil, I have no words for it. Drums are being beaten in the neighbouring jagirs and principalities. This son of the jagir of Pune named Shivba is the offspring of a great soul. He caught by the throat his own officer who had outraged the modesty of a defenceless woman, and used the machete of the law to chop off the miscreant's limbs.'

'Dighe, is the judgement really creating such ripples?'

'Praise, Shivba? Whirlwinds are rising to sing paeans and ballads of your great deed in every direction. Girls of every caste and creed are offering prayers of gratitude to have found themselves a brother.'

'Hail Mai Jagdambe! Hail Ghruneshwara!' So saying, Shivraya closed his eyes in contentment.

'Yes, Shivba, the colossal merits you have accrued by this one single deed, it is many times more than the credit you could have gained by winning a great war.'

14

THE SUVARNAKUMBH OF FREEDOM

Those dense forests and soggy gorges of the Sahyadri! It had been raining by the buckets for the past two months. Suddenly, the rains would take a pause, strewing the glens, the crevasses and the watercourses with dense fluffs of haze and coating the entire region white. It was only lately that the haze had slowly faded.

In front could be seen mountain cliffs rising four thousand feet high—those tall boulders leaping up with their canines snarling at the sky. Bolls of fog sometimes played hide-and-seek between them, or sat playfully on their heads like a white turban on the head of a Kolhapuri warrior.

The distant rumble of water falling down tall, steep cliffs could be heard travelling in from the neighbouring gorges. The birds sitting on the bushes shook their wings vigorously to dislodge the water gathered in their feathers. Little by little, the mist cleared and the bastion of an ancient Sahyadri fort came into view. Glistening wet. On that rain-washed bastion could now be identified small squads of Adilshahi soldiers shivering in the moist, cold wind, recognisable only by their heavy armour and army hats. Otherwise, the incessant rains and the red slime grinding under their boots had given their clothing a thick coat of the red earth of that region. From this distance, the rust-laden men looked like a pack of rhesus monkeys. The rains and the cold biting winds had tormented them to the point of distraction. Even now, as they sat in clusters around tiny fires, the wood and leaves created more smoke than heat on account of being wet.

Tajuddin, the leader of the irregular soldiery, let out a loud whistle of delight. He waved to his colleagues sitting on the bastion and around little fires on the other side, and leapt down from the stone balustrade to the green lawn below. He was feeling extremely happy. He was sure that nobody was likely to be getting into or leaving out of these soaking wet defiles and ravines of Maaval, particularly at this time of the year.

The shortage of reinforcements had brought these men into dire straits. Even if they had money tucked in their waistbands, what could they have got in this deserted fort tucked beyond a jungle trail? Thankfully, they had anticipated this and had had the foresight to save the dried hides of three or four deer, which they would now cut into small pieces and cook in boiling water. That and the vegetables growing in these woods had been their sustenance during these difficult three months. These wet, distressed squads had now begun to come clambering down the narrow, difficult, moss-laden tracks of the fort.

The main descent from the fort was over. The small hamlet lying concealed behind dense vegetation had been left behind. After they had also crossed the ice-cold river in front, a number of them turned around to throw a last, relieved look at the fort high up there, now completely lost in the surrounding mist. There was elation in Tajuddin's voice as he said, 'We will now return here only after Dussehra, well after the rains have departed. Leave alone a man, not so much as a dog can get in here meanwhile.'

Another four days rolled by. A small group of eight or ten horsemen came down from the Subhanmangal fort at Shirwal and got into the gulch of the Kanand river. They were in search of Tajuddin and his squad. A person named Khopade from the Kanap gulch had lodged a complaint against him with the fort-keeper. Tajuddin got wind that there was something untoward happening near their Torana fort. He and his horsemen were resting in a village on the way. The men had been rattled by the sudden arrival of this squad from Torana and gone running back towards Torana with the intention of keeping their jobs secure.

There was the crystal-clear water of the Kanand flowing in front. Tajuddin and his three hundred horsemen hurriedly began wading through the flat, shallow, rustling water. Suddenly, he noticed on the waterbed in front a few shadows. Beyond, he saw some seventy or eighty young Maaval men forming a wall along the riverbank. Every one of them had either a tightly-held sword in their hands or a spear raised high in excitement.

As soon as he saw the enemy lined up on the other side, Tajuddin raised a loud cry of Allah-o-Akbar. The response of Har har Mahadev from the other side was immediate. As the Bijapuri soldiers rushed forward to take account of the Marathas, the Maratha warriors too leapt into the river with their cry of Har har Mahadev. The two forces crashed into each other and converted the river into a battlefield, and a no-holds-barred, hand-to-hand battle began.

Just around then, another contingent of thirty young men came out of hiding from behind the bushes on the other bank and entered the water with shouts of Har har Mahadev. The intense skirmish caused the water to kick up at countless points in the river. As the clash of arms turned violent, the haze on the riverbank rolled in, too, confounding the confusion that prevailed.

This was the first bitter engagement of Shivraya and his braves with the enemy. The boys had together begun to yell 'Attack, attack!!' and 'Kill, kill' with such vehemence that the enemy's heart sank. The Adilshahi men just couldn't fathom how many Maratha men had actually gathered in the surrounding haze, the thick vegetation and the meadows beyond. The level of noise they were creating suggested that an army of a good two or three thousand men had suddenly descended upon them.

While this strange encounter was underway on the riverbed, Shivba, in the company of warriors like Tanaji Malusare, Yesaji Kank, Vishwasrao Dighe, Bhikaji Chor and Dadaji Deshpande, had been waiting at the porch of the Kanandeshvar Mahadev, busy with his surveillance of the area. They all let out a leonine roar and set off for the river. They leapt into the flowing water and began swinging their weapons with vigour.

The sword in Shivba's hand descended upon the enemy like a flash of lightning. The water that had been running clear and transparent some while ago turned red with blood. Disembodied heads of the Bijapuri soldiers began rolling along on the current of the stream. Tajuddin screamed at the top of his voice, 'Run, men, run!' His men didn't need a second order. They swiftly turned around, scampered out of the bank from where they had entered and disappeared into the thick fog.

Soon after, drums of victory began beating near the temple of Kanandeshvar. With loud cries of *Jai Bhavani* and Har har Mahadev, Shivraya and his troops began to climb the slope leading up to the Torana fort. The haze had thinned out a little bit by now. Shivaji looked resplendent in the rays of the setting sun. There was a spark of determination in his eyes. The gash inflicted by a passing enemy sword was still fresh on his cheek. His tunic that flared from the waist was spattered with blood.

That very evening, the green banner with the crescent moon and star was removed, and a red-ochre flag was hoisted in its place. Kanand valley had been captured. The next morning, Shivraya initiated the restoration of the dilapidated bastion of the Torana fort. Masons, artisans and labourers immediately set to work. Since there was a shortage of workmen, the soldiers took crowbars, iron bowls and hoes in their hands, and joined the labour force with great enthusiasm.

One day, a labourer suddenly felt a jolt shoot up his arm when his pickaxe hit something hard under the earth that gave off a metallic sound. The other labourers gathered around and swiftly removed the layer of earth around that spot. They soon came upon a huge copper vessel covered with a lid. Some knocks at the neck and the lid came loose. When they removed the lid, the onlookers gasped in astonishment: the vessel was filled to the brim with gold chips. They men began poking into the earth all around the place, and soon enough, they located six more vessels, all loaded with gold. The very first fort that they had won had yielded such enormous wealth. Shivaji and his men received it as a blessing from Lord Shambhu Mahadev and rejoiced.

The very same day, four horses galloped away in the direction of Pune. The next morning, some palanquins arrived at the riverbank. The first person to alight was Jijausaheb, beaming from ear to ear. She first went to the Kanandeshvar Mahadev temple nearby and offered her obeisance. When the palanquin reached Kanand village, the women and children came streaming out of their houses. 'Aausaheb has come!' they told animatedly to each other, ran into their houses, and emerged with earthen pots full of water to wash her feet. She was, in point of fact, the true Lakshmi of the Maaval region.

After the palanquins and the villagers had made the arduous climb up to the Torana fort, Jijabai offered prayers to the ancient stone statue of Mengai Devi. Then, she cast a long, lingering look at the secret wealth, which had now been transferred into wooden boxes, prayed to Goddess Lakshmi, and took her son in her arms.

That afternoon, she took Shivraya along for a round of the fort. When they stopped before a haveli, Jijau's eyes travelled across the intervening gorge and rested on the peak of a rugged mountain not too far away on the other side.

'Shivba, what's the name of that peak there?' Jijau asked.

'It's called Murumb Deva's peak. But why do you ask?'

Jijau's eyes swept across the bright blue sky, turned below to take in the deep gorges and again came to rest on Murumb Deva's peak. As if still lost in deep thought, she went on, 'I doubt if any king can find a better place than this to build a fort here for his capital city, Shivba. What do you think?'

Shivba let out a loud laugh.

'So, when do you get the work started?'

'Early enough ... but I have a question, Aausaheb. What do you think of "Rajgadh" as a name for this new fort?'

'Excellent! Beautiful!'

―⸙―

After the return from Bengaluru, whispers had begun among the clerks and petty administrators at the court of Lal Mahal that Dadoji Kond'dev was handling far too many responsibilities: 'Quite true. Looks after the maintenance of the Kondhana fort from here and manages the affairs of Lal Mahal too! With age having crept upon him, how much running around can he do, after all?'

'The man is sincere, but the state of his health limits him, doesn't it?'

Word got around one morning that an important document had arrived at the palace from the Bijapur durbar. All ears were instantly cocked. As the chief administrator, Dadoji Kond'dev undid the silk knot of the bag and pulled out the dispatch. As he read it, his eyes lit up with joy. He instantly dispatched the gardener to fetch him a bunch of golden magnolia flowers.

He then adjusted the silk shawl on his shoulder and went towards the private chambers. Bowing before Jijausaheb, he said, 'Aausaheb, you should be the first to taste the sweets.' He offered her a box of sweets and then handed over to her the letter, saying, 'Our prince is being granted the subedari of the Kondhana fort, no less! And at such a young age!'

'Pant, you seem to be quite thrilled at this!' said Jijau.

'Yes, that's quite true. Once the protocol of service to the state seeps into the system, the footsteps acquire an authority of their own.'

Jijausaheb deliberately did not respond to Pant's statement, but her demeanour told Dadoji that something was out of sync there. He discreetly withdrew from her presence. Just then, the hooves of a few horses were heard at the doorstep of the palace. It was Shivba returning with his companions. At a signal from Jijau, the cook and the service boy laid out the food for the gathering. A dozen of them sat down with Shivba for the meal, as usual. Jijau then quietly informed the prince, 'The letter from Bijapur has arrived.'

'Yes, I heard about it, but by now, I guess, half of Pune has got wind of it.'

The meal over, Shivba was getting ready to leave with his friends again when Jijausaheb accosted him, 'So, son, don't you want to see the letter?'

'What letter?'

'The royal letter of appointment that has arrived directly from Bijapur!'

'Oh that! No, we'll let that go. I don't much care for it.'

'What are you saying? The prestigious appointment to the subedari of the Kondhana fort at your age!' Shivraya looked indifferent. Jijausaheb added, 'Doesn't the prince want to have a peep at the fiefdom that the Sultan has offered as a gift? What an insult this would be to the Sultan's benediction!'

Shivraya's face turned red. Tense with suppressed anger, he said in a raised voice, 'Matoshri, you are, perhaps, testing me out with these sarcastic words. But what truly surprises me is the bone headedness of the educated fools who work as administrators in the Bijapur court. This body of mine has not been designed to sit chewing at the stale crumbs of slavery thrown from the Sultan's table.'

He walked up to the court in rage, surprising the officials and clerks who had expected him to walk in dancing with joy. Dadojipant too quietly moved to one side. Shivraya sent word to Siddhi Hilaal to report to him immediately. The cavalry chief was in the stable behind the court; he presented himself in his loose trousers and a Kabuli tunic that reached up to his knees. The years of slavery that had penetrated his system would not allow him to stand erect. 'There are some four hundred youngsters from the Neera and Mulshi valleys who have been standing at the palace doors,' Shivraya snapped at him. 'Have you seen them?'

'Yes, huzoor.'

'If such sturdy young men cannot be accommodated in the army of our independent kingdom, where will they go?'

'Forgive the impertinence, huzoor, but we do not need any more horsemen.'

'Listen, Siddhi Miyan, who are you to decide whether we need more men or not?' Shivba's face had turned stern. In a voice of steel, he passed the order, 'Make arrangements to give honourable appointments to these young men by this evening.'

'But, Rajaji, we need prior sanction for additional recruitments!'

'Whose?'

'The senior Raja's! Shahajiraja's!'

'Khan Saheb, our recruitment here is for our Hindvi kingdom, not for the Bengaluru or Karnataka kingdoms.'

'But, huzoor!'

'From here on, everything should happen as I say, for the welfare of our independent state.'

Shivraya closed his eyes and lost himself in some kind of meditation. The problem was not getting resolved. Every step of the way he could sense the thorns in his path. After a little while, he opened his eyes and looked around in surprise to find that Siddhi Hilaal had still not moved. He was saying to him, 'Please listen to me a little bit, huzoor. Particularly in the matter of the army, we did not have the authority to spend an extra pie without procuring advance sanction from Bengaluru.'

'Even so, you will have to take this decision for the sake of my insistence on an independent state.'

'Huzoor, it is only on account of this passion of yours that we have spent twice the amount allotted to us!'

'Continue doing that. For our swarajya.'

'Prince, it terrifies me.'

Shivraya felt deeply upset at the man's outright refusal. Letting out a deep sigh, he said in a grave voice, 'Thank you very much. Khan Saheb, thank you for having served us so well over the years. However, I am completely driven by my dream of a Hindvi state. If you are not committed to it, then—'

'Raje?'

'—then, maybe, the most convenient thing for you would be to find your way back to Bengaluru.'

Siddhi Hilaal did not spend another day in Pune. The very next morning, he set out for Bengaluru.

⁂

Rajaji, what exactly had you done to your son Shivba at the time of dispatching him from Bengaluru to Pune? What herbal juices, from which mountains, had you fed him? He goes there, and within six or eight weeks, he shows the temerity of gaining control over the mountain forts of our Adilshahi territory one after another! And, this rebellion cannot be seen as childish antics, can it?

He puts us to shame by planting his forces everywhere he goes! What conclusions do we draw from these indiscretions and this misdemeanour? If you have such devotion to our throne here, how can your son turn out to be so intransigent?

Perhaps, you find it amusing to instigate your son to make fun of our Sultanate in this manner. But know that if this kind of folly continues, then the horses of our stables will break their leashes and go galloping into your land to settle scores. And if this happens, not a bird will remain to stand as witness to the destruction that shall be wrought upon your land of the Twelve Maavals.

This threatening letter that Sultan Mohammadshah had sent to Shahajiraja had created immense turbulence everywhere. Shahajiraje immediately had a copy made of it and dispatched it to Pune. Jijausaheb read the letter over and over again and understood the fire that lay behind each word. She had very well sensed the animosity and danger that it portended for the future.

Jijau had travelled that day with Shivraya to the Maaval valleys. The work for the construction of a new Rajgadh had begun in the mountainous region of Gunjan Maaval. Masons, carpenters, and all kinds of artisans and labourers had gathered in thousands to build this fort on the Murumb Deva mountain peak. The work on the temples, lakes and courts in the lower fort was in its final stages of completion. There was a bulge that ran across two miles on each of the three hills, along the main mountain, that was referred to as the trunk.

The construction of fort walls all along this trunk, too, had been moving apace. That mountain fort rising straight up to a height of fourteen hundred metres had begun to look quite forbidding now. Jijau had spotted this site with an unerring eye while worshipping Goddess Mengai at the Torana fort. It had become an unshakeable principle with Shivraya that once a decision had been taken, firm policies would be put into place to ensure its implementation. Whatever obstacles came in the way would simply have to be fought down even to the point of staking one's life on it.

Fighting wars to win forts, losing a fort here and winning one there—these were the standard moves in the game of statecraft. But a king in the southern part of India taking in hand the building of a new fort? This was a phenomenon that nobody had heard of in the hills and dales of these parts for the past two centuries.

Most of the forts in the Sahyadri and the Baglan regions were ancient, dating back to Mauryan and Buddhist times. A few centuries ago, Bhojraja had constructed the formidable fort at Panhala, to which the Yadavas of Devgiri had added a few more. Shivba's enterprise had moved Dadoji Kond'dev to observe, 'Aausaheb, taking in hand the construction of a new fort is the equivalent of a farmer abandoning his cattle and starting a nursery of elephants. It really is testing our king.'

'Well, Pant,' Jijau replied, 'if we are nursing dreams of constructing a strong, formidable palace, we have to make sure that the pillars are strong.'

Dadoji was on the point of saying something when he checked himself. Noticing this withdrawal, Jijau nudged him, 'Out with it, Pant. You wanted to say something.'

'Aausaheb, the artisans and masons of these parts have long ago forgotten the science of fort-making.'

'This is a bit too much, isn't it?' Jijaubai said sarcastically.

'But considering Shivba's tenacity in this matter, we had to send people to Bhaganagar, near Hyderabad. Some workers were brought from as far away as Marwad and Mewad.'

In the heat of the afternoon sun, Jijau was inspecting the construction work. They found a little shelter at the corner of a bastion, a small inspection hut made from the branches of kembal grass. The post gave an unobstructed view of the work in progress. A young boy from Karad, named Arjoji Yadav, had been imbibing the skill of the artisans from Rajasthan and was not too far away from becoming a master himself in the art of fort building. He stepped up to the king, bowed in reverence, and pointed his finger at an edge of the mountain, saying, 'Raje, the work on the Padmavati trunk there is moving on at a fast clip.'

'Arjoji, why call it a trunk? It is a "machi".'

'Machi?' The others were as perplexed as young Arjoji was.

When Jijau laughed out at this analogy, Shivba said, 'See? Matoshri has understood the true import. Like an expert hunter sits on the "machi" or a "machaan" with his arrows or spears and kills the tiger, so will we sit on this "machi", and flay the backs of our enemies.'

'Aah, I have now begun to see things a bit more clearly,' Saibai said with a playful smile. 'When a basket-maker finds a nice piece of reed, he wants to immediately get busy fashioning a nice flute out of it. When a sculptor sees a hard, black piece of rock, his fingers begin to itch for his chisel so that he may sculpt the image of his dreams. So it is with our lordship here; when he rests his eyes on a well-shaped shoulder of a mountain, he loses himself in imagining a fort that he may carve out of it.'

This set off a roar of laughter among the assembly, including Shivaji.

The authorities at Bijapur were deeply upset at the rebellion that Shivraya had sparked off in the Sahyadris. Raghunathpant Korde once informed the king, 'The fort-keeper of Shirwal, Ameen Saheb, has been on a short fuse lately.'

'Reason?'

'Narasprabhu Deshpande has stopped sending the revenue to his fort altogether, which has brought the wrath of Bijapur crackling down upon him.'

'But, Pant, Narasprabhu is one of the frontline warriors for our Hindutva state.'

'That is exactly why a very strongly worded notice that arrived from Bijapur has been pasted on his wall.'

'So, what exactly does the notice say?'

'Well, this is what the notice says in rather harsh language.

Narasprabhu, that brigand Shivaji has infiltrated into the Rohideshvar fort. Also, he is constructing a brand-new fort on the peak of the Murambdev hill, and taking one fort after another under his custody. Have you been sleeping while all this has been going on? With this notice, you are being warned in the strictest terms that if you do not continue depositing the revenue collection of your area due to us, you shall be caught alive. You shall be tied to a horse's tail and dragged all the way to Bijapur and beheaded in a public square.'

Shivba turned grave on hearing the jeering, bullying fizz of the notice. Letting out a sigh, he asked, 'So, what was Dadaji's response?'

'Oh, he responded by declaring in everyone's presence that he would happily embrace death for the sake of Shivba. It would be nothing worse than death arriving tomorrow instead of the day after.'

Everybody in the Maaval region had understood that the Adilshahi grandees had resolved to castrate Shivraya through whatever means, fair or foul. For carrying their mission forward, they had taken in hand their rusted, hurtful swords, and begun inflicting wounds on the minds and bodies of the Maaval subjects and made life miserable for them. Their one single objective was to ensure that Shivba should be stripped of all support and rendered utterly lonely.

Shivba would occasionally be caught in a quandary. He would worry deeply about the state of his subjects, who were standing behind him for an independent state and suffering on account of it. His age at this point was about fifteen or sixteen. The mission before him was as tall as the Himalayas. The temple of swarajya was still very high up there, but dreams should certainly be dreamt. The young and old of the Maaval region were staking their lives for the fulfillment of that dream. Shivraya had often been deeply impressed by the support that the poor and destitute people of Maaval had been giving him. It was imperative that these people who were watching his back be honoured and protected. With this thought in mind, Shivba wrote an encouraging letter to Dadaji Narasprabhu on 17 April 1645.

Rohideshvar Mahadev, the god of our clan, is forever present amongst us. He has already granted us many victories, and He shall continue to fulfill our hearts' desire and grant us our independent kingdom. It is clearly the Lord's desire that this kingdom should come into existence.

The atmosphere in Lal Mahal had lately turned rather grave. The news had reached the Pune markets, the grass markets—in fact, even to the hamlet of Jijapur on the other side of the river—that if Shivba's impertinence went on mounting at this pace, the Bijapur blight would not take too much time descending once again on Pune. The situation was turning more and more explosive with every passing day.

Jijau had handed over a parcel of barren land on the other side of the river to the gardeners' community for their use. The gardeners had gone on to convert this land into a paradise of flowers and proudly christened it as Jijapur. Every day, early in the morning, a dispatch of garlands and bouquets would arrive for use in the palace shrines. When the gardener women began gossiping with the palace maids and talking about the fear that loomed over their hamlet, Shivraya became even more wary.

For some time now, Shivba's frisky horses would refuse to stay confined to their stables. They would go galloping with their companions and comb out the length and breadth of the Twelve Maavals. It had become an obsession with Shivba to go surveying the newly built fort on the mountain-top and the open land around it for further construction activity. That was when the dashing young men of the nearby jungles and hamlets would gather around him. His eyes would forever be searching for the bravest among these strapping young men.

One such boy who had caught his attention earlier was Tanaji Malusare. The manner in which he had caught the king's attention had left an extremely favourable impression of this boy. Shivraya had climbed down the mountain path of Warandh to Mahad to attend a wedding ceremony. There, he had seen this bold, strong, energetic youngster swinging the long, supple blade of his danda-patta with amazing dexterity, knocking down five or six of his fellow-players at one go. Shivba had been so hypnotised at the breathtaking skill of this youngster that he had turned to his companion and asked, 'Who is this boy dancing like a flash of lightning here?'

'He's Tanaji, the son of Malusare of Umarath.'

After the show was over, Shivba called Tanaji over. He patted the boy on the back, removed a gold bracelet from his wrist, slipped it on the boy's wrist, and said, 'Arey Tanha, are these your arms or the primed-up wicks of dynamite? What will you do hanging behind in these hinterlands?'

'I await your orders, sarkar.'

'Come to our Lal Mahal and join our army for independence. Shivraya told his companions, 'Danda-patta and lezim[15] plenty of boys can play, but the zest and excitement I see in this Tanaji, I haven't seen in anybody else. This valiant boy could become a bastion of some fort one day, the striking arm of a brave king.'

Young boys would gather every evening in the villages scattered across the Maaval region. Games would be organised to the beat of lezims accompanied by other percussion instruments. The village would go to sleep watching these games. Once the seniors were fast asleep, the youngsters would sneak out of their houses and head straight for the heaps of hay lined up outside. They would pull out the swords tucked underneath, rush out with them to the empty lands outside the village, and spend the entire night sparring with each other; the others would sharpen their javelin-throwing skills. The furnaces of the blacksmiths glowed all night as weapons were being tempered in every single village. The water sprinkled on the sharpened weapons would turn into hissing steam as it met the hot blades.

It wasn't Shivraya alone; every single boy in the region talked openly about 'our kingdom', 'our self-governed state'. In no time, the army of these youngsters swelled up to seven thousand braves. They were posted to mount a watch over the fort walls and on sensitive cross roads down in the gulches.

The hectic recruitment drive, expenditure on the infantrymen, ordnance, purchase of horses and creation of new stables—the spending

---

[15] Danda-patta is gauntlet-sword, while lezim is a popular musical instrument with jingling cymbals.

kept mounting as ambition soared. Seeing all this, Dadoji's and other administrators' hearts began to beat a mile a minute.

For the past few months, no revenue collection was being deposited at Shirval. Complaints were reported to have reached straight to Bijapur. The dues from Lal Mahal were being sent to Bijapur off and on, in whatever little quantity. But that was only a maneuvre wrought by the skill of the office clerks to avoid a situation of conflict between father and son. Shivraya noticed the goings-on in the court and came thundering down at them. 'Not a pie to be sent to Bijapur from here onwards, understand?' he snapped.

The matter reached Dadojipant's ears. He went to Jijau in a state of high anxiety. 'Playing fast and loose with sending remittances to Bengaluru is not good.'

'All right, we'll see.'

'Aausaheb, even otherwise, the atmosphere in the durbar there is not very healthy. There are a large number of people there who are envious of Shahaji Maharaj.'

Jijau told Dadoji in a calm voice, 'Try taking this up with Shivba too.'

Dadoji was caught in a cleft stick. The Amin of Shirval had sent a written complaint to Bengaluru regarding the complete disappearance of remittances from the Maaval region. Dadoji made contact with Shivba and brought the topic up in a soft voice, 'The money that goes to the senior Raja is not very much, but even that hasn't been sent. I have been getting reminders from him.'

Shivba responded to him in a crisp voice, 'Tell him in a language that he appreciates and be done with it.'

'What should I tell him?'

'Just this much, that he should not wait on the measly amount that is sent to him from this land of stones and pebbles. There are fertile lands on the banks of the Tungabhadra and the Ghataprabha that yield rich harvests. He should meet his expenditure using the money he raises there.'

The atmosphere in Lal Mahal had been turning more and more tense with each passing day. A number of people had begun to wonder if there was a rift in the royal household. Word got around that a very sharp and unpleasant letter had just arrived from the senior king at Bengaluru. The subject was so disconcerting that Dadaji Kond'dev had not even had the heart to read it; when Shivraya and Jijausaheb read it later, they too had been considerably rattled.

The three daughters-in-law, Saibai, Sagunabai and Soyrabai, were rather new to the household, but they too got a whiff of the conflict that had begun to brew between mother and son, and turned quite nervous. When bickerings and protests crop up among the seniors in a household, the antennae of the maids and servants really turn alive, it is said. Shivraya had begun to feel that everyone, from the doorkeeper of the palace to the police officer of Pune, had begun to throw questioning glances at him.

Shivba opened the letter that night and began reading it out to his mother:

> Shivba, my son, what does social observance demand? Dishonesty with one's master means being dishonest with the salt one has eaten. The revolt you have sparked off in the Maaval region against our Sultan Adilshah: it is nothing short of treason and bringing it to an immediate halt will be in the best interest of everybody. Please take serious note of this.

When she heard the contents of the letter, Jijausaheb was greatly disturbed. She sneaked a quiet look at her daughters-in-law from the corner of her eyes. Her heart was beating rapidly. She wondered why Shivba had pointlessly insisted on their presence. The words of the letter seemed to have given quite a scare to Saibai. She turned to her husband, swallowed with difficulty, and uttered, 'Is this really true? Are these words really coming from our father-in-law?'

Shivba, perhaps, did not like this strange doubt coming from his wife. Casting an angry look at her, he said to Jijausaheb, 'Look, please look carefully at this letter. The contents here have not been written by any clerk. They are so clearly in Abasaheb's own hand.'

'All right, then. Read on.'

'Listen, then.'

> Shivba, this mischief that you have got up to, in in the company of a bunch of ragged youngsters from all over the Maaval region, it is creating a deleterious impact on the Bijapuri durbar here. For the present, I just want to say that it will be in everybody's interest that you put an immediate stop to these imprudent activities. The most

convenient and sensible way out of this mess would be for you to acknowledge your offence with an open heart.

It will be best for you to admit before our master, Sultan Saheb, that this misdemeanour of yours was instigated by your immaturity. If the wound is not immediately dressed up and if it is allowed to fester, chances are strong that it will lead to extreme aggravation, to the extent that the entire matter may cause us grievous hurt. Therefore, you must now chant just these two terms day and night: Sultan Adilshah and his merciful heart—and thus free your clogged breath from the obstruction that your own mischief has so pointlessly created. It's only through this penitence that the welfare of not just you and me, but of everyone around us, will be served.

15

ON THE JINJI FRONT

1648

'You who live in the land of the Kanand river, what have you to do with Bijapur? What nonsensical complaints have you brought here?'

'Huzoor, please don't say this,' said Khandoji Khopade with some anxiety. 'If our Sultan Mohammadshah Adilsaheb is unwell, allow us to meet the Queen Mother, the Badi Begum Saheb!' He then looked at Ameen Miyan Raheem, the fort-keeper of the Shirval fort, who had come with him to meet Wazeer Mustafa Khan.

Mustafa Khan looked worried. Mohammad Adilshah had not been keeping well lately and had been staying away from the durbar, preferring to rest in his Saat Manzil palace. If there was any matter that required immediate attention, it was the senior Begum Saheba who would look into it. For the rest, it was Wazeer Mustafa Khan, sitting on the first floor as the prime minister, who would look at administrative matters.

On his way to the palace, Khandoji Khopde had deliberately taken Sardar Bajirao Ghorpade along with him. In his commanding voice, Bajirao let Mustafa Khan have it. 'Please don't forget, Khan Saheb,' he said, 'that this matter is not as simple as it appears on the surface.'

'But Bajirao Saab—'

'Look, we have come only to alert you that if you turn us away from your doorstep today, and if you burn your fingers tomorrow, nobody in Bijapur should lay the blame on us.'

Realising that he should not drag any calamity upon himself, Mustafa Khan asked the visitors to stay on for a while and went into his court.

It took a long while for Mustafa Khan to return, a little out of breath. Along with him came a Telugu Brahmin named Narsinghrao, who functioned as the private secretary of Mohammadshah.

The group climbed up to the third floor of the palace to find Mohammadshah relaxing in bed. He had propped up his neck with three pillows. There were a few lean men around him who looked like experienced physicians. The glittering chandeliers hanging from the high roof, pillars covered with tall mirrors, walls of Persian mirrors—the luxury was such that one could just stand there and keep staring unblinkingly. The imperious voice of a lady fell upon their ears: 'Yes, what have you come to say?'

The voice belonged to a sharp, slender lady who sat in the chamber. Through the diaphanous veil that hung over her face, she gave the impression of being an aggressive person.

It wasn't at all easy to lock eyes with the sharp, blue eyes of Badi Begum. Ignoring the two blabbering Maratha chieftains, she straightaway caught the fort-keeper virtually by his mane and said, 'Tell us, what is the status of the revenue that should come to us from the Shirval fort.'

'Forgive my impertinence, Begum Saheba, the situation there is so dire that not a single post has left our fort for the past four months.' Ameenullah Miyan was sweating as he made this admission.

'What a shameless person you are, Ameen Saheb!'

'But I swear by Allah, Begum Saheba, it's because of that Shiva that the revenue is not being deposited. Begum Saheba, that brat of Shahaji's, has begun to hold his own court there. Moves around in a palanquin, blows the trumpet and pretentiously accepts people's veneration. Even the sight of his vulgar ostentation is so painful to see.'

Badi Begum had Ameen Saheb give her a briefing on the situation in Maaval. She then looked towards Mohammadshah, who appeared to give a nod. Gravely letting out a long sigh, she said, 'The matter doesn't at all look encouraging. If that Shiva had merely attacked a fort and raided the ordnance or even looted the treasure, we would have considered him a foolish robber or rebel; but there is something very different cooking here. What name did you say, Ghorpade? On the Murumbdev hill?'

'Yes, Badi Begum Saheba, Shivaji has undertaken the construction of a big fort there.'

'Would that mean that he has abandoned our mountain forts like Rohida and Torana?'

'There's no chance of that, Badi Begum Saheba. That brat of a Bhosale, once he sticks to a piece of rock, he never lets go. He has appointed his own fort-keepers on those forts, and placed his own guards and observation posts on every one of those bastions.'

Badi Begum looked worried. She said to Mustafa Khan and to all the others present, 'See? There's no childishness in this, nor is there any lack of understanding. First establishing dominance on the fort, then constructing big ramparts there! Abbuji, this boy's movements and daring look to me of a different kind. Begin arrangements for the boy to be buried alive with all his hopes and ambitions, and that too immediately.'

•~∞~•

One day, Gomaji kaka said, 'Jijau, we have been getting jolts upon jolts from Bijapur these days. Just a few days back, our king's intimate friend Randullah Saheb left for his heavenly abode.'

That shocking news had frozen Jijausaheb. She couldn't prevent tears from welling up in her eyes. Making an effort at keeping her grief locked inside, she said, 'I haven't yet met a single Muslim who cared so much about my husband. I remember so clearly, when after the agreement at Mahuli, Shah Jahan had decided to extern Shahajiraje; he had placed his hand upon my head and told me that I could competently take charge of Pune and Supe. How many memories of this kind I carry!'

Jijausaheb distinctly remembered the many favours that Randullah Khan and his son Rustam-e-Zamaan had bestowed upon the Marathas. The father-son duo had won the mountain-sized Bengaluru fort and gifted it to Shahaji.

Turbulent days had arrived. Adilshahi on the one side and the Mughals on the other were looking for opportunities to swallow the infant swarajya whole. The passing away of Randullah Khan against this background was a painful and major loss.

The royal family had not yet recovered from this devastating news when another shock was delivered to them. 'Mohammadshah Saheb has signed a new directive.'

'What's that?'

'As per this directive, the entire army that has been under the command of Shahajiraje should immediately be merged with the Adilshahi army.'

This was a big blow. Since the battle of Bhatwadi, Shahaji had always kept this army of at least eight or nine thousand soldiers from Maaval with him. They were his armour, in a way. It was for the purpose of weakening him that this plot had been hatched in the palace. Shahaji was wild with anger at the hatchet that had been lifted against his private army.

Circumstances had begun worsening with every passing day. To bring pressure on Pune, the Bijapur government had dispatched an army under the captaincy of Khandoji Khopde and Baji Ghorpade Kapshikar towards Pune. Clear orders had been issued for the elimination of that Dadoji Kond'dev and that rebel of a brat who had destroyed the mountain forts.

.ೂಲ್ಲ.

Jijau came close and placed a placatory arm on Shivba's shoulder. 'My prince, in a land where the bravest of men compete every day with each other to bow before a foreign ruler, where slavery has settled itself in every pore of every individual like rust, when a fine young lad stands up in such a land with the flag of independence fluttering in his hands, feathers are bound to be ruffled, a tough test is bound to be taken.'

'Forgive me, Aausaheb, it looks like you haven't properly read the cruel words that Abasaheb has used in his letter.'

'Son, I can not only read the letters well, but understand them well too—those from here and those from there.'

'From there?'

'Look, when our people are working in a foreign state, the rulers there get all the correspondence examined secretly. It, therefore, becomes important for such letters to be written so as to throw dust into the eyes of those foreigners, to hoodwink them.'

'I see, Aausaheb.'

'Yes, Shivba. For the sake of keeping Mohammadshah pacified, our Raja has shown great skill in getting the main issue sidelined.'

'How's that?'

'Our opponents have been screaming that you have seized the Sahyadri forts. Our lordship has clarified to the Sultan that his son has been doing nothing except bringing all the old and dilapidated forts into proper repair. And even where he has taken some new construction activity in hand, he has made arrangements for applying to the government and getting these activities sanctioned when the time for it arrives.'

'Sometimes, I just can't fathom what is going on in my father's mind.'

'Shivba, an intelligent person like you should be able to realise where his father's passion lies—in independence or foreign rule.'

'Independence, of course.'

'Is he a votary of light or of darkness?'

'Aausaheb, I do have hazy memories of Junnar and Pemgadh.'

'Who, then, was the person who had handed the sword of the leadership of seven or eight thousand men to your thirteen-year-old elder brother? You would have been barely five then. You had woken up from sleep in a startled state and gone out running. You had run up to your Shambhu Dada, insisting that you would go to the battlefield with him.'

'Yes, but Aausaheb—'

'Try and remember, son. Emperor Shah Jahan had extended his hand of friendship over and over again, but your father had wanted only the elixir of independence and would have no other joy. I have witnessed with my own eyes, this great man standing on the hill of Dandarajpuri in a raging tempest, looking up at the dense clouds overhead and the stormy sea in front, praying for the health of the son of his loins, pleading with the water to give him shelter for a few days. You were burning with fever. I have seen, son, how your great father tied you to his stomach and took you to the Portuguese fort, standing at their door, seeking royal asylum.'

'Really, Aausaheb, the terrible Ram-Sita kind of exile that fell to your lot—'

'Prince, the Ramayana and the exile that have fallen to our lot are far worse than what had befallen before. This Ayodhya of ours named "Maharashtra" had been fighting to stay afloat in the whirlpool created by the enemy. To save it from sinking, we have suffered the heat of the sun and the assault of wind and rain all our lives. But for that one single mission, we have been enduring the punishment of a permanent separation from each other.'

A few drops of tears had incontinently flown down her cheeks. Softly mopping the moisture away with the end of her sari, she continued, 'I often see our Raja in my dreams. His impassioned words echo in my ears. "Jiu, I feel restless at leaving the hills and valleys of my native place and living in exile here in a foreign land. My state here is of a musk deer that has been taken away from his jungle beat and tied hungry in the corner of a marketplace."'

On the Jinji front, Shahajiraja's base was only at a short distance from Mustafa Khan's base. The two would often meet for consultations, but the meeting of hearts was not happening satisfactorily enough.

Shahaji had stretched out for an afternoon siesta when Kanhoji Jedhe entered his tent. Kanhoji cast an appraising eye at the Raja. His face looked unusually tense. Caught in some whirlpool of thought, Shahaji said, 'Kanhoba, I have been with the Bijapuri durbar for a number of years now. There are some pests in there that simply refuse to get off my back.'

'Nothing unusual about that, Raje. Wasn't it you who once said to me that snakes and their progeny are bound to wrap themselves round a sandalwood tree? In the same way, it is an inherent trait of insecure people to buzz irritatingly around a great man like gnats.'

'That's not how it is, Kanhoji. Sometimes when envy overpowers reason, it transforms into poison. Otherwise, tell me this: our Sultan Mohammadshah is known to be a cool-headed, thinking, intelligent person. But this same Sultan Saheb went into a frenzy of rage and got the hands of my agent chopped off in full view of the court. Such a mindless, despicable act has never been ordered before in a court that regards itself as politically mature.'

'Raje, to tell you the truth, you look extremely depressed today.'

'What else will I be? Strange things have been happening here these days.'

'How do you mean?'

'This Mohammadshah has just issued a strange decree. You know that my cavalry of Maavali men, seven or eight thousand of them, have come with me from my own native land. The decree says that these men have been merged into the Bijapuri army.'

'Indeed very strange,' said Kanhoji Jhede.

'I haven't set much store by this decree. But what I ask is, who has the courage to tear the mane away from a lion? Who has the guts to separate Shahaji's cavalry from him?'

The two then talked about this and that for a while. The Raja said in a despondent tone, 'For the last two days, I have been calling over my brother Mambaji for a talk, but despite being around here in this army camp, he seems to be unwilling to so much as see my face.'

'Could he be upset about something?'

'If he refuses to respond to three messages in quick succession, I suspect he has some mischief up his sleeve.'

'Why?'

'Among the Marathas, relatives may gather physically under one roof, but in heart and mind, they reside in the palace of the enemy. For how long can one endure and foster such relatives?'

◦◦◦

A meeting of the important sardars was in progress that afternoon in a temporary tent erected for Mustafa Khan on the warfront. As Shahaji and Kanhoji reached a little late for the meeting, the big-built Mustafa Khan looked at Shahaji and said, 'Raje,' he said, 'why do your eyes look so red. Had a late night? The party got very colourful, did it?'

'In the turmoil of war, Khan Saheb, we Marathas spend nights with a red-hot cannon as our pillow. Rakish, bohemian revelries like yours are not for us.'

'By party I meant the gathering of your caste-brethren and your co-religionists.'

'Why these barbs, Khan Saheb? If you have the courage, let's settle it face to face.'

Mustafa Khan's face turned red with anger. He snapped, 'Shahajiraje, do you think I am not aware of all the mischief that you have been up to even on this battlefield of Jinji? All of your Hindu kings like Shrirangraj of Penugonda, Trimalnayak of Madurai, Chamraj Wodiyar of Mysore and that Virbhadra of Badnur—will you swear that all of you have not been meeting surreptitiously in your camp?'

'Why surreptitiously, Khan Saheb? I have openly been friends with a number of them, and for many years too.' Shahajiraje's voice had risen quite a few decibels. 'But keep this in mind: I have never sold my honour and integrity for the sake of friendship.'

Not many people failed to register the import of the hot words exchanged between Shahajiraje and Mustafa Khan in the battle-camp that day. A number of the Muslim and Hindu chieftains present there were alarmed.

After that meeting, however, Mustafa Khan became extremely wary. He changed tack. He turned soft and found excuses for reaching out to Shahaji for consultation on every little thing. He pretended to have turned completely docile. But there was a great difference between his daytime masquerades and his wiles of the night.

Scheming Mustafa Khan had little by little brought Sardar Baji Ghorpade into his sphere of influence. He knew very well that the best way of mortally harming a valiant and victorious Maratha was to fire up one of his kinsmen who was sufficiently ambitious and envious.

But, as the days went rolling by, Mustafa Khan was not getting the right signals from Bijapur. One evening, however, a camel-post came and halted before his tent. As servants carried the sweating camels away to a side, the riders slid into the wazeer's tent. In the pitch darkness of the evening, Mustafa Khan had Baji Ghorpade called over instantly. 'Come on, Baji,' he kept saying in a joyous screech, 'our enemy is soon going to drown to his death.'

Mustafa Khan was uncovering the layers off his well-wrought scheme as he explained to Ghorpade, 'Look Baji, our Adilshah Saheb always taught us this lesson: for erecting and maintaining our Bijapuri Sultanate, we need everyone—horses and donkeys as well as the Marathas.'

'Absolutely, huzoor,' Bajirao cackled sycophantically. He couldn't work out whether Mustafa Khan's words were a compliment or an insult.

'It will be great fun if a fine Maratha like you puts the manacles on Shahaji's wrist.'

Baji Ghorpade could not conceal the joy of this important assignment that the Bijapuri administration had given to him. 'We are mavericks, huzoor,' he said. 'But shall I tell you something straight from my heart?'

'Yes, of course.'

'Huzoor, I have always felt that a kinsman should perish while the enemy survives. Put this Shahaji in chains at the earliest. Otherwise, he may quietly slip out and join Qutb Shah.'

All through his life, Sultan Mohammadshah had travelled down the streets of his royal city, seated on the brocaded cushions of a gold howdah, and graciously accepted the obeisance of the citizens lined up on both sides. But one day he had a serious stroke that left one side paralysed and rendered that royal personage half dead.

All that he could do now was to lie in bed and stare mournfully at the chandeliers. All kinds of remedies had been tried—lotions, oils, ointments, pastes, poultices, pills and powders—but none brought him any relief. It was in this state that he would hear complaints arriving every day of that rogue Shivaji from the Sahyadri valleys. It was precisely around this time that the huge Bijapuri army had laid siege to the renowned and formidable fort of Jinji in the south.

Quite a few days had passed since that event, too. Badi Begum let out three or four deep sighs and placed a letter in the Sultan's hand. The sick man groaned and said, 'What is it? Read it out, please.'

'It's an urgent letter from your father-in-law, who is right now the commander-in-chief of your army on the Jinji campaign. He has a request.'

'What about?'

'About putting in chains that Shahaji who is in Jinji too.'

The doctor administered the Sultan his medicine and left. The Begum moved towards her husband's bed and softly sat down in a corner. She informed him that she had sent word for chieftain Afzal Khan to come over.

Mohammadshah's health had been worsening by the day. As a need of the hour, childless Badi Begum had found it imperative that her co-wife's son, Prince Ali Adilshah, be made the heir to the Sultanate. Before the situation worsened further, she was determined to root out the irritants in the Bijapur administration and bring back order and discipline. The prince had to be mentored and seated on the throne.

Complaints against Shahaji Bhosale and his two sons had been creating mayhem in the court. In Maaval, Shivaji was refusing to cool down. In Bengaluru, the elder brother Sambhaji's behaviour was not heartening either. Mohammadshah got into a spasm of coughing. The Badi Begum served him a glass of water from the decanter.

When the massively built Afzal Khan arrived in the private hall, the Begum looked into his eyes and continued, 'When a horse turns recalcitrant, he is thrashed back into submission. If he still doesn't learn, he is simply shot dead, because one doesn't want the other horses in the stable to turn rebellious, too.'

'Ammijaan, I am sure you remember the episode of the famous fort near Bengaluru—' Afzal Khan deliberately brought up a sore issue.

'I don't remember the details, but, yes, you had plunged a dagger into that king's intestines, hadn't you?'

'Over and over again, Ammijaan. This episode had created a storm of protests, branding me as treacherous, but I hadn't cared. I had torn up that Kasturiranga's stomach and pulled out his intestines like one does to a wild deer. Around the same time, look what our big army did to the indestructible neighbouring fort in Bengaluru! And then, it was simply gifted away to that infidel Margattha named Shahaji Bhosale. As if it were not a fort, but a bouquet of flowers!'

'That is at the root of all our problems, son!' said Badi Begum, casting a cold stare at Mohammadshah lying in his bed.

Afzal Khan turned to the Sultan. 'Jahaan-panaah,' he growled. 'I just can't understand the kind of relationship you have with this Shahajiraja.'

'Why? What's your bother?'

'History is witness: as the loyal devotees of Allah, we have destroyed powerful Hindu rajas and their kingdoms of Malnad and Yelwad among others. We have razed to the ground so many Hindu temples and erected madarsas in their place. But then, this inconsequential Hindu sardar named Shahaji Bhosale, why has he become so precious that you refuse to bring him down from his high pedestal? What does it all mean?'

Mohammadshah smiled wryly and asked the Begum for another pillow. Propping it under his neck, he turned towards Afzal Khan and said, 'Afzal Khan, you may be a tiger in swordsmanship, but when it comes to using your head, you prove to be awfully immature. It was not I but my father Ibrahim Shah who had searched out Shahajiraja. After the battle of Bhatwadi—'

'Oh yes, the battle of Bhatwadi! That was where all our aches and pains began.' The very name of Bhatwadi had turned Afzal Khan red with anger. He was so stirred up that he forgot his lowly status and the exalted station of Mohammadshah. He screeched, 'But did that Shahaji have to prosper so much in our land?'

'You are blind. Merely three years after Bhatwadi, the manner in which he conducted raids on Tamil, Madurai and Malabar, dispatched trunks upon trunks full of jewels loaded on the backs of elephants and camels, the way he raised the prestige of Bijapur's treasury ... you should go through the accounts carefully.'

'Yes, Afzal Khan,' chimed in Badi Begum. 'We cannot shut our eyes to these facts.'

'This is absolutely true, son. If there is anyone who has brought far more wealth to Bijapur than any Muslim sardar, it is this non-Muslim Shahaji.' There was a tremor in the old Sultan's voice as he said this.

'Is this really true?' Afzal Khan asked the Badi Begum as he moved towards her. She nodded her head.

'Afzal, son, look carefully at the massive construction work in progress here: the huge structure of the Gol Gumbaz, the palaces and havelis and gardens constructed here within the Mohammadshah complex. After you have seen them, put your ears to the massive doors and listen carefully. They too will openly acknowledge their gratitude to Shahajiraja.'

Afzal Khan cooled down a bit after hearing out Mohammadshah. His voice was softer now as he said, 'What you say is true. But along with the gains that we have made from him, he too would have made some gains.' He gathered a kind of smile upon his face and said, 'My lord, even today, poets and travellers sing paeans to the system of justice and administration in our land. They also sing that in a few days from now,

Shahaji Margattha and his two renegade sons Sambha and Shiva will put the Sultan's clothes on auction.'

'Silence!!!' The word came booming out of the Sultan's mouth like a cannonball from a field gun. 'Afzal Khan—and you too, Begum Saheba, listen carefully. I shall never allow my illness to become a weakness for me.'

The otherwise extremely fair mien of the Sultan had turned scarlet red. His eyes were spitting sparks. The boom of his 'Silence!' was such that the Begum feared for a moment that the chandeliers would come crashing down.

It was after a long while that the Sultan's temper cooled. In the final analysis, the cowherd has to manage his barn, the gardener his lawns and the king his realm. Letting out a deep sigh, Mohammadshah said, 'Don't let all this worry you. Our country and its future hold far greater importance to me than people's favours.'

'Huzoor.'

'Afzal Khan, get ready to set off for Jinji. You shall definitely receive a royal edict from us on the battlefield. Thank you.'

The night had turned enemy for Shahajiraje. His flaming-red eyes seemed to have forgotten what sleep meant. It was after a long, long time that he sank under. But there was no relief there either. He saw strange visions on that pitch-dark island of sleep. Some thirty or forty black forms on horses were in hot pursuit of him. He suddenly felt someone grip him by his wrist and try to pull him out of his slumber. Somehow, he managed to open his eyes to see his younger brother Shareefji standing before him, looking exactly as he had on the Bhatwadi battlefield, bloody sword in hand. He was yelling 'Dada, Dada' in his ear, alerting him to some danger.

The next moment, Shahajiraje sat up erect in bed. He was bathed in sweat and in the grip of an unknown fear. It was now twenty-four years since Shareefji had passed away, and not once had he shown so much as a glimpse of himself in any dream. The king's heart began to race. He instantly dispatched his grooms and servitors to his colleagues, asking them to get ready. In a little while, his experienced friends Kanhoji Jedhe, Dadaji Lohkare and his son Ratnajipant arrived fully armed. They had brought their horses with them, as instructed.

Just then, Shahajiraje's devoted lieutenant Khandoji Patil ran inside and poured into the Raja's ear, 'Something is afoot. We've detected frenetic activity in Mustafa's base. Looks like some kind of treachery is cooking up there, Raja.' Shahaji's anxiety mounted. Meanwhile, his remaining associates also trooped in.

'Give us our orders, Raje,' said Kanhoji, impatiently.

'I suspect the attack on me may be launched this very night. Therefore, go back to your stables, put the saddles on your horses' backs and wait with your swords unsheathed.'

'What next, Raja?'

'If the attack on us does happen, I don't want our entire army to fall under the hammer. Therefore, let's keep our squads separate from each other. Disperse and set off, in the direction of the Sahyadris to the extent possible. The strength of the Adilshahi army would be much greater than ours, but the situation right now is so fraught with danger that we have to strive both to save our lives and our honour. We should not let the stigma of defeat attach itself to our names; we must not allow the enemy any smirk of victory.'

'So, what exactly do we do, Raje?' the assembled men asked.

'Split and move in different directions and save our men; there's not much else we can do now.' Shahaji quietly brought his horse out. He went up to a flat-topped mound and turned his gaze towards Mustafa Khan's base. There, a little distance away, he could see in the blaze of the flambeaus the Khan's men readying themselves for the raid. Since it was the full moon night of the month of Shravan, the outlines of men and animals were clearly visible. The faces of the chieftains standing around Mustafa Khan were visible too. Along with Ambar Khan, Khairiyat Khan and Dilavar Khan could also be seen Balaji Haibatrao, Maloji Pawar and Tukaji Bhosale. And right in front was Shahaji's first cousin, the person whom Shahaji had himself raised with such love and affection—Mambaji Bhosale. The stars in the sky had started turning dimmer.

Seeing Mambaji in that company gave Shahaji a cramp in the stomach.

Shahaji signalled to his men, who began dispersing quietly with their animals.

In the half-light of the setting moon, the three grand forts on the three sides looked like old men sitting with thick blankets wrapped round them. The horsemen had covered their faces with the end of their turbans. The animals were alert too. They didn't let their hooves tap as they slowly began slipping out of the camp premises. Shahaji once more alerted them, 'Make it quick, do you understand? Towards Sahyadri, to meet Shivba.'

Once the horses had trotted out of the base campground, the fifty-five-year-old Shahaji pressed his thighs into his horse. The wind was nippy. Lightly pressing the spurs, Shahaji whispered, 'All right, now, my wonderful beast, become the wind now. No halting from here on.' The animal limbered up and rapidly picked up pace. Skimming, it went over farms and rills and rivulets. There was no stopping now.

They would have been riding for an hour when Shahaji heard calls coming from behind him. He estimated that a couple of dozen horses were giving him chase, desperately trying to close the distance; Shahaji's horse was alert to the danger too. It did not allow its muscles to relax.

They left a big heath behind to encounter a forest river. The horses ran across the sand and the shallow water with great energy. The light was still quite inadequate, and Shahaji's mind was not altogether alert. The voices of the horsemen chasing him could now be heard, among whom the king recognised the yelling, screaming voice of Baji Ghorpade. Blood rushed into his head at the sound of that voice. In the semi-darkness, the horses were treading through the water and galloping out of the other bank. Shahaji's horse failed to make a good estimate of the land under its hooves. It came by a strangely cut tree trunk with a sharp and pointed trunk. In an effort to avoid it, the horse swung to one side and hit the broken end of a rock on the other side. The impact was so strong that the horse fell backwards and hit the pointed trunk. The sharp trunk went right through its thigh.

As the horse lay writhing in its last breath, Shahaji leapt off it on to the sand below but sprained his foot in the process. He got up somehow and made an effort at running, but by then, the chasing horsemen had closed in on him. As soon as he heard Baji Ghorpade's voice, Shahaji pulled his sword out and weapons clashed.

The pain in his leg was so acute that Shahaji found it impossible to gather his energy into his fighting arms. Besides, his was a single sword ranged against twenty-five of the enemy. The lapwing on the neighbouring mango tree let out harsh cries. Baji Ghorpade laughed throatily at his unexpected success. Despite being trapped, Shahaji lunged towards him. 'Treacherous Baji Ghorpadya,' he barked, 'the blot on the name of your family—even if you go and hide in hell, I shall chase you down there, pull you out by the tuft of hair on your head and hack you to pieces. You just cannot escape me!'

16

THE BATTLE OF PURANDAR

1649

The lofty hill of Murumbdev was being badgered by heavy July rains. The sky had simply ripped itself apart, disgorging massive quantities of water day in and day out and yet never emptying itself out. The wind on the upper fort had lost its head and gone dancing insanely all over the place. Its roars got so wild during the night that they would rise over the boom of the cascading rains and create the delusion of thousands of horses galloping in. The construction activities on the fort were far from over. The work on the ancient Rameshwar temple and the palace and courts next to it on the lower plateau was just about half done. But with the rains refusing to relent since the time Shivaji and Jijausaheb had arrived in the first week of June, all construction activities had been brought to a halt.

There was an unbroken two-and-fro of spies and messengers from the south. Jijau's family had moved its camp to the foot of Rajgadh. Work at the fort had not yet been put into proper order; it would continue for a few more years. That was the reason why a few palatial mansions had been built close to the base of the fort. The monsoons had brought with them roaring winds and torrential rains that would forever be dancing their violent duet. The continuous presence of ooze and sludge was an impediment for everyone, particularly women and children. Hence the construction of those residential buildings. A small market had sprung up, too. That patch of land had acquired the name Shivapattan.

Since work at Rajgadh had increased, Shivaji had decided to move his residence to those premises. In any case, with an unpredictable enemy around, living in Pune would have been risky.

The heart-rending piece of news had reached Rajgadh a few days back. It had rattled not only human beings but even the gods in their shrines. Shahajiraje had been arrested in Karnataka. The atmosphere had altogether changed in the fort since the arrival of that news. The eaves that emptied their waters from atop houses and havelis made the heart sadder. But even this appalling news had not caused any change on Jijau's stern face. Saibai and Soyrabai, however, would see in the overflowing eaves all the sorrow that lay concealed in Jijau's heart.

Not even ten days had passed since the arrival of the news of Shahaji's arrest when a conflagration was lit up on the banks of the river Neer. 'Shahajiraja's Shivba has won the Adilshahi fort on the plains of Shirval. The Bijapuri soldiers were humiliated by being stripped of their green tunics.' The news spread like wildfire in the jagirs of Supe and Pune. People were stunned at Shivaji's audacity. A number of them were worrying about the consequences: what new calamity would arrive from Bijapur? The grave shadow of Shahajiraja's arrest lay like a thick blanket upon the entire royal family.

Shivraya arrived, carrying the rain upon his back. Footmen had held velvet umbrellas over his head. Some other grooms had held over it screens of woven grass. But the intensity of the rains in Rajgadh was so extreme that the blast from the sides had wetted the young king considerably. A footman stepped up and peeled the velvet sleeveless jacket off his body.

Wiping his face with the white napkin that another footman offered, Shivba laughed wryly and said, 'Masaheb, the Bijapur people have sounded the kettledrum to mount an assault.'

'Fateh Khan, the disciple of Mustafa Khan. That dimwit was ready to come dancing in this rain like an over-excited bridegroom.'

'What happened then?' queried Saibai.

'The seniors there dissuaded him. They told him that if he went now into the torrential rains of the Sahyadris, he would simply be carried away like turd in the streams there and die. That was when, it seems, he reined in his horse.'

'But, Shivba, what about our own preparedness?' Jijau asked.

'We began our preparations quite long ago. At the blacksmith's anvil, in the foundries, in the weapon-polisher's verandah, the bellows have been pumping day and night. Work has been going on round the clock for making new swords and spears, daggers and axes, and re-tempering the old ones.'

The days were rolling past, but the rains were refusing to subside. The furrows on Jijau's brow were turning deeper. Whenever a spy came reporting from the south, she would ask the clerk on the desk, 'Any news from Bijapur?'

'The news is that the enemy's forces will reach Pandharpur or Rahimatpur even before Dussehra arrives.'

'We've been hearing that Adilshah's spies have been infiltrating our Maaval, carrying bags of messages!'

'Yes, that's true. The spies have been creeping into the havelis of the village chieftains.'

'With what message?'

'The message is clear and open. Ali Adilshah is holding everybody at the edge of his sword. "The army of our Sardar Fateh Khan is moving fast to wrest away the Kondhana fort. Shivaji's revolt shall be crushed. As officials of the Adilshahi Sultanate across so many years, continue to honour and value the relationship. Work with integrity and honesty. Prosperity for you lies in retaining loyalty as in the past. Else you shall all be razed to the ground."'

'Such incendiary language!' snapped Jijau angrily. 'These are not messages, they are threats.'

The young girls who had gone to their mothers' houses to celebrate the festivals of Gauri-Ganpati had returned to their husbands' homes. That was when a miracle began to unfold. Ali Adilshah's forces were espied moving across the Indapur-Pandharpur heaths in the direction of Pune. The perfidious nay-sayers of independence in every village began with their wayward chatter: 'It's two months now since the father was dumped into a prison. Sambhaji is there too. How much time will the Sultan Saheb need to round him up too?'

'They will put chains on this third one here in Maaval and take him there to give company to the other two in Bengaluru.'

'One doesn't become a king by merely twirling umbrellas and waving flags like in a Holi farce, does one?'

There was no shortage of all kinds of news, good and bad, reaching Rajgadh. Deceitful tongues had begun cooking up spicy conversation: 'The Bengaluru jagir of these poor unfortunates has been confiscated.'

'That's not all. As punishment for Shahajibaba's treason, he is going to be buried alive inside stone walls, they say.'

As the days rolled by the atmosphere in Shivapattan turned graver. After all, Shahajibaba was Aausaheb's husband. And the Hindvi Swaraj that had lately taken birth was where young Shivaji's heart and soul belonged. People of action did not cry out their sorrows for the world to see; they absorbed it all like the ever-suffering trees and mountains.

Earlier, too, the armies of the great Delhi emperors like Jahangir and Shah Jahan had tried to swallow the Adilshahi Sultanate whole, but none of them had succeeded in penetrating the four-tiered bastions around Bijapur. How much longer, therefore, would the revolt of these two sons of Shahajibaba last?

Jijau once tried to suggest the path of patience. 'Shivba,' she said, 'if you have to leap ten paces forward, would it be a bad idea to take two steps backwards?'

'Wouldn't stepping backwards mean swallowing the bitter potion of humiliation, Aausaheb?' Shivraya's face was contorted with worry. 'Do we pull down our pennant that has just about begun to flutter atop the Kondhana rampart? The Subhanmangal at Shirval that we have won with such effort, do we return it to the enemy? Do we tell our soldiers at the Torana fort, "All right, boys, abandon the fort and come back"?'

'But, Prince—'

'Aausaheb, just let your blessings always be with me; for the rest, we will create the opportunities sitting astride the neck of destiny.'

Even before the rains had subsided, frenetic activity began at the foot of Rajgadh and in the neighbouring valleys. Not caring for wind or storm, the Maavals of the gorges began gathering at the foot of the fort. They had all heard of the danger that was looming on their Swarajya. One day, the barrel-chested Godaji Jagtap, the one with the thick sideburns and dense moustache, said to Shivaji, 'Raje, that Bijapuri Fateh Khan and Musey Khan are moving rapidly towards the Kondhana fort.'

'Oh? How far have they arrived now?'

'Somewhere close to Jejuri.'

That very afternoon, Shivraya cracked open a coconut at his mother's feet and bowed before her to seek her blessings. Placing the auspicious curd-rice on his palm, Jijau said, 'Raje, don't get waylaid by any sentiments, to the extent that you shouldn't even bother about the kunku that your mother wears on her brow. Go, son, be victorious.'

The rains had given a timely break. The rice crops on the lower lands had grown up to knee-high. About two thousand five hundred of the Maavali youngsters were moving along with Shivraya. The spirited young boys were competing with each other to nudge their horses ahead. The enthusiasm among them was immense, their desire for sacrifice unbounded; not every one of them, however, had any earlier experience of warfare.

The crisis that had befallen their swarajya had buried itself deep into their king's head. The plan to confront experienced warriors like Fateh Khan and Musey Khan had begun to take clear shape in his head. When a big animal has to be hunted in a jungle, beaters hammer vessels and drums to lead it into a place where a trap has been laid for it. As Fateh Khan was advancing towards Kondhana, Shivaji was sure that he would move along the plateau. To be able to challenge him effectively, he took up residence in the Purandar fort on one side. He had already firmed up his plan for snaring the enemy at Shirval.

A number of people had reported that Fateh Khan considered Shivaji's revolt as nothing more than the conceit of a callow boy, merely a rush of blood in a young head. But even so, the experienced Fateh Khan had to test out Shivaji's actual strength. He had to take a taste of the waters in these parts. He, therefore, called over a Maratha sardar named Balaji Haibatrao, gave him a few squads of men, and sent him on an assignment.

The next day, the spies came to Fateh Khan in a state of great excitement. 'Thank you, Khan Saheb. Distribute sweets now.'

'Why?'

'Our army has captured the Shirval fort, and that too quite easily.'

'Easily? What does that mean?'

'As soon as Shivaji's men saw the size of our army from a distance, they ran away like frightened women.'

'Khan Saheb, the sweets?'

'Silence! Don't be so impatient. This could be a honey-trap.'

THE BATTLE OF PURANDAR

The Adilshahi soldiery had barely spent a couple of nights of merrymaking in the Shirval fort when on the third morning, at dawn, a few young men in their late twenties—like Bhimaji Wagh, Santaji Kate, Shivba Ingale and Godaji Jagtap—rode down the slope of the Purandar fort. They entered their horses into the river Neera just as the sky was turning pink. With the monsoons on its last leg, the river was still flowing strong, but man and horse braved it nevertheless, and just when the sky turned lighter, they were at the door of the Subhanmangal fort.

Leading the party was Sambhaji Kavji. Seeing a small crack in the door, he rammed his horse into it, and the latch holding the door snapped. Well-built, tall and supple as a young teak tree, Sambhaji dashed his horse inside. By the time Balaji Haibatrao collected the guts to obstruct his path, Sambhaji plunged his sword straight into his chest and ripped it open. It was with the rising sun as witness that the ochre flag of swarajya was hoisted on the fort. The enemy soldiers surrendered.

Fateh Khan's army was camping that afternoon in a big mango orchard on the meadows of Belsar right behind Purandar. Having finished off a rather long march that had begun early in the morning, the soldiers were stretching their limbs in the abundant shade available there. The water of the river Karha was plentiful for their needs. The men were nodding in the drowsiness that assails one after a sumptuous lunch. On the other side of the stream, they noticed dust being kicked up in the air. It was perhaps a whirlwind, they thought; but before they could arrive at any conclusion, four hundred horsemen emerged out of the cloud and descended upon them like a cloudburst with loud cries of Har har Mahadev. At the head of this charge was Baji Pasalkar, now in his sixties, but fit as any young man could be.

The attack was so sudden and so fierce that Fateh Khan's men couldn't find the chance to lay hands on their weapons. And all that Fateh Khan could do was run for his life and hide behind an embankment. Pandemonium reigned in the camp. The four or five thousand soldiers somehow gathered their wits and stood up to face the enemy. Although the Maratha contingent was very small in comparison, its young soldiers were charged with the fervour of teaching Fateh Khan a lesson.

The young soldier Sarja Mokashi was carrying the ochre banner of the contingent. Inflamed at the colour of the banner, the Adilshahi soldiers began attacking him from all directions, thus throwing him off his horse. Swords clashed and blood spurted from fresh wounds. Seeing what was happening, old Baji Palaskar turned his horse in that direction, shouting, 'Boys, our banner represents the dignity of our contingent.' He flashed his sword, raced his horse into the melee and managed to lift the injured Sarja on his own horse. The horse then turned, and Baji was off with Sarja and the banner in the direction of the Purandar fort. The rest of the contingent followed suit and began racing up the incline leading up to the fort.

Evening had set in. With so many of the Khan's men and animals groaning in agony at the wounds they had suffered, the camp was in a state of turmoil. Body and mind were burning at the humiliation they had been subjected to. Both Fateh Khan and Musey Khan were burning with the desire for revenge. All that they could see now was the highway leading to the Kondhana fort. Musey Khan tried to knock sense into Fateh Khan, 'Khan Saheb, don't pay attention to these small skirmishes. Let's first attack the Kondhana fort. After that, we shall lay Pune waste too.'

'But that Shiva is hiding like a thief in the Purandar fort!'

'First let's set fire to Kondhana and Pune—'

'Musey Khan Saheb, if you too start trembling at the knees like a fifteen-year-old, we will become a laughing stock in the eyes of the world. First Shiva, and then Kondhana!'

'But—'

'No, Khan Saheb, the manner in which this Shiva has been making a mockery of us, it is beyond all levels of tolerance.'

Just then, four horsemen burst out of the bushes in a broken-down state. Their green tunics were torn at a number of places and carried marks of dried blood. Two of them had rags bandaged round their wounds. It was clear that they were carrying the wounds of a battle they had fought a little while ago. Fateh Khan turned towards them in astonishment and asked, 'Where are you coming from?'

'From Shirval.'

'But where is our man Balaji Haibatrao who was posted there?'

'The Margatthyas have destroyed him. The Shirval fort has fallen. The panels of its doors have been tossed into the river Neera in front. Complete annihilation. Shiva's men have robbed our treasury too.'

Fateh Khan's anger had broken all bounds. He immediately called over the tent-men, the quarter-master people, even the royal cook, over to his tent. He told all his chieftains and also the Maratha sardars Mataji Ghatge and Phaltankar Nimbalkar in clear terms, 'You just have these couple of hours to finish your meals and rest. We are then moving forward. We shall not sleep until we have destroyed Shiva and his men.'

·~·

Shivraya was up on the ramparts of the Purandar fort, closely examining the roads that led up to it. He was looking with particular alertness at the foot of the fort and the gorge that lay alongside the river. Soon, his caution was rewarded when he noticed the movement of some Bijapuri squads towards the foot of the fort. He placed his hand on Godaji's shoulder and smiled. The enemy had been drawn into the battlefield of his choice.

·~·

In the manor at Shivapattan, everybody was awake—Jijausaheb, Saibai, Sagunabai, the administration staff—in short, the entire royal household. News had begun to arrive about the battle from Purandar. 'Aausaheb,' gloated the spies, 'the walls of Purandar would never have witnessed such a battle as this. That night, the army of Fateh Khan began its climb up the slope of the fort. The Raja waited for them to reach up to a pre-decided spot and then released upon them such an avalanche of stones and rocks that the Bijapuri men and horses were crushed under their weight. It was only after the enemy was half decimated on the ridge of the mountain that our soldiers opened the doors of the fort and swarmed out like angry bees. The patches outside the Purandar fort were taken over by utter mayhem. That Musey Khan, such a mountain of a man—our Godaji Jagtap got into combat with him.'

'Oh! What happened, then?'

'What could have happened? Our Godaji is instinctively hot-tempered and intrepid. He buried his spear deep into Musey Khan's chest. Musey Khan was also a tremendously courageous man, we must admit. He tried to pull the spear out, but only succeeded in breaking the shaft. At that, Godaji swung his sword upon the man with such force that he split him apart from shoulder to waist, like one chops off a stem from a tree. That broke the spirit of the Bijapuris. Ratna Shah, Minad Khan, Ghatge and the others took to their heels and scampered off in the direction of Bijapur. And like we drive off a fox that gets into our crops, our Bajikaka Pasalkar chased the fleeing Bijapuri men. In all that turmoil, Fateh Khan simply vanished into the darkness, only his Allah can know where.'

For the next hour or two, there was a relay of runners fetching news of victory from the Rajgadh fort. A proud and delighted Jijausaheb loaded the verandah of the Goddess's shrine with coconuts. The shrine itself was lit up with hundreds of lamps. Sweets were distributed with an open hand. The drummers began beating the leather of their drums with enthusiasm. Loud cries of Har har Mahadev could be heard right from the top of the fort up to the Chandratalav lake at the foot of the fort.

But the celebrations came to a grinding halt. The sudden silence that enveloped the air had an eeriness about it. The wind that now could be heard blowing through the fort sounded ominous. Jijau turned towards the meadows to see four Maratha soldiers riding in a hurry through the farmlands. Once they had come near enough, a look at their faces made Jijau's heart miss a beat. 'Yes, Subhaana,' she enquired, 'what's happened?'

'Aausaheb, such a wonderful victory at Purandar, but this tragedy puts a blight of sorrow on it all.'

'What is it? Speak it out, quick!'

'Our Baji Pasalkar went chasing the fleeing Bijapuris right up to the outskirts of Saswad; but there, the enemy suddenly turned upon him in strength. There was a fierce skirmish, but what can one say? Baji kaka, a man as big as a tree, he and his horse put up a strong fight but were brought down in the end.'

Jijausaheb was known for her steely control and composure, but she couldn't hold back her tears. The man who had taken Shivba on rambles and expeditions across the hills, valleys and the high-hanging cliffs of every one of the Twelve Maavals, Baji kaka was Shivba's father's age and was very dear to Shahaji. This misfortune, immediately on the heels of the victory at Purandar, was difficult to bear. Somehow managing to stem her tears, Jijau asked, 'Where is Shivraya?'

'Pasalkar's body has been placed in a hearse decked with flowers. The king has gone walking along with the hearse to kaka's village in the Mosey valley.'

Jijau got a palanquin readied and set off through the tracks made slushy by the recently departed monsoons. It was important for Jijau to offer her condolences to the Pasalkar family personally.

It was these eighteen classes of Maaval—including the herders, guardsmen, fishermen, maangs, mahaars, brahmins, peasants and the Marathas—that had made the first move towards establishing a swarajya, self-rule. It was to pay respect to his senior associate that Shivaji, the king of the poor, was walking over ditches and potholes towards the valley of Mosey. It was along the same track that Jijau, the mother figure of Maharashtra, was moving rapidly right behind her son. Both of them were sharply aware of the value of the blood and tears of the poor subjects of Maaval province.

·⌒⊙⌒·

The manner in which Shivraya had shredded the trained, tough Bijapuri army, ground a big sardar like Musey Khan to dust, brought upon Fateh Khan the humiliation of fleeing back to Bijapur in disarray—all of these heroic events had created a sense of awe for Shivaji in the region of the Twelve Maavals and the thirty-six river basins known as the Chhattis Ners. Everybody was singing praises for this nineteen-year-old son of Shahaji for the exemplary courage and statesmanship he had shown. The Bijapur durbar, in contrast, was badly rattled by the crushing defeat.

The defeated Fateh Khan had to suffer much opprobrium from all quarters, particularly from Badi Begum, who had absolutely lost all restraint in disgracing him. She had promulgated a *firman* that read, 'I shall be happy to welcome cats, dogs and even rats in my durbar, but the doors of my palace and my durbar have forever been closed for that chicken-hearted scoundrel called Fateh Khan. If this reprobate ever dares to show his face again, he shall be buried alive.'

At the same time, Ali Adilshah sent a secret missive to Rajgadh through one of his special spies. 'Shivaji should instantly stop destroying our territories and damaging Adilshahi forts. If this is not done, the gallant Bijapuri soldiers shall enter the Sahyadris and wreak havoc to seek vengeance. Shivaji, before wanting to fly into the sky, take a reality check first. Don't forget, your father Shahaji lies prisoner in our dungeons.'

Shivraya used the services of the same messenger to send a reply, which read, 'It doesn't suit the dignity of the great Sultan Ali Adilshah to fabricate towers of empty threats like these!'

Despite handing such a resounding defeat to the Adilshahi forces in the open battlefield of Purandar, not one person in Rajgadh had breathed a sigh of contentment. Not one among the royal family could forget that Shahajiraje was incarcerated in a Bijapur prison. Saibai would often remind Shivraya, 'Raje, my father-in-law is locked up there. The very thought makes it difficult for me to swallow my food.'

'Patience, Rani Saheb, patience. Just take good care of our Matoshri.'

Days and months were slipping away. Every day that dawned took an eternity to set. While the senior king was being subjected to great agony in an enemy prison, how could there be any joy in the life lived here?

An envoy came from Kanakdurg one day. He brought with him a painting done against a realistic background. The painting showed a herd of some sixty or seventy elephants walking down a jungle track. Every elephant-back was heaped with plundered goods. On both sides of the herd and also in front marched the Adilshahi demons with their hard, aggressive faces, swinging their weapons in their hands.

In that herd was one elephant on whose back Shahajiraja was placed as a prisoner of state. There was not the thinnest of mattress under his thighs nor any covering upon the head. The intention, clearly, was to make him suffer the intense heat of the sun so that he would fall ill. Shivraya, Jijau and Saibai stared at the picture goggle-eyed. It broke their heart to see the presentation of the torture. That evening, the dinner was the most tasteless food they had ever eaten.

The next day, two traders came to pay their respects to Shivraya. The news that they gave of that wild procession was extremely worrisome. A herd of eighty-nine elephants had set off a few months ago from far-away Kanakgiri, moving towards Bijapur stage by slow stage. With the elephants lumbering along slowly, the journey would take a few more months to end. The wealth on the elephants' backs was the treasure that the kings of Jinji had accumulated over two hundred years. All this plundered wealth was now being transported to Bijapur. The elephants were exhausted from carrying that kind of weight upon their backs.

Shivaji understood that the responsibility of parading his father in that disgraceful procession had been placed upon that worthless Afzal Khan. This information sent his heart plummeting into the stomach. Causing accidental deaths, burning down fertile lands and converting them into a barren desert, slaughtering women and children if the need arose, and turning happy households into funereal ones—these were the barbaric arts for which Afzal Khan had earned well-deserved notoriety.

Eight years had passed since Saibai had moved into her husband's house, but she had never before seen anyone in the Bhosale palace under such tension. The withheld breaths of the members of the royal family, their ever-increasing restlessness and worries were a cause for serious concern.

Jijausaheb said to Saibai that night, 'What do we do? I can see an entire mountain of worries collapsing on Shivba's head.'

'Aausaheb, what will happen to the dream of swarajya?'

'It's an impossible question to answer, girl. The boy has nothing but problems laid out before him. He gets a jolt with every breath he takes. If he sets off to save his father, it would mean abandoning the infant *swarajya* over the dung-heap. If he holds the banner of his mission close to his chest, he runs the risk of losing his progenitor forever.'

Memories of Shahajiraja would turn Shivraya's heart heavy. Jijau had often seen him mopping his eyes when in his private chamber. She placed her loving, warm hand upon his shoulder and said, 'What's this, Shivraya? How can the ocean of courage and forbearance inside you develop a breach?'

'What can I do, Aausaheb? Ours is, after all, the artless heart of a Maratha. Humans are a far cry; we stay awake all night even when an animal in our barn falls ill. Here, with my own father rotting in the enemy's prison, how can I ever get a peaceful night's rest?'

'That's true, Shivba.'

Immediately after Purandar came this other good news from Karnataka: Sambhajiraja had defeated Faryad Khan's army at Bengaluru. He had defended his jagir with the heart of a fearless warrior. This news provided some joy to the royal family. But all things considered, the privations being suffered by Shahajiraja, his incarceration, as also the worry of a potential assault from Bijapur were enough to keep them restless. The snakes in the grass, however, were having a great time; in fact, their strength had begun to wax.

That morning, the women of the area were doing their washing on the bank of the stream flowing next to Shivapattan. Enthusiastic Maalvanis had lit up felicitation lamps and burst firecrackers both at Rajgadh on top and Shivapattan below to celebrate Shambhuraja's victory at Bengaluru. The washerwomen of the palace had arrived at the bank with their load of clothes. A woman who was a relative of Jijau asked in a sour, loud voice, 'Last evening, our Bhosale people were bursting crackers about something. Know why they were celebrating?'

'What about?'

'Our elder prince Sambhajiraja destroyed Adilshah's soldiers there in Bengaluru. He won a victory—'

But mean-spirited minds had no appreciation for such information. On the contrary, their tongues found more pleasure in spreading poison. 'Shahajiraja's days of grandeur are over now.'

'He has been dumped into the darkness of a dungeon. There's no chance of Shahajibaba seeing the light of the outside world during his lifetime. The Bhosale lineage has been stamped out now.'

The Maavalis had foregone the pleasures of their household and come out to hold aloft the banner of swarajya; it was important to keep their morale high. Jijau looked extremely grave. Shivraya was aware of how much she loved her husband. He had knowledge of all the storms and calamities they had faced together. He had now begun to feel that he himself was responsible for the adversities that had struck his father.

As the days of the senior king's incarceration stretched on, the discord between Shivraya and the Adilshahi officials intensified. There seemed to be no resolution. At Bijapur, Mustafa Khan, Badi Begum and Ali Adilshah himself had decided to teach Shivaji a lesson.

It was not as if there had been no dialogue between the two sides. The agents of both sides were constantly on the move, but the dispute just refused to get settled. The Bijapuris first demanded custody of the Kondhana fort near Pune and the Kandarpi fort in Karnataka; the problem would be resolved only after that, they declared. On the other hand, indications also arrived that these two forts alone would not satisfy them. Deeply upset at their stance, Shivraya had arrived at the opinion that he would rather give his life than hand over any fort to anybody at all.

But as the days rolled by and Shahaji continued to suffer in prison, Jijausaheb's distress increased. She was finding it difficult to keep up a brave front. She had stopped eating adequately and begun losing her vigour. The women in her service were shocked at her state.

One day, when Shivraya returned from court to his private chamber, he saw Saibai there, looking bedraggled like a rain-soaked vine. 'Why do you look so distraught, Rani Saheb?' he asked worriedly.

'Raje, Aausaheb has not eaten a morsel for the past four days.'

'What are you saying, Rani Saheb?'

'How can half a cup of milk last her for an entire day?'

'Look, Sai, calamities will come. Assaults will happen. What can a person do except face up to them?'

'What are you saying, Raje?'

'Well, to be absolutely honest, no. No, Sai, there can be no compromise, whatever happens. I cannot give away big forts like Kondhana and Kandarpi.'

'Forgive me, Raje, but does Aausaheb's life have any value?'

'How do you forget one thing, Sai?'

'What?'

'When I was barely ten years of age, on the banks of the Tungabhadra, on way to Maaval, what lesson had our Abasaheb taught us? He had asked us to learn a lesson from the Muslim emperors, from the Adilshahs, that they would part with their knee-joints, even the pupils in their eyes, but never part with their forts.'

'Be that as it may, Raje. What do desperate women like me do when God has thrown such a challenge at them? ... But Raje, please do find the time to meet Matoshri.'

Saibai's words hit him hard. He said in a grave voice, 'Well, all right, let's go meet her right now.'

When the Shivaji reached his mother's doorstep, what he saw inside made his stomach churn. The state to which worry and starvation had reduced her was more than the king could bear to see. There were black bags under her shining eyes. Her wide brow was marked deep with worry lines. His mother had countered so many calamities and disasters, but never had she been reduced to this level of emaciation. He leapt forward and went on his knees by her bedside. He held her wrinkled hands in his. As always, Jijausaheb caressed her son's head lovingly. Deeply stirred, Shivaji placed his hands upon her forehead and asked, 'Aausaheb, where have I erred?'

'No, prince, nobody is at fault. Even before you ask me, let me tell you that I am not upset with anybody. On the contrary, I can only instruct you to stay on your mission. Don't make any compromise.'

'What are you saying, Matoshri? Isn't Destiny putting us to a severe test?'

'No, Shivba, it's nothing like that. I have no complaints at all. Similarly, you have no reason to feel guilty either. But—'

'But what, Aausaheb?'

'I remember again and again the dark night at the foot of the Devgiri fort. Storms arrive in one's life, whirlwinds of calamities swirl around us, but that was a night when a mountain of catastrophe had crashed upon our heads. I don't think any woman would have confronted such a disaster as that. Every piece of string that existed in my parents' house had been snapped brutally. It was as if the winds had shredded the sails of our poor boat. A wicked lightning descended upon my tree-like father under whose shade we had flourished. My young brothers were slaughtered, and their flesh and blood sprinkled all over the place. I had been reduced to a state when I didn't even know which way to run! On the other side was the two-month foetus in my womb! Where could I go? I was merely a woman, after all! All my fortitude, my breath, nay, even my flesh and blood had begun to melt and disappear. I was very close to wanting to end my life at that point. It was at the last moment that loving hands rested on my back. I recognised that touch. They were the hands of my three brothers, giving me courage. They were telling me not to jump into this black abyss of destiny. Hold on to the staff of life. Dam this river of sorrow and show the courage to nurture the child in your womb. I trembled from head to foot. It was that touch that helped me stay on with you in my womb. It was much later that I realised that it was the kunku on my brow, my husband, that had tapped me on my back. His touch had given me courage by taking the form of my slain brothers.'

'Wah, Aausaheb, you have given an altogether new identity to the Man of Destiny who is my father. I feel blessed.'

'Shivba, all I can say is that Shahajiraje is not merely Jijau's husband, but a part of God that has come our way. Every bit of me is aware of his virtues and his sacrifice. In the Ramayana, Rama and Sita did live in exile for fourteen years, but they stayed together. But in my case, I was compelled to looking after the sinking Ayodhya of Maaval, and suffer the exile of staying away from my husband for a lifetime. I have endured all of that. I am proud of the fact that not even goddesses would have been blessed with the kind of husband I have.'

'Aausaheb, please stop worrying. Your words have given me the elixir of life. But please do me this favour: please have your food.'

'But, Raje?'

'At this moment, all I can say is this: the force of the merits earned by my parents is so strong that there is no scope left for anxieties. Profit, loss, fines, penalties, all that we shall see later. But the kunku on my mother's brow shall not lose its lustre.'

Shivraya's tortured thoughts had finally defeated his courage. His father had to be saved, whatever the cost. From here on, he stopped caring for a handful of forts.

The prayer got delayed that evening. The priest, his deputies and the servants were waiting for Saibai to arrive. Saibai had, after hearing the conversation between mother and son, come to know how the gods had again and again put the royal family to the severest test.

She sent a message to the temple that she herself would preside over the puja. Accordingly, she went to the shrine and finished with all the rituals.

She emerged from the shrine after a long while, feeling like a fresh breeze of consciousness was blowing through her. As if she had been given a divine blessing.

The decision had been taken; the horses would set off at dawn for Bijapur, carrying the banner of truce. The keys of both the forts under the custody of the Bhosales would reach Adilshah's durbar in the next two or three days.

Shivajiraje was surprised to see Saibai walking hurriedly towards the bedroom. The smile on her face was more radiant than the hibiscus flowers she was carrying on her tray.

Saibai smiled mischievously and asked her husband, 'Tell me, Raje, is this Adilshah the only powerful person in this whole wide world?'

'Meaning?'

'Your lordship just needs to search out someone more powerful than him. There is bound to be an entity somewhere in the world that can throw a scare into Adilshah.'

'Like who?'

'Raje, could we not make the armies of Delhi go and stand on the Bijapur border?'

Jijausaheb and Shivaji were dumbfounded. They exchanged enquiring looks. They were sure that they had arrived upon a singular political weapon. Saibai had so casually offered a remedy that was beyond the reach of even the greatest political experts. Shivaji laughed and said, 'Aausaheb, your daughter-in-law has turned out to be a brilliant person.'

'Her idea is so perfect, I have no words for it,' Jijausaheb responded enthusiastically. 'Really, Balraje, even if street talk of something cooking between us and Delhi reaches the ears of the Bijapuris, they will turn jittery. At the very least, nobody in Bijapur will be so foolhardy as to harm your father.'

Shivraya's eyes lit up. The worry lines on his face melted away. He walked away immediately, in the direction of his court.

Raghunath Pandit departed from the fort that very night with all his paraphernalia. He had been provided with the swiftest and the longest running horses. They were instructed to reach Gujarat post-haste. Shah Jahan's son Murad Baksh was posted as the governor of that province, and a letter had to be delivered to him for forwarding to the emperor. Another contingent was due to leave the next afternoon for Agra with an exact copy of the letter.

The remedy recommended by Saibai held immense potency. Shivraya was convinced that it had the power to destroy from its very root the dangerous disease that had been afflicting swarajya. Shivraya had also hinted that if the need arose, he would even be willing to accept the mansabdari of the Mughals against the Adilshah. Emperor Shah Jahan, on his part, had started putting the fear of God in the hearts of the rulers in Bijapur. He had gone to the extent of sending letters directly to Shahajiraja in prison, expressing great concern about his health and happiness.

The Delhi emperor's two-pronged strategy had turned out to be a masterstroke. On the one hand, using Shivraya as an excuse, he had brought pressure to bear on Adilshah; on the other, he had shrewdly managed to keep the Marathas and the Bijapuris entangled in the south.

Around that period, a sealed letter from Emperor Shah Jahan was delivered at Saat Manzil. The Badi Begum read it instantly along with the the prime minister to understand the subject matter. Then, she carried the missive to the hall where Mohammadshah lay ailing, and read it out to him:

> Observing basic courtesies, we had handed Shahajiraja to Bijapur as a friend. We hear that some differences have arisen between the two of you. The news that has reached here is that you have put him behind bars as a prisoner of state. We have no interest in your mutual quarrels, but taking good care of his health and ensuring his physical well-being are your legal responsibilities. We pray to Allah-tala every day for the good health of both our friends in the Deccan.

Badi Begum had been seriously upset with this interference from Delhi. Before presenting the letter to her husband, she had read those words a number of times, and the heat emanating from them had made her distinctly restless. But right now, her entire attention was focused on gauging Mohammadshah's reaction. After a bout of violent coughing, Mohammadshah said, 'Let's alert our associates and sardars: the atmosphere is not conducive. They must keep their cool. That Shahajiraja possesses a big fortune and has great influence.'

Starting from Agra-Delhi to Rajgadh to Bijapur to again Gujarat, where Prince Murad Baksh was governor, things had begun moving rapidly. The horses of political maneuvering had been galloping unrestrained, often leaving the Adilshahi schemers bloody-nosed. With everything slipping out of their hands, all their efforts were concentrated on saving whatever cutlery they could.

Under the circumstances, they were left with no option but to compromise.

In return for Shahajiraje's release, Adilshah demanded the Kandarpi fort near Bengaluru from Shahajiraje and the Kondhana fort near Pune from Shivraya.

Shahajiraje and his son had to part with two forts that were very dear to them. When he actually handed over the charge of Kondhana, Shivraya was deeply grieved. But for the sake of his father, the aging Shahajiraja, he was left with no other option but to compromise.

17

ASSAULT ON JAWALI

1655

Jijausaheb had turned quite emotional lately. She had given strict instructions to Shivraya, 'You will never step out of the fort without informing me.'

'How will it do for a brave person like you to show weakness, Masaheb?'

'Shivba, it worries me sick that you have turned so solitary these days. Nobody going in front of you, nobody coming behind you. And my elder one, my Shambhu, so pointlessly perishing there in the south.'

News had come of the passing away of Shivraya's elder brother Sambhaji and snatched away all joy and contentment from the fort. Down in the south, Appa Khan, the fort-keeper of Kanakgiri, had revolted, and Shahajiraje had dispatched his son Sambhaji to crush the revolt on behalf of the Adilshahi durbar. When a siege was laid round the fort by Sambhaji's contingent, a cannon ball had flown out of the fort's bastion one day and taken the prince's life away.

The news had shattered Jijausaheb. For one, the boy had begun going out with his father from an early age to learn the lessons of managing campaigns. She had always carried inside her the regret of not having spent enough time with him. And now, for him to depart from the world when barely twenty-three was a devastating blow.

Saibai would often tell her, 'Please, Aausaheb, get a hold on yourself. How much more can you grieve?'

'How can I forget my dazzling young prince, Sai? He was just thirteen when he worsted the enemy in the battle for the Junnar fort. My adolescent boy had fought a tenacious battle with Shaista Khan of Delhi and prevented him from entering Sangamner for many months.'

People said that he had died only because of an accident. But here was a person who had only lately fought for the defence of Bengaluru, and forced Farhad Khan of Bijapur to withdraw to Bijapur in shame and humiliation. How, then, could a person as brave and as perpetually alert as him have walked into an accident?

It was some time later that the truth of this mysterious occurrence came to light. A big scholar from Shahajiraja's court named Jairam Pinde had come visiting Pune from Karnataka, and he had brought some hard facts with him. 'When the prince marched to Kanakgiri, he had Afzal Khan's army accompanying him. Afzal Khan was the person who had compelled Shambhuraja to lay fuses of mines around the Kanakgiri walls. But contrary to what had been arranged earlier, Afzal Khan's forces did not supply him with the help that had been promised.'

'So, it was a deliberate plot, then?'

'Something even worse has reached my ears. That devious devil of a man Afzal Khan had sent a secret message to that rascal Appa Khan, promising to have his prey stand at the mouth of his fort, so that he could then consume him at will.'

When these facts came to light, Jijausaheb's heart wept tears of blood. Shivraya too was grief-stricken. Memories of his brother came flooding. He remembered his last meeting with Sambhaji that wet morning on the banks of the Tungabhadra. How he doted on his younger brother! While bidding him goodbye, he had said, 'Shivba, if you get so much as a whiff of any problem, just send me word. Then watch how I bring the entire Deccan along with me to the Sahyadri to help you.'

⁘

A person with whom one had decided to travel a few miles shoulder to shoulder, if that person were to turn his back on his benefactor, deliberately sow thorns along the path, what could this deed be called?

A poor widow from the Musey valley had come and been sitting in a corner of the court for quite some time. When she had come this way eight days earlier, Shivajiraje had handed over this subject to Netaji Palkar. The matter was delicate. The help extended to a poor woman during the episode of the Patil of Ranjha had gained great exposure and brought great praise and appreciation for the king. Now that the head accountant of a town had forgotten his status and sexually exploited a poor widow, outraged her modesty and disappeared, Shivajiraje was deeply agitated. 'Who is this corrupt official that has brought such shame to the government he serves?' he fumed at Netaji.

'Rango Trimal is the name of that rascal.'

'If our servitors, ministers and state servants indulge in such despicable acts, what ideals will our subjects follow?'

'Raja, we have been desperately trying to apprehend him, but unfortunately,' said Netaji, with his head bowed, 'we have not been able to catch him.'

'But where could he have gone? Disappeared into the earth or flown up into the sky?'

'Forgive me, Raje, that bastard has escaped to the Jawali principality. Our horsemen had gone there to arrest him, but they had to return empty-handed.'

'Why?'

'That Morey of Jawali absolutely refuses to hand the man over to our charge.'

There was considerable ruckus at the court today. One complaint followed another with regard to one Chandrarao alias Yashvantrao Morey of Jawali; and like a man who had seen the world, he had stopped caring a fig for anyone at all.

The dissension with Morey had been making Shivaji quite restless. Talking disparagingly about Shivraya with a number of *deshmukhs* and *deshpandes* had become a habit with him.

When Jijausaheb entered the court, everyone bowed to offer obeisance. Shivaji growled, 'You see, Masaheb? This is that Yashvant. Now he talks of standing up against our swarajya.'

'Who? Morey?'

'Yes, that's the man. It was just six or seven years back that he had come holding the apron strings of Maanakubai, and stood in this court like a timid cow. How could he have sprouted horns now like a belligerent bull?'

'Send him a timely admonition, Raje.'

'Admonition? We have already sent him warnings, Aausaheb. But look at his language, so spiteful, so uncaring! The response he gave to Netaji's letter just the other day … why don't you tell Aausaheb about it, Netaji?'

'This Yashvantrao Morey just lets his tongue go wild and spews out whatever acid he wants to,' said Netaji. 'He said: "Go tell that son of Shahaji Bhosale, this is the eighth generation of Moreys ruling on the throne of Jawali. Our lineage connects directly to Chandragupta Maurya."'

'Yashvantrao seems to have forgotten those days,' said Jijausaheb, her face tense with anger, 'when he would wear his soles out at our doorstep in Rajgadh in the company of Maanakubai? He would actually cry. We sent our soldiers to ensure that his adoption ceremony happened without hindrance. It was under our protection that he ascended the throne of Jawali. And now, he turns back on us like a snake and hisses? This is the height of ingratitude.'

'But, Masaheb, have you any idea how far this tyrannical Morey has spread his tentacles?'

'Tell me.'

'This Morey has been taking his gripes straight up to Bijapur, inciting the sultan to mount attacks and snatch back the forts that Shivaji has taken away. He's been provoking him to raid the swarajya lands.'

'Is this news of the transfer of the governor of Wai true?'

'Yes. That Afzal Khan—the Bijapur administration has sent him from Wai to Kanakgiri in the south,' said Shivraya. 'Actually, this Yashvantrao was not such a bad man, but Afzal Khan's company has given him airs, and he has begun to fancy himself quite a bit.'

'Now that this bother of Afzal Khan has gone southwards, you should play your hand, Raje.'

'What hand?'

'Permanently curing this Jawali headache?' suggested Saibai softly.

'See, Aausaheb?' laughed Kanhoji Jedhe. 'How sharp your daughter-in-law is! How well she understands when to spice a dish on the stove!'

This brought on a burst of laughter from everyone around.

The villagers of Palsul, from the glen of Rohida, had arrived with a complaint. Ramaji Wadkar was an ordinary farmer in the village of Chikhali near Panchgani. Differences had arisen between him and Yashvantrao some time ago. Just to settle accounts, Yashvantrao entered Chikhali with a bunch of swordsmen. There was a carnival of sorts going on in the village in the name of the village deity, and the place was bustling with visitors, wrestlers and devotees of the deity. But without caring for the assemblage, Yashvantrao's men came down upon Ramaji Wadkar and hacked him to pieces with swords and axes in the presence of the entire village. He was slaughtered like a stolen goat in the middle of the street.

But Yashvantrao's passion for revenge had still not been slaked. One day, the terrified relatives of Wadkar reached along with other villagers to the court at Rajgadh. 'Raja, give us justice, please,' they wailed in unison. 'Either arrange for us to live in peace or slaughter us all.'

'What's the matter?' ask Shivaji.

'That Morey first killed Ramaji in his own village, and now he is making life difficult for his one and only child.'

'What has happened?'

'That poor boy of Ramaji's had taken fright and shifted to faraway Palsuli in the Rohida glen.'

'So, then?'

'These demons of Jawali tracked him down. Yashwantrao's goons dragged him out and hacked him to pieces. Where will his children go and live now?'

'But, then, the Rohida valley does not even fall within Moreys' territory!'

'That's our complaint, Raja. His tyranny recognises no limit now. Who do we poor subjects depend on now except our king?'

The wailing of the villagers was a heart-rending sight to see. It disturbed Shivraya greatly. When Musey Khan and Fateh Khan had come marching to Purandar, Shivba had felt nothing at all in giving them battle. But now, this was happening in the neighbourhood of his kingdom—a situation was arising in which swords would clash in the lap of the Sahyadris; it was an extremely painful development. Shivba said in a grave voice, 'Masaheb, mounting an attack directly on Jawali is a difficult adventure.'

'It's the gifts that nature has given him and the support he gets from the narrow passes and gorges of the Sahyadris that have given him this arrogance, is that right, Raje?'

'Oh yes, he is rich, all right. But far more potent than that is his twelve-thousand-strong cavalry. He also has an extremely intelligent brother in Hanumantrao and two fearless sons.'

'It's good you brought up Hanumantrao, Raje,' said Jijausaheb. 'Why don't you contact him through one of the aggrieved men?'

'Hanumantrao lives separately on the other side of Jawali, in Chaturbet. But he is the Deewaan, the prime minister, of Jawali. Brilliant man, great thinker. Which is why people call him "Vichari", the thinker.'

'Can we talk him into joining our mission for swarajya?'

Shivraya looked at his mother and smiled wryly. 'Yashvantrao, Hanumantrao and Prataprao are very close to each other. Deewaan Hanumantrao is a blind admirer of Yashvantrao; therefore, trying to create a divide between the brothers won't be a prudent strategy.'

'Well, all right, see how you want to handle it. But they say, don't they, that having a jealous neighbour is dangerous?'

'A tyrannical neighbour like Morey is a landmine,' said administrator Raghunath Sabnis. 'Nobody knows when it will blow up and cause all-round destruction.'

The time was just right for an assault on Jawali. Mohammad Adilshah had been very unwell in Bijapur for the past few months, keeping the Badi Begum and all the others deeply involved in caring for him. If an attack were mounted on Jawali at this time, there would be no help forthcoming for the Moreys.

It was afternoon time and Chandrarao alias Yashvantrao Morey sat in his court leaning against a bolster. He was twirling his substantial moustache that grew on his pale-yellow face. From the window of the palace could be seen the sharp slope of the Nisani ghat far away. A few farmers and soldiers sat on the bench in front.

As he lay relaxing with some haughty thoughts of his own, he heard the name 'Shivaji' and his eyes turned red. The prime minister of Jawali, Hanumantrao, and his middle brother Pratoprao stood in front, holding a letter with shivering hands. The subject was incendiary, but not reading it out was not an option either. Hanumantrao looked at his brother and said in a squeaky voice, 'Dadaraje, actually Shivaji had no business writing such a bitter letter.'

'Arey, Shivaji who? That Bhosale?'

'Yes.'

'What has he set out to teach me? And Hanumant, why are you standing there shivering? Read what is written and be done with it.'

'He ... he ... writes—Yashvantrao, during the time of problems with the adoption episode, you had come grovelling to our court. As per the discussions that had taken place then, you may go ahead and enjoy your province to the full. But you had better stay loyal in our service as per your commitment. The complaints that have been pouring in against you and your mounting impertinence shall not be tolerated any further.'

'Arey wah, arey wah, is this how Shiva writes?' Yashvantrao said, making fun of the letter and receiving an appreciative giggle from those around him. 'Go on, read the rest of it.'

'Stay dutiful. If you continue with your insolent behaviour, we shall destroy your Jawali, put you in chains, and drag you all the distance here.'

Yashvantrao burst into a roar of laughter at hearing the last line. Like the rumbling of rainclouds, the sycophants surrounding him echoed his laughter. Signalling them to silence, he told Hanumantrao, 'All right, inform that Shivaji immediately—you have begun calling yourself a king these days. But what are you the king of? Of a durbar, or of an entertainment show? Stop this meaningless noise of yours. How can you ever dare to call yourself a king? With the blessings of God Mahabaleshwar, it is we Moreys who are at the pinnacle here in all of Konkan region.'

The exchange of letters gathered momentum. A new letter arrived from Shivaji four days later that read, 'If you continue with your audacity, we shall come personally at the head of our army, arrest you and annihilate you.' To which Yashvantrao responded with a challenge, 'If you want to come to us, why wait for an auspicious moment? Why come tomorrow?

Come today. Come, experience for yourself how we rip the skin off those who have the temerity to enter our Jawali jungles. Dare, if you can, to enter these jungles. Not one single person shall return alive.'

Rajgadh had suddenly begun buzzing with activity. Shivraya's army was as big as the Moreys'. Once the flame of enmity had been lit, there was no saying in which direction the fire would spread. Wisdom did not necessarily lie in destroying the enemy's town because it had burnt down yours. It would be important to think through all the strategies with discretion—cajolement, bribe, punishment, blackmail. A number of points were being placed before Shivraya, various scenarios were being discussed. During the discussion, Jijausaheb said, 'This Hanumantrao Morey has two daughters of marriageable age, they say, beautiful and intelligent.'

'Yes. The elder one is Jaishri and the younger is Rupmati.'

'*Ago bai*, the king has even the names of the girls pat!' Jijausaheb laughed , causing Saibai to blush.

'Masaheb, it is true that these girls are beautiful, sweet and courteous, but they are not Hanumantrao's daughters.'

'So, then whose?'

'Yashvantrao's. Since Hanumantrao had no children of his own, he adopted the two girls when they were infants. He now plans to get them married with pomp and show.'

'Think. You are twenty-two now. The two families could be tied in a bond of mutual benefit. The results may be fruitful.'

Shivaji had decided to bring the Jawali matter to a head as early as possible and under any circumstances. He had begun a detailed investigation into the province, its people, its facilities. Raghunath Ballal Sabnis and Sambhaji Kavji had made secret trips to the region. Shivaji's spies had picked up every grain of information they could find on Jawali, Mahabaleshwar and the Konkan belt sloping on the other side. If the occasion arose, a confrontation could ensue; accordingly, a rough battle-plan had been drawn out on paper. Detailed discussions were conducted on how assaults could be launched on Morey's territories like the Joharbet, Chaturbet and the Shivthar gorges near Mahabaleshwar and particularly in the Jawali gorge.

One afternoon, Sambhaji Kavji and Raghunath Ballal Sabnis entered Jawali with a marriage proposal from Rajgadh. They had for company twenty-five horsemen and a hundred young Maavali soldiers.

Right next to the Moreys' residential palace was the court palace where Hanumantrao would conduct the business of running the state. Very often, he would go over to his house in Chaturbet, located at the foothills on the other side. He had a big stable of horses there. More importantly, his two daughters, Jaishri and Rupmati, lived with him there. Yashvantrao lived in the palace with his mother and his old grandmother Manaku and his younger brother Prataprao.

It had been decided that the formality of meeting the prospective bride would happen later; meanwhile, the preliminary talks could be done now. Hanumantrao was very well aware of the extraordinary profile of Shahajiraja's son. He knew that the boy was extremely accomplished and handsome. But far more importantly, he knew that Yashvantrao had got his Jawali some five or six years back only on account of this young king. He had very clear memories of the event that Yashvantrao had so conveniently forgotten.

Sambhaji Kavji and Raghunath Ballal Sabnis had barely settled down in the court and begun their conversation when Jaishri walked in. She possessed a beauty that would have attracted anyone. When she saw the guests in the court, she got flustered. Hanumantrao introduced her to them, saying, 'This is our Jaishri,' and instructed her to bring jaggery-water for the guests. When she came in with the maids, who carried pieces of jaggery and water in beautifully engraved silver bowls, he told her, 'These guests have come from Rajgadh.'

'*Ayya*!' she exclaimed, 'from Shivajiraja?'

'Yes. They have brought a marriage proposal for you.'

She blushed deeply at these words, pulled the velvet curtains and disappeared behind them like a gust of soft wind.

Within minutes of the conversation warming up, Hanumantrao's face turned tense. His brother Yashvantrao occupied a place of great reverence for him. And here were these men from the Bhosales' court, who had begun to openly complain about him. Raghunath Ballal Sabnis was saying rather blatantly, 'Our Raja doesn't like your brother's conduct at all. When he was in need, he had come crawling like a ladybird and stood in front of our king.'

'What are you saying?'

'Simply the truth. Gratitude is something that has got washed out of the Moreys' blood. The attainment of power seems to have wiped out common courtesy. How can you join the enemy with such alacrity?'

'Don't shoot your mouth off. What evidence have you got?'

'Have you forgotten the Bijapuri sardar Baji Shyamraj who had marched in with an army of ten thousand men a few months ago?' said Raghunath Ballal Sabnis. 'Your brother Yashvantrao had offered him full support. The two of them had met and conspired in the jungle near the ghats, like a pair of owls, planning to finish off Shivaji through an act of betrayal—'

'Shivajiraja then raided the jungle at night and drove you off,' Sambhaji Kavji added. 'This is how you people turn traitors to your salt!'

'Silence, Kavji! Not another foul word against my elder brother!'

'Look, Hanumantrao, we give you this last opportunity for rectifying things. Present yourselves immediately in our king's court with all the documents that you have forcibly snatched from your poor subjects and your other forged documents.'

'Who has the time to present himself in the court of beggars like you?'

'In which case, get ready to die!' said Raghunath Ballal as he stood up in anger. Sambhaji quickly unsheathed his sword. The very thought of an outsider pulling out his sword in his own palace was intolerable to Hanumantrao. When he noticed Sambhaji sidling in towards the Moreys' court, he plucked out the sword that had been hanging from the wall. Hanumant Morey was an excellent swordsman. He clanked his weapon against Sambhaji's. Sambhaji himself was a magician with the blade. When their weapons began to clash, some of the Morey swordsmen on guard outside came rushing in.

A skirmish suddenly flared up. The twenty-five swordsmen who had accompanied Raghunath and Sambhaji joined in. The other Maavalis too got into the melee with sticks and spears. The commotion of the face-off reached the palace next door. The drums atop the ramparts began to beat, signalling a hostile engagement. The horses stabled barely a loud call away were untethered, and the Morey horsemen leapt on their backs.

When Sambhaji heard the sounds of hooves, he understood what was happening. When they realised that Moreys' men were soon going to descend upon them, they slipped out of the skirmish and dispersed along with the other Rajgadh horsemen. Very soon, they and the Maaval men had vanished into the jungles.

When the soldiers from Yashvantrao's palace arrived, they saw the dead bodies of two of the Bhosale horsemen and one of their soldiers. A little further up, they saw twelve of their own men lying dead, too. A number of their men were groaning in agony as they were grievously hurt. Yashvantrao stared in dismay at the bloodbath that had taken place on his premises. Then came into sight something that turned Jaishri and Roopmati into stone. Hanumantrao's head lay on the ground, severed from his body. That blow had obviously come from Sambhaji Kavji's sword. Jaishri trembled violently at the sight and fell into a swoon with a loud wail: 'Baba!!!'

After their raid on Hanumantrao's palace, Sambhaji Kavji and Raghunath disappeared from the spot like the wind. They took shelter in the dense bushes that lay on either side of the river Koyna that flowed small and narrow in those parts. They then rapidly climbed up the slope of the Nisani ghat and reached the ancient temple of Mahabaleshwar on top by nightfall.

When somebody informed them that the king was in the Purandar fort, Sambhaji barked, 'You must be mad!' The horses galloped back through jungles and bushes, through hills and dales in a straight line.

They were unsure where they would find the king—whether in Rajgadh or in the Purandar fort. After riding all through the night, when the contingent reached near Nasrapur, they were astounded at what they saw. There, next to a wide stream, Shivraya was standing in preparedness with his army. He had brought over three thousand Maavalis from Rajgadh and an equal number from the plateaus of Purandar and Karha, all of them straining at the leash to get into action. The enthusiasm of Kanhoji Jedhe was unfettered.

Even in the morning haze, Shivaji recognised the bull-like frame of Sambhaji approaching along with the spies. He hurried forward and asked, 'Yes, Sambhaji, what chances of getting all those confessional papers, those fraudulent land documents of their poor peasantry from Hanumantrao?'

'Raje, we pleaded with the man, but he refused to listen to us.'

'As the twists in a rope do not disappear even after burning, so do the arrogance and conceit of the Moreys refuse to part with them. So, then?'

'Hanumantrao pulled out his sword and stood in our way. In the skirmish that followed, he lost his life.'

Shivraya's face turned tense with worry. No arithmetic of life submitted itself to an easy solution. His dream of fulfilling his objective without bloodshed was broken. He froze where he stood and gave himself to contemplation like a yogi. After some time, he came to; his face shone with the light of some new resolution. Addressing all those present, he said, 'Come along, let's mount an immediate assault. Yashvantrao will soon gather an ocean of men under him. Let's punch a hole in him before he does so.'

The soldiers as well as the animals that had gathered in the town of Nasrapur had already tired themselves out considerably. They came upon the river Krishna near Ghom just before sunset. The animals were given their fodder. Bags of green gram were tied to the snouts of the horses. Man and animal recovered their breath and felt refreshed, and again resumed climbing the Mahabaleshwar mountain range. Shivaji was in a hurry. The Moreys had the strength of fifteen thousand men. The assault on them had to be made before their scattered men could be brought together.

On the third day, after taking a holy sighting of the Mahabaleshwar temple on the brow of the mountain at the crack of dawn, Shivraya began to climb down the Nisani ghat with his army of six thousand soldiers. At around the same time, the same number of soldiers were climbing down the Radtondi ghats into the Jawali valley under the leadership of Raghunath Ballal and Bhimaji Dahatonde.

The goddess of war danced her violent dance that day in the valley of Jawali. Yashvantrao Morey had an army of fifteen to seventeen thousand men; besides, they enjoyed familiarity with the jungles, mountains, rills and streams of the area. Yet, Shivraya's forces had energy, surprise, and great vigour on their side. The Morey forces realised that the gods and tides of war had turned against them. Some seven thousand of their men and an equal number of animals had been slaughtered. Although they fought with great intrepidity, when they noticed in the afternoon which way the war was tilting, both Yashvantrao and Prataprao slipped away and lost themselves in the shrubbery nearby. But Tanaji Malusare was not giving up easily. He chased after them.

The ochre flag was hoisted over Jawali, but Shivraya's attention was not on the flag at all. When Kanhoji Jedhe noticed this, he asked, 'Raje, are your eyes searching for anybody specific?'

'Where's our Tanaji Malusare?'

By sheer coincidence, the moment he uttered the name, out sprang Malusare, astride his horse from the bushes in front. Shivaji called out loud, 'Arey, Tanoba, where are the Moreys?'

'I was virtually holding the Moreys' horse by its tail. Rode straight after them like a bullet.'

'How, then, did a gallant soldier like you come back empty-handed?'

'Failure fell to my lot, Raje,' said Malusare, looking down.

'Impossible! Absolutely impossible! We had been sitting here, absolutely certain that our valiant Tanaji would only return with the crown of success on his head.'

'What could I do, Raje? What could I do when someone more formidable than me stood in the way?'

'How's that possible?'

'Raje, the man who confounded me was a person named Murarbaji Deshpande. He belongs to our Mahad province and hails from the Kinjloli village. A Kayasth Prabhu by caste. Tougher than the catechu tree. He fought like a man possessed for his master Yashvantrao Morey.'

'What exactly happened?'

'Well, when Yashvant's army got battered, he began his final efforts at escaping with his life with a few trusted men. He headed towards the sharp fall at a cliff on the tail-end of the Nisani ghat. I was there, ready to pluck the wings of that wild bird, because he was not being able to find the courage to leap over the death-dealing cliff. Just then, Murarbaji Deshpande ran in like a spirited horse, and threw a stout rope down the cliff. He took the help of the bushes, lifted the Morey brothers on his back, and managed to reach them to safety below.'

Shivaji lost himself in thought. This conflict had taught him a new lesson. Whenever he came across an unattainable fort or a valiant young man anywhere, he would be desperate to take them into his fold. He returned to the present and asked Tanaji, 'But where is that Murarbaji now?'

'I searched for him among the herders in the jungle. I got to hear that towards the last stage of saving his masters, he slipped into the dark gorge.'

'So, has he died?' asked Shivraya.

'Well, no, he's not dead, I hear, but he's seriously injured. He has found himself a safe and secure place where he can lie concealed till his wounds heal.'

.ᴏᴎᴇᴏ.

Shivraya opened up his court in the Jawali palace and began carefully planning the next steps for the campaign ahead. Within four or five days, a special force was made ready and dispatched to conquer the Wasota fort of the Moreys lying in the Sahyadri range. He felicitated his brave victors and rewarded them. He looked among the remaining men of the Morey army and picked out the healthiest warriors among them. Seven thousand new soldiers were thus recruited to serve in the swarajya army. Thousands of energetic horses were inducted into the swarajya cavalry.

There was immeasurable wealth lying in the Morey palace, of which Shivaji took charge. He gathered all the royal ladies and children of the Morey household, including the extremely old Maanakubai, seated in palanquins and doolies, and had them sent over to the Purandar fort. Even before this contingent had reached there, Aausaheb had personally made arrangements for the accommodation of the guests.

Once he was assured that the Jawali gorge was totally under his control, he dispatched Nana Palkar and Raghunathrao down the ghat to Konkan for some new enterprise. No one knew what that enterprise was, but little by little, things began to come to light.

Shivaji had won Jawali and attached it to his swarajya, thus gaining for himself immense advantages. Starting from Supe, Jejuri and the Karha plateau, the western frontier of the swarajya had joined the sea along the Konkan coast. He had, of course, taken possession of the Moreys' stables in Mahad and Poladpur, and now, his men and horses had started doing the rounds of the Bankot bay beyond Mahad. That was where he had begun to construct factories for building boats and ships.

Silence descended upon Yashwantrao Morey's territory and upon all his near and dear ones. There was no sign of Yashvantrao, Prataprao and the two princes of their clan. But within a month's time, information began to trickle in. The Moreys had taken shelter in the Rayari fort that lay under the guard of the huge gulches and gorges of Konkan. They still had a force of three thousand men with them. Posting them strategically around them, they stayed concealed in the fort like snakes in a pit.

Shivajiraja himself led a force to lay siege to the fort. It was an immensely strong redoubt. There was just one single narrow path that led up to the fort. Otherwise, it lay surrounded on all sides with walls so straight and tall that access was possible only to wind and rain, not to human beings. White haze could often be seen hugging the bastions in a tight embrace. Clouds would descend from the sky morning and evening, pay their respects to the fort, and move on. Shivaji fell deeply in love with this fort. Turning to old Gomaji kaka, who stood next to him, he pointed towards the fort and said in a voice soaked in passion, 'Kaka, very soon I shall have this amazing fort in my control. When that happens, I shall name this mesmerizing fort "Raigadh".'

'What did this son of a good man like Shahajiraja gain by causing all this bloodbath? All this strutting like a king with a fancy umbrella over himself, all this drama of moving around in a palanquin accepting people's obsequies, and then, after all this fanfare, going and slaughtering people belonging to royal households!'

'What humiliation! That aristocratic family running into its ninth generation—Shivaji's street-side vandalism has turned them to dust.'

'Just look! Wears a mask of such humility and benevolence and hides such a malevolent face behind it!'

'Yes, such naked, brute violence! Plundered his kingdom, stole his horses, burnt down his Jawali. And did he stop there? No way. That poor Yashvantrao lay in prison and begged and pleaded for his life, but what did our man do? Chopped off the head of that defenceless man. Ruined the lives of those two innocent young boys of his!'

'What a shame! The wicked deeds of these feudal lords and their tyrannical banners are going to burn down one of these days. Just watch!'

There was no holding the tongues of these feudal lords of hereditary estates.

Shivraya, ensconced in Purandar, was getting the drift of the wind blowing outside. First-hand, second-hand, and the gripes and curses of a number of people were reaching him. Reticent though he was, his distress had added much to the distress of everybody else in the fort. One afternoon, he opened his heart out to his mother. 'Masaheb, the battle of Jawali refuses to give me a moment's peace. My conscience berates me. I sometimes feel that I am—'

'A murderer? A sinner? That you killed Yashvantrao pointlessly? That you hanged his two young sons there in Pune?'

'Yes, every word that you have said is true.'

Jijausaheb said, 'Raja, haven't you forgotten a few things? It was barely seven years ago that this Yashvantrao had come with Maanakubai and planted himself in our court. How he would lament the obstacles in his way! He was basically not the son of the Morey of Jawali but the Morey of Shivthar. With the entire world ranged against him, his adoption proceedings were not coming to a close. Did anybody else send a squad of soldiers to help him? Who was it that stood behind him during that time?'

'We did.'

'That Adilshah didn't come from Bijapur to help him, did he? And what did he do? He turned round at us like a snake, didn't he?'

'That's quite true, Matoshri. I had never intended to take his life; on the contrary, my desire was to have him as a friendly kingdom bordering our swarajya.'

'Shivba, both your perspective and your direction are appropriate, because this forest region in the middle, from Mahad to Wai, always has been the heart of the Sahyadris and shall remain so.'

'I am in complete agreement, Masaheb. All the goods that come from foreign countries land in harbours like Chiplun, Dabhol and Harne in Konkan, and are sent to the rest of the country through the ghats of Mahabaleshwar. If one thinks deep enough, this route has become the windpipe of the Sahyadris. Therefore, if the breathing apparatus of swarajya had to be kept functional, it was critical that we win Morey over—either through friendship, or through arm-twisting, or through war. That was why I had to take such an extreme step.'

'That's just what I've been saying, Shivba. It was he who deliberately chose the path of depravity and led himself to rack and ruin, we didn't.'

'The sad thing, Matoshri, is that after Jawali had fallen, we had imprisoned only Yashvantrao. But he was so obsessed with the idea of destroying us that both he and his sons wrote all those treacherous letters to our enemies in Bijapur. He shook hands with that traitor Baji Ghorpade, tried to gather other aggrieved Maratha sardars around him, and plotted to destroy us root and stalk. What other option was I left with, Aausaheb?'

'He had to be punished, Shivba.'

'Aausaheb, a king so often has to take unpleasant decisions like a king. Otherwise, there is no saying when he will lose the reverence of his subjects.'

'Shall I give you a piece of advice, son?'

'What a question, Masaheb?'

'Well, then, the elder Morey girl is still unmarried; as a matter of fact, she is still in our palace. She must be devastated.'

'What are you thinking, Aausaheb?'

'Don't lose this wonderful opportunity of applying the salve of love on the grieving heart of this young girl, son.'

'Masaheb, I will do as you say, but on one condition. If this daughter of the Moreys, this Jaishribai, is willing to accept my proposal with all her heart, only then will this auspicious event happen; else not.'

⁘

It rained very heavily all night. The Purandar fort was drenched. The Morey family had been housed in a spacious hall in the palace. Jaishri opened her eyes, still feeling quite drowsy. There was no royal physician there. The only people around were her grandmother Maanakubai and her mother Sitabai.

The tragic events of the past couple of months—the travel through the jungles, the forced residence in the Purandar fort, then, her marriage to Shivraya—the memories of all these events would often leave her distaught. Hanumantrao's disembodied head, her brothers Krishnarao and Baji, hanging by a noose—seeing them there had been enough grieving, breast-beating and lamentation. When Jawali had fallen, she had been sure that her head would explode. However, within a gap of a few weeks, she had applied the kunku of Shivajiraja on her brow and in the parting of her hair. Her relatives had cried assault; the rest of the subjects saw it as justice done. It was, perhaps, the outcome of this sequence of events that for four days she ran a very high fever. Last night, the fever had reached its high point.

It was with the intention of consolidating the swarajya by bringing together formidable and beneficial forces that Jijausaheb had made Shivraya enter into multiple matrimonial alliances. Saibai and Sakunabai were followed by Soyrabai of the Mohite family, then Putlabai from among the Palkars, Sakvarabai from the Gayakwad family, Jadhav's daughter Kashibai, and Ingale's daughter Gunvantabai. Thus, she had brought home beautiful, virtuous and accomplished girls as her daughters-in-law. Yashwantrao Morey and Hanumatrao Morey's daughter Jaishri was also as consummate as she was beautiful.

Jaishri's mother Sitabai, Jijausaheb and the extremely old and infirm Maanakubai had sat till late in the night by Jaishri's bed. Both would frequently touch her throat to feel her temperature. Some time after she had consumed the potion given by the physician, she broke into a profuse sweat.

The next morning, when Jijau came in, Jaishri was looking somewhat better. The rays of the sun were picking the brightest colours they found in the environment. When she saw the women of her own household and those of her husband's all gathered together, she laughed merrily. She turned towards her sister and asked, 'Roopmati, tell me honestly, whom among these three did I bother the most last night?'

'How can you call this bothering, girl?' said Jijau.

'Please forgive me. I was sleeping the sleep of the dead. However, someone had taken my head in their lap and was caressing me like a small child. I remember hazily that the person was also wiping the sweat on my brow.'

Everybody laughed when Jaishri said this.

Jijau smiled and said, 'Last night was a strange one. Everyone was despairing of your life. The physician had also declared that his medicines were not working. In the latter half of the night, Shivba had himself come to ask about your well-being. He was the one who had taken your tired face in his lap.'

Jaishri was flustered. When she looked in confusion towards Jijau, she merely nodded.

Turning red, she turned towards her mother and said, 'What's this? Should the king have been troubled on account of a mere fever?'

Finding the girl so tensed, Jijausaheb said, 'Your husband is not merely your husband, but the patron of all his subjects. It is the king's duty to take care of every needy person among his subjects. Besides, the two of you are tied to each other for life.'

Tears began to flow copiously down Jaishri's cheeks. As Jijau moved closer to her, Jaishri held her back by stretching out her arm. 'Please, Aausaheb, let my tears flow. This purging will lighten my heart. These are tears not merely of sorrow, but of joy too. For the past couple of months, the boat of my life has been crashing into all kinds of obstacles. To be honest, I carried a lot of anger in my heart for his lordship. He was the person who had razed my mother's house to the ground. I was furious at this unjust king, and so outraged.'

'Girl?'

'But then I began thinking about it carefully. As per the laws of morality, different rules apply on the battlefield and in politics. On a battlefield bathed in blood, what value do poor women and children have? They are looted, raped, slaughtered and their bodies are thrown away like dogs. Bullocks and horses can be useful and are therefore carried away by enemy soldiers, not women and children.

'Whatever calculations exist behind the hostility between the Bhosales and the Moreys, let them be. But you didn't brutalise me for being the daughter of the enemy, nor did you throw me away on the dung heap. You created a space for me in your home.'

'Girl, this eventuality is known by various names like Fate, Destiny, Fortune, and so on,' said Jijausaheb.

One afternoon, a company of about seven hundred Pathans assembled in front of the court. They were in the age range of adolescence to mid-forties. Tall and broad-chested, most of them were sharp-nosed and handsome. They had short or long beards on their fair, pink faces. The assemblage was pleasing to look at. Their arrival had created turmoil in the court. Soldiers, horsemen and even the common multitude had gathered, looking at them appreciatively.

When the king arrived in the court in a little while, the Pathans let out a loud cry of 'Long live Shivajiraja!' and bowed before him in respect. Their robust health, energy and desire to meet the king could not be concealed.

Shivajiraja came straight to the point. 'Where are you coming from?'

'Rajaji, we are coming straight from Bijapur. Till a fortnight ago, we were working in the Adilshahi army.'

'I see. But why did you decide to come here?'

'Rajaji,' said a senior among them, 'we have come here with the desire to live under your benediction and fight under your banner.'

'But why did you leave Bijapur?'

'Raja Saheb, today's Bijapur is no longer the Bijapur of Adilshah Ibrahim Saheb's and Mohammadshah Saheb's times. Those good days have long disappeared. All that happens there now is backbiting, petty squabbles and betrayals.'

'We had made up our mind to leave their service,' chimed in another Pathan. 'The only question was where we should go next.'

'When we thought of a master who would hold us in esteem and value our work, it was your image that sprang before the eyes of our group.'

'We, therefore, just picked up our swords, got on our horses, and came straight here.'

The court clerks standing in the back rows were quite sure that their king Shivraya would issue an immediate order for their recruitment into the army. Shivaji, however, merely cast his eyes at the gathered group and said, 'You have travelled a long way.' He instructed his administrators to make arrangements for their food and stay, and then, turning back to face the Pathans, he said, 'Stay here for a few days. We shall discuss everything else at the appropriate time.'

Barely two or three days would have passed when some of the courtiers began whispering in the king's ears. 'To what extent can we trust this foreign community, Shivraya? If they have turned their backs on a generous master like the Sultan, how, then, can we be sure of their loyalty to us?'

Shivaji was disturbed at these differences of opinion cropping up in his court. He snapped at one of the advisors, 'Why do you expect betrayal from them?'

'It appears that somebody is deliberately trying to cause you and your kingdom grave harm from a distance by playing this shrewd game. At first, they will talk sweet and gain our confidence. Then they will infiltrate our army. Keeping up the pretence of loyalty, little by little they will gather intelligence on our strengths and weaknesses, and pass it on to the enemy. Then they will revolt and make us fall flat on our faces.'

'But how can this be possible?'

'Right from Kabul, across Delhi-Agra to Bhaganagar and Bijapur, right up to the Kutubshahi at Bidar, this religion has spread like some wild weed. Once religion matches religion and beard meets beard, then how much time will it take for them to roar 'Subhan-allah, let's attack', and burn our fledgling swarajya to the ground?'

Shivaji realised that his associates were dead set against allowing the Pathans entry into their army. He decided to gather information about them through his spies. He found out who these Pathans were and where they had come from. These men had worked earlier with Randullah Khan, and with Shahajiraje, too. Lately, however, unwarranted interferences from Mustafa Khan and Badi Begum had upset them greatly, and they felt humiliated by their despotic behaviour. That was why they had abandoned Bijapur and decided to join up with Shivaji.

During that time, the responsibility of Pune's security lay in the hands of Gomajibaba Pansambal. Knowing him to be a wise and trustworthy person hailing from Aausaheb's father's town of Sindkhed, Shivraya sought him out privately for consultation. He brought up the subject of the Pathans and said, 'The fact is, kaka, that at first sight, these Pathans have left a good impression on me. But our sardars and administrators are dead set against allowing them inside our army. They straightaway cite their religion as a sore point. For them, a different religion is inextricably associated with betrayal.'

'Shivraya, you will not be able to resolve the issue by raising the point of different castes and creeds. The direction of the wind cannot be changed by trying to hide behind the excuse of different religions. Think it out with a clear mind, Shivraya. Your great father Shahajiraje, your grandfather Malojirao, your mother's father Lakhojirao, all of these accomplished and powerful people spent their entire lives serving one Islamic kingdom or the other. How, then, can you raise the issue of the Hindu religion, and keep people of that other religion out of the scheme of things?'

'Thank you, Gomaji kaka. What you're saying has given me a clear perspective.'

Two days later, as they sat talking after dinner, Jijau expressed her admiration for Shivaji. 'I congratulate you, Shivba. You have judged the Pathans correctly. You did the right thing by inducting the Pathans into your army.'

'Arey wah! Aausaheb agrees with my decision.'

'Of course I do, son. It won't do for a king to think in narrow terms like caste and faith?'

'That's very true, Aausaheb.'

'Balraje, this has held true since ancient times. Why else would our ancestors call the raja "Prajapati", "Prajapita" or "Bhupati"? He is the husband, the father, the caretaker of all his subjects.

18

PRABALGADH—THE GODDESS OF WEALTH

1657

Queen Jaishri informed Shivaji enthusiastically, 'Raje, the people of Chehul have come to meet you.'

'What's left to be done for them? I've already brought them relief from the grips of Kanta Gujra.'

The crowd from Chehul, numbering into the hundreds, entered the palace grounds with heaps of garlands strung from marigold and magnolia flowers. Placing the garlands round the king's neck, they sang out, 'Raja, it was only because of you that our record books and our jewellery have come back to us. Otherwise, that Kantya Gujra would have sold off the entire town.

Shivaji, too, was extremely pleased that he had taken charge of an old, highly cultured township on the seacoast and begun the construction of a harbour wall there. He had ordered the flogging of a usurious person named Kanta Gujra after retrieving the documents and jewellery in his possession and returning them to their rightful owners. The people of Chehul, therefore, had felt very grateful.

He had many things to do all at the same time. Other than the four or five hours of sleep that he squeezed out, the remaining time he spent in resolving issues. Fighting on seemed to have become the default state of his body. Recently, Shivaji's Maaval forces had vanquished the Adilshahi forces and taken over the fort. He had undertaken the reconstruction of the Gheriya fort on the Kharepatan coast in Maalvan. The four-hundred-and fifty-year old walls constructed by pouring lead on the rocks in the sea were extremely strong. The work on adding extensions to this fort was in full swing.

He was like a man possessed at all times of day and night and would undertake the three-day ride to the Kharepatan coast. He was determined to make the fort walls stronger.

Shivraya renamed the fort at Gheriya as 'Vijaydurg'. He had taken the help of the Portuguese artisans and technically sound officers in the region for increasing the fort's size and strength. Actually, the technicians working in the Portuguese administration did not have the authority to help any native king. But little by little, Shivaji had forged intimate relationships with the adventurous sailors, traders, big artisans, architects, language experts and hunters from all the countries.

A number of Portuguese officials would visit Maalvan from Goa under the pretext of hunting. They would stay for a few days in tents of palm leaves erected on the beach. They would then find the time out and go help Shivaji. They would be thrilled at meeting a native king who was so keenly interested in new technologies and in construction work.

Shivaji's queens were astonished at the labour their husband was putting in day and night. Often, they would go to Jijabai and complain, 'Matoshri, please tell your son to take it easy. How much should a person strive after all? His lordship is forever toiling as if a war is in progress.'

'After all, Aausaheb,' Jaishri would say in half admiration, 'however valiant a person, isn't it out-of-place for a single person to carry the load of seven?'

'But if he were ever to listen to us,' complained Sagunabai, 'if he were to sit down and rest a bit, then would he at all be the raja we know?'

As soon as the bay in the north of Konkan had come within his grasp, Shivaji's blood had begun to bubble for gaining Prabalgadh. A Rajput sardar named Keshari Singh was the fort-keeper working for the Adilshahi administration there. In Shivaji's memory was imprinted an image from when he was barely six. His parents had taken shelter in Prabalgadh for a few days. The torrential rainfall, the moss settling in the crevices of the fort walls, that ball of red and gold against the greenery that he had seen from the window of his sick-room, the dense greenery everywhere and the white haze that would descend on it, these pictures had etched themselves permanently on his heart and mind.

One day, Shivaji pitched his tent at the foot of the fort and sent his cavalry of two thousand climbing up the slope. He was aware that the force placed there and its ammunition were in quite a dilapidated state, and he expected the fort to fall to his men within a couple of hours. However, when four or five hours had gone by and there was neither any message from up there nor any sound of the victory bugle, he began pacing restlessly.

That was when Madari Mehetar came racing down on his horse and reported, 'The fort-keeper Keshari Singh is fighting with great vigour, Raje. It may take us a few more hours to gain charge.'

Shivaji immediately decided that there was no point in pushing his men into the fire of that counterattack and wasting time. The groom brought his horse over, and he jumped on to its back. Just as he was spurring his horse to leap forward, he heard the sounds of horns and trumpets. A wave of satisfaction swept over his face.

They began the climb immediately—the king on his horse and his queen Sagunabai in a palanquin. As they were excitedly moving up through the red Konkan soil and all the denseness, they were met by Barhiji Naik riding down. Barhiji immediately turned his horse round and began climbing up again with his master. He began talking with great enthusiasm: 'Raje, that fort-keeper turned out to be a very tough character. He fought on with great tenacity.'

'Have you taken him prisoner?'

'No, Raje. Despite our repeated requests to him to surrender, he refused to put his sword down. His armour was soaked in blood. He caused us a lot of damage. Finally, our Daduji Babaji got so irritated that he swung his sword hard and sliced off his head from the body.'

The horses were still moving up the narrow trail. The riders then saw a cloud of smoke balloon up into the sky. Shivaji assumed that the Rajputs at the fort would have cremated Keshari Singh's body, and he urged his horse to move faster. Very soon, it was Tanhaji Malusare who was spotted coming downwards. As soon as he was near enough, Shivaji asked, 'So, how's it going, Tanhba? Why were Keshari's men in such a hurry to cremate his body?'

'No, Raje. Keshari's head had rolled into the bushes and has still not been located; so how can the body be cremated? That was Chanda Rani's pyre.'

'Who's Chanda Rani?'

'Keshari Singh's beloved wife. Her relatives had been pleading with her to desist, but she refused to listen to anyone. She lived by the code of the Rajputs.'

'What code?'

'After the husband is defeated in war, the wife cannot allow another man to touch her; she therefore commits "jauhar" by jumping into the funeral pyre. That what the pious woman has done.'

Shivaji jumped off his horse and leaned against a tree, as if unable to trust his legs. Everybody turned anxious, including Sagunabai. The king's eyes turned moist and his face turned red. Nobody had ever seen him in this state before. Tanhaji stepped forward, held him by the wrist, and enquired worriedly, 'Maharaj, what is the matter?'

'Arey, Tanhaji, why didn't you prevent Keshari Singh's wife from jumping into the fire? She was my sister by religion. Why didn't you prevent her from committing jauhar?'

'The practice of Rajput women to commit jauhar is holy, but when would Rajput women want to leap into fire? When the dark shadows of the wicked Mughals would fall upon them from Delhi. You should have told this sister of mine that this assault was not of the Mughals, it was of the Marathas—the Marathas who would be willing to sacrifice their lives for their sisters if the occasion arose. If this message had reached her in good time, she would, perhaps, have not lost her life.'

This news had made Shivaji utterly distraught. He did not feel like mounting his horse again. For the next hour, he travelled with the others on foot up the twisted, slushy trail. A number of heart-rending events had occurred by then in the fort above. After Keshari Singh's death, his two young children and his old mother had disappeared; they had run away from the palace out of fear. Search was on for them.

When the Maavali soldiers saw the king himself coming over to take charge of the fort, their faces lit up. He first paid obeisance to the two old stone statues of Maruti and Ganesh. He then went to the holy pit of the Rajput ladies, where two of Chanda Rani's friends had joined her in entering the flames, and paid his respects to them. Then he enquired affectionately after the health of his injured soldiers.

The Raja stayed overnight at the fort. The sun had set, but there was no sign either of Keshari Singh's severed head or of his relatives who had gone missing.

It was midnight when the guards on duty came and said, 'Maharaj, we have combed through every bush and shrub in this fort, but there is no trace of anything at all.'

'But how is this possible?'

'Raje, we suspect that there is a secret passage out of this fort through which Keshari Singh's mother and children have quietly slipped out.'

The next day turned out to be more fruitful. Keshari Singh's head was finally found; along with his body, it was placed on a funeral pyre as per the custom. There was no call at all for the king himself to be present for the cremation of the fort-keeper, a person who worked for the enemy. But the king made it a point to be present there and place a sandalwood log on the pyre. As the smoke rose up to the sky, the Raja's eyes went beyond the smoke to see a strange sight. There, on the other side of the haze stood a dignified-looking old woman, with two ten-year-olds holding on to her apron. They had obviously come out of their hiding to pay respects to the dead man. The king recognised them as Keshari Singh's mother and sons and had them taken to the palace.

The king's heart melted at the state of the old woman. He explained to her, 'Your son was a brave warrior. My soldiers requested him to lay down arms and surrender, but he went on fighting for his master and became a martyr.'

He then stepped forward and placed his head at the old woman's feet. The sheer humility of the king stunned Keshari Singh's mother. When she began to cry, the king said, 'What's happened has happened. The transaction of war is over. Matoshri, what can I do for you?'

'My parents' house is in Devalgaon Raja that lies on the way to Warhad. If arrangements can be made to have us sent there—'

'Why not? Everything shall be arranged. Please don't worry.'

The Raja immediately issued orders for a palanquin to be requisitioned for the old woman. He also arranged for two strong horses for her grandsons. Supplying them with enough provisions, he sent them on their way with all due respect.

He then felt like taking a round of the fort. Instead of doing it on horseback, he decided to do it in a palanquin. As the palanquin-bearers were carrying him through some dense vegetation, an interesting event occurred. As the palanquin squeezed its way through a thorny bush of berries, some of the thorns caught Shivaji's velvet jacket. While a servant rushed forward to disentangle the clothing from the bush, Shivraya observed the next bush carefully and found it to be slightly unusual. When he went closer to examine it, a strange thought crossed his head and made him tremble with excitement. He immediately ordered his men to dig below the bush.

The diggers had barely gone three feet deep when they came upon some old masonry work below. Soon they unearthed twenty-two silver vessels filled with gold coins from Akbar's times. They dug deeper and wider to locate four large bowls full of hons and long, thin rods of gold. Everybody, including Shivaji, was amazed and thrilled at this unexpected find.

Shivaji looked at the palace from the spot where he was standing. About nineteen years ago, he had looked out from a palace window towards the exact spot where he now stood and had sensed the flash of gold as a small child. As he stood there reliving the memories of his childhood, he didn't know how to explain this phenomenon. Could it have been a mere coincidence?

19

A CHALLENGE IN THE DURBAR

MARCH 1659

'Alert, all, with due respect and reverence.' The frequency of this call of the durbar herald had reduced substantially; it had lost its tremor, too. The durbar orderlies who had strutted around with silver canes in their hands, now seemed to have lost themselves behind the pillars of the court next door. The state of the royal court of Bijapur had turned grave.

Letters had reached everywhere—from Madurai to Karvar and right up to the borders of Bidar—inviting all the sardars, umrao and ghazis of the Sultanate.

The durbar was choc-a-bloc full of grandees. Nineteen-year-old Ali Adilshah sat in state on the throne, a crown studded with diamonds and pearls on his head. To his right sat the ladies of the royal family behind a diaphanous curtain, with the handsome, dignified Badi Begum sitting in front. Her real name was Taj-ul-Mukhaddiraat, alias Alia Janaab. She was in her fifties, and authority was written all over her face and demeanour.

She was witness to almost a decade of Mohammadshah's illness, his death two years ago, and the ascension of Ali to the throne under her patronage. Her aggressive gaze swept over the assembled durbar and rested on Ali's face. She was satisfied that the Sultanate had been inherited by Ali, who was at least of her husband's blood, if not hers, and not gone to some adopted third party.

Badi Begum turned her sharp gaze towards the left, where she saw Prataprao Morey of the Jawali principality standing like a timid cow. He had been living in Bijapur since Shivaji had ransacked the Morey principality a few years ago, quite like a beggar lying on the steps of a mosque. He lay rusting here with just one single desire: that the Sultanate should destroy Shivaji and hand the principality of the Moreys over to him.

Her features and her pink complexion strongly reflected her Iranian-Turanian lineage. When she looked at Prataprao, her deep blue eyes suddenly sparkled and her face turned grave. She unconsciously clenched her delicate, jewel-bedecked fingers. That was when Prataprao standing in front, sobbed out, 'Begum Saheba, our Jawali! Our Jawali! Shivaji burnt it to ashes.'

'Prataprao, easy. Show some patience.'

'That rogue Shivaji slaughtered my brothers Yashvantrao and Hanumantrao. He hanged our boys in the bazaar of Pune, harassed our girls. Begum Saheba, I must receive justice at your doorstep, I must.'

The old wazeer had anticipated the topic on which animated discussion would take place today. He ran his fingers through his dense white beard. Up there on the table in front lay a contour map of the Sahyadri mountains done in wax. Tiny flags were stuck in places to mark out important spots. Pointing at the various landmarks with a stick, Wazeer Mustafa Khan said, 'Benevolent Ammijaan, this is the coast of Konkan. These are important harbours, like Dabhol, Harne and Murud. There is constant movement of foreign ships in these harbours. This is the jungle track that leads out of here. All goods, cannons, ordnance, market places—everything—are serviced through this solitary path that crosses a check-point here. It then goes through the dense Jawali forests, travels past the Radtondi ghats, begins climbing down to get into the Taighat, and then goes through Wai —'

'Yes, yes, I know all that. It's on these valleys that the recalcitrant Shiva has established his control. Comes up with new perversities every day. He has snatched back the Kondhana fort, which has always been our pride, and tossed the dust of the Subhanmangal at Shirval into the Neera river. That traitor, he ripped our Musey Khan into pieces outside the Purandar fort; we couldn't even retrieve his dead body.'

'But Ammijaan, the worrisome thing is that this Shiva is trying to gain control over the Konkan forts now. If these subversive activities of his continue, the foreign powers too will stop paying heed to our orders.'

'How wonderful those earlier times were! I had become used to hearing victory bugles blowing in this Bijapur city every day. Whose evil eye could have brought our grandeur to dust? That no-gooder Fateh Khan! Returning home vanquished, beating his breast like a woman of the street! I have confiscated his properties and forbidden him from ever stepping into the durbar. He now haunts the ruins outside the town like a mad dog, I hear.'

Taking careful measure of the Begum's mood, the wazeer said, 'Begum Saheba, it is, after all, a matter of administration and politics. Shouldn't we handle it with some discretion and patience?'

'I understand this talk of politics very well. Don't forget, I was born in a palace. My father was a sultan, my husband was a sultan, and now this person who sits on the sultan's throne—this Ali Adilshah—is no less than my son. So, my son is a sultan too. I understand full well what negligence can lead to and what insurgency means.'

The entire durbar was terrified of Begum Saheba's fury. Nobody dared to look up at her face that had turned red as a beetroot. Her indignation had gone beyond anyone's expectation. Foreseeing the pitfalls that lay ahead, Sultan Ali Adilshah climbed down from his throne, unsheathed his sword, lowered himself on one knee and roared, 'I await your orders, Ammijaan.'

Looking at the gallant pose that the sultan had struck, the rest of the courtiers were also sufficiently charged up. Every one of them roared, 'Your orders, Begum Saheba, your orders!'

Begum Saheba directed the durbar's attention to the betel leaves that had been rolled up and kept in a golden plate. Picking up a roll was the traditional symbol of accepting a challenge. Lifting her eyes from the plate and scanning the gathering, Begum Saheba threw the gauntlet, 'Is there any brave young man in the gathering who is willing to head towards the Sahyadri mountains right now and decimate that Shiva?'

The sheer dimension of the challenge put the skids under the courage of the gathering. All present lowered their eyes and looked furtively this way and that at their neighbours. When the Begum sensed that the expected response to her challenge was not forthcoming, her voice turned sharper still as she snapped, 'Anyone? Any person in this mortuary called our durbar, who has the courage to lead my army and rip that Shiva to shreds?'

The Begum ran her flaming eyes over the durbar, but she couldn't persuade a squeak out of anyone. She then flung this statement sharp as a dagger at the gathering, 'Is this a durbar at all? Or is it a marketplace for goats and sheep? You disgust me!'

'Please wait, Begum Saheba,' came a stern voice from behind. 'For Allah's sake, wait!'

Heads turned to see a huge bull of a man making his way to the front. Six feet and a half in height, barrel-chested, strong as an ox—everyone's eyes lit up as Afzal Khan moved forward. The man came and stood before the throne, and roared, 'Forgive my impertinence Begum Saheba, but how can this durbar be allowed to drown itself in the sea of pusillanimity in such a hurry? How can you forget this lion of Bijapur that stands before you?'

Everybody in the durbar began chanting in unison, 'Afzal Khan! Afzal Khan!'

'I am that Afzal Khan who put that Shiva's father in chains and made him dance on the streets of Bijapur with manacles on his wrists. I am that *Kufr-shikan*, the destroyer of evil, Afzal Khan.'

Afzal Khan swung his gaze at the entire durbar with great hauteur. He then took five steps forward and lifted the betel-leaf roll between his fingers. As he then raised it up, the gathering broke into a deafening applause and shouted, 'Wah, brave-heart, wah!' 'Wah intrepid ghazi, wah fearless warrior!' 'Long may you live!'

The hubbub of delight refused to die down. Badi Saheba signalled to the sultan who promptly called Afzal Khan closer. He then handed to the man a jewel-studded sword and put expensive clothes on his massive shoulders as a mark of honour. All the sardars and dignitaries broke into loud felicitations. Delighted at the development, Badi Saheba addressed everybody and asked, 'Does this durbar need to be introduced to *Qaatil-e-kaafiroon*—the slayer of infidels—Afzal Khan?'

'No, no, not at all!' came the response from those present in the durbar.

'Just a couple of years back, this Afzal Khan had performed a miracle in the battle of Bidar. He had managed to trap the Mughal prince Aurangzeb.'

Afzal Khan's face turned red at the memory of that event. He said in a hoarse voice, 'That Aurangzeb had so neatly fallen into my trap that it could well have turned into the darkest night of his life. I had made all arrangements to make him prisoner and take him dancing through the lanes of Bijapur like a cock in a carnival. But Allah, what could I do?' He wiped a tear off his eye and snorted angrily, 'If the wazeer of that time had not accepted a bribe and betrayed us, history would taken another direction altogether, for sure.'

This passionate declaration by Afzal Khan stunned the durbar. But Begum Saheba quickly pulled the people out of the quagmire of sentiments and said, 'Afzal Khan, we like facts, not fiction.'

'Why, Begum Saheba, haven't you enough faith in me? Ammijaan, there is no need to take such a fright at Shiva's new antics.'

'Afzal Khan Saheb, you still haven't stepped into the battlefield. Get into the Sahyadris first, the land of Shiva and his Maavalis.'

'I shall do all that is required to raze the enemy to the dust. Once I get into the gorges of the Sahyadris, that Shiva will run hither and thither to save his life. I swear here in open court in the name of Allah: I shall tie that man up in chains, drag him here, flogging him all the way, and tie him to the leg of this throne.'

'Wah, wah, Afzal Khan, may you live long!' roared the durbar.

Wiping warm tears off his cheeks, Afzal Khan raised his heavy hand and screamed, 'There are just two demons whose wicked shadows fall upon our Bijapur—one is Aurangzeb and the other is this Shivaji. The first escaped because of good luck and the treachery of our own wazeer; but this Shivaji shall not be allowed to live at all.'

That very evening, Badi Begum had Afzal Khan called over to her royal palace, Anand Mahal. Nobody else was present for this meeting in the big hall except Sultan Ali Adilshah and a few of the closest relatives.

Immediately after the discussion in the durbar that afternoon, Afzal Khan had made a beeline for the armoury to take stock of the weapons and other battle equipment. He had got so engrossed in his inspection that dinner time had arrived before he knew it. That was when Badi Begum's message had reached him. He quickly got up and made his way to Anand Mahal.

Even before he had taken his seat, the Begum's words fell upon his ears: 'There can be no doughtier and more loyal person in the entire Sultanate for this difficult task than you.' All present nodded their heads in agreement. Looking proudly at Afzal Khan, the Begum continued, 'If anybody other than you had stretched his hand to pick that paan of challenge, I would myself have shooed him away, saying, "Son, this is beyond your capacity."'

'My real strength lies in your blessings, Ammijaan,' said Afzal Khan, in a voice thick with emotion.

'I remember the day so distinctly when our wazeer had released Aurangzeb from prison and you had come storming into the durbar, livid, swinging swords in both your hands and shouted, "Do whatever you have to do, but immediately bury that treacherous wazeer who has caused such harm to our nation." The fire you displayed that day, the wrath, the spirit, Subhan-allah! I was completely mesmerized.'

'Shukriya, Ammijaan.'

The begum had actually arranged a grand dinner that evening for the senior grandees and close relatives. But it was the topic of the grand expedition that had taken complete hold of the Begum's mind. Even as they sat down to their meals, the conversation remained confined to the adventure ahead. Putting down a half-eaten chicken leg in his plate, Afzal Khan laughed and said, 'Begum Saheba, sometimes I feel that maybe we are making too much of a small thing. Should a small nudge to a dozen of our forts in Maaval by Shahaji's son make us think of him as a big danger?'

'Afzal Miyan, don't get deluded by that boy's tender age; keep an eye on his firm and tall intentions. The person who slaughtered our brave Musey Khan, the boy who destroyed Fateh Khan not only in battle but in life—he is no other than that insolent kid of Shahaji's.'

'Forgive me, Ammijaan,' replied Afzal Khan, looking down. 'We shall be alert during every moment of this enterprise.'

'I have deliberately called you over for the second time today. That Bhosale brat is the biggest danger that hovers over our Sultanate today. The perfidy of the father-son duo cannot be ignored at all.'

'Is it the son who is foolish or the father who is double-dealing?' asked Ali Adilshah.

'I think the father is a bigger rascal. At the drop of a hat he breaks out into platitudes like "Serving the Sultan is my religion", and then moans, on the other hand, that his son is not within his control. How wonderfully clever, Shahajibaba! This is what is called, "You laugh there and I shall pretend crying here."'

In the same meeting, Badi Begum admonished Afzal Khan to be alert about a number of things. A number of black arts were practised in that belt of Konkan. There were any number of demons, ghouls and hobgoblins haunting that region. A lot of witchcraft like sorcery, exorcism, killing and obstructive black magic were prevalent there. Afzal Khan should, therefore, stay at an arm's length from any inducements of trickery that Shivaji might try on him.

Afzal Khan was taken aback at the scale at which Badi Begum had busied herself preparing for the campaign. Twelve thousand of the highest quality of horse and men, ten thousand infantry, three hundred and fifty big and small cannons, over a hundred elephants, over three thousand bullocks of the Kathiawad breed for pulling the cannons and other load, seven hundred camels—such was the army that had been assembled for the war.

Not depending on Afzal Khan alone, Muslim and Hindu sardars like Siddhi Hilaal, Ambar Khan, Rustam-e-Zamaan, Yaqoot Khan, Ghulam Barbar, Baji Ghorpade, Jhunjaarrao Ghatge, Jivaji Devkate, Mambaji Bhosale, Kalyanji Jadhav, Shankarji and Pilaji Mohite, Pahelwan Khan, Prataprao Morey, Rehmat Khan, Hasan Pathan and Sardar Pandhare had been assigned for the campaign.

As soon as the meals were over, all the officials who had been asked to report gathered in the next hall. Badi Begum then called each one of them and took account of their preparations in the areas of weapons, clothes, food, ordnance, animals, money and espionage accounts. She then asked for the accountant to present himself. A dark, heavy, flabby Telanga Brahman presented himself, head bowed in submission. The white ash marks on his forehead and on his ear lobes stood out starkly against his dark skin. Straightening the flat turban on his head, he stood humbly, waiting for instructions. The Begum asked him, 'Narsaiyyaji, where are Afzal Khan's papers?'

The accountant undid the knot on the silk kerchief he was carrying and brought out a well-arranged sheaf of sparkling white papers, which he handed over to Afzal Khan. Perplexed, Afzal Khan asked, 'Ammijaan, what is this?'

'We have made all arrangements for at least three years' worth of food, fodder and weapons. But if any other need crops up, these *dolas*—'

'I still haven't understood, Ammijaan.'

'Son, these *dolas* are royal edicts, genuine documents for any future transactions. The stamp and signature of the Sultanate have been imprinted on them.'

'But why? Is there any need for them?'

'Of course, there is, son. With these documents, you can issue royal edicts from anywhere at all. They give you the authority for calling over reinforcements from other states too. All the senior generals coming with you will be directly under your command. You will have the authority to reward or punish them, encourage the army to perform at its best. In short, for this campaign, not merely elephants, horses and cannons, but the entire Adilshahi administration is with you. All that I want is victory. I want Shiva.'

'Ya Allah,' murmured Afzal Khan in a charged voice, arms raised upwards, 'both my prestige and the Bijapur crown are in your hands now!'

'Look, Afzal Saheb, I just want Shiva—dead or alive.'

It was quite late in the night now. Many of the aristocrats attending the meeting had left. A few of them were simply hanging on. Ali Adilshah was there too. Suddenly, something seemed to have occurred to Badi Begum, and she signalled for Afzal Khan to follow her out. They went into the next hall. Looking at the conspiratorial demeanour of the two, the doormen quickly pulled the door close.

In the silence of that hall, Badi Begum pulled him down to sit next to her, and said, 'Another very important thing, Afzal. You may go chasing that Shiva like a hunting-dog, but keep one thing in mind.'

'What's that, Ammijaan?'

'Don't ever go chasing him into the jungles in the inner mountains.'

'Ammijaan?'

Trying to impress upon him the gravity of her message, she said, 'Don't trust that son of a devil, even an iota, even when pretending to make friends with him. There are birds that fly free in the jungles there. But there are some hunters in those dense mountains who can whistle beautiful lilts; these lilts lure those birds into traps that these hunters have laid out. This is how that Shiva too can lure you into his magic trap by creating sweet music. Remember, therefore, that the whistle you hear in the jungle is not a piece of music but the sharp edge of a sword.

20

'IF YOU GO, YOU WILL NEVER RETURN'

APRIL 1659

Dawn had begun to break. In front was the huge shrine of the sufi saint Hazrat Pir Amin Chisti. The early morning wind was nippy, making the flames of the lamps in the alcoves flutter. The entrance to the shrine was half-lit. The shrine itself looked extensive. The pir baba, however, was never comfortable inside. He would always be sitting on a tattered reed mat near the worn-out steps. He was as thin as a dried bamboo stick—nothing but skin and bones. Somewhere in his seventies, he wore a startlingly white beard. He sat there like a small boy, contracting his body into a small bundle.

Afzal Khan and his favourite wife Ladli Begum stood before the baba frozen with fear. Both of them looked severely anxious. Afzal Khan had doubled himself up before the old man as he groaned, 'Baba, for the past twenty-five years now, I have left for a campaign only after taking your blessings. I have always carried with me my destiny and my favourite elephant Fateh Lashkar. But a strange calamity has descended on me now. My dearest elephant died at the very first stop we made. What does this utterly unexpected event portend?'

The mystic looked at him piercingly. Actually, he had no eyes. Only deep, dark cavities where the eyes should have been. But he could see with absolute clarity with the divine eyes of his spirit; that was what thousands of his disciples and votaries believed.

He too looked very worried today. In the cold of the morning, he extended his dark, gnarled, shivering hand towards the guard of the shrine, who stood with a flambeau in his hand. Pir Baba took the flaming torch from him and shone it upon Afzal Khan's person. He first saw Afzal's footwear; then, moving upwards, he saw his legs as strong as teak logs, then the tunic above it, the strong chest filling the tunic out, and his muscular arms. Afzal Khan was so generously built that during a day's ride he would need to change three horses; the sturdy animals would become breathless carrying him about.

When the mystic raised the torch further up to see Afzal Khan's head, his heart missed a beat. Atop Afzal Khan's thick, bull-like neck, where he should have seen his head, he saw nothing at all. When a young tree is struck by a stormy wind, its leafy head gets blown away, leaving just the trunk oozing out some kind of resin. That was just what Pir Baba saw of Afzal Khan—his neck bereft of the head, warm, dark-red blood flowing out of the top of the neck. It was like the milk-and-curd *abhishek* flowing down the statue of Mahadev, the god of the infidels. This prior vision of a burning future caused the pir baba to shiver involuntarily, and he immediately moved the torch away. 'What happened, Baba,' asked a deeply worried Afzal Khan, 'what happened?'

Suddenly, Pir Baba's face turned dark as a moonless night sky. He looked deeply distressed and frightened. It was only because he held Afzal Khan in immense affection that he advised him in a mournful voice, 'Please listen to me, son, abandon the dangerous thought of leading this campaign against Shivaji.'

'But why, Baba?'

'What can I say, son? I do not see a single ray signifying victory here. All that I can see is devastation.'

'But, Baba, I have lifted the paan of challenge!'

'So what?'

'I have sworn in open court, Baba. This campaign is now a matter of life and death for me,' responded Afzal Khan with determination. 'Even if Allah-tala orders me to abandon it, I shall not be able to do it.'

Pir Baba held Afzal Khan by the hand and said in a sharp voice, 'If you go, you will never return.'

Afzal Khan's wife Ladli Begum had been listening to this conversation between the master and his disciple. She had never seen the pir look so wan. She had never heard him say such dreadful things in all the twenty-five years she had known him. This prediction had virtually broken her spine. She almost collapsed at his feet. Pir Baba was never known to wear any kind of footwear; the frequent encounter with stones and thorns had turned his soles thick and calloused. Rubbing those hard, leathery feet with her soft hands and releasing hot tears on them, she said, 'Hazrat, every single time you have talked of victory and on every single occasion, Afzal Saheb has hoisted the flag of success.'

'But, in this campaign I see only calamities and more calamities,' replied the holy man, tremulously.

'But from where could all these misfortunes arrive?'

'What if this Shiva is backed by a more powerful master and a holier intent?'

'But, Baba—'

'Don't argue any more, children, and listen carefully. For Afzal to start a war now is the same as deliberately leaping into the pit of certain destruction.'

These words of defeat and destruction coming from the mystic's mouth had utterly shaken both Afzal Khan and his wife. They had never dreamt that such a frightening prospect lay ahead of them. If the old man had merely said, 'You shall lose,' it would not have mattered much. But terrifying words like 'certain destruction' and 'you shall not return' emerging from his dark, dry lips felt like their hearts had been branded with red-hot skewers.

It was time for them to take leave. Many preparations had to be made for the massive enterprise. But in the hope of getting some concession from a person he held in high reverence, Afzal Khan said, 'All right, Baba, whatever is written in my fate will happen. But please do me this little favour. Give me a few tips for finding some relief somewhere.'

'Yes, son. There are a few rays of light I can see, rays that will perhaps lighten the burden of the mountain of worry hovering over you.'

'Like what, Baba?'

'Once you are in Shivaji's vicinity, do not get caught in the densely rocky areas of the Sahyadri. Whenever you have to meet him, make sure you meet him at the foot of a hill.'

'What else?'

'Another very important thing. When in the middle of a battle, do not remember anybody very close to you. If you get trapped in this desire for a dear one, you are done for.'

Despite the desperate circumstances, Afzal Khan smiled at this observation. Lifting his four-and-a-half-arms-long sword, he said, 'Baba, this naked sword is my only close companion and my dearest one. There is no one else.'

Baba remained ominously silent. Not being able to digest this silence, Afzal Khan shouted like an irritated child, 'I swear by the name of Allah, neither my mind nor my heart will ever get snared by any infatuation for anyone.'

'Subhan-allah,' responded the pir with a smile. 'Son Afzal, there is nobody else in this Sultanate who maintains a harem of sixty-three wives. If the memory of even one of these beauties infiltrates into your mind and causes your hand to shiver, you and your army will get wiped out.'

Afzal Khan's life up until this moment had been merely a game of climbing up the rungs of success. Joining as a mere trooper with Randullah Khan, he had gone on climbing till he stood in the first rank of the Bijapuri generals. He would refer to himself proudly as Afzal Khan Mohammadshahi. His effort was at presenting himself not merely as an intimate of Mohammadshah, but as a close relative. And the royal durbar was gracious to him, which helped him wear the feather of intimacy with comfort.

Pir Baba's prophecy had seriously undermined his self-confidence. This augury had been followed by a series of accidents. As his army was leaving the precincts of Bijapur, another of his elephants had gone out of control and crushed some eight or ten of the citizens under its feet. As they had moved forward, the staff of the main banner atop an elephant in the vanguard had snapped in the middle during the very first watch. Besides, as they were bidding the city goodbye, such a violent storm had broken out that it had kicked up tons of dust and rubbish in the air. For some time, the sky had turned so dark that it looked like evening had set in at noon. Making it more ominous were swarms upon swarms of crows flying over the army to the left as well as to the right.

The campaign was expected to go on for a long time. Hence, Ladli Begum had come over to the camp to make sure that Afzal Khan's personal effects were in order. She stayed on for the next night too. Looking at her accomplished husband in such a worried state, she was very shaken too. As both of them sat in their tent in a gloomy mood, news arrived that the master of the elephant stable of Adilshah, Jange Khan, was waiting for him outside his tent.

The event of the master of the stables presenting himself had attracted a crowd of onlookers. When Afzal Khan and his begum came out of the tent, they saw a huge and extremely handsome-looking elephant standing there. It had been decorated from its head to tail. It was caparisoned in shining brocade. On top of it was placed a sandalwood howdah. Its two tusks had been covered in thin sheets of gold.

The sight of the grandeur in front made him suck his breath as he said, 'Arey, Jange Khan, this is the sultan's elephant. Why have you brought it here?'

'My dear Khan Saheb,' said Jange Khan with a laugh, 'I have brought a message to you from our master, the Sultan. Don't let the passing away of Fateh Lashkar upset you. His stable is huge.'

'Wah! Many thanks.' The gloom that had clouded the faces of Afzal Khan and Ladli Begum vanished at the sight of this gift.

Ladli Begum was immensely proud of her husband's accomplishments. She herself was the daughter of a sardar in the Qutbshahi Sultanate. She sent a thrill through her husband's heart when she said, 'In the entire Bijapuri Sultanate, it is Mohammadshah Saheb alone who built the Gol Gumbaz mausoleum for himself. Have you heard of anybody except the Sultan constructing a mausoleum for themselves when alive?'

'No one at all. Who, after all, can afford such expensive indulgences?'

'But, Hazrat, you have done so. You alone have got a mausoleum constructed five years ago which is as beautiful as the Sultan's.'

A new thought suddenly crossed Afzal Khan's mind. He extended the stay of his army at Torve by another two days and informed his officers accordingly.

He called for his horses and set out of his tent in the middle of the night. The horses crossed the Mahidari hamlet while the cold wind blew.

The guards were rattled at the arrival of the Khan at this odd hour of the night. That grand mausoleum with its sturdy walls, those graceful arches, those pillars thick as the trunk of a tree, the well laid out garden in front, the overall sense of sacredness and elegance of the building, the Khan was overcome at the sight of the place, and his eyes turned moist as he said in a hoarse voice, 'This is my hallowed resting place.' A seven forearms long and three forearms wide cavity had been created in the floor. The thought that his bier would be lowered into that space one day filled him with awe. He looked at Ladli Begum as he murmured, 'Ya Allah, such an expensive and matchless tomb!'

'You are another Sikandar, my lord.'

'But, Begum, do you think my body will be able to reach this place?'

'Allah!' groaned the wife in dismay, 'I'd rather die than hear you talk of death.'

The next day, the soldiers began rolling up their belongings. Ladli Begum was very heavy of heart. She knew well how the pir baba's pronouncement had crushed her husband's spirit.

If you allow any thought of a beloved person drift into your head at the time of battle, you and your army will be destroyed. These words of the pir had etched themselves on his heart as if with a chisel. The pain was excruciating. He told his wife, 'Look, Ladli, my women will continue showering their love on me and my thoughts will ever be swirling in the whirlpool of their memories. My body, therefore, will never be able to reach here from the mountains, and my mausoleum will remain empty for centuries to come.'

'For Allah's sake, stop discussing this morbid topic, my lord,' the Begum beseeched him with folded hands.

Immediately after that, she got busy charting out a plan. At a little distance from the mausoleum, Afzal Khan had made for himself a pleasure palace on the extensive farmlands there. He had poured all his artistic instincts into the construction of this colossal structure. For one, he had a great fascination for water sports and eroticism. When there was no campaign or war to conduct, he would spend his time indulging his passion in this pleasure palace. A massive, square well named 'Surang-bawadi' had been built there of walls made of dressed stone. A three-storeyed palace constituted one of the walls of this well. The lowest floor was almost half submerged in water. Afzal Khan's young wives, beautiful as fairies, would play their water games in that huge square well. The upper two storeys had many big halls. The residence of the wives was on the second storey. From there, dressed in wet or dry clothes, these beauties would move up to the well-appointed terrace on the third floor to bask in the soft rays of the morning sun. Ladli Begum decided to spend the night in this pleasure palace in the company of all her fellow-wives. Accordingly, before it had turned dark, Afzal Khan and his sixty-three wives gathered there. The entire night was then spent in gourmandizing, splashing around in the baths, bonfire, singing, dancing and every other kind of merrymaking. It was a night spent in a paradise of voluptuous indulgence.

The next morning, the air was wet with dew. Fresh out of their baths, Afzal Khan and his sixty-three wives stood shivering in the cool breeze at the platform of the well. They were all dressed in new clothes. A number of these wives were of tender age. On the outer side of this pleasure garden stood armed guards under the command of Afzal's three sons. The eldest of the boys, Prince Faazal Khan, stood next to his father.

Afzal Khan's face, distorted with pain, was a piteous sight to behold. Ladli Begum too appeared to be under tremendous stress. It was only out of some mysterious determination that she was moving around frenetically. The air was damp, the sky was overladen. Ladli Begum estimated that all her fellow-wives had arrived. Then, in an authoritarian voice, she said, 'Sisters, there is nothing left for us now. We have to do now what the wives of our infidel enemies do.'

'Just tell us, aapa, and we shall follow. You are our elder sister,' they responded in unison.

Ladli Begum resumed, 'We have been seeing every day, how our master, the Khan Saheb, has been straining himself through these doomed times. It is campaign time, so I shall not say much. It's just this, there's just this one thing that tests us out—death. Jauhar.'

Some of the very young among the wives were taken aback. 'How can this happen, aapa?' they screeched. 'What will happen?'

Ladli Begum pulled out from her waistband a sharp, glittering dagger. She lifted the weapon up to her chest and said, 'It's either this dagger or the water in this well. One way or the other, we have to destroy ourselves for the better fortune of our beloved husband.'

Saying this, the seniormost wife leapt towards the royal well. Some other wives of her age leapt up with her and somehow held her back. The other women ran past and leapt to their deaths in the well.

While this was happening, there was a loud cry of pain from behind. One of the younger wives, terrified for her life, had somehow found her way out of the palace and was racing across the farm. Someone, however, flung a dagger at her from behind that found its mark and brought her down. Her half-dead body, bathed in her own blood, was carried back and flung into the well. The person who had shot her down was Afzal Khan's eldest son, Prince Faazal Khan. He was doing his bit to ensure a better future for his father. The bodies of the wives who had stabbed themselves to death were tossed into the well. Most of them, however, had preferred death by drowning.

The senior wife was now reassured of a religious duty performed. She was the only wife left now. This shocking sacrifice of lives stunned the firmament. Overwhelmed by the grief of separating from her husband, Ladli Begum walked up to him and hugged him tightly as she said, 'My master, may Allah tala grant you success. Saying this, she shook herself free and ran towards the well. Afzal Khan leapt after her and gathered her in his embrace again. 'Where are you going, Begum?' he screamed in a grief-stricken voice. 'If you also leave me, my entire garden will be devastated. How will I then live in this ravaged world?'

She tried frantically to free herself from Afzal Khan's iron embrace, but the husband in torment refused to loosen his grip. She twisted and turned and managed to extricate the dagger from her waist, which she then plunged into her stomach. The blood turned Afzal Khan's tunic red too. 'Begum, begum!' he screamed like a stricken deer. As she turned limp in his grasp, she placed her hand on his head and said with her dying breath, 'My master, forget my grief and now go tear that Shivaji apart.'

⁂

Afzal Khan's army was moving rapidly towards Solapur.

Once a shrewd man gets it into his head to take to crooked ways, his brain begins to buzz. Right from the beginning of the campaign, Afzal Khan had decided to use the weapons of discrimination and dissention among his men.

Shivaji was creating this façade of being the savior of all of Maharashtra, including the Maaval region. Taking this as his backdrop, Afzal Khan had begun giving a lot of importance to Maratha sardars like Jhunjaarrao Ghatge, Pilaji Mohite, Pandhare-Naik, Katey, Kharate, Kalyanrao Jadhav and Shankarji Mohite. During discussions, he would seat Mambaji Bhosale right in front and address him as chachaji. Seeing this increasing importance given to Mambaji, the other Maratha sardars would mutter, 'Whose uncle is this Mambaji? Shivaji's or Afzal Khan's?'

Afzal Khan's gargantuan army was nothing short of a mobile carnival. Those ten thousand spirited horses, an equal number of infantrymen, seven hundred camels, upwards of three thousand bullocks for carrying the foodstock, fodder and other paraphernalia, a regiment of a hundred elephants, the carts carrying the three hundred big and small cannons—whenever this caravan went past a village, people would gather and stare at it with awe. Afzal Khan had at his disposal a number of howdahs on which he could travel in ease and comfort, but he was never seen travelling on any one of them. In fact, he was hardly ever seen sitting in one place. He seemed to have decided that relaxing at any point was a terrible sin. All that he wanted to do was to get into the land of the Maavals and destroy Shivaji as early as possible.

Afzal Khan's horse would always be running up and down the massive spread of the army. He paid careful attention to every contingent. He would personally check who needed what and when. The army was rolling across the hot sand of the river Seena. The twenty-five-odd bullock carts carrying the ordnance were placed at the tail end of the caravan. This precaution was being taken to ensure that if something untoward happened and if some careless spark reached the gunpowder and caused it to explode, the entire army would not be put into disarray. The steel rims of the wheels of the bullock carts would rub against the hot sands of the riverbank and throw off sparks. Afzal Khan realised that this could cause the dynamite to catch fire.

He immediately halted the movement of the ordnance wing, and stood scratching his head for a while. He then sent his men hunting for banana groves and ordered them to bring the long, wide leaves of the plant, and had them tied to the frame of the bullock carts like mud flaps, thus blocking the sparks from flying up.

The news of the Khan having departed from Bijapur began reaching the banks of the Krishna and the Twelve Maavals right from summertime. There would sometimes be an element of truth in it, but most of the time it was spiced-up bazaar gossip. What news? Oh, he has reached Tuljapur and has razed Goddess Bhawani's shrine. Some travellers were willing to swear on oath, 'That Khan put Ma Bhawani's statue in a sack and had it ground to dust.'

Later, the information arrived that he had reached Pandharpur and had made life miserable for the local Brahmin priests and traders. He had also smashed the statue of Vithuraya and thrown the statue of God Pundlik into water. Such, and many more, were the stories that were being spread across at breakneck speed. Leaving Pandharphur behind, Afzal Khan's army was moving stage by stage along the Mhaswad road and had reached Malwadi. He had caught hold of Shivraya's brother-in-law, Saibai's brother Bajaji Nimbalkar, and tied him to a cannon. He had also threatened to have him crushed under an elephant's legs. This harassment of Bajaji had even reached Shivraya's ears. There was this sardar named Naikji Pandhare who was travelling with Afzal Khan. Establishing secret communication with him, Shivaji requested that Bajaji be somehow released from Afzal's custody. Finally, the maverick Afzal released the man after a ransom of sixty thousand hons was paid to him.

There was also talk of Afzal Khan racing northwards. On his way, he would send raiding parties of three or four thousand men from the Indapur-Baramati side and create mayhem and terror. A number of Deshmukh and Deshpande landlords had shifted allegiance to him. Many of them seriously believed that Shahajiraja's son would not be able to withstand the impact of Afzal Khan's colossal forces. Out of self-interest, desperation and the desire to ensure a future where they would continue to live in luxury, men like Sultanji Jagdale of Masoor, Khandoji Khopde of Utravali, Vithoji Haibatrao of Gunjan Maaval and numerous others had found it prudent to hop over like a bunch of frogs to the secure shade of Afzal Khan's army.

.ᴓ.

It was a hot afternoon in the market by the Indapur fort. Suddenly, a loud cry went up in the fort as well as the marketplace: 'Run, run! That Afzulya has arrived!' A cloud of dust could be seen over the road that came past the Akhluj heath. A few horses could be seen coming racing in from a long distance. Going by what they could see, the soldiers and horsemen at the Indapur post and in the fort quickly began gathering their belongings. The big and small tents were brought down and the grooms and footmen began loading the weapons in bullock carts. There was bedlam everywhere. People threw their belongings on horses, donkeys and bullocks and began fleeing in the direction of Pune.

Jyotyaji Mane, the thanadar, the station head, of Indapur, wrapped his kerchief tightly round his head, got astride his horse and began exhorting his men, 'Move, move. Let's shift base to Pune.'

While this winding up was in progress, a battalion of five hundred horses came galloping in from the direction of Barshi. When they saw no less a gallant than Tanaji Malusare at their head, the fleers were flustered. But Jyotyaji was in no frame of mind to listen to anyone. When Tanhaji noticed this, he spurred his horse and brought it to obstruct Jyotyaji's path and shouted, 'What's this I see, baba? The son of a Maratha displaying such eagerness to flee?'

'Have you got cataract in your eyes, boy? Look there at the heath in front. That's Afzal Khan's men rolling in like a storm.'

'Afzalya's forces are going to move from behind Mhaswad towards Aundh and Rahimatpur; this is confirmed news.'

'So, that cloud of dust moving in from the heath?'

'It could be one of the small-fry sardars of that Khan. But should a veteran like you abandon your post for fear of such minnows?'

Tanaji got his horse to circle around Jyotyaji's and said in pent-up anger, 'Try fleeing while I am here. It was while defending this station in Indapur that my cousin had taken a cannon ball on himself and died. That's why I say, I shall not let anyone flee from here. In any case, by whose orders are you abandoning this post?'

'The king's!'

'Shivajiraja's? What rubbish! My king exhorts people to confront the enemy, not run away from them.'

'You want to see the orders? Well, here they are.' Saying this, Jyotyaji pulled out a missive from his bag, unfolded it and said, 'Read this now—empty out all the forts, posts and castles that lie in the way of Afzal Khan's movement. Pack up your belongings and begin moving into the hills of the Sahyadris.'

Tanaji's eyes bulged out as he read the words and saw the royal seal. It carried the signature of Moropant. It was impossible for an edict like this to come out of the state court without the king's order. As he read those contemptible words, his head buzzed. He jumped off his horse in a rage, removed his headgear and tucked it in his armpit, ran his fingers through his hair and roared, 'Why go running into the mountain range? To leap off a cliff like a helpless woman?'

Tanaji stood there in a state of extreme anger and desperation. His mind had turned numb.

Afzal Khan's armies reached close to the village of Vadooj. Wave upon wave of villagers would gather around to see his caravan of thousands of horses, camels and infantrymen. When the Khan's caravan halted at the outskirts of the village, the man himself came forward on his stallion and growled at the gathered villagers.

A big bullock cart was rolling past as Afzal Khan stood there. On the cart was loaded a four-arms long wooden cage in which was imprisoned a red-faced rhesus monkey. The kids of the village had begun crowding round it and teasing the animal. Some of the more impertinent boys sitting atop a nearby tamarind tree had begun throwing stones at the cage. The poor monkey was stamping in rage and fear at being harassed thus.

Mambaji brought his horse from behind and began shooing the boys away. 'You insolent rascals! Go away!' he shouted. Hearing that, Afzal

Khan nudged his horse forward and addressed Mambaji, 'Why, chachaji, why are you shooing the children away?'

'These are irrepressible fiends, these kids. Pointlessly riling up the poor animal.'

'That's not what it is, chachaji,' Afzal laughed sarcastically, 'they are only practising.'

'Practising for what?'

'When we make our return journey to Bijapur, we shall have the same bullock cart and the same cage. Only, it won't be this monkey inside.'

'Khan Saheb?'

'It will be your cousin's son—Shivaji. Every child from every village shall throw stones and dung at him and rile him beyond endurance. These children are practising for that pantomime.'

Afzal Khan had ordered a halt on the heath that lay between Aundh and Rahimatpur. Very soon, they would cross the bed of the river Krishna. There was tumult everywhere when they arrived at the very frontier of swarajya land. Fear and pressure were on the rise. Gossip in the markets and villages was turning spicier with each passing day. Afzal Khan had moved forward traversing through Tulzapur and Pandharpur. A conference was in progress in the big tent, and the twenty-two sardars from Afzal Khan's army had formed a semi-circle around their leader. The Khan needled Mambaji by saying, 'Chachaji, you Margatthas are scoundrels and your gods are very dangerous.'

'What are you saying, Khan Saheb? You haven't left the gods alone, or their priests? The poor pujaris complain that you have raised your cudgels against them and their priests, and crippled them.'

'Where?'

'In Tulzapur and Pandharpur.'

'Look, chachaji, don't think that Afzal Khan is a fool. I used baked tiles to take water from the lake of Begum Talav to all over the city through underground channels. I have spent days at the smithy and in stone quarries when the blacksmiths were fashioning their weapons and the masons were dressing stones. I have supervised the construction of huge mausoleums. I very well understand the difference between genuine and fake statues, understand?'

'What does it mean?'

'My friend, these innocent devotees of Bhawani had kept a fake statue of the goddess in the temple. That was exactly what those rogues at Pandharpur had done and hidden the genuine statue of your Vithoba in the river.'

'But what I have been saying, Khan Saheb, is, why should you pointlessly go after our pilgrimages and our idols?'

The Khan laughed heartily at this and said, 'Chachaji, I understand the difference between real and spurious. I am known as the *Shikanda-e-butaan*, the demolisher of idols. Down there in Madurai and Jinji, I have demolished a number of temples and reduced hundreds of idols to rubble. Even Aurangzeb is nothing in comparison to this *Qaatil-e-kaafiroon*.'

Afzal Khan's voice suddenly rose a few decibels. The Marathas in the assembly froze. Laughing loudly and in the voice of a bully, he went on, 'You are making such a ruckus because I got just a hundred or two people flogged with sticks. But do you at all know the real Afzal Khan? If I wanted, I could have razed all of Tulzapur and Pandharpur to the ground along with their temples.'

Looking at this fearsome avatar of Afzal Khan, the Maratha sardars developed cold feet. Both Mambaji and Jhunjaarrao Ghatge mewed in a sycophantic voice, 'We are grateful for your generosity and the favours you have bestowed upon us.'

'Look, this was not my generosity but a compulsion. There are about a hundred and twenty-five thousand men in this Bijapur army, of whom a good forty thousand are Marathas. That was the reason why I didn't bother your gods and your temples much. I really have no interest in your deities.'

'So, then?'

'I just want my Shiva—dead or alive.'

21

AFZAL KHAN AT THE THRESHOLD OF SWARAJYA

Shivraya's horse climbed up the steep cliff of Rajgadh and reached the upper shelf. Right in front was the Rameshwar temple, and the construction of the court building was still in progress. The scope of the fort was huge. The effort of bringing all the building material to such a height on the backs of bullocks and donkeys was immensely taxing. It could well take a couple of years more for the construction work to be over. The horse came to a halt and a groom immediately came and took the animal away towards the stable.

The horsemen, soldiers and villagers assembled there looked extremely anxious. The Raja asked Raghunath Billal Sabnis, 'Yes, Pant, what's the hassle here?'

'Nothing. The palanquin passed by just a little while ago. Aausaheb has returned from Purandar.'

'Hmm? She was going to stay there for a few days!'

The Raja began his climb up the sharply rising stone steps that led to the top of the fort. Whichever way he looked, he saw deep worry lines on all the faces. Well, yes, if the news that he had been hearing while returning from Konkan was true, there was every reason for worry. He would have hardly climbed four or five steps when he saw two dispatch riders coming hurriedly down the steps. They were carrying missives from the two espionage heads, Vishwasrao Dighe and Barhiji Naik, who had been assigned the task of keeping an eye on Bijapur. Three or four days had gone by since Afzal Khan had left Bijapur for the Maaval region at the head of an immense army.

The preliminary estimation was that Afzal Khan's would target Purandar, Kondhana and Pune, but if the man decided to turn adventurous and singled out Pune alone for a straight assault, the consequences for the kingdom of swarajya would be grave. Hence it was important that he not be allowed to climb down the Purandar mountains to move forward; he should be kept busy on the Karha plateau, and hopefully be slaughtered there when the opportunity arose. This enterprise needed the participation of a truly vigorous and fearless warrior.

It was only recently that the commander-in-chief of the swarajya had passed away and the Raja had placed the responsibility of that position upon the shoulders of Netaji Palkar. Nobody ever had the slightest doubt about the courage and valour of the man. The Raja had therefore sent Palkar instructions that the Khan should be kept busy in the regions of Supe, Saswad and Purandar; on no account should he be allowed to come down the ghats. Netaji, therefore, had put himself on high alert and was guarding the region with unblinking attention.

The Raja entered the courtyard of the palace and looked towards the structure in front. Through the arched windows of the elevation, he could see the eyes of his queens looking out eagerly for his arrival. When he entered the ground floor hall, he saw Dharau the wet-nurse and Jijabai waiting for him in the passage. Jijabai had in her arms the fifteen-month-old Sambhaji. The king heard the otherwise cheerful child crying. And the moment it sensed the presence of its father, the baby reached out to him.

Shivraya held little Shambhu to his chest and sent his fingers through its thick head of soft hair. Restlessness and sleeplessness were evident from its face. The Raja asked solicitously, 'Matoshri, is all well with Saibai Rani Saheba? Why does young Shambhu look so upset?'

'The royal physician has strictly forbidden the mother from keeping the infant close to her.'

'The royal physician doesn't seem to have diagnosed her right. I had issued an order for a palanquin to be dispatched to Karad for fetching that doctor from Kashi.'

'Yes, of course. The great physician Adhikarrao Shastri from Kashi had come visiting four days back,' replied Jijau. She added, with a touch of worry, 'It was he who examined the child and arrived at the diagnosis.'

'What diagnosis?'

'What we had all been fearing.'

'Matoshri?'

'Yes, Shivba. Our Sai has come down with tuberculosis.' Jijau's face was racked with pain as she uttered these words.

'Hey Shambho!' Shivraya murmured and closed his eyes, but just for a moment.

Saibai's fellow-wives were sitting in the hall around her bed. Lakshmi and Putlabai were gazing at her unblinkingly. The Raja was seeing his favourite wife after a gap of a month. What met his eyes broke his heart. She had turned pale and lost a lot of weight. Her resemblance to an emaciated deer shocked the king.

Both of them were desperately trying to lift each other's spirits. Looking at her husband's grave mien, Saibai smiled and said, 'Could your lordship have forgotten? We had to leave for a certain place as soon as you returned from Konkan.

'To Phaltan, to my mother-in-law's house. The ritual of offering obeisance to Goddess Nimjai of your village Nimbalak has still not been done.

'All my sisters and all my fellow-wives are going to be there too. To taste the sweetmeats of my mother's house.'

'Wah, that's great.'

'Raje, we got so busy immediately after our marriage that your lordship couldn't return to his in-laws' doorstep. There are so many other things that have been left unfinished.'

'Unfinished?'

'Your haldi ceremony has still not been done.'

'Why do you want to coat me in turmeric now?' asked the king with a laugh. Jijau and the others joined in the laughter, too.

'Don't laugh it off. There are certain rituals that my people observe. All of them remain due. My visit to my parents' house for the confinement during little Shambhu's time remained due too.'

'Listen, Rani saheb. You recover a little bit, then we'll set off immediately.'

'Where does the Raja have the time?'

'It will have to be squeezed out for my darling queen.'

'But that blight upon destiny, that Afzal Khan has set out with his huge army.'

'Oh really, Rani Saheb, you have heard the news too?'

'How can I not hear it? I am your other half. I keep a tab on every breath you take.'

Shivaji placed a loving hand upon her head and then stood up. Exchanging a few words with the physicians there, he left for his court on the upper fort. Gomaji Pansambal, Raghunath Ballal Sabnis and Jijabai had gathered there to discuss the next step forward. Jijau's face showed the exhaustion of her travels.

Everybody was fully aware of the storm clouds that had gathered not merely on the upper fort but all across the swarajya because of Afzal Khan's imminent assault. Everybody knew that for all his accomplishments, he had a cruel and perverse nature. He could go to any length for the fulfillment of his mission.

'Shivba, till date, our battles have been fought inside our own mountainous region.'

'Yes, Masaheb.'

'Even during the battle of Purandar, the tall hills around the fort gave us an edge over the enemy. When we had raided posts like Junnar and Kalyan, the forces there would have been not too large.'

'That's true, Matoshri. All right, now, Pant,' Shivraya turned towards Raghunath Ballal and said, 'what do the letters from our espionage chiefs tell us?'

'Raje, our spies have informed us that Afzal Khan has marched out in all readiness with an enormous army. At least ten thousand horses, fifteen thousand foot-soldiers, elephants, cannons, everything. Besides, it is important to find out who all join him on the way. He has a regiment of big-built Pathans, resilient Turks to man his artillery, and a number of Afghan and Telanga swordsmen. In the words of our spies, the army he is moving with looks strong as a huge steel wall.'

As the meeting stretched on, the ominous silence across the fort became more and more burdensome. In the palace and on the temple parapets and ledges, murmurs became tenser. Dinner time had slipped away, but people were more anxious about what they would hear than what they would eat. But again, this discussion was happening at the highest level, and they would not let anything spill out in the open.

They sat down late for dinner. People like Kanhoji Jedhe, Tanaji and others were sitting with the king.

'I think, Raje,' said Kanhoji Jedhe, 'we should try our best to resolve the matter through dialogue.'

'If we let the enemy come down upon us as always, we would no doubt be praised for our valour and chivalry, but—'

'But what?'

'The enemy ready to descend upon us is like the scourge of Destiny. If things go off-course even a little bit in the open battlefield, it may mean the end of us. Death for everybody—you, me and our newly born swarajya.'

Shivraya was quite prepared for an open conflict, but circumstances didn't look favourable for such a move. Taking a deep breath, he said, 'Afzal Khan is absolutely on fire. He has his sword aimed at my chest. Even if he creates a charade of coming to some settlement, what runs through his arteries isn't blood, but deceit. Even if he sees a hairline crack, he will leap for the throat.'

'Isn't there some honourable compromise in sight, Raje?' asked Jijabai.

'Masaheb, I suspect that under these circumstances, words like compromise and accommodation are going to sound insipid and flaccid.'

'So, then, what?'

'We should first take some skin off his knees and elbows, injure him a bit before we bring him to sit down with us for negotiations.'

'But what could be the Khan's reason for going to such extremes?'

'By wiping us out, he wants to prove to the world that Shivaji and his Maavali army were nothing but bubbles on the surface of a wave.'

'But, Raje, his army is thrice as strong as ours. If our spies are to be believed, he is carrying food and fodder that will last him for three years.'

'Be that as it may,' responded Shivraya with unshakeable resolve, 'whatever happens, we shall not be cowed down by his growls. And there is absolutely no stepping back.'

'But—'

'Oh, cut out all these buts. What is the worst that can happen? We may lose our lives,' roared Shivraya like a hermit with a sword, 'but we shall gain immortality for all times.'

⁂

How to respond to Afzal Khan's assault was a question that had been tormenting the Raja's mind. A meeting was in progress in Rajgadh in the yellow light of flaming lamps and torches. Kanhoji Jedhe, Raghunathpant, Moropant, Tanaji Malusare, Shivaji Jedhe and some other of the king's closest confidantes sat there raising the temperature.

It was clear that Afzal Khan would pounce upon them aflame with vengeance. The important questions, therefore, were how to confront him and where. If they were to strike camp at Purandar, Afzal Khan would then hold Pune at the end of a rope. It would give him a golden opportunity to bring immense pressure upon Shivaji. If he were to set fire to Pune, there would be no alternative left except to surrender.

Rajgadh was the second option. It was a big, strong fort, but because of its height, it would not be possible to maintain a really big army there. The main problem would be of water; but if the Khan were to lay a long-drawn siege, everything would begin to fall short—soldiers, goods, equipment, ammunition, everything. Shivraya looked at Kanhoji Jedhe and said, 'Kanhojibaba, we need to find such a strong, unique and difficult place that .... 'Have you ever seen the game that herder boys play during the monsoons with planks of wood in the hills of Maaval?'

'Yes, it's a bit like kabaddi. Go running through slime and sludge, dodge the opponent attacking from the front and exhaust the rivals.'

'Perfect. If the enemy lays siege to one mountain valley, slip into the other one, and from there to the third. Make him vomit blood. He shouldn't even dream of coming close to victory.

'Yes, the enemy is mighty as a mountain. But, perhaps, God and Destiny have thrown him before us to test us. For flattening him on his back, we have the privilege of choosing the battleground and shrewdly luring him into it.'

Afzal Khan's march upon the swarajya proceeded relentlessly. One day a messenger arrived from Bahirji Naik with the news that Afzal Khan was on the Mhaswad road and was perhaps on the point of crossing the river Krishna at Rahimatpur. Within two days, the change in route had become known to everyone.

Shivaji sat with his advisors contemplating on the best battlefield on which to confront the enemy. It was night time and everybody was lost in the discussion. Suddenly, the king was startled. He sensed that somebody had come and stood at a distance from his huddle of officials. When he peered into the darkness, he saw the outline of a big-built person standing there. He immediately cried, 'Netaji kaka? How have you suddenly arrived at the fort? And where have you come from?'

'From Purandar.'

'But my orders were for you to stay put there!'

'We were in need of some more dynamite there.'

'But you could then have dispatched someone else.'

'I found it important to dust my feet at your door. That is why I have come here in a hurry.'

'But how can that be? You are the commander-in-chief of the swarajya. You should know that there are important discussions in progress here.'

'What are discussions going to bring? Just a waste of time.'

The overbearing tone and tenor of the man embarrassed everyone present. Nobody had ever dared to address Shivraya in such arrogant language. A senior, much respected person like Netaji letting his tongue loose in this manner left the audience stunned. Jijau was flustered too. Moropant, who sat next to Palkar, said in a whisper, 'What are you doing, Netaji? Lower your voice.'

'You shut up, Pant. The manner in which this Khan has been flaying our skin and humiliating us all along his way here, how can you seniors not see it?'

Noticing that the conversation was taking a dangerous turn, Jijau used her rank and age to say, 'Netaji, come aside with me, please. What exactly do you want?'

'What is left now to ask? The Raja told his soldiers not to give battle at Indapur. They did not. Told us to abandon Baramati, so we tossed it in the lap of the enemy. And now the orders are that we must abandon some new posts. Arbitrary orders are being issued every day to that effect.' Netaji's words had now begun to carry a trace of dejection.

'But, Netaji—'

'No, Masaheb, no. I fall at your feet, but please don't stop me.' As he said this, he broke into a loud sob; he couldn't hold back his tears. In a thick voice, he said, 'As an ordinary soldier of the swarajya, I want some answers. As a snake enters a hen coop and begins swallowing chick after chick, this Afzulya has begun swallowing our posts one after another. And now the Raja talks of emptying out Supe and Shirval without putting up a fight—what name should I give to this act?'

Everybody present in the meeting broke into a sweat. It was no different from firing real gunpowder from a cannon with a cracked barrel. On the one side, Netaji was blasting away without restraint; while on the other side, Shivaji simply got into a blank yogic posture and listened. This was no young, immature brat getting into an argument with the king; this was no less than a person who was known as the 'jewel in the sword' of swarajya. It was Netaji himself that had come and rammed himself straight into the king.

When a boat moves through stormy waters, the waves begin to lash at it. Stormy winds blow in and blow away, too, but the barge-pole that navigates the boat stays steady as ever. That was Netaji Palkar, a sturdy, tenacious general. When he walked in front of an army, he gave the impression of a sharp, straight cliff moving along. His axe-shaped, luxuriant moustache was turned up at both ends. He held the bragging rights for all masculine games like swordsmanship and danda-patta. But his favourite exercise was this: the presence of a tall hill or a rocky peak before him would always be seen as an impertinence which he needed to set right. He would tighten his stole round his waist and race up to the top barefoot, before anybody else could. Once he was on the peak, he would peel his wet vest off his chest and wring the sweat out with delight. He would throw a scornful look at the hillock under his feet, as if to say that he had put it in its place.

As was his physical exertion, so was his food consumption. When he sat in a row with other diners, he would need a constant supply of chicken. He could easily polish off five birds at one sitting.

Palkar was born in the village of Tandli, which was a little distance from the river Ghod. From his boyhood, he had earned the reputation of being an excellent lancer, a top-class archer and a wrestler who could bring down rivals sequentially one after another. He had opened up a gymnasium for the wrestlers living around the Ghod. When Shivraya had gone propagating the idea of swarajya to Maaval, Palkar had not been able to hold himself back. He had immediately gathered ninety rugged horsemen from his gymnasium and presented himself at the Lal Mahal for a meeting with the king.

When a camphor wick comes close enough to a fire, it is bound to flare up. Within months of his arrival, he had moved up to the front rank of Shivaji's most trusted men on the strength of his exploits. Since he was six or seven years older than the king, he would be addressed as Netaji 'kaka' as a mark of respect.

This, then, was the hero among the soldiers of swarajya, who was now talking so insolently with the king, sending the awestruck listeners into a swoon. The Raja preferred to stay mute for a little while. A tense silence reigned. At a sign from the king, the venerable Kanhoji Jedhe took Netaji affectionately by the arm and had him seated next to the king.

Taking everybody into confidence, the king said, 'Look here, Netaji kaka, we had instructed you to block the enemy and not let him move towards Purandar—'

'When did I say no to that? Going by your order, I have been standing on the field holding on to that end. That is my strength. But for how long do I keep standing there like a stake planted in the field?'

'That is a part of our strategy. It was I who had given the orders that our men should move out of their stations with all the equipment, and move slowly towards the mountain ranges in the west. Listen, kaka, our strategy has still not taken final shape. Keeping in mind the trouble that the enemy can cause, it will be dangerous to expose the moves of the army to the ordinary soldiers.'

This explanation riled Netaji even further. 'When have I ever claimed to be an "extraordinary" soldier, Raje?' he growled.

'Look, Netaji kaka, I have been observing for some time that you have quite unnecessarily been fanning yourself into a flame.'

The discussion went ahead. Netaji had been much appreciated recently for having resolved some land disputes with great efficiency. That was why his opinion carried a lot of importance in the ongoing conversation. Netaji could not suppress the current ferment in his heart. Not being able to hold himself back, he broke away from the topic of conversation and said passionately, 'Listen, I have a secret and extremely important piece of news.' He had fixed his sight on the map that had been drawn on a board.

Everybody was again perplexed. They began wondering what porcupine's burrow Netaji had set out to hunt. Shivaji said, 'Yes, kaka, let's hear your news.'

'Afzal Khan is only feigning to be moving towards Pune. However,' he said, placing his finger at a spot on the map, 'he will actually cross the Krishna here, near Rahimatpur.'

'You have identified the Khan's direction perfectly,' Shivaji smiled and said. He was impressed with Netaji's sharp intellect and the keenness with which he was observing Afzal Khan's movements. 'What would be your advice, then?' he asked.

'What advice? This is your golden opportunity.'

'For what?'

'For launching a sudden attack and drowning that Afzulya right there in the Krishna.'

'Don't you consider the move risky?'

'Not one bit. My four hundred horsemen are waiting in the woodland of Rahimatpur, ready to leap into this river of fire.' He looked expectantly first towards Shivraya and then at Jijabai. Realising that he was not getting the desired response, he became frantic and pleaded, 'Listen, Raje, listen. Masaheb, you at least listen. My heart is ready to burst. Once that Afzulya is buried in the sand of the Krishna, all the other knots will open up on their own. Clogged noses will be cleared for breathing.'

Everybody was startled at the audacity of the move suggested by Netaji. While they stayed silent, Shivraya responded calmly, 'All right, Netaji, I accept your proposal and grant you my permission. And there's a good chance that you will succeed in your daring adventure. But what do we do with the remaining twenty-five to thirty thousand soldiers who are with him?'

The question brought Netaji's enthusiasm down a few notches. 'Yes, that's true,' he said at a lower pitch, 'something will have to be planned for them, too.'

Jijausaheb smiled inwardly as Shivraya continued, 'That's just what I have been saying, Netaji kaka. These half-baked adventures can backfire and hurt us badly. A slight slip and we could lose our entire kingdom. We can see that there is a cannon all primed and waiting to burst inside you, but let's make sure that it is pointed in the right direction.'

On the one side was the Sonejai range of mountains, and on the other was the Pandavgadh range. Between these two ranges, the Krishna had found its way down the Sahyadri in twists and turns, and was now flowing through the plains. The township of Wai lay on its bank. The water from the early monsoon rains of the month of Aashaad was making the river froth. The reddish-brown flow was moving rapidly downwards. On the other bank stood huge royal tents and pavillions. Behind them spread thousands of smaller tents. This year, the farmers had sown nothing on their farms. It was on their massive, widespread fields that the Bijapuri army had pitched its camp.

The huge cavalry, the foot-soldiers, the caravan of camels, a hundred elephants—they had all lodged themselves there. Alongside them were also some Deshmukhs and Deshpandes from Maaval who had joined forces with them, along with the fort-keepers, cavalry sardars and other soldiers who had arrived from Belgaum and Athani right up to Solapur. Together they amounted to well over fifteen thousand men. On a huge ground in the camp were hundreds of cannons and the thousands of bullocks and carts that would pull them. On one side, under strict army surveillance, was stockpiled all the gunpowder. On exactly the opposite end were arranged huge heaps of animal fodder. The twenty-five thousand plus animals needed that fodder to keep their gums busy.

At the cusp of the month of Mrig, when it begins to rain seriously, the small tents were given a roofing of grass. This was a land of heavy precipitation, thus requiring the sheaves going on the roof to be tightly packed and well laid out. The need for dry grass, therefore, ran into thousands of cartloads, and the gatherers spread themselves far and wide to round up all the material that would go into the making of a relatively leakproof roof. Gathering dry grass from locations as far as Masoor, Karhad, Kaasheel, Vita and Phaltan right up to Baramati was taxing the stamina and the resources of the gatherers.

The need for water for an army this size was also immense. The water-supplying community of bhishtis had rounded up two thousand male buffalos that would carry leather bags with water. An army market had sprung up where the Jain and Marwadi traders had opened up shops to sell sweetmeats and trinkets. There were farriers, grooms, footmen and odd-job boys everywhere.

Actually, Afzal Khan had planned to take Shivaji prisoner and drag him to Bijapur before the rains arrived. But there were serious limits to the speed at which his monstrous army could move with its cannons, elephants and the bullock carts loaded with all the paraphernalia. Now, when the rains had offered them a break, the activities of the bhishtis and their buffalos, camels and horses had resumed to finish off whatever work had been suspended.

Afzal Khan too took advantage of the lull in the rains and set off on his horse in the company of Ankush Khan. As they turned a corner past the bazaar, they saw a crowd of youngsters practising war drills. Some three thousand young men from the Maaval valleys had been freshly recruited into the army, and they were being taken through their paces by the army captains from Bijapur and Hubli. Hundreds of feet were stamping in the slush riding horses, throwing javelins, doing sword fights, climbing ropes and a host of other activities. The slime under their feet had turned into a thin, ankle-deep paste, making it difficult to find foothold. Surveying the youngsters throwing themselves enthusiastically into the activity, Afzal Khan asked, 'Where are these kids from?'

'They come from this region, Khan Saheb, from its hills and valleys. The strongest among them have been recruited under your instructions.'

'Wonderful! Otherwise, the kids from our Bijapur, Bagalkot and Shimoga can just about manage to ride their horses on open plains. What can they know about the defiles and gorges in the jungles of these parts, or about the wet, slimy tracks that run through them?'

'Absolutely right, Saheb.'

'These lads will be immensely useful in our battles ahead. If you want to get into the water, you must carry with you people who can knock the teeth off of the crocodiles living in it, Ankush Khan.'

'Forgive my impertinence, Khan Saheb, but as your personal friend—'

'Speak without fear.'

'Khan Saheb, the lustre that shone on your face earlier seems to have dimmed a bit.'

'It's quite obvious, Ankush Khan. Worries increase when facts turn out to be different from dreams. I had sworn to take this Shiva into my custody within two months. Four months have now gone by, but, forget putting him in a cage, I haven't had a single sighting of him, even from a far distance.'

'Where, then, is the point in sitting on your hands, cooling your heels, Saheb?'

'This Afzal Khan is no half-baked warrior. The world shall very soon see my exploits. It's a matter of just four days.'

'You shall see, Ankush; these forests and hills and rains on which this Shiva prides himself, it's exactly in these dense jungles that a miracle shall occur that the world shall watch with awe.'

When Afzal Khan returned to the private hall of his manor, he found the heavy-bodied but stoutly built Krishnaji Bhaskar Kulkarni waiting to welcome him. Krishnaji was the sergeant and the revenue collector of the city of Wai. A Puneri turban on his head, a flaring *barabandi* tunic, the folds of his crisp, serrated-edged dhoti coming down from his waist in a flare, these were evidence that Krishnaji was particular about the way he dressed. Krishnaji and Afzal Khan had known each other for a long time. They had been friends since the time that Afzal Khan was the governor of Wai.

In the middle of the monsoon month of Aashaad, a crucial piece of news had arrived from northern Hindustan. At the cusp of the Mrig period of the almanac, Aurangzeb had declared himself emperor and conducted a grand coronation ceremony at Agra.

The news had set Afzal Khan's body on fire. He couldn't get out of his mind the events of something over a year ago, events that would often drive his sleep away. The role that he had performed in the campaign of

Bidar-Kalyani, the way that he had dragged Aurangzeb to death's door, these memories even today had the power to leave him utterly distressed. 'Ankush, my friend,' he said wanly, 'as they say, when Allah wants to shower His blessings on someone, He rips the sky apart.'

'What are you talking about?'

'Take this Aurangzeb's case ... Barely eighteen months ago, the scoundrel lay in my prison like an ordinary prisoner. Then he managed to escape by bribing our wazeer ... and today he has become the emperor of India.'

'It was that sinner's destiny, what else?'

'Destiny? Who is this whore called destiny? Tell me, Ankush Miyan, that criminal who was willing to lick my feet like a dog for saving his life, he becomes the lord and master of the Peacock Throne of Hindustan. And look at my shredded destiny now—look at the slime through which I am wading here in Wai, shouting "Shiva, Shiva!"'

Ankush decided to maintain a few minutes of discreet silence. After Afzal had vomited out the bile gathered in his stomach, he said, 'But, Afzal, you would have heard the other thing too.'

'What thing?'

'An agent of this Margattha Shiva was present at Agra for the coronation ceremony.'

'What rubbish! What can Shiva possibly have to do with Aurangzeb?'

'That I don't know, but the name of his agent is Sonepant Dabeer.'

'Well, so, this Shiva might have sent his agent there. But who would even have looked at this dog at the Agra durbar?'

'That's where you are wrong. This man was standing unobtrusively in a corner of the durbar.

'And then?'

'I say this in the name of Allah. As Aurangzeb was proceeding towards the throne in all his pomp and glory, he noticed the Maratha-looking man there and asked him, 'Are you Shivaji's agent?'

Ankush Khan noticed the marks of extreme agitation and repugnance appearing on Afzal Khan's face and decided to hold his tongue. He didn't want the man's anger to go shooting through the roof. But what he had to reveal was so pressing that he couldn't hold it for long. Irrepressibly, he said after a while, 'Aurangzeb not only took cognisance of Shiva's man, but he also sent for Shiva expensive gifts of clothes and jewels.'

The news of the respect given to Shivaji's man in the Agra durbar left Afzal Khan tossing in bed all night. He had Krishnaji called into the inner chamber. Not knowing exactly what had upset Afzal, poor Krishnaji began relating tales from the Agra durbar with great relish. That was enough to trigger Afzal Khan off like a drunk elephant.

It was dusk. The roar of the flooded river would keep sounding high and low in intensity. Lamps were being lit on the second floor of this sandalwood palace. The Khan's specially invited guests were due to arrive any time now. The musicians had begun to tune their instruments for the dance soiree that would happen in the evening. That was when Afzal Khan screamed at a footman who was passing by, 'If, after a minute's time, I hear the sound of anklet bells, I shall have the necks of everybody chopped off. Stop this dance and music immediately.'

All the sounds and movements in the palace came to a sudden stop. Krishnaji found the first occasion and slipped out of the hall without soiling his dhoti.

Afzal Khan's particular worry was this: he had got the Bijapur wazeer Mohammad Khan, the man who had helped Aurangzeb escape, torn apart in the public square in a fit of vengeance. Was it possible that Aurangabad would not have heard of this incident?

Afzal Khan did not stir out of the palace for the next two days. His head had turned into a sieve with all the thinking he had been doing. There was one mystery that he was struggling to solve. Why would Aurangzeb have gifted Shivaji with robes of honour? It was after much thought that he arrived at the conclusion: it was not a frivolous gesture or an act of wanton generosity. It was a well-thought-out political move. Once Aurangzeb had settled down in his throne at Agra, he was bound to come down to the Deccan. His old dream of swallowing up Bijapur had still remained unrealised. When he did come down for that mission, he would want the Marathas to be on his side, or at least to stay neutral.

Two days later, he again sent for Krishnaji Kulkarni. 'Listen, Kulkarni,' he said, 'have you ever seen the decomposed body of a dead man?'

'Shiv, Shiv, Shiv! Oh Kedarnath!' muttered Krishnaji, cringing. 'Khan Saheb, why are you talking of such inauspicious things so early in the morning?'

'If this face-off with Shivaji keeps getting postponed indefinitely, that is the kind of stench that will spread everywhere.'

'So, spell out your orders for us, Khan Saheb. What should this servant do?'

'Kulkarni, you are an old player in this mountainous playfield. Go, get into those jungles of Jawali and establish contact with Shivaji. Make sweet talk with him, make as many false promises as you have to. Just lure him out into these lower regions and get him to stand before me.'

'Forgive me, Khan Saheb, but this does not appear to be within the realms of possibility.'

'Why?'

'Shivaji is not stupid. If you order me, I shall do as you say, but I request that you take a reality check. Why would Shivaji step out of his secure post at Pratapgad Jawali, my lord?'

'What rot you talk? Look, Kulkarni, do what you have to but get that Shivaji to stand before me.'

22

NETAJI PALKAR

It was an evening in the month of Bhaadrapad. Behind stood the Rajgadh fort, as tall as a mountain. Down at the foot of the fort was the market of Shivapattan. Out there was Parjanya Mahal, the king's monsoon palace. The heaths and jungles down there had reached total satiation with the torrential Aashaad rains they had received. In all four directions could be seen dense green paddy fields. Between them flowed raging streams. In the paddy fields and on the paths, there was water and more water—clean and beautiful.

The green paddy plants around had begun to pick up a tinge of yellow. Greyish-white clouds had made the sky their playground. The wind rattled the trees in the jungles and punched holes in the fog that gathered around the mountain tops.

A big stream flowed at some distance from the Parjanya Mahal, where peasants, administrators, soldiers and people from the royal family had gathered in large numbers. A big funeral pyre of sandalwood logs had been erected on which the body of Rani Saibai was placed. The pile had then been topped with large quantities of jungle flowers. These were days of heavy rainfall. Because of the surveillance mounted by the Bijapuris everywhere, it had not been possible to convey the news of her passing away to friends and relatives in many towns and villages.

The mourners were not many in number, but those present were submerged in immeasurable sorrow. On the other side stood all the ladies of the royal family, along with Saibai's fellow-wives—Saguna and Jaishri.

Gomaji Pansambal and the wet-nurse Dharau would take turns taking infant Shambhu Raja in their arms and keeping him distracted. The event that was unfolding in its presence was beyond its understanding.

The servants were trying desperately to set alight a lump of dried dung-cake by rubbing flintstones. The sparks came, but they were not enough to create a fire. A strong gust of evening wind would defeat their efforts. Some soldiers blocked the wind by holding blankets around the servants, but they weren't succeeding. Sufficient fire refused to be lit. Meanwhile, a small shower also blew in and left.

Somebody standing in the back row murmured, 'The deceased is waiting for some dear one to arrive, perhaps.'

'Her heart could well be set for the arrival of the king.'

'But how can that be? The queen had made the king swear that he would not abandon his duties to attend to her,' said one administrator.

'What can one say about anything at all?' said Aausaheb with a sigh. 'This husband-wife relationship is one mysterious tangle of silken threads.'

Just then, the sound of horse-hooves reached the assembly's ears. The animals crossed the paddy fields, galloped through the fog that rolled along the ground and the grass that had grown waist-high. The heavy downpour and the sludge through which the horsemen had ridden had smattered their clothes with mud and slime. The king leapt off his horse and went up to the sandalwood pyre, where he looked at his late queen for a long while.

His face showed the contentment of having reached before the funeral pyre was lit. With little prince Shambhu resting on one arm, he took the golden vessel filled with water from the Ganga that the priest handed to him. Together, father and son poured some of the water into the dead queen's mouth. The scene caused a number of onlookers to break into a sob.

A dried stick of the nirgudi shrub was lit, with which father and son set alight the pyre. As the gathered priests chanted the mantras, the flame gathered strength, and father and son began circumambulating round the burning pyre. The balls of smoke that shot out of the burning heap went up to become indistinguishable from the fog and the clouds hanging above.

The king stood for a long time, with his little son in his arms, staring at the flames that were transporting his beloved wife into the next world. He could see her soft, kind face peeping out at him from the smoke. The breeze that blew past him had taken on Saibai's voice and was whispering in his ears, 'Why did his lordship risk his life thus to come galloping through the jungles and mountains? As promised, I shall always be hovering close to you. Hundreds of thousands of stars break out in the dark of the night sky, don't they? It's through their eyes that this simpleton of a woman shall watch the ever-expanding arch of your success.'

Circumstances demanded that the king return immediately. The situation at Pratapgad was balanced on a knife-edge of life and death. . .

The king returned to Parjanya Mahal and gave himself a hot-water bath. He then sat down for his meals of *jhunka* and *bhaakar*, and then began preparing for his return. Just then, the rain picked up intensity and began drumming loudly on the palace's roof. It came pouring down the roofs in buckets. The king walked out of the hall. Old Gomajikaka came forward and held him affectionately by the wrist, saying, 'Duties must always come first, Shivraya, but just look at the sheets of water descending from the sky.'

'But, Gomajibaba—'

'I know, I know. I know what you want to say, but can you see anything at all? How will your horses see where they are going in this rain? How will they know whether they are falling into a pit or ramming against a rock? The loss will ultimately be ours, won't it?'

'That's absolutely right, Shivba,' chipped in Jijausaheb. 'Even the gods are helpless before the forces of nature. It's best that you leave early in the morning.'

The soldiers slept wherever they could find a place in the palace. The downpour continued. Gomajibaba stretched himself out in a small area close to the entrance. He was, however, reasonably alert. Suddenly he heard the knob of the front door being rattled. When he made his way to the door and opened it, the first thing he was greeted with was a gush of wet wind. He then saw some fifteen or sixteen men standing out there bathing in the rain. They were soaking wet, right from the turbans on their heads to the slippers on their feet. In front stood the generously built Netaji Palkar with his thick, axe-shaped moustaches and sideburns. The grooms sleeping in the verandah got up and took Netaji's horse from him, and walked it to the stable.

Gomaji got into a conversation with the housekeeper sergeant. Netaji had with him about two hundred and fifty horsemen waiting in the stable. Fodder was arranged for the animals, and the army-kitchen staff were woken up and put to work for readying meals for the late-night guests.

The palace kitchen stoves were lit for the important among Netaji's soldiers. Shivaji was awake too. He first ensured that Netaji got out of his wet clothes and changed into fresh ones, and then called him into the private chamber, where Jijausaheb had also arrived. The Raja asked him in a worried tone, 'What's going on, Netajikaka? I had issued fresh orders for you to mount surveillance in and around Pratapgad. What are you doing so far away from your post?'

'There was an urgent need for it.'

'But how can you so carelessly abandon your assigned beat?'

Despite the hustle, Netaji smiled sweetly and said, 'How can I abandon my beat, Raje? Keep one thing in mind, Raje: as the range of our horses increases, the extent of the beat expands too. Worry for the king's safety nags the mind to distraction.'

'Meaning?'

'You may have closed your eyes for a bit, but the enemy is unblinkingly awake. Unfortunately, the Khan has got to hear of the Rani Saheba's passing away, and your journey across the jungles to this place.'

'What are you saying? I just can't believe it,' the Raja responded point-blank. 'Raje, I have confirmed news that the Khan plans to attack you on your journey back. That's why I came running here. I have done what I saw to be my duty. Whether you want to agree with it or not is your call.'

Shivraya, however, shrugged off Netaji's fears. The dense Sahyadri forests, the torrential rains, thick fog in the air, all of these taken together meant that the chances of an ambush were virtually non-existent. He just dismissed the subject. Much of the night had passed away. It was important to catch at least an hour or two of rest. That would also give time for the horses to recharge themselves. Hopefully, the rains would abate too. He had, therefore, made up his mind to leave at the crack of dawn.

Netaji sat in the palace kitchen, consuming his *bhaakari* with some spices. After he was finished with his meals, Shivraya, Jijausaheb, Netaji,

Gomajikaka, Kanhoji and young Shivaji Jedhe sat chatting in the hall. Netaji was determined to lay out all that was hurting inside him. He said in a sorrowful tone, 'Tell me this, Raje, whoever has come into this world to live until eternity? Who is going to escape the embrace of death?'

'What you say is quite true, kaka.'

'That is why, Raje, I join both my hands and beseech you. Instead of living on the horns of a dilemma, would it not be better to kiss death on the cheek and set off from here?'

Both Shivraya and Jijausaheb were stunned. They exchanged glances, which suggested that they should hear out Netaji's grievance. Handling and nursing a champion were no easy tasks. Netaji was by instinct a dazzling star, a scorching wind. There was no saying when he would set himself alight, like a heap of hay, to descend upon the enemy like a forest fire.

It was, perhaps, as a visceral warrior that God had sent him to the earth. He knew the pedigree of every sword he saw; knew exactly how an arrow could best find its mark. He had as much knowledge about every cannon-piece as an Agra Muslim artisan did who had spent his entire life pouring molten metal into casts in a cannon factory. While creating him, God had casually tossed in every single attribute that one would expect to find in a valiant warrior. But because of these very virtues, he was as difficult to handle as a lump of burning coal in the palm of one's hand.

The Goddess of War had taken total possession of Netaji from the moment Afzal Khan had stepped out of Bijapur. Getting into battle with him, defeating and crushing him altogether had become a monomania for him. Both Shivraya and Jijausaheb were sharply conscious of respecting the man's sentiments, however obsessive or impractical they appeared to them. It was barely two or three months ago that they had appointed this hot-blooded fighter as the commander-in-chief of the Maratha cavalry, a position that had earlier been occupied by a veteran like Bhikaji Dahatonde.

Netaji was designed to relish and flourish in all kinds of conflagrations. It was in that spirit that he snapped at Shivraya, 'Raje, at least now you may confess. Was that scheme of mine bad at all?'

'Which one, Netaji?' asked Jijausaheb.

'Matoshri, I had fallen not only at the Raja's feet, but yours too. What an opportunity that was! As if worked out after a study of the almanac. I could have confronted him as he was crossing the river Krishna at Rahimatpur, drowned him right there, and buried him in that wet sand. But you didn't listen to me. Now, he has reached Wai.'

Shivraya raised his voice a decibel and said, 'Look, Netajikaka, a kingdom cannot be run on blind, instinctive soldiery.'

'Before entering into the Sahyadris, when Afzal Khan had been advancing, swallowing all our posts like Supe, Baramati, Phaltan and Shirval, I had been imploring with you to stop him on the way, to break the teeth of that demon. I had not wanted a single one of our stations to fall into that devil's lap, but you would not listen to me.'

Netaji's emotional state was like that of a possessed devotee who whips himself to appease a god. How was he to be reined in? His rant refused to stop. 'You did affix to my turban the feather of the commander-in-chief; for that I thank you from the bottom of my heart. But this feather has nowhere satisfied my hunger, Raje. If I were to swear by God and lay it out plainly to you, this disease called Afzal Khan has completely consumed me.'

Despite the gravity of the situation, Jijausaheb put in a word of admiration, saying, 'Which means, our Netaji can see only Afzal Khan in the manner that Arjun in Mahabharata could only see the eye of the fish!'

'Yes, but what's the use, Aausaheb, if I am not given the opportunity to send my arrow straight into that eye?'

He then suddenly turned silent. Perhaps, the shock and the dangers involved had discomposed him. He heaved a deep sigh and continued, 'I've been trying my best to explain to you, but are you taking me seriously at all? The enemy has sent two thousand soldiers into the jungle to bring the Raja down.'

The night had nearly passed. Dawn would break shortly. The Raja avoided giving a straight answer to Netaji. The two hundred horsemen who were to leave with him got ready. He took the blessings of Goddess Jagdamba and his mother, and left. Within a short while, the contingent disappeared from sight.

Shivraya had disappeared from his sight without so much as looking at him. That he should walk away thus, without so much as a word to him, hurt Netaji deeply.

Dawn had begun to break. Jijau went inside and, after setting something in order, returned to sit at the head of the council hall. She had sensed the presence of Netaji and his men standing outside in a grim mood. In a little while, she saw Netaji and his friends stepping in soft-footedly. When they had come close enough, they placed their swords and spears at Jijausaheb's feet.

As he was laying his sword down, Jijau noticed tears streaming down his eyes. He bowed to her, deferentially, telling her through body language that he was off and there was no saying when they would meet next.

When she saw Netaji's form receding towards the door, she felt what a bird does when it sees its chick moving out of its sight. In a commanding voice, she pronounced, 'Stop, Netaji. Behave yourself and turn round.'

There was such weight in her voice that Netaji's feet froze in mid-step. He then slowly turned round and stood before Aausaheb like a student in a seminary; the others followed suit. Netaji noticed the teardrop that hung in her eye, refusing to come down any further. In the same intimidating voice as before, she ordered him, 'Netaji, pick up your weapon.'

When Netaji continued to stand there, still as a statue, Jijau rose from her seat and lashed out, 'If you refuse to pick up your weapons and stand up for the dignity of swarajya, keep this in mind: it's Lakhoji Jadhav's warm blood that flows through my arteries. Besides, if you are so sure that the king's life is in danger, why do you stop at merely offering advice? Why are you caught in this vicious battle of egos and sitting it out cold? All right, then. Look at the lustre of the kunku I wear in the name of Shahajiraje. Anybody there? Gomajikaka, let's move. Get the grooms to bring the horses out immediately. Keep this in mind: even at this age, when I lift my sword, I shall not sheathe it without splitting that Afzal Khan's throat.'

Jijausaheb bent down and picked up Netaji's jewel-studded sword. At that, Netaji Palkar broke down completely and threw himself at her feet. Placing his forehead on her feet, he cried out, 'Aausaheb, you are the mother of Hindvi swarajya. Please forgive us.'

Jijausaheb patted Netaji affectionately on his back, and handed over the jewelled sword to him. 'Netoba, this madness that resides inside you for swarajya, it's for this singular quality that not merely men but even animals fawn over you. But you have to be patient. The dream for which you are burning yourself like a lump of camphor, that dream will surely come true.'

The very next moment, Netaji and his men trooped out, leapt on their horses, and disappeared like the wind.

~~~

The precipitation on the trees was unceasing. Sludge underfoot, rains overhead, dense shrubs and bushes on the left and right, over impossible hilly terrain and across narrow trails, the Raja's horsemen were racing on without a break through this darkness. Suddenly, they heard the sound of a large body of water falling from the heights of the hills ahead. Man and animal instantly surmised that there was a big waterfall ahead. The Raja, however, rode on, uncaring for the force with which the water was descending. His men followed him excitedly. But the force of the water was beyond combating. It was this very patch that the king had crossed on his way to Rajgadh. But the incessant rains of the night had transformed a small stream into a powerful river.

The water rose up chest-high for the animals, and their eyes turned white with fear. Kanhoji Jedhe then suggested, 'Let's turn around. We should find a flatter patch of land from where we can cross this stream.'

The horses turned around. In the blinding downpour, a hillock came into view. That was when they heard the cry of 'Allah-o-Akbar!' and 'Deen Deen!' emerging from the bushes ahead. Suddenly, the enemy forces hiding in the wet, dense greenery ahead came down upon them with great fervour. The Raja and his men were taken aback because their own strength was far from adequate to confront the assault. The enemy had planned this attack on this unfrequented jungle trail. Swords clashed and a bitter hand-to-hand battle ensued. The Raja remembered Netaji's warning and realised too late that the man's information was right; so was his decision to come running to warn him. As the fight progressed, the darkness of the night dissipated and the wet green jungle of the Sahyadris became visible.

Old Kanhojibaba created mayhem. The others also ran in, and a hot skirmish ensued. The enemy were not too many in number either, but they were fired up with the motivation of finishing Shivajiraja in this wet wilderness. The warriors in front halted for a few moments behind the green bushes, and then they froze. The next moment, the sound of men and horses withdrawing through the dense green vegetation could be heard. Within a short time, the adventurous band simply disappeared into the greenery of the forest.

There was no alternative except to cross the valley in front and to take a roundabout route from the other side towards Pratapgad. On the right side were hills as tall as trees, while on the left were deep gorges and sharp, broken cliffs. The trail in front was ragged and extraordinarily narrow. Shivaji surmised that the enemy would deliberately have withdrawn for a short while. Danger lay ahead on the trail in front. Therefore, the rain-drenched horses moved forward, gingerly, waddling like ducks. Another deep valley lay ahead, through which a stream of cold water was gushing. Shivaji stood at the top of the hillock for a while. Everybody was staring like an alert herd of deer at the track that was running into the forest on the other side of the runnel.

Shivaji's squad hung on there for some while, but their restlessness was rising by the minute. There was danger in tarrying here too long. The rainfall would continue and they didn't have enough food and fodder to last them for long. Also, the battlefields in the jungles of Jawali had begun to flare up. It was imperative, therefore, to do all that they could and cross the stream in front. The Raja then noticed some movement happening in fits and starts on the bank of the stream in front. The Bijapuri horses were lying in wait for them. He consulted with Kanhoji. There was no choice but to fight through the danger that stood beyond the stream, and move ahead before their supplies of food and fodder ran out.

The best strategy would be to come suddenly upon the enemy, as the heavy vegetation offered them concealment, too. They climbed off their horses and began descending slowly and carefully through the slime and mud, pulling their horses behind them by their reins. Not much time would have passed when loud cries of 'Har har Mahadev!' and 'Jai Bhawani, Jai Shivaji!' rang out from the vegetation on the other side of the stream. The Raja and his company just couldn't fathom what was happening behind there, because the dense screen of trees and bushes had blocked their view. Some of the Maavalis, however, couldn't contain their curiosity and somehow managed to shin up the trunks of the slippery trees to find out. From that elevation they saw the battle that was being fought right on the other side. It was the loudness of the cries of 'Har har Mahadev!' and 'Allah-o-Akbar!' that gave them some idea of the intensity of the encounter.

Shivaji's group now began to descend the twists and turns of the slope rapidly. The horses were struggling to find a decent foothold on the wet earth and would often skid. The track, however, was refusing to end. It was after a long time that they began to hear the flow of the stream below. But amazingly, there was no other sound to be heard. Everything except nature had turned strangely silent. The slope finally ended, and the Raja and his men ran to the bank of the stream.

The sight that met their eyes left them stunned. Some two hundred bodies of the Adilshahi soldiers lay either bobbing in the stream or scattered on either side of it. The ones that had died in the stream looked like washed and cleaned fish. The two banks, however, carried splashes of blood mixed with the mud into which it had gushed out. Shivaji could count barely a dozen or so blood-stained head gears of the Maratha kind on either side of the stream. Someone had wiped out every last man of the brave and hardy band that Afzal Khan had dispatched for annihilating the king. Utterly overwhelmed at the sight, Shivaji and Kanhoji stared dumbly at each other.

Who that someone could be was obvious not only to everyone gathered there, but to the very trees and bushes that had been witness to this exploit. Shivraya spoke in a tone full of awe, 'Where even the wind cannot reach, there goes racing our dear, beloved Netaji.'

The deeply stirred Kanhobaji could only mutter, 'What does one say about our wild Palkar? He just floated in here, slaughtered the enemy and disappeared? He could at least have hung back to receive a pat on the back from his master!'

'He wouldn't hang back here. He is aware that the enemy has laid siege around the forest from Wai onwards, and his king is still not at his station. That has sent him flying back to his post.' As he said this, Shiavaji's heart turned soft and sentimental. A light drizzle was falling upon him and his company. Wet in body and wet in heart, he turned towards the gathered Maavalis and remarked, 'Wah, kaka, wah! Why shouldn't this Shivaji consider himself blessed as a king when he has subjects that adore him so and lions like Netaji who stake their lives for him?

23

THE DIPLOMATS MEET

SEPTEMBER 1659

Afzal Khan was a hedonistic person. He loved music and dance. People used to say only in half jest that in the matter of beauty, drinks and dance, there was no old cadger more colourful than Mahtab Khan among the Mughals and Afzal Khan among the Adilshahis.

Right since his days as the governor of Wai, Afzal Khan had owned a huge palatial manor there. The halls were arched, and in the middle of the quad was a large fountain. There was a special hall for entertaining guests. On the second floor facing the river Krishna was a pleasure hall with walls of mirrors. Dancing girls and women of pleasure had arrived in the army camp from the markets of Bhaganagari, Burhanpur and Pune. The artistes and the musicians accompanying them would be paid more than they expected. But this time round, our Khan Saheb was not being able to extract pleasure from all these merry-makings. After a day of running hither and thither, he would sometimes get pulled towards an evening of music and dance, but the joy he had anticipated would never arrive.

The beautiful young girls dancing in all their frenzy, their seductive gesticulations and provocative gestures, the inviting looks in their almond-shaped eyes, their rhythmic movements to the beats of the tabla—nothing could hold his attention too long. Bit by bit, he began to understand why he had lost the faculty of enjoying these soirees. The beats of the tabla would remind him of the cannons booming on the castle ramparts; the mournful strains of the sarangi would remind him of the keening of the womenfolk of dead soldiers and bite into him like the edge of a sharp sword. Even as he sat watching the frivolous merriment being enacted in the dance hall, he would get the sensation of being surrounded by the devilment of the Margathhas and being squeezed to death in it. He would then jump up like a deer that had slipped from over a cliff and scream, 'I don't want these indulgences, I want war! I want Shiva—dead or alive.'

Afzal Khan would often wonder whether his Pir Baba had given him a baseless scare. But on the other hand, he could see how the secret squad he had sent into the jungles had been so thoroughly wiped out. Here, in his camp at Wai, hundreds of thousands of rupees were being converted to excreta every day.

The grand proclamation he had made at his departure from Bijapur—that within two months and a half at the most he would put that Shivaji Bhosale in chains and bring him dragging through the streets in a procession, with drums and trumpets and all! But four months had been blown away like dry leaves since the campaign had begun; the month of Shraavan had gone and Bhaadrapad was now upon them, and his mission had not even seriously begun. This loss of precious time had left Afzal Khan tense and agitated.

Since he hadn't slept well that night, he had sent for his sardar friend Dundey Khan early in the morning. His body having turned stiff from many nights of sleeplessness and restlessness, he had surrendered it to the masseur that morning.

Stretched out flat on the bed, his well-built, muscular body looked like the trunk of a massive tree. The masseur boy Shaukat was a skillful artist. Taking a swab of cotton, he had daubed his master's body with oil and was now pumping and pummeling it in the manner of a wrestler, kneading the extra flesh, pulling his fingers and toes, exerting himself to the limit while the master lay groaning in pleasure.

While he was thus being given a rubbing, Dundey Khan sat against the opposite wall, resting against a bolster. 'There are two things I find necessary for taking Shiva alive into our custody, huzoor,' he said.

'What are they?'

'Getting into the dense jungle belt of Jawali with all our strength and tearing apart that Shiva's abdomen—'

'Well, that's not possible. Next?'

'Or else, laying out a careful web or threatening him with dire consequences and compelling him to come to the negotiating table. I don't see a third way.'

'That is our problem, Dundey Khan. That Shiva is extremely shrewd, the rascal. He understands full well that coming down from his mountain redoubt is no different from walking straight into the jaws of death.'

Afzal Khan's worrisome response left Dundey Khan perplexed. He looked up and down at the tall, lean, wheat-complexioned, eagle-eyed Muslim boy doing the massage and then looked enquiringly at Afzal Khan.

'Oh, he's a good cook, this boy. Lives somewhere in the vicinity of Bengaluru. Other than being a good cook, he gives a good massage too.'

The expression on Dundey Khan's face flipped. Losing all restraint, he yelled at Afzal Khan, 'Forgive me, Khan Saheb, this boy giving you the rubbing cannot be one of us by a long stretch. I suspect he belongs to the enemy camp and has been sent here to keep an eye on us.'

Dundey Khan's words virtually set a cat among the pigeons in the palace. Shaukat was shivering uncontrollably as the minions of the palace came running in. Afzal Khan's face turned stern as he clapped his hands, indicating to his men that the boy be arrested. Pointing his finger at Shaukat, Afzal Khan roared, 'Catch hold of this chap. Take him into the next room and pull down his trousers. Check him out thoroughly.'

The men did as they were instructed and dragged the trembling Shaukat into the next room. Afzal was so curious about the outcome that he could not stay away for long. He dashed into the room and, after a while, came out laughing merrily. He announced to the gathering that he was properly circumcised and was a co-religionist. The assembled servants and guards also broke into laughter.

Everybody was happy that Shaukat Miyan had escaped a painful death. Afzal Khan expressed the wish to be served the tasty Krishna water fish, and instructed Shaukat Miyan to cook the delicious curry that he prepared so well. The boy bent low and took leave of his master. Looking at his receding figure, Afzal Khan told his minion Qutb Miyan, 'Always keep an eye on this fellow, anyway.'

'Why, Khan Saheb?'

'In spite of being one of us, he doesn't look like one of us.'

Vengeance and hatred were forever keeping Afzal Khan's blood on the boil. The monsoons were not allowing him to settle down comfortably. Expenses were mounting all the time; but far worse, his reputation was taking a beating like never before. He sent for Krishnaji Bhaskar Kulkarni to report to him immediately that morning at his palace court. 'You belong to a faithful Brahmin family from the Wai region,' he told him on arrival, 'and you have been in the service of Bijapur for many generations.'

'Absolutely, huzoor.'

'Your pen drips honey and your sword lets out fountains of blood.'

'I don't need these praises, huzoor; just issue the orders.'

'Go immediately to Shiva, then. Magic spells, breast beating, songs and dances, soft talking, do whatever you have to, but bring him to Wai for a conversation with me at any cost.'

'But, huzoor—'

Without letting Krishnaji complete his sentence, Afzal Khan held him by both his hands and said, 'Arey, Krishnaji, this not an order, this is a plea.'

·~·

'Ankush Khan, when someone wants to cross the river for matrimonial purposes, it can never do to depend upon one single boat.'

'Rightly said, Miyan,' said Ankush Khan with a laugh. 'If that boat were to capsise, the entire marriage procession would be gone.'

'But, Ankush Miyan, this time an agent won't be enough. We must find some close relative of Shiva's ... some insider.'

'We have the exact man in the army, that Mambaji Bhosale, Shahaji's first cousin!'

'I've already tried him, but it appears that there's not much love lost between Mambaji and Shahaji's family. Looks like some old grouse. Besides, the man has now turned old. We need a shrewd, sprightly young man who can sit in Shiva's tent, get into his heart, and persuade him to come down from that mountain to meet me. After that—'

'I suppose, it is Mambaji who can lead us to the person we want.'

'Yes, that sounds right. You go visit Mambaji this very evening.'

That evening, both Ankush Khan and Dundey Khan had a long sitting with Mambaji in his tent and had their dinner together. Very early the next morning, Ankush Khan and Mambaji went visiting Afzal Khan in his manor. They had with them a handsome-looking boy of around twenty. Ankush Khan first sneaked into Afzal's bedroom and informed him of his success. The three then sat in the outer hall, waiting for Afzal Khan to come out. Meanwhile, Afzal Khan happened to peep out and he got a good view of the boy, and was immediately disappointed. He returned to the inner hall.

After some while, he called Ankush Miyan and Mambaji inside and said, 'The boy is certainly handsome, but we don't need any dancing boy for this purpose. I had wanted you to locate someone close to Shiva who would be able to reach that cunning fox's den in the jungle.'

'*Ajee* Khan Saheb,' retorted Mambaji irritably, 'if you will not let us even speak, how will we make our next move?'

'But what do I gain by taking this young boy in my embrace?'

'Khan Saheb, it's through him that you will find the perfect medicine for your ailment.'

'Who is this boy, anyway?'

'His name is Khelkarn Bhosale, and he is the son of my brother Kheloji Bhosale and Gaurabai.'

'The Kheloji who was my sardar at one time? The person who was hanged by a tree in Aurangabad?'

'That's the one. The son of the woman whom Mahtab Khan had beleaguered near Nashik on the bank of the Godavari.'

'Ah, now I get it, Mambaji. He is your nephew.'

'That's just what I've been saying. Both my sisters-in-law Gaura vahini and Jija vahini—that is Shivaji's mother—were very dear to each other. They shared an intimate relationship. When Shivaji was first put into a cradle, it was this Gaurabai who had gone to sing the verses for blessing the infant. That boy sitting outside, Babaji is his name, is Gaurabai's son.'

'But you just said his name was Khelkarn?'

'Khan Saheb, Khelkarn is the name he is known by, but his official name is Babaji.'

Afzal Khan called the boy inside and explained to him the nature of the assignment. The first impression of the boy was that he was the silent kind, but it soon became clear that he was a responsible young man who spoke with precision and thought with clarity. He told Afzal Khan with great self-confidence, 'Look, Khan Saheb, the matter has settled quite clearly in my head and there's no need for me to say much. I shall go to Pratapgad and meet Shivajidada. I shall explain just this to him that he is ruining his life by playing paltry games with an elephant. Because of him, the entire Bhosale clan is suffering losses too.'

'That is wonderful,' Afzal Khan whooped in delight. 'Where was this boy hiding all these days?'

Babaji declared that plenty of care would have to be exercised. Even if it required making multiple visits to the jungle of Jawali, he was ready for it. He told Afzal Khan that he would have to be assigned a few guards and would have to be trusted completely. He turned emotional as he said, 'My aunt Jijaukaku and my mother are devoted to each other. When my father met his unfair and unfortunate end, both Shivajidada and Jijaukaku were genuinely aggrieved.'

'Look, son, you will get all the help you need for this errand.'

'Please hear me out carefully, Khan Saheb. We are talking of an extremely delicate family matter here, and therefore, it is important that I reassure myself about a few things. He may very well trust my word and agree to come over. But what if you commit some treachery upon a person who is the pride of our Bhosale clan?'

'How can you think of such a thing, son? My only aim is that the misunderstanding that is troubling Sultan Saheb's head with regard to Shivaji should be cleared. Your Shivajidada is quite like a younger brother to me. I shall hold him by the finger and take him to Bijapur and bring back amity between him and the sultan. This can lead to nothing but advancement for him. Besides, I shall grant you a ten-thousand-horse mansab too and take you places.'

The past three months had seen incessant, torrential rains. Today, however, there was no trace of rainfall across the Sahyadri hills and valleys. After having drunk water to their heart's content, the jungles had begun to look bright and lively. The sky was cloudless too. The intelligent and industrious Arjoji Yadav had wrought a miracle: he had put to work thousands of labourers and fulfilled the promise he had made to Shivraya. He had completed the construction of the massive bastion and the walls of the Pratapgad fort in a short period of two years. He had, of course, benefitted considerably from the advice of Moropant Peshve. This was a brand-new fort constructed by the Raja himself. The entire neighbourhood was happy that the Raja had shifted residence to this fort during the monsoons. But there were worries too over the news of the gigantic army that Afzal Khan had assembled at Wai on the bank of the Krishna.

In the verandah inside the palace sat the plump Krishnaji Kulkarni and three Adilshahi grandees who had accompanied him. As Krishnaji was mopping his face with the cloth on his shoulder, Kanhoji Jedhe arrived. This experienced old gentleman had seen fifteen to twenty monsoons more than Kulkarni had, and was familiar with every town and hamlet located between Bijapur and the Maaval region. Krishnaji rose to his feet immediately and bowed low to greet Kanhoji Jedhe with due respect.

As soon as Kanhoji saw him, he said, 'Arey Krishna, you have arrived at the most inauspicious time to meet the king.'

'Why?'

'Illness. Krishnaji, if you see the debilitated state in which my king is, you will also be dismayed.'

'How did this happen, Kanhojibaba?' He looked properly concerned.

'He's burning with fever. He finds it difficult to stand up, and when he's up, he finds it difficult to sit down,' Kanhoji said, breathing heavily. He then narrowed his eyes and asked, 'But tell me, Krishna, what could be the reason for you to have travelled up through these difficult jungles, and that too during these rains?'

Krishnaji took Kanhoji to a side and whispered in his ear, 'I've brought an important message from Afzal Khan.'

'Oh my God, from Afzal Khan Saheb?' Kanhoji's face turned dark with worry. 'God help me, but I don't know how it's going to work out.'

'What are you saying?'

'Arey Krishnaji,' said a visibly tensed Kanhoji in a voice that seemed to choke in his throat, 'don't you utter the name of Afzal Khan here. The fear of that man has settled deep into the heart of our king like a poisonous thorn. The very utterance of that name seems to turn the king into a nervous wreck.'

Krishnaji pulled at the cloth on his shoulder and gave it a shake. He was daunted at the thought of having to go back to Wai empty-handed. 'Wait, Kanhoji,' he pleaded. 'Don't disappoint me so much. Do me this little favour, at least.'

'What's that?'

'Khan Saheb has given me this urgent and highly confidential letter.'

Kanhoji shut his eyes and lost himself in some thought. Then he said, 'Look, Krishnaji, I don't find it right, either, to have to send back such an important Adilshahi official like you empty-handed. Moreover, the letter has come from Khan Saheb, no less! What prestige he enjoys! Fifty battles he has fought till now, and not in one of them has he ever withdrawn or suffered defeat!'

Kanhoji then suggested that an effort could be made for Krishnaji to meet the king, but for that to happen, he would have to stay behind for a couple of nights. Krishnaji happily accepted Kanhoji's advice.

The next evening, Shivraya sat with a shawl wrapped tightly around his shoulder and a monkey-cap pulled over his ears. He looked like a person who had been bed-ridden for a couple of months. His voice had turned thin and weak too. When Krishnaji held out the letter from Afzal Khan, Shivraya found himself too weak even to stretch out his hand and accept it. Instead, in a faint voice, he mumbled, '*Aho* Pant, why don't you read the letter out yourself?'

Krishnaji adjusted his headgear, mopped his face, and began reading the letter from the Bijapur general:

> Raje Shivaji Bhosale, you are an ambitious and intelligent person. When the Nizamshahi sank, you established unprovoked and illegitimate control over the mountainous region and the forts in it that had gone to the share of the Mughals. We have received complaints that you even took control of Kalyan and Bhiwandi, and razed to the ground the mosques—

'Stop! Stop right there, Pant.' Despite feigning illness, he couldn't keep his anger away. 'You may throw all kinds of accusations at this Shivaji here, but being accused of desecrating religious places, that I shall not tolerate even in my dreams.'

Krishnaji was taken aback and looked deeply embarrassed. The Raja got his hold back on himself and said, 'All right, Pant, read on. Don't worry. Read whatever is written.'

> You seem to suffer from the delusion of having become a king. Accordingly, you sit on a golden throne, carry the symbols of an emperor, stage the drama of delivering justice before the subjects—do not care for intellectuals or accomplished persons. Therefore, you are advised to immediately return to the all-conquering Emperor of Delhi the forts that you have illegitimately taken into your possession, and to hand over to us all the land that lies between the Neera and the Bheema rivers. Doing this will save your life and will be an act of wisdom.

Looking at the changed demeanour of the king and the timidity he was displaying, Krishnaji felt more emboldened. He said enthusiastically, 'Please do meet our Khan Saheb once. He has said this on oath that he will persuade our Sultan to return to Shivajiraja all the forts and lands that he has won or confiscated. As for the coastal region of Konkan, he will take it from the Sultan and place it round your neck like a garland of flowers.'

'Wah!'

'You just have to come and meet him at Wai.'

'No, Pant, no, don't be so insistent. Actually, I feel ashamed at the thought of presenting myself before him with my guilty face.'

The meeting went on until quite late in the evening. Arrangements had been made for Krishnaji Bhaskar's overnight stay at Pratapgad. He was surprised when he noticed that he had been housed in a room at the extreme corner of the guest house. But after having spent a very taxing day, he soon fell into deep slumber. Very late in the night, he got up with a jolt. Out there, the mountain winds were screaming, and inside the guest house, somebody was knocking on his door.

Krishnaji jumped out of his bed with a start and peeped through a crack in the door before opening the latch. In the orange flame of the flambeau, he saw Shivaji standing there, wrapped in a shawl to guard himself against the roaring wind. There were two other torch-bearers with him.

Beginning in a hoarse voice, he said that he had something extremely important to say to Krishnaji privately. Fixing him with his sharp gaze, Shivaji said, 'Krishnajipant, you are a Brahmin by caste and a Hindu by religion. Tell me something on oath, then.'

'Ask, Raje.'

'Tell me honestly what the Khan has in his heart—real amity or treachery.'

'Well, this is a difficult question to answer.'

Giving an answer to this question was altogether beyond Krishnaji's ken. Gathering his wits, he managed to say, 'It is not Afzal Khan alone, but I too believe that this deadlock should be sorted out once and for all through dialogue.'

However deep one digs into a deep well, what becomes visible on the surface is just bubbles. One thing was clear, however, that as a servant, Krishnaji's ultimate allegiance lay with Afzal Khan. Nevertheless, Shivaji made a final effort and said, 'Look, our kingdom here is of gods and Brahmans. Wake up to the loyalty you owe to your religion. See if you can stretch yourself and do something.'

'I certainly shall,' replied Krishnaji with a smile. 'I shall definitely try to protect your interest. But I shall have to take care that this dhoti of service that I wear doesn't come undone as I move forward.'

After his two-day stay, as Krishnaji took leave, he was felicitated in style. He was given gifts of three sets of clothes, a pearl set, gold bracelets and medals, and an Arab horse of the best breed. He was also given five thousand hons in cash. Besides, Shivraya also handed over a letter for Afzal Khan and an invitation for a visit to Pratapgad.

Pantaji Bokil was instructed to accompany Krishnaji as the Raja's agent for handing over the invitation to the Khan. Pantaji Gopinathkaka was basically an official with the Jadhavs of Sindkhed. He had come over to the Bhosales after Jijau was married into the family.

Barely eight days had passed when Babaji Bhosale returned to the Wai camp. Everybody gathered around him. His handsome face looked happy at the new assignment entrusted to him. 'I have a feeling that I have been successful in bringing about a change of heart. But I may have to make a few more trips to Dada's palace.'

'But why have you returned mid-way?' asked Ankush Khan.

'Oh, that's a family matter. There are some dissensions among us Bhosales regarding the distribution of lands in Sandaskhurd and a few other places. It's with regard to this matter that the king has asked me to seek some responses from Mambajikaka and get back to him immediately.'

That night, uncle and nephew sat in the Bhosale tent. Before the conversation began, Mambaji stepped out twice and swept his eyes all around the canvas walls. Assuring himself that the entire Khan camp was fast asleep, he asked, 'So, Khelya, did Shivaji give ear to your talk?'

'What do I say, kaka? I went there all right, but Shivaji dada has now sent me back to you.'

'What does he say?'

'He has just sent a reminder that hitting with a stick in the middle of a flow does not split a river into two. Therefore, as a father-figure, you should show largeness of heart and move over to his side.'

'Ah, I see.'

'To tell you the truth, kaka, the very voicing of your name released for him a flood of memories. He asked me to tell you of the times when you carried him on your back all over Pemgadh. He wondered whether you would have forgotten about it, but he simply can't. He wondered why you have abandoned your own barn full of animals and are wandering elsewhere. At this time in your life, why should you stay under the wing of an outsider and at his mercy like an old stag? He said that he loved you dearly and saw no difference between his father and you.'

'He's someone who has erected his own world.'

'Mambakaka, I too believe that blood should meet blood.'

'How is it possible at all now, my boy?' said Mambaji, wiping the moisture off his eyes. 'Tell my Shivba, I have long crossed the river of distances and reached the other bank. Fruitless sparks of conceit, bickerings and property have long ago burnt the bridge that lay between us. Forget it, there is no point in raking up this matter.'

Mambaji let out a deep sigh or two. Shrugging the subject away, he said, 'Arey, but do you remember what you had gone there for? To persuade Shivaji to come over for a meeting with Khan Saheb, right? What happened to that?'

'What do I say, Mambakaka? When I saw the extraordinary world that Shivajidada has erected around himself, I completely forgot why I had been sent there. I saw the poor people of Maaval gathered around him like bees gather around a flower. They have accepted Shivajidada as someone more revered than their gods. The warriors gathered there stand on one foot to offer their lives in the service of their king. What do I tell you, Mambakaka, about what I saw in that land—that wise king of the poor, that lion with a compassionate heart, that lustrous jewel that has emerged in the land of rocks and stones. I became his devotee there and fell at his feet. That was why I couldn't lift my tongue to sing the praises of Afzal Khan in that sacred place.'

'Have you lost your head, boy? Shhh!' Panic-stricken, Mambaji quickly stepped out to peep at the darkness outside his hut and returned. 'What kind of talk is this, and in whose camp? Don't you value your life?'

'All right, Mambakaka, here's the truth,' said Babaji in a choked voice. 'If you ask me, the real euphoria lies in fighting battles on the side of an extraordinary person like Shivraya. If I can die for his sake, I shall consider it a pleasurable death.'

Mambaji felt completely unsettled at hearing this eulogy from Babaji's lips. He wiped the sweat beads that had suddenly formed on his face and under his chin.

'Mambakaka,' Babaji continued, 'I can swear with my hands at the feet of Mother Bhawani that if ever Rama and Krishna were to take birth in the Bhosale clan, they would be astounded at the respect that my Shivajidada commands. Come along, stop wasting your time in this suffocating camp. Come with me to the Gokul that my Shivraya has built for the poorest of the poor. Come with me to swarajya. I have come to pick you up.'

The wind picked up outside. The canvas walls began to flap. Along with these sounds came the flapping of sixty or seventy chappals and loud shouts of 'Catch the bastard! Beat him up!'. Mambaji realised that it was his tent that was being raided. He took in hand the burning torch that was stuck outside his tent, but it slipped out of his hands and went out—went out or was put out, difficult to say. There was complete darkness in the tent for a little while. Stamping their feet as they came, the swordsmen and the lancers among the crowd began searching through Mambaji's tent.

Meanwhile, Ankush Khan came over to him, and the two together began running hither and thither. Mambaji cried in a deeply offended voice, 'Look at this useless brat. I had never thought this fellow of mine would turn out to be such a traitor. Comes and stays in my tent, eats my salt and then, at a critical moment, tells me to join Shivaji!'

The search went on for a long time, but Babaji had melted into the darkness. The search was abandoned, and a call arrived from Afzal Khan. Deeply remorseful, Mambaji went with his head bowed to meet the Khan. He was subjected to some grueling cross-examination. He finally managed to drag himself back to his tent.

The night had almost rolled by and soon it would be dawn. Everybody in the army camp had fallen into deep sleep. The barking dogs had also done their duty for the night and toppled off listless. There was no way that Mambaji could go back to sleep. He sat at the edge of his bed in the company of four of his closest associates. Cold wind blew outside. He stepped outside to the little temporary shrine he had erected along the canvas wall of his tent, and touched his forehead to the idol there. From there he went to the rear of the tent, where he kept sacks of fodder for his favourite horses.

He reached out to pull one of the sacks. A little stone pit had been created there for keeping various things. Mambaji sensed some movement there in the darkness. He whispered softly, 'Khelya, come on out, quick.'

Babaji jumped out the next moment. The profusely sweating uncle-nephew duo looked around carefully. Complete silence everywhere except for the sound of the pre-dawn breeze. 'All right, now,' Mambaji whispered. 'You are a good swimmer. Some of my men will accompany you up to the river. Keep some distance from them and walk briskly.'

Babaji placed his head at his uncle's feet. The old man lifted him up and gave him a tight embrace. Wiping his eyes, he said, 'Khelkarna, tell my Shivaji this. Tell him his invitation gladdened my heart to its very core. But this body of mine is teetering at the lip of the abyss of old age. After an entire life of running around, my bones have begun to rattle. At this age, there is no strength left in my limbs for making big leaps. Forgive me, my boy, but do tell my Shivba that he may go ahead and shake hands with the devil if he is compelled to, but he shouldn't place any trust at all in this son of a bastard Afzal Khan. Go, go tell Shivba that he should keep growing. And he must always draw strength from Ma Bhawani.'

24

THE TREACHEROUS TRAIL OF RADTONDI

OCTOBER 1659

Afzal Khan had been frantically searching for a way to eliminate Shivaji, through fair means or foul, through a daring raid or whatever else. But success had been eluding him, thus enraging him further. The matter needed urgent resolution, but resolution was nowhere in sight, making life miserable for him. Under these circumstances, when he heard that the agents of both sides were arriving for talks, he felt a little hopeful.

Krishnajipant and Gopinath Bokil entered Afzal's palace together. Both of them informed the Khan that Shivaji had taken a fright, and more importantly, he was deeply contrite over whatever offences he had committed. He had also sent an extremely expensive dress for the Khan along with an incomparable necklace of jewels as a peace offering.

As Shivraya had instructed Krishna to do the reading of the letter, Afzal Khan placed the same responsibility upon Gopinath Bokil. In an extremely mellifluous voice, Bokil presented Shivaji's words in a soulful manner.

> We are too small to eulogise on Khan Saheb's effulgent personality.
> There is no match to the strength of your arms and your splendour.

'Wah wah. Beautiful. Read on.' Afzal Khan's face had begun to glow at these words.

You have ornamented the world with your extraordinary deeds of valour. Alongside, you also possess a heart that is pure, beautiful and transparent. No one can ever locate a single evil thought in the folds of its petals.

'Wait, Bokil,' exclaimed Afzal Khan with a laugh. 'We had heard of the great swordsmanship of your Shiva. Is he a poet too?' With that, he signalled to Bokil to continue.

Khan Saheb, we are aware of the extraordinary personality we are communicating with through this letter. The fact is that we do not possess the strength to look into the eyes of a great person like yourself. There are no ifs and buts in my mind with regard to your esteemed self. Without carrying any doubt in my mind, as per your demand, I am ready to surrender not just all the forts, but Jawali, too, in the bargain. I am eager to lay down my sword at your feet.

'Wah, what a clean-hearted and bright boy this is! Read on, Bokil.'

In furtherance of the word I have given, I am eager to obey your command. But my humble request is that Khan Saheb should wind up his unnecessarily prolonged stay in the township of Wai. Instead, he should take the benefit of the clean, pleasant air of Pratapgad. He should tour around the old and fabulous forests here with his army to his heart's content, experience the post-monsoon beauty of this region. The meadows have turned as attractive as the most expensive velvet shawls that Khan Saheb can imagine. The world here is covered in the white blooms of the sonaki flower—

'Stop, Bokil. I don't like this last part of your Raja's letter.'

Both Gopinath Bokil and Krishnaji were perplexed at Afzal Khan's response, and responded together, 'Khan Saheb?'

'That's right. I can discern the vicious intent hidden beneath your king's honeyed words.' With that, he glared in both directions. 'No, this cannot happen.'

'But, Khan Saheb—'

'Go tell that Shiva, not even my dead body shall travel to the Pratapgad forests. He will have to come down here to meet me.'

Where has your fire gone? Our army of twenty thousand men sits there, for four months, like a bear with a stomach ache, and finds itself incapable of arresting an ordinary boy like Shiva? What is our *Qaatil-e-kaafiroon* Afzal Khan Saheb doing?

When Khairiyat Khan, who had arrived from Bijapur, was reading out the missive from the Badi Begum, her tall personality, her sharp, stringent face and her lacerating eyes were floating before Afzal Khan's eyes. Hugely upset, he tore the Afghan turban off his head. When Khairiyat Khan froze, he shouted, 'Keep reading.'

'Forgive my impertinence, huzoor,' Khairiyat pleaded, hands trembling, 'I don't have the courage to read further.'

'Read!' roared Afzal.

Khairiyat swallowed hard and somehow read out the next words, 'If you don't want to fight the proper way—'

'Then what? Read on, Khairiyat!'

'Then a new brave-heart will be sent to the field.'

Afzal Khan was a proud man. He did not appreciate the language that the Begum had used. 'All right, stop,' he screamed and got up. He began pacing the hall in circles like a wounded wild pig. He would sometimes go up to the window and look out at the flooded river in front. He had whipped himself out of control. 'See this, Ankush Khan? Do you see this, Khairiyat Bhai? This is what fate can do. The *Qaatil-e-kaafiroon* who has rendered over fifty kings and grandees homeless in the Deccan, before whom the shameless whore called defeat has never dared to stand for a moment, that is who Afzal Khan is. And today our Begum Saheba has called this loyal slave of hers incompetent!'

In a fit of rage, Afzal Khan picked up his turban and his sword, and began to move out. 'Miyan Afzal Saheb,' stuttered Ankush Khan, worriedly, 'Where are you going?'

Afzal Khan's livid face was telling a story of its own. When he saw fear written over the faces of his sardars, he heaved a deep sigh and said, 'A government that does not know the meaning of appreciation, staying on in that government is inviting disaster.'

He dictated in his response to his chief administrator that if the Adilshahi of Bijapur considered him so incompetent, they should by all means go ahead and appoint a new commander-in-chief to replace him. That done, he walked off towards his bed chamber with long strides.

Afzal Khan came into his bed chamber and sat down heavily like a traveller who had just returned exhausted from a long journey. After a while, when he heard footsteps in his hall, he did not even care to raise his head. He knew for certain that nobody except Ankush Khan would have dared to step into his chamber. In a voice filled with exasperation, he said, 'Why are you hounding me like this, Ankush Khan? I am not going to change my decision.'

'Wah, Afzal Bhai, if Bijapur is expressing disappointment after four months of waiting, why is it such a terrible thing? Afzal Bhai, a person like you has to be true to his salt.'

'But what is my fault?'

'Bhai Afzal, there are a score of big sardars in the Sultan's durbar, but along with being in the service of the Sultanate, you are the one and only big trader, a person with his own ships riding the waves, the only other person who runs a factory for issuing gold currency in his name other than Adilshah Salamat himself. Can another Afzal Khan ever be born in this Adilshahi kingdom?'

This reminder from Ankush Khan softened Afzal Khan considerably. He had already begun considering reining his anger in when Ankush Khan spoke again. 'And who can forget those sixty-three innocent, beautiful sisters-in-law of mine? They were all daughters of great grandees, belonging to the most renowned families. When they had married the grand, consummate high official that was you, what dreams they would have brought along with them! Those sisters of mine who gave the ultimate sacrifice of jumping into the well for their land and for their husband's victory, are you now setting out to grind their sacrifice into dirt?'

Ankush Khan's points were well chosen, and Afzal Khan was no longer left with the strength to counter them. Ankush Khan continued to remind him of the beautiful mausoleum he had built for himself, the advice of the pir baba and a number of other things. This assault of Ankush Khan's was so debilitating that Afzal Khan was not even left with the energy to pick up a glass of liquor for himself.

'Moving into the mountains of Jawali means taking the army into Shiva's land.'

Afzal Khan had nearly a couple of dozen senior sardars in his army, who had been dinning it into him, 'Afzal Miyan, let's not rush into Jawali and invite sure disaster.'

Krishnaji Bhaskar had returned from Pratapgad empty-handed, bringing the news that Shivajiraje was avoiding any meeting with him. Afzal had made rapid advances from Bijapur to Wai in the hope of taking the king into custody. On reaching Wai, he had been extremely excited at the thought of quickly crushing Shivaji. He had sent secret squads for killing him; he had sent Babaji Bhosale in the hope of luring him out, but all his plans had fallen flat.

The monsoons had left him with little option but to set camp at Wai. Besides, the familiarity of the Marathas with the Sahyadri mountains had become a serious headache for him.

Afzal Khan suddenly decided to change tack. He decided to fold up the Wai camp and set out for Pratapgad. When his chieftains got this information, they had crowded into his palace, uncaring of his arrogant and dictatorial nature. Most of them had begun to scream, 'Listen, Afzal Miyan, the affectionate invitation that Shivaji sent through Krishnaji is a total eyewash. Please listen to us.'

'Listen to us. You will walk into a trap. You will regret it.'

Dundey Khan slapped his sword on his thigh and said in a mournful voice, 'If you don't listen to us, all that you will get is ruination.'

'Silent! Silent, Dunde Miyan. A senior and experienced sardar like you crying like a screechy young girl is something I cannot stomach.'

'Khan Saheb, the poor girl cries for the welfare of her husband. These tears that flow from my eyes flow not for you and not for me, but for my beloved country Bijapur,' he said in a tremulous voice.

Emotions were running high at the meeting. Afzal Khan, therefore, stayed silent to help calm everyone down. After some time, he adopted a solicitous tone in the hope of converting his sardar allies. 'My brothers,' he said, 'why are you feeling afraid? How can you not see that Shiva has been reduced to the state of ailing sheep and goats at the sight of our all-conquering army? And the Makka and Madina of the brutish Margatthas, what are they called? Oh yes, Tulzapur and Pandharpur. Our very name caused not just the people there but even the gods to shiver in fear. Our army has been marching ahead with live torches, and in contrast, what happened to their half-dead soldiers? At their posts in Supe, Indapur and Thane and others? Those emaciated, cowardly men merely heard of our arrival and ran for the mountains.'

In the end, everybody had to bend to Afzal Khan's will. Here was a person who, until yesterday, had been talking about laying traps and playing games. Nobody was able to solve the puzzle of this sudden change of mind. There was one thing, however, that had happened that could have brought about this turnaround.

The letter that Krishnaji Bhaskar had brought from Shivaji had been read out and the purport fully understood. But as Krishnaji was about to leave the Khan's room, he had said, 'Huzoor, Shivaji has given me a private letter for you.'

Afzal Khan quickly took the letter. It read:

Jung Bahadur Khan Saheb,
Actually, I had wanted to come running to you, searching for support at your sacred feet. But then, I have committed so many grievous offences against a venerable, lionhearted sardar like you, that the very thought of showing you my sinful, guilty face fills me with shame. As a misguided youngster, I feel excited at the thought of one day kissing your holy feet and ridding myself of my sins. You have been an old associate of my father, which makes you my uncle by this relationship. That is why I have decided to take guidance from you at every step and bring my life back into order.

As of now, I request that huzoor suffer a little discomfort by making this trip to Pratapgad. The sight of you and this meeting with you will automatically wipe out whatever little doubts remain. We shall not be spending much time here after that. I shall hold your finger, and we shall set off for Bijapur through this jungle via Bamnoli and Vasota. The confusion will be resolved only when I touch the feet of Ma Badi Begum Saheba in her Bijapur palace. Hence the supplication that huzoor makes this visit to Pratapgad. Give this blind person a pair of eyes; grant this destitute some support. We shall then immediately leave for Bijapur.

Afzal Khan was thrilled at reading the letter. In the middle of the night, he dispatched his servants to the army tent and had them bring over the famous wooden cage. He had it placed in the hall next to his bedroom, and issued strict instructions that no footman or servant should come anywhere near there. He then began examining that cage like a solitary ghost.

Afzal Khan kept walking around the cage all through the night. He was as delighted with it as a kid could be with a balloon. His eyes could see Shivraya imprisoned in the cage. He would snap his fingers and laugh villainously as he screamed, 'Catch this hell-hound Shiva!' He would punch the cage with his fists.

By dawn, the Khan's eyes had turned blood-red and droopy. He punched the cage one more time and laughed as he said, 'Shiva, you are very smart, aren't you, boy? You've been dreaming away of luring me into your trap with all these honeyed words, haven't you? But what do you know? When a hunter gets trapped in a jungle, slips, or runs out of luck and falls into the jaws of a wild animal, that's when that ferocious animal sits on the hunter and tears open his chest, pulling the stomach and intestines out. The joy of that moment is like no other joy. Young man, if you have a net, I have a super-net. Laugh while you can. This *Qaatil-e-kaafiroon, Shikanda-e-buniyaad-e-butaan*, the demolisher of idols, Afzal Khan is coming over to meet you.'

Even before dawn had broken, the army camp had been taken over by frenetic activity. Afzal Khan had had the tents brought down. All the paraphernalia had been loaded on the backs of bullocks and donkeys. The men began to march even before the first cock had crowed. After three months and a half of lazing around, the horses had finally been let free. When the cold wind of early dawn hit their nostrils, they became animated and began kicking their legs energetically.

Only twenty big elephants and eighty large cannons had been left behind in the Wai camp. The rest of the army had moved with all its equipment.

By the time daylight began to spread, they had reached Kusgaon. By the time the sun had turned hot, they had reached Chikhali. Breakfast was consumed standing. As the army-kitchen boys receded, the bhishtis came with their leathern bags and poured water into the cupped hands of the soldiers to wash the food down. Then the march resumed.

In the afternoon, when the army reached the climb of Taighat, the Bijapuris got their first taste of the Sahyadri jungles. With the rainy season having just got over, the jungles and the tracks inside them were still wet. When the horses began to lose their footing on the moist, slimy earth, the riders got off their backs. They realised that the only way to make them climb the ghats was to pull them by their reins. It was a good thing that Shivajiraja had requested Khan Saheb and taken a few big elephants under the custody of the Maavalis about ten days back. The animals had used their trunks to dislodge a few big and small trees, after which the horsemen had cleaned out the rest of the vegetation, creating a passage that could be used. It would otherwise not have been possible for the Khan's army to move through these ghats.

Before the elephant herd began its climb, ten or twelve thousand horses had travelled up the sharp slope. The hooves of those horses had whipped up an enormous amount of muddy slush. Often, getting an estimate of the stones on the way would be difficult, causing the donkeys to teeter and fall with all the load on their backs. A few horses had knocked themselves into the rocks on the way and broken their backs. As they screeched in intolerable pain, their owners could not take it any more; they nudged them to the edge of the cliff with great difficulty and pushed them into the gorge, thus delivering them from pain forever.

As the mahouts egged their elephants to climb up the ghats, they got first-hand knowledge of what the pain of death meant. Often, they would skid over the muck and mire, and fall on their faces or on their sides. The thick skin on their knees would get ripped off, and the huge beasts would let out horrible screams. Some of the smarter ones would swing their trunks to get a grip on the thick branches of trees, and try to pull the huge weight of their bodies up.

The animals urinated copiously and groaned as they climbed up the near-perpendicular cliffs of Taighat. The horses were subjected to merciless flogging, while the elephants shrieked with pain when the goads of their mahouts buried themselves deep into their flesh.

There were about thirty-five thousand horsemen, foot soldiers and non-combatant groups, and well over twenty thousand animals, along with enough food and fodder to last them a month—taking them across and over the ghats was a miracle by itself. Three full days were consumed in the exercise.

The army trudged on. In front were huge, unscalable mountains, and on the right were deep crevasses. It wasn't that such ancient trees, thick, thorny bushes and jungles were utterly unfamiliar to the Bijapuris soldiers. Some of the men and animals had moved around in the jungles of Shimoga, but the vegetation there was shorter, flatter, sparser and thinner. It was the difference in scale that had brought them to desperation. 'What kind of ghost-land does this Shiva live in, Ya Allah!' they groaned.

'What massive trees, these! So dark inside here! The sun simply doesn't reach the jungle floor here. Why did our Adilshah Saheb have to push us into this fearful hell?'

And then they would hear a loud, resonant voice coming from behind. 'Arey brothers, *khair khuda ki*. May Allah bless us. Let the land be Adilshah's and ruination and hell be Shivaji's lot.' Everybody turned around to see the huge, six-foot-and-a-half figure of *Qaatil-e-kaafiroon* Afzal Khan himself striding energetically towards them. He would stand next to a marching group with one hand resting on his waist, and exchange a few words with his soldiers. He had with him for company Khairiyat Khan, Musey Khan, Ankush Khan and, surprise of all surprises, Krishnaji Bhaskar. The brisk manner in which he walked showed that the man had well internalised the pulse of this jungle.

The soldiers would greet their leader with '*Assalaam-o-alaikum*' and '*Fateh ho meherban*', wishing him victory in battle.

From Gurhegar and Bhilar, past Lingmala, right up to the jungle river named Venna, the land was flat. It took the army another two days to cross the huge jungle atop the mountain to reach the Venna. They camped at Met'tala.

At around midnight at Pratapgad, the grandees and sardars had finished with their work for the day and were getting ready to depart for their residences. That was when a message arrived from Moropant for an emergency meeting. Within half an hour, they had all assembled in the meeting hall.

Tanaji Malusare and Netaji Palkar sat in the front row, very close to each other. As they sat exchanging whispers, the others began to speculate on what the two revered leaders could be talking about. Other senior people like Kanhoji Jedhe, Moropant Pingale, Gomaji Pansambal and Pantaji Gopinath soon trooped in. Immediately after this, the herald announced Shivaji's arrival. All rose to their feet and greeted him with reverence. Shivaji came and sat in his designated seat.

The days had turned hectic. The news that evening had been that Afzal Khan had left Met'tala and had reached almost up to the edge of the Radtondi ghat. Early the next morning, he would begin climbing down from there.

Fixing his gaze at Malusare, Shivaji said, 'Yes, Tanajirao, what information have you gathered?'

'Maharaj, the entire world knows what a wicked and eccentric person this Afzulya is.'

'That's quite true. If you leave aside the fact that he is a brave warrior, the rest of his black deeds can rival a coal mine. Even in Bijapur there are plenty who are aware of his vicious nature. Proceed.'

'Two months back, Rani Saheba Saibai passed away down in Shivapattan. As you were returning through these dense Sahyadri jungles after performing the last rites, these scoundrels had mounted an attack on you in the middle of a raging storm—'

Shivaji immediately turned his admiring gaze at Netaji Palkar and said, 'Yes, that was a narrow escape. The entire credit for it goes to our Netajikaka here.'

Shivaji looked here and there. His fingers involuntarily gathered into a fist, which he tapped lightly on his thigh and said, 'Let's come to the point now, shall we?'

Tanaji stepped forward and placed a rough, hand-drawn map in front of the king. Immediately recognising the salient features marked on the map, Shivaji said, 'This looks like our Radtondi ghat.'

'That bastard named Afzal Khan is camping for the night at the exact central pointnt between the Met'tala houses and the Radtondi cliff.'

'That's right. Tomorrow at dawn they will begin their descent. But what exactly have you two got in mind?'

'Maharaj, just give us a signal. We shall go racing there and come crashing down upon that Khan and his army when they are in the middle of their descent. We shall arrest that rogue like one shuts a frog in a bottle, and bring him over.'

The daring plot of the Tanaji–Netaji twosome captured the imagination of all present. Their excitement mounted and their breathing became faster. There was silence everywhere. Breaking that silence in a grave voice, Shivaji said, patiently, 'You are all aware that the Khan was not at all ready to step out of Wai and come towards Jawali. We had to beg and plead with him. In fact, we even mowed down a few trees along the route to make his journey easier.'

'Yes, Raje.'

'We didn't have enough elephants with us to uproot those trees, so we called over their herd and cleared up the passage for them.'

'That's just it, Raje. On account of their exercise of bringing down those trees, our Maavali soldiers have now become very familiar with all the jungle tracks, the secret trails and even the stones scattered in those parts. Just give us the signal, and we shall destroy that Afzulya, along with his entire army.'

'Hold your horses, Netajikaka. Pull the reins on the winds blowing through your head.'

The Raja's voice went on rising; it turned hard as he spoke. The gathering was confused; in fact, frightened. The Raja said gravely, 'We have given the Khan our word and invited him to meet us in our own verandah. Would it suit the dignity of us Marathas to waylay him in the jungle like thugs and robbers?'

'But, Raje, is that man himself as white as freshly washed rice?' growled Netaji. 'Could you have forgotten Kasturiranga of Shira? It was this demon who had invited that great king for a conference and throttled him to death. It was through deceit that he had brought about the death of your elder brother Sambhajiraja. He stooped so low as to put your father

Shahajiraja in chains. Why should we have any qualms about killing a brute like him?'

'Look, Netajikaka, I have not moved an inch away from my mission. But I don't understand why you always have this fascination for precipitate action.'

'Because, Raje, this Afzal Khan has been an enemy of the Marathas across a hundred births. Since I heard of his departure from Bijapur, I haven't slept well for a single night, nor have I had a contented meal. Let me burn down this monster that lies at the root of a thousand of our problems.'

'But it is not as if the Khan stands unprotected there for you to conduct such a daring raid as you suggest.'

'Why be afraid of that? I shall gain the merit of having died a valorous death while defeating Afzal Khan.'

'Arey wah, Netaji,' said Shivaji, disappointedly, 'Valorous death! Why are you so eager to gain martyrdom and become a stone in a mausoleum?'

'What are you saying, Raje?' Netaji asked in an offended tone.

'Only the truth, Netajikaka. However much you want to walk to your death, how can we allow a hero like you to die just like that? On the contrary, I dream of building a magnificent temple of Hindvi swarajya by assembling together a number of sacred stones like you in an appropriate manner. This is how that dazzling temple will be made. Till as long as there are sun and moon in the sky, people will sing ballads to our swarajya.'

All of those listening were moved at their king's words. Their spines tingled. Netaji, however, was not happy. He said passionately, 'What the Mughals and what these Adilshahi men! They are all beads strung together in the necklace of deception and violence. There is one single thought that bothers me, just a single one. If this dilly-dallying continues, it may just result in an outcome we do not want.'

'No worry, kaka. This is a game of *mantra-yuddha*. Haven't we been able to needle the Khan out of the security of Wai and lure him into the unknown jungles of Jawali? That's *mantra-yuddha*, confounding the enemy's head. This Shivaji shall live by his word. I shall observe the ethics of a king. If a king has to die, well, then, so be it; but the ethics of humaneness must live on.'

'But, Raje, if the enemy is sitting on your chest, shouldn't we use our weapons against him?'

'Netajikaka, where weapons become useless, techniques become the weapon; and where techniques become ineffective, that's where *mahamantras* have to be called in—getting into the head of the enemy and filling it with delusions. In these dales and hills of the Sahyadri, we want to adopt the policy of *mantra-yuddha*, play mind games with the enemy.'

That declaration stirred up everyone. There was endless work to do the next day. Hence the king called the meeting to a close. The company was on the point of stepping out when the Raja remembered something and called out, 'Please stop for a moment, friends. I have to say this in the presence of all of you. Whether it is Tanaji or Netaji, all of you who are so concerned about my life, these priceless sentiments you mustn't abandon. However, without trapping that Afzal Khan in any gorge, we have to show that man the sky above the battlefield.'

Just then, someone from one of the back rows remarked loud enough for the king to hear, 'But, Raje, how can we trust this treacherous man?'

'Since he is our guest, we shall give him the first choice of whether he wants to fight the battle with dignity or wants to resort to subterfuge and deception. But if he is nursing the dream of using brute force and brainless trickery and crushing me like a flower, then we shall not rest easy before tearing open his jugular like a tiger.'

When the fifth morning dawned, Afzal Khan's forces came to the lip of the Radtondi ghat. When they saw the slope dropping at an angle of seventy degrees in front of them, their hearts turned to water. However, there was no choice but to go skidding down it as best as they could. Both men and animals were finding it nearly impossible to get a firm foothold. Horses would suddenly lose their balance and go crashing into the trees below. The men could utter no other words except *Ya Allah* and *Ya Khuda*.

However difficult, a horse would still have a chance to somehow squeeze and twist and sway to maneuver around a rock or a tree. But the near perpendicular slopes of this ghat had made life utterly miserable for the army elephants. They were loath to take the next foot forward. Their mahouts began to belabour them with sharp goads that would pierce deep into their leathery skin and draw blood. The poor animals would be left with no choice but to stake their all, shut their eyes and step forward. So often it happened that the mahout sitting on the elephant's neck would get distracted, and his head would crash against the branch of a tree and smash open like a watermelon. Most of the elephants had the smaller type of zamburak cannons tied with leather straps either on their backs or on their flanks. Although they were considered small, they were still very heavy. The animals would surely have preferred death to carrying that kind of load down the sharp drops of the slopes.

On the first night, only half the ghat had been negotiated. When visibility sank to zero, the animals sat where they had stood. The bhishti boys had brought water dragging down in their leathern bags. When the poor brutes touched the water that was served to them in big bowls, their eyes literally watered. The odd-job men and the women and children accompanying the army appeared like ghosts in the darkness. The fodder they carried should really have been a feast for the animals. But they were so drained out that they would barely have taken a mouthful or two when their eyes turned heavy and they lowered their necks to one side.

The next morning at breakfast, the floor of the gorge, the small thatch-roofed huts there and the narrow span of the jungle river Koyna became visible through the branches of the trees. They had finally seen the end of the Radtondi ghat. All the animals, bipedal and quadrupeds, heaved a sigh of relief.

As they were walking, they suddenly heard loud explosions on the top. The men turned to look around, but before they could realise what was happening, a section of the upper edge of the Radtondi cliff came tumbling down the sharp slope in a cloud of dust. Concealed in the dust were huge rocks that fell upon men and animals, triggering off loud screams and groans.

The squads hurried as fast as they could down the sharp slope. Work began to extricate the bodies of the men and animals that had been buried in the landslide. Afzal Khan immediately went down on his knees and sent his prayers for help to Allah.

The corpses of about a dozen horses and some twenty-five soldiers were laid out on the grass. On the other side, a huge, baby-elephant-sized stone had rolled over the legs of three soldiers and pinned them down. The impact had cracked their bones and created a pool of blood underneath. Although they were begging for help by screaming out the name of Allah, the place was so dangerously narrow and so much in the line of the stones falling from above that it was not possible for anybody to run to help them.

That was when a giant of a man, huge as the pillar of a temple, went running towards the stone. He dug space for his fingers below the stone, kneeled on the ground, and heaved with all his strength. He groaned and keened and gnashed his teeth, and with super-human strength managed to roll that massive stone aside. The three trapped men were somehow pulled out of the jaws of death. Physicians and other soldiers ran to help them out. Everywhere there arose a loud cry of 'Wah, Sayyad Banda, wah, bhai!' Afzal Khan pulled a diamond ring out of his finger and slipped it on Sayyad Banda's finger.

The bhishti boys were trying to pour water into the mouths of the semi-conscious men who had been saved from a gory death. Afzal Khan looked at the mountain in front of him with determination. Then he narrowed his eyes and began examining one side of the mountain with greater concentration. On top of it he could see the ramparts of the Pratapgad fort and his entire body broke into a shiver of excitement. He looked to the left and he looked to the right, and mumbled some verses from the Kor'an.

By the evening, the tent-boys and other labourers had reached the stream. About five hundred men had gathered there at a spot, screaming and shouting. Afzal Khan too reached there and started at the sight of the hubbub in front. Suspecting that something was terribly amiss, he pushed his way into the crowd with Ankush Khan and Khairiyat Khan. 'Move, move aside,' they shouted, pushing their way into the crowd. What they saw in front was the flag-bearing elephant of the army, stuck in the quagmire by the stream. The durbari howdah on its back was on the point of toppling off.

Horsemen, foot soldiers, artisans, all of them together were trying to scoop out all the boggy earth around the elephant's massive legs. But the earth beside the stream was extremely soft and slimy, causing the huge animal to sink deeper and deeper into the liquid earth. It appeared that the effort to extricate the animal had been going on for some time. The harder the animal applied pressure to lift any of its legs out of the mire, the deeper it slipped into it. It had begun to screech piteously for fear of its life.

Khairiyat Khan's eyes settled on something and his face looked terror-stricken. He just could not fathom how he should break it to his commander-in-chief. He finally gathered his courage and blurted out, 'Huzoor, that howdah on the elephant's back—'

'Yes, I can see it.'

'It's not the howdah alone, huzoor, do you see our army's green banner tied to it?'

When Afzal Khan saw what Khairiyat Khan was talking about, he broke into a cold sweat. The most auspicious piece of any legion is the elephant that walks right in front of the army procession carrying its banner. Khan suddenly felt a huge hole form in his stomach out of fear. He remembered the inauspicious death of his lead elephant Fateh Lashkar as they were on the point of stepping out of Bijapur. Ya Allah, what calamity was this? Why should it again be the lead elephant that should get stuck in the bogs at the final stage of their journey? What was one to make of this misfortune?

The very next moment, he handed over his jewel-studded sword to Musey Khan and, uncaring for the royal clothes and the diamond necklace he was wearing, he leapt into the slimy water and began wading towards the elephant. With his immense strength, he caught hold of the elephant's trunk and began screaming, 'Pull! Apply all your strength!'

When the soldiers saw their commander-in-chief entering into the ooze, some other soldiers also jumped in. They began pushing and pulling and doing all that they could to loosen the sludge's grip on the elephant. The animal, however, had got so deeply embedded that there was no way it could be stirred out. On the contrary, it was sinking deeper and deeper. Terrified of the bad omen that it represented, Afzal Khan threw all his strength into the effort. The soldiers gathered around could see his face streaming with perspiration.

After all his formidable efforts had failed, he waded out and stood at the bank, looking broken. His entire body was stinging with pain. All that one could see of the elephant now was the top of its back and its head. Afzal was deeply frustrated by his failure at saving the elephant. He felt as if the hills and mountains around him were mocking him. He took a bow and some arrows from an archer who was standing close by, and strung the bow. He let fly two arrows in quick succession that found their mark in the two eyes of the unfortunate animal. The calamity that had descended upon him had actually turned Afzal Khan completely blind.

Little by little, the hapless animal sank completely in the water reddening from its blood.

The rays of the sun had started disappearing, stretching the shadows of the mountains longer and longer. The entire mountainous region had started gathering the gorges of Jawali and the narrow stretch of the Koyna river into its arms. The golden rays of the setting sun had begun to dance on the brow of Pratapgad. There, at the rampart that carried the flag, stood Shivraya along with his associates. For a long time, he had been intently watching the slope of the Radtondi ghat right in front.

Finally, his enemy for life had arrived with his entire force, and set up camp within the range of visibility.

25

AFZAL'S CAMP ON THE KOYNA BANK

FIRST WEEK, NOVEMBER 1659

The best battle formations may sometimes be breached, but the pattern of the human mind is inscrutable. Breaching that is a near impossible task.

Afzal Khan's thoughts had been racing back to Bijapur for quite a few days now. There was little doubt that not Badi Begum alone, but all of Bijapur would have their eyes turned in this direction. A hero from whose name the word 'defeat' had stayed away by miles in every single campaign—what was that *Qaatil-e-kaafiroon* doing for so long? Why wasn't the good news arriving of Afzal having killed Shivaji and drowned his entire army?

Since the time power had passed over from Sultan Mohammadshah into the Badi Begum's hands, she had put on display her experience as a sharp, acerbic lady. The biggest of chieftains would be in dread before her strict discipline and despotic ways.

What an amazing life that woman had lived! What times had she seen roll past her! Born as a princess to Qutbshah, married to Sultan Mohammadshah, and now ruling the Adilshahi Sultanate by proxy, she had experienced and established her dominance across the entire spectrum of power, starting from her father's palace to her husband's, across many decades. What will to authority and action she exuded! When Aurangzeb had returned north to fight his battle for succession, this shrewd, masterful Badi Begum had played all the tricks in her bag and compelled him to return to her all the land he had won from the Adilshahi.

The love and trust she had showered upon Afzal Khan was enough to cause many heads to turn. It was he who had insisted on and succeeded in hacking the wazeer Khan Mohammad to pieces in the public square. Begum Saheba had never uttered a word of admonition against the violence with which the deed had been perpetrated.

Afzal Khan had lately been haunted by strange, perplexing doubts. Whenever he stood before Begum Saheba, he felt like she looked at him with wonderment. Why had he often noticed her observing him through the corners of her blue eyes? What secrets lay behind those soulful eyes?

That poor, pitiable elephant that had been lost to the quagmire yesterday—what reason did he have to blind the poor animal so cruelly? Why should a front-ranking military leader like him have fallen prey to such impulsive behaviour? But, again, why was Allah causing such inauspicious events to happen? The predictions made by the blind mystic Baba Chishti with regard to the campaign and the inauspicious hindrances and ill-omen that he had been encountering were not designed to place him in any zone of comfort.

Staying awake till late in the night meant that he rose late the next morning. The moment word spread around the camp that the Khan had finally woken up, frenetic activity began everywhere. Personal servants, disciples, grooms and cooks set to work with gusto.

As soon as he returned from a ride around the camp, he would invariably think of his masseur Shaukat. He had now become habituated to having his body daubed with oil and rubbed down. Therefore, word had been sent to Shaukat.

The masseur was waiting for him with his bottle of oil and cotton swabs. When he was being daubed with the oil prior to being massaged, Afzal noted that Shaukat looked unhappy. 'Any problems, son?'

Shaukat's eyes filled with tears. Meanwhile, Afzal's son Faulad Khan had come over to stand beside his father. Before Shaukat could respond, he piped in, 'Abbu, this poor boy wants to go back home to Bengaluru.'

'Why?' Afzal Khan asked in a weighty voice.

'I feel afraid, Khan Saheb.'

'Afraid? In my camp?'

'How do I say this, huzoor? Without hiding any facts, I had declared openly that earlier I had worked as a cook in Shahajiraja's kitchen.'

'Shaukat Miyan,' intercepted Faulad Khan sternly, 'why don't you tell it straight to Abbu?'

'How do I say it, Khan Saheb? A few of Shivaji's men had come secretly to meet me a couple of days back.'

'Why?'

'Their argument was that I was an old servant of the Bhosale household, therefore I should arrange to meet Shivaji once.'

Afzal Khan absorbed this news silently. Then his eyes suddenly brightened and he said, 'What is there to be afraid of, son? Of course you should go.'

Shaukat froze at the very thought of this deed. Afzal then placed an affectionate hand on his shoulder and said, 'If you do go into Shivaji's tent, we shall benefit more than anybody else. What do you say, Faulad?'

'Absolutely, Abbu.'

All kinds of new formulations began floating in Afzal's head.

Feeling relaxed after Shaukat's massage, Afzal got up from the mat. A special bathroom had been made for him by raising a brocade partition. He poured plentiful warm water over his naked body. Immediately afterwards arrived his breakfast. He polished off four chickens stuffed with corn and roasted on coal braziers to the accompaniment of raw green chillies.

A conference began with his senior captains. Through the window of the canvas wall of his tent he could see the Pratapgad hill. Straight, tall and impressive, it looked frighteningly ready to come crashing down upon whatever lay below. What if that Shivajiraja sitting there suddenly decided to mount a raid at some odd hour of the night? What if he had already planted a large army inside the jungle? What if this conflict turned out to be a long drawn out one? Multitudes of such doubts and questions were biting into his restless head like ants.

The Khan had to leave his tent in a hurry. But before that, he called Qutb Miyan over alone for a quick discussion. He whispered softly into his ear, 'We are leaving for a surveillance of our camp to ensure that the army has been well laid out. We will have to put up another tent in the Jawali township.'

'Another tent, huzoor?'

'Yes, it is necessary, Qutb Khan. Why just an enemy, even a friend should not know where I go during the day and where at nighttime.'

When he stepped out of his tent, he looked very happy. His attention drifted to the narrow span of the Koyna river. His eyes swept around the dense green mountains and valleys that stood mounting guard in a rough circle over the land in front. He cast his gaze to the left and the right of his tent. Last night, it had turned dark by the time they had arrived, but during the day, the scene in front of his tent was extraordinary. About four or five acres of land had been cleared of its trees and vegetation around the main tent. Small tents had been erected there in rows for the occupancy of the Khan's personal staff like servants, grooms, clerks and butlers. In the open yards in front were tied the elephants and horses. On the slope that lay to the rear of the tent, plenty of stacks of grass and dry sticks had been erected.

Afzal Khan closely examined the mattresses, pallets and other items of spreadsheets and upholstery. When he came out, he scrutinised the large twenty-two link tent that had been erected. He then asked his captain, 'Qutb Miyan, what kind of magic is this? This luxury of muslin cloth, these green frills around, who has wrought this miracle?'

'These are gifts from our enemy Shiva, my lord.'

'What rubbish are you talking?' responded Afzal Khan, twitching his head and widening his eyes.

'That's the truth, huzoor,' broke in the tent-master with a low bow. 'Our labourers and artisans were never put to any trouble. Even before we reached here, Shivaji's men had got these tents, tent walls and their frills stitched at Mahad and delivered here.'

It was very important for Afzal Khan to ensure the best possible movements of his men and animals during the battle and to work out the complex arithmetic of attacks and counterattacks for that purpose. He had stepped out to do a careful appraisal of the land from that perspective. Off and on, he would look up at the top of the hill on the left and the Pratapgad fort that rested atop it.

Looking at the wide open space on both sides of the river, the traders of the army market had opened up their shops. The sweet-meat sellers had put up their stalls of sweets and fruits, while a number of Gujar-Marwaris had opened up their trunks of pearls and precious stones. As for meat-shops, the soldiers had never had it so good since departing from Bijapur. Shivaji's message had gone to all the butchers from Mahad, Poladpur and Khed right up to Bankot. The butchers and sheep-traders from those areas had brought along with them four thousand goats and sheep. With ample food now becoming available to them, the Bijapuri solders were thrilled.

Afzal Khan was moving along the bank of the Koyna. He reached one end of the valley that lay in front of Pratapgad. The Koyna was entering into this valley after describing a crooked turn in the valley beyond. At this junction, an elephant-trunk-like length of hill was descending near the river from the Ambenali ghat on top. Afzal Khan turned the head of his horse from that corner towards Jawali that lay on the other side of the hill. Suddenly, he heard his name being called out from behind. Turning round, he saw Prataprao Morey galloping towards him in a hurry. His face looked grim.

He brought the muzzle of his horse close to Afzal Khan's and pointed towards the bushes on the other side of the river. 'Look, look, Khan Saheb, at the ruined Hashamgadh of the Moreys. There you see the spire of our temple. You may even see the deserted, orphaned walls of our palace. It is that Shiva of the Bhosales who has taken away our kingdom, our grandeur, and reduced everything to dust. Khan Saheb, give us justice.'

'Don't worry, Prataprao, it's only a matter of a few days now.'

'The more you delay, the sooner this Shiva will turn into a lion. Kill him first. Let's finish him, huzoor.'

In the valley on the yonder side, too, could be seen temporary, mobile stables, camel sheds and crowds of soldiers. The camp of the Bijapuri army had spread up to there. Surveillance posts and guard-sheds had been erected. Afzal Khan had wanted to take no risk at all. That was why he was paying personal attention to the finer aspects with the greatest care.

Khan's band entered into the deeper part of the valley in front, where they came upon a village called Dara. Right behind this village was a hill that ran up to eight hundred meters in height. On the right could be seen a slope that appeared to have been cut down straight. That was the Nisani ghat. However hard he tried, he could not work out how Shivaji's men and horses could have climbed down that slope in the middle of heavy rains. From this side ran a trail through the dense forests of the

Haatlot ghat towards Khed in Konkan. Then there was the extremely difficult route that went down from the Dhavlya ghat towards Mahad, as also the Gopyaghat route that went dodging through the Rajgadh jungles. Such were the big and small pieces of information that Afzal Khan had been gathering assiduously from all available sources. Working out some preliminary plans in his head, he reached his tent near the Paar village by evening time.

The next afternoon, after Afzal and Ankush had eaten their lunch together, they sat down for some conversation.

'Ankush,' Afzal said, 'stop being scared. That Shiva will be wiped out in the next two days or four … the poor chap. Once we have finished him, we shall have a grand celebration here—marijuana, drinks and all.'

'Forgive me, Afzal Bhai, facts always carry a dreadful look about them.'

'What rubbish are you talking?'

'Please wake up from your slumber and tell me this: how, in the name of Allah, is your army going to survive in this jungle? How?'

'What rubbish is this, Ankush Khan?'

'If you delay matters even by just four or six days, our men and animals will die of thirst.'

'Ankush Khan, stop blathering. Have you started drinking during day time?'

'Afzal Miyan, I hope to God you snap out of your colourful dreams,' Ankush snapped back. 'You have no knowledge about these mountains and valleys. It's now three weeks since these Hindu hellhounds finished with their Diwali festival.'

'So?'

'Look, when it rains here, the entire sky descends upon these mountains.'

'Therefore?'

'But even after an ocean precipitates here, does the water stay on the ground for too long? The jungle streams here flow for just about a month, or another week at the most, after which they suddenly dry up.'

'Ya Allah!'

'Another eight or ten days from now, you will see the wives of these herdsmen here travelling with their earthen pots as much as ten miles to fetch water for their cooking.'

This information caused the earth to crack under Afzal Khan's feet. He said in a terrified voice, 'Into which well, then, will we push our twenty-five to thirty thousand soldiers and twenty thousand animals for slaking their thirst? We will be utterly ruined.'

He looked upwards at the sky and then immediately lowered his eyes and looked around. The crags of the Sahyadri mountains sat like a set of demons all around him. He somehow managed to croak in a choked voice, 'Ya Allah, till yesterday I believed that Shiva was fighting this battle against us all by himself; but now I know that he is not alone, nature too participates with him in all his demoniacal activities.'

⁂

Shivraya sat with his feet hanging down from his ebony bed. Between his legs sat Shaukat on a comfortable cushion. He had some warm sesame oil in a shallow bronze vessel near at hand. He would dip his fingers in the oil and give a strong rubbing down to the Raja's knees, calves, ankles and feet. Shivraya looked at his timid, shrunken face, and smiled.

The Bijapuri messengers who had arrived with Krishnaji Bhaskar were sitting in the hall on the other side of the palace. Getting his legs massaged was only a charade. It was after proper administrative sanction that Shaukat had come to Shivaji in the company of the two messengers. Shivaji noticed his restlessness and invited him into the inner parlour. Shaukat got up immediately and followed the king inside. He undid the string of his pajamas and pulled out Afzal Khan's tunic that he had smuggled in with him tied to his chest. Shivaji spread it out using both his hands and said in a note of concern, 'This Afzulya's height is much more than that of an ordinary person. Seems to possess a big, strong build.' He then smiled pleasantly and pressed four gold coins into Shaukat's palms. The poor man was thrilled.

As he took Shivaji's leave, he said softly, 'Raje, there is one more very important piece of information.'

'Yes, Dighe.'

'What I am going to tell you now has been kept extremely confidential. The only person who knows about it there is Faulad Khan.'

'All right, say it quickly then. Those two Bijapuris who came with you are waiting in the hall. They might get suspicious.'

'Afzulya owns a number of ships on the coast of Goa.'

'I know that. What else?'

'When he set off from Bijapur, he brought along with him three of those ships. They are lying anchored on our coast. All fully equipped, with some four thousand soldiers aboard it.'

Shivraya asked, 'On which harbour?'

'On the Dabhol coast on the other side.'

'The purpose?'

'That devil has big dreams—to put you in chains and drag you all the way back home. His route will perhaps be either through Pandharpur or the Miraj-Athani road to Bijapur. If the news goes around that you have been captured alive and if the people rise in opposition to the Adilshahi forces in an effort to free you, if they try to block the Khan's progress, he then proposes to change his route and take you from the Konkan side to Dabhol, and whisk you overnight to his ship. He can then take you straight to Goa.'

The king was astonished at this intelligence coming from Vishwasrao Dighe, who was playing the role of Shaukat in the Bijapur camp. Putting an affectionate hand on his shoulder, Shivaji said, 'What stress you have been under on our account! Even got yourself circumcised to complete the disguise of being a Muslim.'

There were tears of pride in Vishwasrao's eyes as he said, 'Circumcision is nothing—for the sake of our beloved swarajya and at a single command from your kingdom, this slave is willing to sacrifice his neck.'

Shivaji sent for a bamboo stick, and with it, began to take a more exact measurement of Afzal Khan's tunic. For a moment, he felt disturbed too. He did his calculations carefully. If he were to stand in the presence of Afzal Khan, his forehead would just about reach the man's chest. The enemy was truly a giant.

The python lay coiled up by the side of the river. The war was no longer at the doorstep; it had come close to the chest now. The armies of both sides were carefully taking an estimate of each other, looking for strengths and weaknesses, and waiting to pounce at the first opportunity that presented itself. A tiny spark somewhere and the explosives stacked in the arsenal would blow up.

That night, Shivaji lay tossing and turning in bed, when Gomajibaba entered the bed chamber and informed him that Bahirji Jadhav Naik had come to meet him. Shivaji immediately stepped out in his vest and britches flaring at the thigh. Out in front, Bahirji and his three companions were waiting for him. They bent low to offer their respects to Shivaji.

Shivaji was delighted at the disguise in which Bahirji and his friends had presented themselves. Their turbans shaped out of finely twisted red cloth, steel bracelets, footwear with triple-layered soles of hard leather, rough, warm blankets on their shoulders and long bamboo sticks with bells at the handgrip—they were indistinguishable from the Maandesh herders one found standing in the bazaars of Malwadi.

Shivaji, too, was fired up with the desire to take a round of the outside world. He threw a blanket on his shoulder and took a stick in his hand, wrapped a herder's turban round his long, silken hair, and the four of them stepped out of the fort. Of course, as a precaution, fifty armed bodyguards had split into smaller units and were walking soft-footedly at sufficient intervals from each other ahead and behind the king.

Bahirji carried in his arms a small, fortnight-old lamb close to his chest. The four of them slipped out of the fort from the rear gate, and, walking through the darkness, they hit the jungle. There were settlements of herders and shepherds on the way. The cold had just started to set in, causing fires to be lit in the localities round which the menfolk gathered. A few farmers had gathered around a bonfire to warm themselves. The fire was fed with fresh, sun-dried twigs and was crackling with each gust of wind. One of the farmers had rolled himself into a tight bundle and was sleeping peacefully. A couple of tippers from the fort also joined this group of peasants and herders. Small talk flowed freely. A soldier voiced his opinion, 'Man, I feel really scared. Standing up to this Afzulya means finally dying in the end.'

'Chhey! How can this happen?' challenged the other soldier. 'Arey Waadya, our king's own readiness is like that of a tiger.'

'Listen to this chap! It means that the worm still hasn't reached your ear. Arey, till date, this Afzulya has fought fifty battles in a row, and won every one of them. He doesn't know the meaning of the word "defeat", it seems.'

'So, Gonduba, what could be the real miracle behind this?'

'It could be the blessing of some Muslim guru or some pir baba.'

The faces of the three men looked dull with worry. One of them said, 'What's written in one's destiny cannot be dodged.'

Grumbling like a wet jungle-cat, another man said, 'It doesn't seem at all like the trumpets of our king have been heard in this jungle.'

The conversation startled Bahirji and the others who were with him. Their faces were creased with worry. Shivaji's face, however, was as impassive as ever. But unknown to him, a couple of beads of sweat did break out on his brow and trickle down.

Sleep did not visit Shivaji that night. As Jijausaheb had prophesied long ago, Afzal Khan's campaign was turning out to be a trial by fire for Shivaji. Up until this point, his soldiers had been involved in hit-and-run skirmishes, guerilla raids and counter-raids. Shivaji had immense faith in the audacity of Netaji Palkar; but it was critically important that the six thousand horsemen with him should have the skill to come down upon the enemy with equal zest. He had equal faith in the gallantry of Kanhoji Jedhe and the recently recruited Babaji Bhosale, Moropant Peshve, Tanaji Malusare, Shilimkar, Raghunath Ballal Sabnis and other such warriors.

When Afzal Khan's immense army was climbing down the Radtondi ghat for two and a half days in a continuous stream, those foot-soldiers, those thousands of horses, those seven or eight hundred camels, those elephants, they had looked like a massive wave of water cascading down those sharp slopes. It was a sight that had filled the hearts of the soldiers hiding in those jungles with dread. One thing was clear: a bitter confrontation with an army so strong and huge was necessary; this would give his valiant men the experience needed for the evolution of a powerful state.

Since the time Afzal Khan had crossed the Krishna river at Rahimatpur, someone had circulated this information among the Maratha soldiers that Afzal Khan was invincible; that he had never in his life faced defeat, not once in the fifty or fifty-five campaigns that he had led. This, unfortunately, was also a fact. The Maratha men also had faith in things like good and bad omen. It was, therefore, important to pull the arrow of Afzal Khan's invincibility out of their chests. But it would have to be done skillfully, thought Shivaji.

Little by little, Shivaji sank into the pool of semi-oblivion. His eyes closed. Suddenly the aroma of frankincense hit his nostrils. He saw the beautiful image that Arjoji Yadav had sculpted by chiselling the monolithic stone-front of the palace—the image of Goddess Bhawani astride her lion; her angry, flaming eyes; the red vermillion powder on her massive brow; the unsheathed sword in her hand. He could almost hear the lion roaring with its jaws wide open.

By and by, the statue transformed itself into *Rann-Chandika*, the goddess of war. Shivaji jumped out of bed and sat before Goddess Bhawani in the expectation of her blessings. She stepped out of the stone statue as the embodiment of the goddess of war. Mounting on her lion, she advanced a few steps. Jasmine and prajakta flowers came down in a shower upon her head. Shivaji removed his headgear and bowed down reverentially before the goddess.

She touched his head, lovingly, running her fingers through his hair, pronounced a few mantras, and handed over to him the jewel-studded sword that she had been carrying. Shivaji placed his head at the goddess's feet, at which the goddess again caressed his hair in blessing with her soft hands. Shivaji was delighted beyond measure. In a little while, she melted into the air.

Shivaji woke up with a start. His face was bathed in perspiration. He looked this way and that in confusion, but could find nobody around.

·ೂಲ್ಲ·

A map of Pratapgad had been placed before the conference. All the officials, big and small, were to occupy their assigned seats this afternoon. In the morning meeting, Shivaji had impressed it upon them again and again: 'Afzal Khan is a born betrayer. He simply cannot be trusted. He broke my elder brother Sambhajiraje's trust, and brought upon Aausaheb the sorrow of a lifetime. He is not just any enemy.'

'Don't worry at all, boy,' said old man Kanhojibaba Jedhe. 'This Kanhoji has sworn to fly your flag. I will fight alongside my five sons.'

'Kaka, we have decided to meet at the Jani top the day after tomorrow. But who can ever trust this treacherous enemy? Therefore, it is good to post our men there right from this afternoon. Up, up everyone, tie your bands round your waist and get ready for battle.'

As the attendees began to rise, Shivaji called out to them in a loud voice, 'Wait, all of you wait, please. There is some thrilling news yet to be given to you.'

Everybody was agog with excitement. What good news could the king have brought?

'We now have absolutely no reason left to nurse any kind of fear. The knot has been undone. Bhawani Mata herself came and gave me her word last night.'

'So, who brought the message?' asked Netaji.

'It was Tulza Bhawani herself. Friends, you may call this event a dream or a prophecy, but she paid me a visit last night.'

'What are you saying, Raje?' They were utterly stunned at this declaration.

'What can I tell you about her ferocity, her grandeur? And what does Mata Bhawani tell me? "When that wicked Afzulya brought the sledgehammer down upon my statue and smashed it to pieces, as the chips fell, some sparks flew and one of the sparks set my *pallu* on fire. That fire has melded with the sharp edge of your sword. Don't worry, son. It is through the burning edge of your sword that I shall severe that sinful Afzulya's head."'

The awe-inspiring peroration delivered by Shivaji worked wonders and rid the gathered warriors of fear. If Mata Bhawani herself had decided to pull out her sword and stand up for the welfare of their army, then Afzal Khan didn't stand a chance. They were now so drunk with the passion for battle that they walked out of the hall growling like a pride of lions setting out on a hunt. Shivaji himself accompanied his friends out of the hall into the courtyard. As they were walking, Kanhoji and Netaji's attention drifted towards the sculpture of the goddess carved in the front wall of the palace. Heaps of jasmine and prajakta flowers lay at her feet.

Shivaji saw the flowers too, and suddenly noticed something glinting among them. He strode rapidly to the statue, and moved aside the flowers that lay on top. What he saw there turned him into stone. It was like he had been hypnotised. Kanhoji narrowed his experienced eyes and took a look. His eyes began to shed copious tears of joy as he spoke. 'Take it, Shivba, take it. Pick up the blessing that your Bhawani has sent for you.'

It was an extraordinary weapon. Its hilt was studded with many kinds of jewels. Everybody was ogling at the divine weapon. Nobody, including Shivaji, had ever seen such a dazzling weapon. Such a weapon didn't exist in the armoury of the greatest of kings. What was it, after all? A miracle or a personal gift from the mother goddess?

One thing was absolutely clear: the glittering sword that lay there in the heap of flowers and the weapon carved in the stone statue of Bhawani Mata belonged to the same lineage.

This unprecedented event had shaken up all of Pratapgad. Everybody gathered there—sardars, the small and big captains, the administrators, including Netaji Palkar—were so charged up by that magical moment that they broke into a loud cry: 'Jai jai jai Shivaji, jai, jai, jai Bhawani!'

26

PRIMING THE SPRING TRAPS

The fire of retribution was burning in the hills and valleys of Pratapgad. The snake and the mongoose had caught each other in a murderous hold, and each was snapping at the other, squeezing it, biting it, lashing at it with its tail, tossing it this way and that in the hope of smashing it to death. Both the forces had begun grappling with each other in a do-or-die effort.

Afzal Khan was in a big hurry to kill Shivaji and rush back to Bijapur. The reality had dawned upon him now: if he did not extricate his army from this jungle as early as possible, he would invite doom upon his men and animals. He was eager for a quick confrontation with Shivaji so that he could save his forces from a miserable death before the water in these valleys dried up. Besides, it was common knowledge that despite their familiarity with every vine, every blade of grass of these Jawali jungles, Prataprao Morey's forces had been handed a resounding defeat by Shivaji and his men.

Whenever the Bijapuri soldiers sat around a bonfire, their terror-stricken conversation would always circle around the desperation to escape from the devil-infested jungle. Allah tala could not give them a bigger blessing than this, they all unanimously agreed.

In sharp contrast, the conversation in Shivraya's camp centred around the duplicitous moves that Afzal Khan was capable of playing. There was no doubt in anyone's mind that he was a doughty warrior. Besides, if he did come to grief, only his army would be annihilated; the Sultanate of Bijapur and its people would continue to remain safe and sound as ever.

But everything that the Marathas had—the horsemen, the foot soldiers, their belongings, the throne that had been acquired with such blood and sweat, its ochre banner, all the dreams that had been dreamt for the future—Shivraya had put everything at stake on the outcome of the battle in Jawali. If they won, there would be no victory bigger than it; however, if they lost, everything they had built with such love and labour would be consigned to dust. The only option for staying alive, therefore, was to fight and hold victory by its wrist, and bring it dragging into their camp.

Every single day that passed felt like eternity to both the armies and their generals.

An eagle sits atop the tallest rock in sight and carefully surveys everything below in the depths of the valley. The eagle named Shivaji had identified his prey. In fact, he had even beguiled the prey into entering the jungle of his choice. The eagle now had just one caution to observe: the enemy was utterly unpredictable. From the top, they did look like chicken feathers. But after the fateful leap was made by the eagle, if the enemy turned out to be a porcupine hiding under the feathers, the consequences would be disastrous. Care, therefore, had to be exercised that not only were lives prevented from being lost, the mission of swarajya should remain unharmed too.

The tempers in Afzal Khan's tent ran high. He was pacing to and fro in agitation. The others present there, like Musey Khan, Faulad Khan and their experienced agent Krishnaji Bhaskar Kulkarni, looked worried. Everybody had come down on Pantaji Gopinath like a ton of bricks. Afzal Khan barked, 'Do you consider us fools? How many days since we arrived in this tent?'

'Two days, huzoor.'

'Arey, Pantaji, tell us when we will be able to meet your king Shivaji.'

'Definitely within the next fifteen days, huzoor.'

Pantaji's reply sent Afzal Khan's anger flying through the roof. Stamping his feet like a spoilt child, he said, 'Do you realise what you are saying? And to whom? No way, Pantaji. Telling you clearly, inside of three days, that Shivaji has to meet with me. If that doesn't happen, the consequences will be catastrophic. This is my last warning to you.'

Letting out a deep sigh, Pantaji Gopinath said, 'I swear by my mother, Khan Saheb, our poor king is really terrified—'

'Stop, Pantaji! Stop your foolish prattle about your king being terrified. If you say that again, I shall slice the tip of your tongue with my sword. You won't even know where it has fallen.'

The sight of Afzal Khan's angry avatar scared the life out of poor Pantaji. Nervously adjusting his headgear, he wondered how he would plead his case before this fiend. However, in a low, squeaky voice, he plodded on, 'When has my king ever said no to a meeting? Here's his heartfelt supplication that I present before you, Khan Saheb: let the dust of your feet grace our doorstep immediately, Khan Saheb. Please accept our hospitality.'

'What do you mean, Pantaji?'

'Hospitality. Our king desires to throw a grand dinner for you.'

'A very shrewd Brahmin you are, Pantaji. What hospitality? What dinner? You want to talk sweet and thus trap me and my army alive in these mountains? Ankush Khan, tell this over-smart *Bamman* that either he resolves this issue right now, or he shall not walk out alive from this tent.'

'Huzoor, I swear by Mata Bhawani, our efforts—'

'Look, we can't travel up and he can't come down, but isn't there some place in the middle?' Afzal Khan said, desperate to bring about the meeting.

'You have stolen words from my mouth, Khan Saheb. Let's try for a place somewhere in the middle, as you say. Let the two of you meet and undo this intractable knot.'

Forgetting the dignity of his position, Khan pulled Pantaji into his embrace. He even pulled his cheeks lovingly. Seeing his changed mood, everybody in the tent felt relieved. Everybody's eyes showed a spark of victory—just a day or two more, and that would be the end of Shivaji.

Krishnaji Bhaskar Kulkarni and Gopinathkaka made numerous tours up and down the hill. Everybody was desperate for this suppurating wound to be treated one way or the other.

The two parties agreed to meet on a flat spot where a temporary tent could be erected; a spot that lay somewhere in the middle of the sharp slope descending from Pratapgad. The spot that best met their needs was known by the name Jani top.

'We don't need cowards! We need fearless men who are willing to stick their chests out against death,' Afzal Khan roared at the officials lined up before him. 'Go back to your tents and carefully handpick from your contingents the smartest, toughest and bravest boys. I don't want any more than two hundred and fifty or three hundred of them.'

The officials set to work. Within a few hours, a crowd of eighteen hundred men had assembled in the open space before Afzal Khan's tent. Faulad Khan and Musey Khan took them to the riverbank on the other side, and had them line up before a slope. In front were bamboo groves, and on either side were woods of ancient trees. It was in this secluded place that the final selection would be made. Due care was being taken that the Marathas on top of the hill or hiding in the jungles would not get wind of this exercise.

Instead of assigning the responsibility to anyone else, Afzal Khan himself stepped into the arena. In that secluded spot on the bank of the stream, the men were divided into groups. To test their mettle, they were put through the toughest of exercises. They were told to run along the bank, then cross the river to the other side and run up the sharp incline in front. Strong, strapping young men were drained out in no time, their clothes soaked in perspiration.

Afzal Khan then gathered them in an open patch of land. He first pruned out three hundred men who had been found inadequate either in intent or stamina. He then stood on a high ground before the remaining fifteen hundred. The walls of Pratapgad fort could be seen above through the branches of the trees. He deliberately made Musey Khan and his son Faulad Khan stand next to him as he addressed the men, 'Friends, each one of you holds in his hands the flaming torch of Bijapur's honour.'

Dundey Khan intercepted to add his bit, 'Boys, you are truly fortunate. When our commander-in-chief shall begin climbing up the slope of the Radtondi ghat after slaying Shivaji, it's just you, young men, who will be walking alongside him.'

Afzal Khan resumed in his strident voice, 'Trapping Shiva and killing him shall be my job alone. But your responsibility will be greater than mine. When we signal to you by blowing our horn, your job will be to, with everything you have got in you, under the leadership of Musey Khan and Faulad Khan, scamper up the the hill to Pratapgad with all your might and main.'

'Yes, Khan Saheb, we shall run,' shouted the assembled men.

'Even if you spit blood in the effort, you cannot stop. Whatever the difficulties on the way, there is no stopping your dash towards the top of Pratapgad. On reaching the top, you have to give battle to whatever enemy you encounter and loot their armoury, their treasury and whatever else you find worth plundering. Whoever comes in your path should be instantly slaughtered. That rascal Shiva who sits hiding up there in the fort, it shall be my responsibility to hold his living or severed head in my armpit.'

Afzal Khan was drenched in sweat as he continued addressing his men. 'Warriors of Islam, look at that ghat of Radtondi,' he said, pointing fervidly to his left. 'Look carefully. Two days later, before the sun's rays have dimmed, I shall have demolished the entire Maratha army. I shall then carry with me this Shiva, dead or alive, to the top of that ghat. And when I turn around and look at the Pratapgad hill, I shall see the Adilshahi flag fluttering in the breeze on the bastion there. Only after that victory shall I say my evening namaz.'

Once the rendezvous had been decided, it had become imperative for Shivaji to check the place out for himself. He shed his royal finery, and the embroidered brocade turban with the royal crest on it, and put on the simplest of clothes after finishing his morning prayers. He also wrapped himself in a white shawl. His silken hair hung loose over his shoulders, making him look like a hermit.

He descended from the upper part of the fort and then came out of the fortress altogether with a few select companions. They rapidly climbed down the steps of the main gate. Ahead and behind, maintaining a fixed distance between them, moved Shivaji's Maavali guards. Their eyes darted to the left and right in the manner of a rabbit looking for beasts of prey. Until recently, Kanhobakaka would always follow the king like his shadow, but he was senior to Shivaji by thirty-five years. He was actually

Shahajiraja's associate from Karnataka and had accompanied him both to the battlefield and the dungeon. The two valiant soldiers who had trained under Kanhojikaka were Jiva Mahal and Sambhaji Kawji. They were also riding down the steps with Shivaji today.

Looking at Shivaji's drawn face, Kanhoba asked, 'Shivba, has the meeting been confirmed for the day after tomorrow?'

'Yes. The earlier, the better.'

'Don't you think that it's being hustled a bit?'

'Kanhobakaka, if the edge of a cliff has collapsed upon you, if the rubble is all over you, suffocating you to death, the only remedy for saving one's life is to clear the rubble.'

'Shivba?'

'Yes, kaka. Through whatever means, the outcome of this battle should be decided as early as possible. Either this disease called Afzal Khan gets destroyed, or all of us get wiped out.'

Shivaji reached the Jani top. He swept his gaze over the space that measured barely three quarters of an acre. He had issued instructions the previous night, which had brought in all kinds of artisans like carpenters, blacksmiths, bazaar-masters and tent-masters, even before the king himself had arrived. He had commanded that the pavilion to be erected should be as grand as a hall in a palace. Labourers and artisans were busy putting into place walls of brocade, glassware like chandeliers and vases, small pillars of sandalwood and other such big and small items.

Finding the work proceeding to his satisfaction, the king returned to the fort immediately. Appearing before a dangerous man like Afzal Khan required that he have a few brave and energetic men beside him. He had been mulling over whom to pick for this job since the previous evening. As he was walking back up the hill now, he turned around to look surreptitiously at the dusky and massive-built Jiva Mahal who was trailing him. Jiva and Tanha were the two sons of Dev Mahal who had sculpted Kanhoji's life for him. When Shahajiraja had dispatched Kanhoji to Pune to help Shivaji settle down, the two boys had joined Shivaji's service.

The next person Shivaji looked at was Sambhaji Kavji. Sambhaji was as strong and resilient as the trunk of a teak tree. He had the reputation of being an immensely powerful but eccentric man. He was from Maaval and was another of Kanhoji's disciples. On a bet, he would lift a horse as if it were a lamb or a pup, and carry it around in his arms. When Shivaji turned to take a second look at Jiva and Sambhaji, a smile became visible under old Kanhoji's white moustache. Shivaji too responded with a soft smile.

Then he climbed up to the fort and arrived at his court, where all the senior chieftains were waiting for him. In court, every moment was being applied to chart out political moves and battle strategies. Even before Shivaji had arrived, a big map had been drawn on the floor with white rangoli powder.

Taking the pavilion as the central spot, Shivaji began to plan the field placement. Jani's hillock could be seen even from the window of the secretariat. He first explained the importance of that spot. 'Can anyone tell me what kind of acquatic animal this Jani's hillock resembles?'

When no senior leader like Netaji, Annaji Datto, Kanhoji Jedhe, Shivaji Jedhe and others could give an answer, Shivaji said, 'This spot looks like an upside-down crab with its legs spread out. See, this is a crab-leg-like path that descends straight from the fort to the spot. Here's this extremely narrow and almost invisible path filled with thorns and brambles that comes fromParghat, past the Vardayini temple. And here's another one, that descends from the spot and reaches the enemy's camp.'

'Raje, this place looks extremely mysterious and spooky to me,' said Annaji Datto.

'Well, there is no mystery here. Whatever spookiness there is can be assigned to nature. It is altogether concealed by the dense vegetation around. It isn't visible at all from down there, by the river, which is where Afzal Khan has his tent. But this spot is specially advantageous to us. Because everything happening in the pavilion will be easily visible from one side of the fort.'

As Shivaji was talking, his voice turned serious. 'There is a possibility of a skirmish erupting suddenly on this spot. If our guest, Afzal Khan, feels threatened even in the smallest degree, his bodyguards and, immediately after, his band of warriors will come dashing in and jump at me like rabid beasts of prey. It will be imperative to intercept them on the way.

So, here's the plan. You can see these dense, thorny bushes of the stinky ghaneri and the karvanda plants on the rear side of the pavilion. Kanhojikaka, Shilimkar, Annaji Datto and Annaji Pasalkar will conceal themselves with their men in these bushes. You will have to block the path of the men who will rush from below towards the pavilion. Once we have succeeded in the task, you must race down towards the bank of the Koyna.

A message arrived from the army kitchen. It was now afternoon and Shivaji headed along with his colleagues to have lunch in a smaller manor opposite the palace. The food was plain and simple: some rice and *machan bhaakar* served on plates made of leaves, and a thin gruel made of gram flour served in leaf-bowls. Also placed before everyone was an onion smashed into two halves using the fist. This was the staple of the poor peasants of the region, and this was the king's food too.

There was one single whisper that was circulating among the diners: there had been no sign of Moropant Pingley anywhere for the last two days. It was odd that he wasn't present at the meeting that was underway since the early hours of the morning.

'How could nobody at all have seen him?'

'Difficult to fathom. Well, we can understand that he may have been sent on some secret assignment by the king, but what about his foot soldiers? Where are they?'

The foot soldiers that went with Moropant generally had units from Jedhe, Narayan Brahman and Tryambak Bhaskar too. Everybody was perplexed as to where this force had gone and on what secret mission the king could have sent it.

Every moment was precious. Babaji alias Khelkarn had wanted to have a secret word with the king, but no time could be found for it. The king had earlier welcomed Babaji into the fold, and rewarded him with the robes of a sardar. As they were moving from the dining area to the durbar, Babaji held the king's hand in a hurry and slipped into his palm some consecrated grains of rice. Shivaji laughed out in delight and said, 'What? Despite the hustle, you have managed to slip in a ritual for your nuptials?'

'What can I do, Raje? My mother has grown old. She has arranged for a betrothal close to our village. But there is no cause for worry, Dada. The auspicious day has been fixed for the month after this battle gets over.'

Shivaji would have wanted to discuss this betrothal with a great sense of affection and involvement, but the entire jungle around Pratapgad had turned heavy with the smell of gunpowder from the hidden cannons. Nobody had the time to see the colours of anything other than war.

'Wah,' responded Shivaji. 'Please tell my Gaurakaku that her Shivba and my Matoshri will reach the marriage pavillion well before the auspicious hour. No worry at all.'

All the sardars assembled in the durbar once again. The meeting between Afzal Khan and Shivraya was due to happen the day after the next. Concern and anxiety regarding this meeting were not limited to the people living inside the fort; even the goat herds of the jungles, nay, even the trees and bushes were on edge.

Three or four days had gone by since Afzal Khan had pitched his camp by the side of the river. The clash of the two armies had got the wraiths of cold fear to go dancing through the jungles of Pratapgad and the hills and valleys in the vicinity. People living in the hamlets and the mountain bluffs were afraid of stepping out of their huts. Animals that would go to graze in the jungles were now being kept tethered in their barns. Even the birds that ordinarily created such a racket on the tree-tops had stopped flying out much.

Secret messages had arrived from Bahirji Naik and Vishwasrao Dighe: it would be a serious mistake to believe that Afzal Khan was taking it easy now that the meeting had been fixed. He was, in fact, extraordinarily restless. His spies had spread themselves across the jungle trails to learn what Shivaji was planning.

Shivaji's eyes rested on the top of the cliff on the other side of the valley. He tossed a question at Sardar Babaji Bhosale, who was sitting in front, 'So, Babaji, you shall be manning the post on top of the Radtondi cliff, won't you?'

'I am staking my life on it, Dada.'

'*Aho*, if this Afzal Khan gets worsted, from which direction will he flee for his land? Via Wai, right?'

'That's right, Raje. We shall give him a bitter engagement. Nobody shall be allowed to cross the road to move any further. Even at this moment, my men are sitting in the bushes of the Met'tala village with their weapons primed.'

'And you?'

'Me? As soon as this conference is over, I shall rush to my post through the valley on the other side.'

'Wonderful.'

Shivraya was laying out before the conference how and where the various units had been posted. Kanhoji Jedhe, however, had been looking very restless for some time. He suddenly addressed Shivaji and said, 'Shivba, when a turbulent river has to be calmed down, the jaws of the powerful, sharp-toothed crocodiles in it have to be smashed first.'

'What do you mean?'

'Afzal Khan is going to come up to this pavillion to meet you. Your plan to intercept him on the way is commendable. But there is his huge administrative camp that has been pitched at the foot of Radtondi and Pargaon. More than a thousand camels are parked there. Big and small cannons, a stockpile of explosives and some eight or ten thousand of his soldiers are going to station themselves there. How can we hope to win unless we break their backs there?'

The assembled chieftains were startled. Kanhoji had put his finger on the most dangerous hole in their plan. Shivraya, however, laughed loudly and said, 'All right,' he said, 'come with me to the verandah of the palace.'

This grand palace was situated on the uppermost part of the Pratapgad fort. Its verandah was located at such a great height that it commanded an unparalleled view of the valleys through which the Koyna river flowed. The rear side of the fort gave a panoramic view of the prodigious slope leading down to Konkan, the hills and valleys of the Western Ghats. Shivaji looked down towards his left side, where one could see among the hills a flat patch of land. At a signal from Shivaji, Gomajibaba picked up the flagstaff in the verandah and waved it in the air. Everybody was stunned when they saw an immediate response of a flag being waved from the patch which lay in the denseness of the jungles.

As the grandees looked in amazement at Shivaji, he informed them with unconcealed delight, 'Our Moropant Pingale has ensconced himself in those woods there.'

'And his army of four thousand foot-soldiers?'

'They too have joined him there. They would have reached last evening.'

'But this is a miracle!' exclaimed some of the men around him. 'How could an army of four thousand men have climbed down this massive slope and travelled such a long distance through such thick jungles without the enemy getting wind of it?'

'Well, these valiant Maavalis left last evening by taking a detour through Konkan. They got down close to the village of Kaneshvar near the valley below there. To make sure that the enemy spies did not get wind of their movement, they did not light flares while crossing the jungles. They just used flints for crossing the difficult streams and defiles. It was after a difficult night of travel that they managed to reach there.'

It was a tale that stirred the hearts of all the listeners, including Kanhoji Jedhe. Addressing them all, Shivraya continued, 'On the night previous to our rendezvous, Moropant will do the two-hour climb to the top of the hill where there is this ancient temple of Goddess Vardayini. Then, at the crack of dawn, before even the first ray of the sun knows of it, our men will go into hiding in the gorge there in the middle. Then, finally, when they receive the signal of a cannon being fired from Pratapgad, within half an hour they will burst upon Afzal Khan's main army camp like a thunderstorm and wash it away.'

Shivaji was explaining the proposed movements with the help of a map that lay in front of them. At a little distance, just behind Jani's hillock, was another pit, in which would hide some fifty or sixty men. He said, 'Hiroji Farzandkaka, you shall be in charge of this unit. As soon as there's trouble in the pavilion, you have to spring out of the pit. You should reach the pavilion in a few leaps and tackle the enemy.'

He assigned the hills, stations, trenches and clefts on all sides of the Jani top to the assembled sardars with great precision. Referring to all the hillocks and hideouts around, he continued, 'On the eastern side of the Jani hillock is this small hill that the people here call the Mahaarwada Tape. In a rupture there, some six or seven hundred of our foot soldiers can easily be accommodated. As soon as the ruckus breaks out in the pavilion, these soldiers must make a rush for Afzal Khan's tent in the camp.'

Pointing his finger to the south of the pavilion on the map, he said, 'This broken trail that comes from the direction of the Vardayini temple and leads up to the pavilion, this will be in Shilimkar's and Annaji Datto's charge. The slope of this ravine is so steep, so narrow, that people can't easily walk through it, or even crawl through it, for that matter. They can only scrape their butts to move forward. There is danger here.

'We came into these jungles along with our forces under heavy rainfall before the month of Aashaad. I shall never forget the welcome and cooperation I received from the boys and even the women from every little village, every household, every hamlet of these parts. Our enemy Afzal Khan entered these jungles with all kinds of guns and cannons loaded on the backs of roughly two hundred camels. He is going to rain fire upon us, but we have no reason either to be afraid or to lose our confidence because the very god of nature here in the Sahyadris is fighting on our side in this battle. I am confident that the red soil of this region shall easily set fire to the sulphur that his cannons disgorge upon us.

'Our enemy has massive kitchens and cooks, but we don't. Our soldiers have to take shelter in villages when the rains arrive. Following instructions issued by Masaheb and me, rations were supplied from the fort to every household in this region. While this is true, the actual labour of cooking the food and serving it to our men was done by my mothers and sisters in these villages.

'We shall move heaven and earth to ensure that Afzal Khan's army does not flee from our land. And when all hell breaks loose on the day after tomorrow, you will not get anything to eat in these dense jungles. That is why, women and children from the villages you pass by shall stand waiting for you at the outskirts with bundles of bhaakari and onions. Without even dismounting from your horses, you shall just pick up those bundles and gallop ahead. Keep in mind that these *naachani bhaakaris* that can easily last for a couple of days will turn out to be the tastiest dishes of our swarajya.'

His eyes began to search for someone. Then he called out loudly, 'Where is our Shivaji Jedhe?' Shivaji Jedhe, who was standing right by his side, came forward and bowed in respect. Raja Shivaji asked him, 'Where are your helper boys? Has the selection been made?'

'Of course, Raje. They are waiting for you in the compound of Kedareshvar on the other side of the wall.'

Shivraya walked down to the ground in front of Kedareshvar in the company of Shivaji Jedhe and Hiroji Farzand. A hundred and fifty boys were to be recruited as helpers, and the crowd out there was well over two hundred. At a signal from Shivaji Jedhe, a contest of danda-patta took place. It was followed by a round of swordsmanship. With the exception of barely one or two, the rest of the boys were all strong and audacious, and were bubbling with enthusiasm. Fifty, however, were pruned out. But when the king noticed the great disappointment on those faces, he took them all into service.

For the critical meeting with Afzal Khan, each of the boys was examined for his particular skill and appointed for a task that suited him most. Seating them all in front of him, Shivaji said, 'While offering the Khan our hospitality, some of you will serve paan, while some others will stand fanning him or his grandees. Some of you will serve water. Some of you will play disciples, and some will stand outside the pavillion, loitering around, pretending to put in order the footwear of the officials inside. You have to be perfect in your roles. But, finally, boys, what is your ultimate task?'

'Just tell us, Raje, we will offer our lives.'

'Every single one of you will be provided with a dagger or a switchblade to carry in the fold of your dhoti or tucked in the string of your trousers. On the surface, you will be ordinary helpers; but in truth, you will be rugged Maavali fighters. If Afzal Khan plays foul, if he attacks us, or if he and his men try to rush out of the pavillion to climb up to the fort, then you have to whip out your hidden weapons and fight every foot of the way for your motherland. You shall perform the ultimate duty of destroying the Khan with your own hands.'

'Your wish is our command, Raje. We shall give up our lives for you.'

It had begun to turn dark. As Shivaji turned to return to the durbar, Sakanya Gurav met him on the way. Tucking his horn under his armpit, he bent and touched the king's feet. Shivaji smiled as he instructed him, 'Sakanya, my friend, you shall come with me to the pavillion the day after tomorrow. Don't worry about whether we'll win or lose. Your job is to blow your horn from the very pit of your stomach. That shall be the signal for the cannons on top of the fort to go off. When the cannons on our fort are fired, our soldiers hiding in the jungles and hills and defiles, shall hear them and jump out like locusts and chew the Bijapuri forces to extinction.

27

THE CHALLENGE AND THE BATTLE-OBSESSED CHAMPIONS

The time had come for bidding each other luck and setting off for war. Around this time, a servant brought on his shoulder two bamboo laths with a pair of knee-high wicker baskets hanging by each lath. The mouths of all four baskets were covered with leaves. Many eyebrows shot up, wondering what the baskets contained.

The sardars and the army captains were due to reach their assigned posts by nighttime. It was important for them to find suitable spots from where they could best perform their roles. In anticipation of his rendezvous with Afzal Khan, Shivaji had sowed units of his army at strategically advantageous points. But nobody had any idea what front had been assigned to Netaji Palkar and his first-class cavalry. Netaji himself was unaware of it. Surprisingly, however, he hadn't shown his usual impatience by questioning Shivaji about it in everyone's presence. But in the court, conjectures were being exchanged in the back row. How did Netaji suddenly manage to vanish from the fort as soon as any meeting got over? What magic wand did he possess?

It was quite late now; the officials were in a hurry to leave. Looking at all his grandees and chieftains, Shivraya said, affectionately, 'Look, among the Mughals, and even in the Adilshahi Sultanate, there is this custom of giving a token gift to soldiers who are departing for the battlefield. Some give gold ear-studs, some others give jewel-studded necklaces, or whatever else.'

'Why are you embarrassing us, Shivba?' Kanhoji Jedhe said. 'Ours is the Hindvi swarajya of the poor and destitute. Why do we need gifts at all?'

'But we shall not let you depart empty-handed today.'

'Raje?'

'Yes, I have brought a unique item to offer to you as gift.'

At a sign from Shivaji, the servants placed the leaf-covered baskets before him. After the leaves were moved aside, Shivaji picked out fresh yellow fruits with a trace of green in them. As he distributed them among his men, he said, 'These are wood apple, or bel fruit as we call them here. It is very sweet, this jungle fruit.'

'Raje, where did you find this fruit?' asked Hiroji Farzand.

'It's right there outside Kedareshvar's temple door, on the other side of the wall. This year, the tree is loaded with fruit. The bel fruit and the leaves of the bel tree are Lord Shankar's favourites. Try the fruits out.'

Shivraya distributed the first few himself; later, others took over. He turned emotional while bidding goodbye to his men. 'I feel,' he said, 'that it would be a kind of deception to leave a few things untold to a warrior. My brave soldiers, I tell you this clearly, the blessings and support of Mother Tulza Bhawani are with us in abundant measure; I do not have an iota of doubt that we shall emerge from this campaign victorious. But, my friends, please do not carry any delusion in your minds. This enemy of swarajya, this Afzal Khan, is the most wicked and villainous person of this era.

'A war is a game played with life as stake. In this whirlpool of war, anything can happen—absolutely anything. Afzal Khan can just turn out to be singularly fortunate. But assuming for a minute that he unfortunately succeeds in killing me—'

'Don't! Don't, Raje, don't utter such words!' some objections were heard in the gathering.

'Honesty is a quality that the leader of an army needs to possess. That is why I have to tell you this: if that unfortunate event presents itself, please do not sit down to grieve. Don't let grief eat away time that is as precious as gold. Keep fighting. If you fall short of weapons, pull out bamboo sticks from the jungles. Make lances out of the branches of trees and smash open the enemy's head. If you don't have enough swords and spears, use your teeth to tear open the enemy's skin. It won't do to pour milk or curd or butter upon the god of our Hindvi swarajya. You have to bathe him in warm blood if you want to drive away the darkness of slavery. Please do not expend your time in shedding tears for me.'

The audience was overwhelmed. 'Assuming that by the evening of the day after tomorrow, the boat of my life sinks, who, then, will look after this state of swarajya?'

On hearing this coming from the Raja, some of the men assembled there began to cry incontinently. Even an intrepid warrior like Netaji let out a loud sob and got up with the intention of walking out. Shivraya, however, held his hand tight and said, 'Please wait, Netajikaka. Listen, all of you brave Maavalis: after me, my responsibilities will be taken over by my mother Jijausaheb and Netaji Palkar. My little son Shambhu has been deprived of his mother's love only some while ago. I have decided to hand over the cradle strings of these two infants—Shambhu and Swarajya—to the mother of all of Maharashtra. All of you now have to defend with your lives this "Swarajya Lakshmi" that has come into being because of the aspirations of the poorest of poor among our subjects.'

'Raje, Raje, why are you talking this language of final settlements?' Netaji cried.

Shivaji said, 'Endorsement for your great deeds comes even from my enemies across multiple births. They refer to you as Shivaji's alter ego. I am telling this openly to everyone here that after Shivaji, there is only one person who has the ability to pluck out a fistful of stars from the sky; it is just Netaji Palkar.'

The wind was howling outside. It was shaking down the bel fruit upon the roof of the durbar. The gong of the bells from the temple of Kedareshvar could be heard. The atmosphere in the durbar had turned poignantly tender. Shivaji folded his hands, invoking Bhawani Mata, and rolled out his final piece like a rallying cry, 'My esteemed Marathas, when the shadows of the evening begin to lengthen on this Pratapgad, the wheel of history will certainly stop, even if for a fleeting moment. The astounded present will raise itself on its toes and look with excitement at the jungle trail that runs from Gopya's ghat towards Rajgadh. At that very moment, our Matoshri Jijausaheb at Rajgadh will have fixed her expectant gaze on this same trail. That is the reason why I want to remind you. On the morning of the day after tomorrow, even before you pull your swords out of their sheaths, you have to make a very important decision: how do you want to spend that evening? Putting up a vigorous fight, severing Afzal Khan's head, spiking it on the point of your spear and taking it in a procession to Rajgadh to the accompaniment of drums? Or, hanging your heads and carrying my dead body on a litter, and finding ways to sneak it out of the battleground like a bunch of thieves?'

The response to Shivraya's question came in the form of a loud roar: 'No, Raje, no! We shall fight. For the sake of your pride and in response to your call, the men of these mountains will fight, without a doubt. But as it happened with Hanuman in the jungle, the trees of the jungles of the Sahyadris shall also uproot themselves and break the spines of the Bijapuri army. We shall grind the enemy into the dust; we shall blow the trumpet of your victory.'

Instead of sleep, it was wakefulness that was sitting heavy on Shivaji's eyelids. The life of unremitting strife that his parents had lived stood before his eyes. He remembered many incarnations of his mother Jijausaheb. Even while he was in her womb, she had been required to face up to unimaginable grief. The slaughter of her father and three brothers in the Nizam's durbar had crushed her as if she had been run over by a stoneroller. Then, the various uprisings and rebellions by the lord of her life, Shahajiraje, for trying to break the noose of slavery. The demands of time had certainly compelled Shahajiraje to wear out his heels at the doorsteps of the Mughals sometimes, the Nizamshah at some other times, and later the Adilshahs. But each one of these forced services had caused his wounds to resurface and suppurate. The breathless running around that he did chasing his dream of swarajya, in fact, the cruel chase to which he was subjected, the new Adilshah's failed experiment at the Pemgiri fort, from Ahmadnagar to Pune, from Pune to the horrific descent to Konkan done in the torrential rains, the entreaty to the Portuguese at the Cheul fort, seeking sanctuary for saving the life of wife and child, the rejection of that appeal—the wandering and the running around were not yet over.

In recent times, Matoshri Jijausaheb had finally begun to look happy. With the arrival of Shivraya, the soft rays of independence had just about started playing upon the hills and dales of these parts. Then arrived the dense, dark cloud named Afzal Khan. He killed Jijau's elder son through deceit and deception. He branded Shahajiraja a criminal and slapped manacles upon him. And now, that foe had taken the shape of Destiny, and entered into the womb of the Sahyadris to destroy the infant swarajya. It was unfortunate that out of the leading twenty-two sardars that were with him, eight were Marathas and Brahmins. These sardars were quite ready to pick up the dung that lay in the enemy's barn and call it gulaal. Ranged against them was a boy named Shivaji, just entering his thirtieth year, who was turning his blood into water, endeavouring day and night to keep the ramparts of swarajya safe.

Sleep was simply refusing to visit the king. The night's maw was wide open.

He suddenly remembered something and called Kanhoji immediately. Since the old man himself was awake, it took him no time to arrive. 'Forgive me, kaka,' Shivraya told him, 'there was one thing that I had brought to court, which I simply forgot to distribute. But this item should be distributed to all the sardars and other officials holding their spots. It will then automatically get distributed to the soldiers.

'As you command.'

'Quartermaster Guna Mohite will still be in the warehouse. I had instructed him to be present there.'

'But tell me what this special thing is!'

'Yes, of course. Here is a sample.' So saying, he pulled out a piece that he had kept with himself.

It was a small pouch made out of plain, thin cloth. Shivaji pulled a smaller pouch out of it and showed it to Kanhoji who opened the knot at the mouth. Inside the pouch were a dozen or so pinches of tobacco leaves and a lump of wet lime. Kanhoji didn't know whether to laugh or cry. Making a sour face, he said, 'I know that our king will not dismiss his soldiers' efforts to entertain their small indulgences and addictions, but—'

Shivaji smiled softly and said, 'Kanhojikaka, these jungles of Jawali and Pratapgad are soaking wet. They are crawling with leeches that bite sharper than a cobra can. They draw blood. Our army has to spend two nights and three days in those thick bushes. The leeches are going to make life miserable for them. Horses and bullocks too will lose their mind suffering the bites. These men of ours have to sit there in hiding without letting the enemy get the faintest whiff of their presence. No flares for them either. In the pitch darkness there, they would not even be able to procure herbs that may work against the leeches. So, what is left then? Tobacco!'

Kanhobaji was delighted to hear the king speak of tobacco's virtues. He bowed to him with great contentment.

The Maavalis left in the darkness of the night to distribute the tobacco pouches. Using this opportunity to meet Kanhoji, Jiva Mahal held the old man by the arm and asked in jest, 'Nayak, I fall at your feet, but let the other mystery also be resolved.'

'What are you asking about, Jiva?'

'Tell me this about our Netaji Palkar—what kinds of herbs and leaves does he derive nourishment from?'

'Herbs and leaves—what do you mean'

'Well, how does he suddenly disappear from the fort like some spirit?'

Kanhoji broke into a loud laughter. 'The mystery behind our Netaji is the bigger mystery name our Shivba.'

'What are you saying?'

'Nothing but the truth. When Shivba was a boy, his father Shahajiraje would often tell him the story of the invincible fort of Devgiri. Long ago, once, the enemy had laid a siege around the fort. In a few months, they ran out of grains. The people inside the fort could not escape because there was just one secret passage to sneak out of such a huge fort, and the enemy had blocked it. Thousands of men and animals died in the fort from starvation. To save the lives of whatever few were left, the Yadava king of Devgiri had to bow before the enemy in abject surrender.'

'So, how does that story connect here?'

'That's just what I'm telling you, Jiva. Netaji's disappearing act has nothing to do with leaves and herbs. When this fort was being built three years ago, the king had instructed the architect Arjoji Yadav to lay out four secret passages in the design of the fort. I stay with Shivba almost like his shadow, but even I don't know all the secret passages very well. It's just one or two others like Netaji with whom Shivba has shared the secret.'

The thought that he would finally be face to face with Shivaji that afternoon sent Afzal Khan's spirits soaring.

He had already planned what he would do after the meeting was over. Excited by the possibilities the future held for him, he began to bring all pending matters to a neat closure.

He finished his second prayer of the day, handed over the prayer mat and the rosary to his footman, and walked over to the other hall of his luxurious tent. 'Where is all the equipment, son?' he asked Faulad Khan. At a signal from Faulad Khan, a servant brought a bamboo basket five feet long and a foot and a half in width and height. The aroma in the hall suggested the use of tender bamboo. The bamboo strips had been so skillfully woven that it looked like a perfectly well-made wicker box. The footman soon brought in a couple of baskets of some kind of herb.

'What are these herbs for?' Afzal Khan asked.

'If in the process of being taken captive, Shiva gets seriously injured, then he can easily be lowered into the basket and whisked out. Anticipating the nature of the wounds, physicians have been kept on the ready. No time need be wasted.'

The image of a Shivaji tightly bound in ropes and blood dripping from his wounds thrilled Afzal Khan. A unit of ten strong camels stood ready before his big tent. The men riding the camels were strong, strapping young men, too. Besides, a company of seventy spirited horses were also ready and waiting for a signal from their master.

'Abbu, the camels are, of course, going to move fast, but I have deliberately arranged for horses too. The reason is that right up to Rahimatpur, it is Maratha country. Besides, because our prey is big, proper guard will have to be maintained. Also, if the camels happen to get tired or if they fall ill, the horses will prove useful.'

'That's very good,' said Afzal Khan. 'If we take this middle route and travel night and day through Rahimatpur, Aundh, Vita and Jat, we will be able to hit the outskirts of Bijapur by the third night.'

'Yes, Abbu, absolutely. But you must wind up this drama of meeting Shiva quickly and hand the merchandise over to us. We will then set off at express speed.'

Afzal Khan left hurriedly for his private tent to effect a change of clothes. Just then, sardars Dundey Khan, Musey Khan, Ankush Khan, Khandoji Khopada and Shankar Mohite reached him. Their faces looked tense with worry. Although they stood mute, the tremor in their breaths did not go unnoticed. 'Yes,' he asked brusquely, 'what is the matter?'

'Afzal Miyan, what is the point in our valiant commander-in-chief's exposing himself to danger?

'What are you saying?'

'Why should you yourself go to meet Shiva, putting your life in danger? Any one of us can go there, and we swear by Allah, we'll come back with what you desire.'

'Ankush Khan, you fool! Look at you, all scared of that mountain rat.'

'Shiva is an extremely dangerous man, huzoor. These hills of the Sahyadri look very frightful too; difficult to figure out,' Dundey Khan found the courage to say.

'Please listen to us, Khan Bahadur,' Khandoji Khopade said in a desperate tone. 'I place my head at your feet as I say that this son of Shahaji Bhosale is an extremely vicious person. Don't get into close proximity with the boy. Please don't go yourself.'

'Yes, Shiva is dangerous. Yes, he is a vicious rogue. That is the exact reason why I shall not show the immaturity of sending a half-baked soldier to meet him. Otherwise, the scheme we have laid out with such hard work will fall through.'

Khan walked into the dressing area in long strides. He put on a vest of thin weave. Two footmen rushed in with the thin chainmail made of interlinked steel rings that he usually wore. The footmen tried to put it on him from behind. The half-sleeves settled on his forearm, but the front flaps refused to meet across his chest and stomach. The sight of those flaps made Afzal Khan laugh. His stomach had really bloated. During the monsoons at Wai, he had done nothing but spend his days in utter luxury.

Besides, the goats that were supplied there came straight from Mhaswad, animals that had been fed on dry fodder, leaving the Khan with no option but to gorge on the delicious meat to his heart's content. It, therefore, did not surprise him at all that he refused to fit into his mail armour as he did before.

The footmen got ready to make a dash for the armoury to see if a mail could be found that would accommodate their master's well-fed body, but Afzal Khan's roar froze them where they stood. 'Go away, you fools. Why do I need an armour at all? How much time will it take this Afzal Khan Mohammadshahi to dispatch this puny wax doll to its maker? Go away, and don't fret yourselves.'

There was a well-arranged stack of shervanis and kurtas that lay in the clothes-room. He nixed the thought of wearing a shervani too. His eyes fell on a yellow muslin kurta that lay at the bottom of the heap. When his marriage procession had arrived from Bhaganagar, he had worn a kurta exactly like this one on his first night with his beloved Ladli Begum. He always looked at the kurta as a good omen.

When that kurta had become old and worn out, his Ladli Begum had got another one of exactly the same colour and texture stitched for him. That kurta had turned a little tight, too, but the Khan was glad that it had not turned as traitorous as the armour. He wore it and admired himself before the mirror, hands in the pockets. Memories of Ladli Begum came flooding in, filling him with grief. He remembered the royal well where his sixty-three wives had drowned themselves for his sake. Afzal Khan was distraught. In the mirror, he saw a smiling Ladli Begum. He cried to her in a mournful voice, 'Please stay on for some more time. That sinful Shiva's life is about to come to an end.'

28

THE CONFRONTATION

This very important day dawned when Shivraya was twenty-nine years old. It was *Marg Shirsh Shashti*, which means the day of Champashtami—10 November 1659.

The sky was heaving anxious sighs over how the day would unfold. The precincts of Jawali, that little Koyna river, twisting and turning through the mountains to find its way down, and the area around the foot of Pratapgad—all of them could feel an unceasing rumble in the stomach. The stars switched themselves off in a hurry at dawn. The rising rays of the sun began playing restlessly on the heads of trees and bushes.

Whatever the amount of sleep gathered the previous night, half an hour or three quarters, it was important to be at the Kedareshvar temple at dawn. Shivajiraja tied his dhoti around his waist, tossed a length of white cloth over his shoulder and stepped out. Bare-bodied, fair-complexioned, tall brow, and a thick head of hair falling over the shoulder—the impression he gave was that of a wise hermit. Giving him company were Kanhoji Jedhe and Ganoji Govind, a sergeant in his army.

As they were climbing down the stairs, Shivaji murmured, 'If somehow a clash can be preempted through dialogue, if a bloodbath can be prevented, it will be a blessing from Mata Jagdamba.'

'But what if the enemy carries black thoughts?' asked Kanhoji. 'What if he initiates violence?'

'Then, of course, Afzal Khan and his entire army will be destroyed.'

'Our soldiers are lying in wait at their assigned posts.'

'Excellent.'

'Their eyes are fixed upon your meeting with the Khan this afternoon. Once the cannon atop the rampart is fired to give them the signal—'

'As it happens,' said Shivraya, 'the moon is going to rise a touch late this evening.'

'Meaning?'

'There will be plenty of light available from the stars to keep the battlefield colourful.'

The priests at the temple had made full arrangements for the prayer. Fresh flowers, twinkling lamps, small earthen receptacles for ghee, aromatic incense sticks—the atmosphere exuded a sense of peace and well-being. The perfume of musk pervading the air gave it a sacredness that was exhilarating. The prayer was performed with due diligence. Shivajiraja distributed gifts to the priests, as per tradition.

The diaphanous screen of darkness was slowly pulled away from the sky. The soft, early flush of the morning sun glimmered gold and pink on the Pratapgad ramparts.

As soon as breakfast was over, Shivaji began to prepare for the meeting. He wore a steel mail-chain, thus securing his chest and back from harm. He then put on a steel helmet, which he concealed carefully under his embroidered official turban. The jewels embedded in its crest winked in quiet splendour. He then put on a sparkling white tunic, upon which he sprinkled ochre water. He then put on his shalwar trousers. He concealed a *bichhua* in one long sleeve. This dagger's name was taken from *bichhu*; its sharp, thin blade curved like a scorpion's tail. Inside the other sleeve, he concealed a unique weapon called the *wagh-nakh* or the tiger's claw.

He stepped out of his palace with the grace and power of a lion emerging from its den. He had with him as bodyguards Jiva Mahal, Sambhaji Kavji Kondalkar, Bhanaji Ingale, Sambhaji Karvar, Siddhi Ibrahim, Yesaji Kank, Krishnaji Gayakwad, Soorji Katke and Vishwas Murambak.

As he was walking out, his eyes drifted involuntarily towards the image of Mata Bhawani sculpted on the front wall. He bowed before her, took the fresh golden magnolia flowers that Kanhoji handed him, and placed them at the feet of the goddess.

He felt overwhelmed. He thought of his mother and father, the ordeals the two had faced throughout their lives.

Thinking of their relentless perseverance, Shivraya broke into a fervent prayer: 'Oh you thousands of gods who reside in the hills and jungles and rivers and defiles of the Sahyadris, so often have my parents dreamt of bringing independence to this sacred land, but tyrannical powers and the devastating winds of Destiny have defeated the realisation of their dream thrice over. History tells us that when one generation retires, the next one picks up the cudgels with intrepidity. It is in this consecrated land that I have sworn to plant and nurture the sapling of swarajya. Responding with a resounding yes to our call, the poor denizens of these Twelve Maavals, who have no clothes on their backs and no weapons in their hands, have always stood with us to cross the threshold of death. We have been striving for many years to fulfill our life's mission of creating this temple of swarajya.

'That is why, O Mata Bhawani and Shiv-Shankara, the bhaakari on the skillet, the calf in the barn and the birds of the jungle are all waiting for your commitment to our cause. The meeting is going to be so decisive that either the enemy will survive or we will somehow manage to come out waving our flag of victory. In simple words, in this inevitable conflict, one certainly has to die while the other comes out victorious. That is why, O Mata Bhawani, O Shiv-Shankara, we supplicate before you from the bottom of our hearts; please put into our begging bowl the gift of success and success alone. Please bring us and our swarajya out of this trial in good shape.'

With that, the king stood up, determination writ large on his face. He looked to his left and right. He had the feeling that the deep gorges of Sahyadri were looking at him with expectation. At that moment, a wind came blowing in from the valley beyond, and the leaves on the trees trembled. Those bidding farewell to Shivaji were overwhelmed. The vines, that playful wind, the swaying trees were overwhelmed too. It was as if all of nature and the entire region of Jawali was wishing him the best of luck. He was conscious of it in every limb, which was why his steps had gained firmness and speed.

The Paar crossing had been left behind. Crossing the river, the twenty-two bearers of Afzal Khan's palanquin were moving with rapid steps. Carrying almost two hundred kilos of his enormous body was a taxing job. The carpenters had used a single log of the sticky, resilient gum tree for making the central beam of the palanquin.

That colossal body and that heavy carriage were squeezing the last ounce of strength out of the bearers. The difficult climb arrived immediately after the river was crossed, and it tested the stamina of every one of those hardy men. Knees aching, calves throbbing, bodies bathed in sweat, they slaved on without letting their steps miss a beat.

The two envoys—Krishnaji Bhaskar Kulkarni and Pantaji Gopinath—were walking alongside the palanquin, keeping pace with it. Pantaji was valiantly playing the role of a wedding guest who was representing Shivaji in Afzal Khan's procession.

Among the Khan's main bodyguards were strapping young men like Pilaji Mohite, Shankarji Mohite, the massively built Sayyad Banda, the Khan's nephew Rehmat Khan and Pahelwan Khan. Behind the bodyguards was walking a company of fifteen-hundred armed foot-soldiers, all of them handpicked by the Khan himself.

The procession climbed up the incline to reach the top. That was when Pantaji Gopinath's attention was attracted by the long retinue of the Khan's fifteen hundred men stretching like a tail, rapidly closing the distance with the procession. Pantaji's heart sank into the pit of his stomach. He immediately stopped and asked, 'Krishnaji, what's this?'

'What happened, kaka?'

'This carnival of soldiers trailing behind the palanquin?'

'Now, who is going to explain this to the Khan, kaka?'

'Look, Krishnaji, the agreement was that there would be exactly ten men accompanying him.'

'But—'

'All right, now, you tell me this. Do you want to go up there to meet our king or just take a round of the empty pavilion?'

'What do you mean?'

'Look, things will happen exactly as agreed upon. Otherwise our king will not take four steps out of his palace up there.'

When the argument between the two envoys began to heat up, it fell upon the Khan's ears. The fifteen hundred men halted. Afzal Khan signalled to the palanquin bearers to stop, and called his envoy. Krishnaji came scurrying up to him.

'What's the matter now, Krishnaji?'

'Khan Saheb, it was with such difficulty that this meeting was arranged. Now, you have gone and spoiled it all.'

'Why? What happened?'

'Khan Saheb, even otherwise that Shivaji is so terrified of you, to the point that he can't gather the courage to even stand in your presence. Now, when he sees this contingent of fifteen hundred following you, he is not likely to so much as peep out of the fort window. How, then, will the meeting happen?'

'Khan Saheb, please listen to me,' pleaded Sayyad Banda softly, 'under whatever excuse, just let this mouse get into the pavilion. Then see how we bury him alive. You just have to stand and watch.'

'Huzoor, why are you spoiling the milk for such trifle? You are like a massive tree and he is just a blade of grass.'

'Is that so?'

'What else, huzoor? Just a little while more—'

'—and that will be the end of him.'

'Well, all right,' said Afzal Khan. He was pleased at the confidence of his men in their ability to crush the enemy. From where he stood, he could see the spire of the pavilion among the trees at a slightly higher altitude. Drunk with conceit, he too began to think that the need for the company of fifteen hundred to be pressed into action wouldn't arise. He signalled to them to stop right there.

The palanquin again began moving rapidly forward.

.ཽ໑ྋ.

Shivaji was still in the fort, receiving a steady stream of reports from the pavilion below. Afzal Khan had arrived at the pavilion, and was pacing the pavilion restlessly. Another herald brought the message that there was a huge giant of a man called Sayyad Banda who had entered the pavilion along with Afzal Khan and was standing next to him like a wooden post.

Shivajiraja got into high alert. It appeared that the man had mischief up his sleeve—why else would he want Sayyad Banda to be present with him inside the pavilion?

He immediately sent a sharp message to Krishnaji in the pavilion. 'Does the Khan seriously want me to see him? If yes, then that Sayyad Banda should immediately be sent out of the pavilion.'

―⁂―

Right behind Pratapgad, towards the Konkan side was a village called Rankadesar. In the middle of a crowd of a thousand horses in the jungle there, Netaji Palkar's horse stood frisking. He looked immensely restless. Amused at his leader's state, Raghunath Ballal Sabnis went near Netaji and asked, 'What's going on, Commander-in-Chief?'

'Why?'

'Why are you making your poor animal dance like a horse in a marriage procession?'

'Well, call it nervousness if you have to, Raghunathrao. On the one side, I have no doubt that Afzal Khan will get the thrashing of his life today, but—' Netaji halted mid-sentence and then resumed in a worried tone, 'it is absolutely necessary for us to know in which part of the jungle he has parked three thousand of his best horses.'

'How can this be found out at such short notice?'

'Arey Raghunath, we absolutely must know the answer. I have been uneasy since last night. I dispatched Bahirji and Vishwasrao's best spies on this assignment this morning.'

'Oh come on, what difference will it make?'

'You are a fool. When there is a war afoot, death waits for you at every step. During such times, we must have every conceivable information on the enemy's strengths; else ruination can't be too far.

―⁂―

The strong-built Jiva Mahal stood at the door of the pavilion. After looking at him sharply, Afzal Khan turned his eyes towards Gopinath, as if asking, 'Who is this good man here?'

In answer to that question, Gopinath looked at the formidable personality of Sayyad Banda and let his eyes ask, 'So, where have you brought this specimen from?'

The Khan understood the ifs and buts of those silent questions and signalled to Sayyad Banda to go out. As soon as Banda had left, Gopinath signalled to Jiva to wait outside.

That was when a person of average height, but extremely handsome and charismatic looking, walked in, dressed in sparkling white. The brocade on his turban and the pearls in the crest shone with a grand lustre. The sharp nose, the soulful eyes, that thick black beard that belonged to a hermit, and that semi-circular sliver of a crescent moon drawn on his wide brow. The grandeur that this man exuded startled Afzal Khan for a little while. But immediately after, it struck him that his prey had now arrived within the range of his grasp, and that delighted him to no end.

Keeping his eyes fixed upon the slim person dressed in white, shorter than him in height, he asked, 'So, Krishnaji Kulkarni, is this the person that you call Shivaji?'

'Yes, huzoor.'

Shivajiraja then turned towards Pantaji Gopinath and asked, 'Is this the person who is known as Afzal Khan?' To which Pantaji nodded.

Throwing a look at the expensive drapery and the other jewel-studded paraphernalia around him, Afzal Khan asked Shivajiraja mischievously, 'This pavilion glittering like the ceiling of a king's palace, these beautiful strings of precious stones, these chandeliers that cost lakhs of rupees—my question is, why does the son of a farmer feel the need for all this grandeur?'

'How can the son of a female cook ever understand these urges?' retorted Shivaji with some asperity.

The dart of 'female cook' hit and ripped open an old and deep-seated would inside Afzal Khan. It was like sprinkling salt on a fresh wound, and its burn reached right up to the very root of his brain. It was with the greatest effort that he managed to put a lid on his reaction. This was not the time for petty bickerings. This was the wild jungle of the enemy, and here was the prey that had come walking into his grasp. It would be better to take the sweet-talk route and then finish the matter once and for all.

He somehow digested the rage that had welled up in his chest, and turned to Krishnaji with a smile. Krishnaji bent his large body low with reverence before Afzal Khan and, using all the political acumen he possessed, told Shivaji in dulcet tones, 'Raje, here is the opportunity to turn your ordinary life into a golden one. Why miss it? Go, bow before our Khan Saheb and take his blessings.'

Shivaji looked daggers at Krishnaji and communicated to him with his eyes that he would never belittle himself thus.

Afzal Khan, meanwhile, was finding it impossible to accommodate the self-esteem and pride of the young man who stood before him. He roared, 'Shivajiraje, abandon your obstinacy and your conceit. Who gave you the authority to invade and take control of our Adilshahi forts and castles?'

'Khan Saheb, every one of those forts are holy territories for the people of this Maaval land. They have been the jewels that our ancestors always wore.'

'Raje, as it is, because of your arrogance, you have erected towers of errors and sins. Consider it a stroke of fortune that you are meeting in me a man with a clean heart. Come back to your senses and start walking on the path of truth. I am quite willing to take you with me to Bijapur and plead before Sultan Ali Adilshah on your behalf.'

Afzal Khan was trying every trick in his bag to make Shivaji lower his guard and come closer. 'How do I tell you?' he proceeded. 'Whatever property, land and forts you had taken away from the Adilshahi Sultanate, I shall arrange to have them returned to you. Come, don't be afraid. You are, after all, the son of my friend Shahaji, and that makes you my nephew. Let's forget all bitterness and embrace each other.'

Without waiting for Shivaji's response, Afzal Khan lunged forward with arms outstretched and took him in a bear hug. Even as he did that, he quickly maneuvered to pull his prey's neck under his armpit, and began twisting it with his vice-like grip. Shivaji, however, had anticipated this kind of move. He whipped out the dagger hidden under his sleeve and thrust it into the man's side. The blade ripped past the tunic and its tip went grazing against the mail inside.

Afzal's squeeze was so tight that for a moment or two Shivaji felt like he would choke to death. But holding himself with all his reserve, he shook out the *wagh-nakh* from his other sleeve and plunged it into Afzal's belly with an upward motion, ripping the skin apart. Afzal Khan's grip on his neck loosened, at which the agile Shivaji brought the dagger back into play and shoved it inside the Khan's soft belly, turning it in a circular motion that brought the Khan's intestines hanging out. Even so, as Afzal Khan doubled up in pain, he pulled out his sword and brought it down heavily upon Shivaji's head. The weapon clanged against the steel helmet under Shivaji's headgear. Afzal Khan squealed like a stricken animal, 'Betrayal! Betrayal!'

At this scream for help, Sayyad Banda ran into the pavilion, sword flashing. Looking at him, Shivaji lifted his sword. Just then, Jiva Mahal dashed in, sword at the ready, and said, 'Wait, Raje, I'll take care of this demon.' With that, he lifted his double-edged sword and brought it down upon Banda's shoulder with such force that the blade ran right through the shoulder blade and sliced the entire arm off the body. The movement was so swift that Banda saw his arm fall and the sword clattering on the ground even before he could feel the pain.

Blood was gushing out of Afzal Khan's eviscerated stomach. He somehow tied his stole round it and began to move out of the pavilion. Plenty of blood had flowed into his shoes, too, which made walking a slippery task.

Krishnaji Bhaskar advanced towards Shivaji with his sword swinging. Shivajiraje found this act rather strange. However, without caring for propriety, Krishnaji brought his weapon down and stabbed Shivaji, who, even though wounded, managed to save himself from fatal harm. 'What are you doing, Krishnaji?' the still astonished Shivaji bellowed.

Uncaring for his remonstration, Krishnaji swung his sword again. He had sworn to be loyal to his Bijapuri master. Shivaji now raised his sword and swung it at the advancing man. Krishnaji lost his balance, fell upon his side, and was rising up again to make a fresh assault when Shivaji's sword penetrated his stomach and went right through the spine. His corpse fell with a thud on the floor.

Afzal Khan's footmen and palanquin-bearers came running towards the pavilion, screaming 'Treachery!' Afzal Khan's massive body was bathed in blood. The cloth round his stomach had not done much to stem the flow of blood. When he saw the palanquin, he somehow managed to stagger towards it, and went limp so as to fall into the carriage. The palanquin-bearers hurriedly pushed the rest of him inside and began carrying him down the slope with loud shouts.

As the Khan's men ran for their lives in the direction of the river, shouting, 'Run! Flee!', the Marathas chased after them, roaring, 'Catch them! Don't let them get away!' In the lead was the mighty Sambhaji Kavji. He took after the palanquin, shouting, 'Bearers, set the litter down and save your lives!' The bearers, however, were paying no heed to his orders. Sambhaji caught up with them and swung his blade at their calves. As they fell screaming, the palanquin fell free on the ground.

Seeing the ferocious Sambhaji Kavji striding towards him, Afzal Khan screamed piteously, 'Help! Save! Treachery!' Sambhaji grabbed Afzal Khan by his long hair and swung his sword viciously, separating his head from the body. Blood gushed out from the headless neck and fell to the earth below.

Shivraya was now moving rapidly towards Pratapgad, with Sambhaji Kavji and the other Maavalis close at his heels.

Inside the pavilion, the moment Afzal Khan had raised his sword against Shivraya, Mansha Gurav had completely ignored the mayhem and bloodbath that had followed and begun blowing on his horns with all his might, just as Shivraya had ordered him to do. As soon as the men on top of the fort had heard the horn, they had set fire to the three cannons they had kept primed and ready. The boom of those cannons had brought the jungles and gorges and defiles on the slopes all around the fort suddenly alive. As the leaves trembled and the trees shivered, throaty battle cries of 'Har har Mahadev!' burst from behind every tree and bush. 'Shivaji Maharaj ki jai!' was the call that began echoing together from thousands of mouths across the entire mountain range.

When the Bijapuri men heard these battle-cries from every direction, they were petrified. 'Ya Allah! Ya Khuda!' they screamed in unconcealed fear.

The tumult rising in the jungle rattled the main army camp of Afzal Khan. Musey Khan and Faulad Khan quickly leapt upon their horses and galloped in the direction of the pavilion. They had with them a cavalry of two thousand horsemen. Musey Khan egged them on with shouts of 'Come on, you devotees of Allah, move forward. We shall slaughter that Shiva today.' The unit was advancing with great vigour. Having no knowledge of what had happened to his father, the disoriented Faulad Khan was urging his horse fast up the slope.

The unit couldn't have proceeded very far when they saw five men running down the slope, their clothes spattered with blood and muck. They were screaming as they clambered down, 'We have been destroyed. That Shiva has killed our Afzal Khan Saheb. Khan Saheb has been slaughtered. We are ruined!'

The earth-shattering news turned Musey Khan and Faulad Khan to stone. The inconceivable had happened! They leant upon the mane of their horses and began to howl without restraint. But they were cruelly jolted out of their grief by the loud victory slogans of the enemy; they seemed to get closer with every passing moment. This was no time for crying. They gathered their wits and rode towards the fort.

A little while later, when the loud cries of victory began to echo out of every rock and hill, tree and shrub, stream and gulch, accompanied by the terrified screams of the fleeing Bijapuri soldiers, they knew that their army had been shredded. They thought it wiser to turn around and save whatever they could of their camp down below. The colossal stack of arms and ammunition, of grains and fodder, that lay there should at no cost fall into the enemy's hands. They spurred their horses to greater speed.

There was tumult everywhere. The deranged cries of the Bijapuri men reached every leaf and bud. 'Shiva has slaughtered Afzal Khan. We are finished.'

The foot-soldiers of Moropant Pingale's unit, who had climbed down from the Vardayini temple, began moving forward. Seated on his horse, Moropant galloped up and down through his forces, urging them to move faster. 'Come, my brave soldiers, let's swallow up the Khan's army before it gets dark.' Once they reached their destination, they began laying the enemy camp to waste.

Meanwhile, the Maratha squads that had been hiding on the bank of the Kumtha also came running in with loud cries of Har har Mahadev from across the Paar crossing. In the melee, Faulad Khan, on his way back to his camp, saw his cannons. He shouted at the gunner standing there,

'Quick! Quick! Light them!' The gunner spotted the Marathas scrambling down the hillock towards the river and fired a few zamboorak shots at them. Faulad Khan was sizzling with the desire for revenge, and he made a few efforts at hitting back, but the roaring wave of destruction that had begun to roll in his direction was refusing to stop.

The wind that was blowing across the river in the direction of the camp wreaked further havoc. It carried a few sparks from the firing cannons and dropped them on a stack of dry fodder that stood behind it. The blaze threw a million more sparks in the air, which, again, the wind promptly carried to the rows upon rows of fodder that stood all around them. It soon looked like an entire mountain had caught fire.

The entire army camp had now descended into chaos. Before the gunners could set alight more cannons, Moropant and his men ran across the shallow waters of the Koyna and crashed into the camp with a loud uproar.

Then there were those two thousand men who had been hiding in the rupture that fell between Mahaar-tape and Jani's hillock. They too scrambled out of hiding with cries of Har har Mahadev, and rushed towards the Khan's base camp. The fire that had been lit ran in circles across the camp, roasting whatever men and material fell in its mad circuit.

Musey Khan attempted to salvage whatever he could of his camp from this multi-directional assault. As he spurred his horse this way and that, a lance thrown by a Maratha soldier found his horse's neck and then penetrated into its chest. The unfortunate animal teetered on its hind legs for a moment and collapsed into a pool that its own blood had begun to create. Musey Khan fell off his seat. Faulad Khan leapt off his own horse and dragged him back to relative safety. When he saw the spray of the blood all over Musey Khan's face and clothing, he lost courage and looked around with terrified eyes.

The news of Afzal Khan's death had spread everywhere now like a gust of wind. The death of their leader had squeezed the very last drop of courage and spirit out of the Bijapuri horsemen and foot-soldiers.

The sun was sinking rapidly into the western horizon. The shadows falling across the Koyna waters had begun to turn darker. The Bijapuri men were horror-stricken: what would happen to them when the jungle was taken over by darkness. The cold fear of death made them begin to flee in the direction of the Radtondi ghat, and behind or towards the Makarand ghat on the other side.

Faulad Khan too read the writing on the wall. He had no doubt left now that the jungles here, the river, the wind, even the sky had joined forces with the Marathas. He desperately whispered to Musey Khan, 'Let's move out, chacha. What is left here to stay behind for?'

'Yes, son, it's best that we move out.'

Hundreds of the fleeing Bijapuri soldiers were trying either to climb up the Radtondi ghat, or taking the back-breaking route behind the Paar crossing in the direction of the Wasota fort. As they struggled to find their footing up the Radtondi slope, they were harried by bunches of Maratha foot-soldiers and even horsemen springing out like fearful wraiths from behind bushes or out of gullies. Musey Khan was so driven out of his wits that he screamed, 'These demon Maavalis of Shiva! Why aren't they at least letting us run away?'

As they neared the upper cliff of Radtondi, Musey Khan and Faulad Khan saw a bunch of a couple of dozen Bijapuri soldiers belabouring somebody. As they went nearer, they saw that the men were kicking and punching Prataprao Morey, who was screaming in agony, 'Please don't beat me! Please don't, for God's sake!' When Prataprao's eyes fell on the two, he pleaded with them, piteously, 'Please save me, Khan Saheb! What's my fault?'

'You filthy pig! It was you who were offering proofs like so many pieces of sweetmeat! You were the rogue who lured us into these haunted jungles!'

'Crush this fellow,' shouted one of the soldiers. 'He's the one who has ruined us.'

'Please have mercy on me, Khan Saheb.'

'You are a filthy dog,' Faulad Khan snapped. 'You deserve this.'

'Please don't say this. If you have to seek revenge on Shivaji, you will have to come back into these jungles.'

'Of course, we shall come back!' growled Faulad Khan.

'When that happens, will you be able to find a bigger turncoat Maratha than me to lead you through its secret passages and trails?'

'Yes, this, of course, is true.'

Prataprao was delivered a few more slaps and then made to rise. He turned out to be useful as a way finder through these jungles. He began taking Musey Khan and Faulad Khan along the path that went through the Medha ghat towards Satara.

⁂

While Shivraya was climbing up to the fort, with Sambhaji Kavji riding alongside him, carrying the severed head of Afzal Khan, some among the Bijapuri warriors had begun to run up the slope to attack him. Hiroji Farzand's unit blocked their way and slaughtered them.

The companies led by Pasalkar, Baji Sarjerao, Kanhoji Jedhe and Annaji Datey descended rapidly towards Afzal Khan's base camp.

Netaji Palkar and Raghunath Ballal Sabnis's cavalry of four thousand men stood next to Rankadesar village on the slope behind Pratapgad that descended into Konkan. If Afzal Khan's army were to climb down the Konkan slope, it would be Netaji's responsibility to block their way.

As soon as he heard the cannon boom at Pratapgad fort, Netaji pulled at the reins of his horse. His stallion immediately raised its forelegs high in the manner of saluting some royalty. Netaji gave a cry of 'Let's go. Har har Mahadev,' and began climbing up the incline.

Netaji still hadn't rid himself of his real worry. He still hadn't been able to find out where Afzal Khan had hidden his best cavalry of some four or five thousand horses in this jungle. This unit, if not neutralised in time, could inflict serious damage on Shivraya, whose words had been ringing in his mind. He could relive the scene word by word.

'Netajikaka, the most important of responsibilities rest upon your shoulders.'

'Just issue the orders, Raje.'

'As soon as you hear the boom of the cannon on the fort, you have to dash up towards the jungle, make sure that the jungle is completely under your control, and then go galloping towards Radtondi. Ride through the night through Gureghar and Taighat, and mount your assault upon Afzal Khan's main camp at Wai by breakfast time. Will you be able to traverse this immense distance through the jungles in the darkness of the night, and reach there in time?'

'Raje, the mission is tough, that's true; but what else am I here for?'

'That's what I have been saying, kaka. You will be able to fulfill your mission only if you can move at the speed of a shooting star.'

His horse's hooves had been drumming the ground frenetically since the cannon had boomed. Keeping a sharp eye on the probability of some Bijapuri forces loitering hereabouts, Netaji was galloping up and up, spurring his poor animal mercilessly till it was spuming froth from its nostrils.

Just as he had crossed a stream, he saw Shaukat closing in with four other horsemen. When they had come close enough, Netaji shouted, 'Yes, Miyan, what's your news?'

'Come with us.'

'Where?'

'I will give you the key to the treasure you have been hunting for.'

Netaji laughed out with pleasure. He looked at Raghunath Ballal Sabnis and said, 'Take five hundred horses with you and go where Shaukat Miyan leads us.'

'Forgive me, chief, this can't happen. Our Shivajiraje too would not want it.'

'What are you saying, Raghunathji?'

'Netaji, how do we place our trust in this miyan, especially in the middle of a battle?'

'Yes, that's true, but—'

'I know, I know, Netaji. He may have brought some useful information from the enemy camp to our Raje out of greed for money. But this rascal has spent nights in Afzal Khan's tent. Should we then trust him and sink our entire contingent?'

'Arey Raghunatha, you remember when we had gone to your grandfather's house in Penn, your grandmother Gangubai had served us some river fish cooked in Konkani spices?'

Raghunath Ballal Sabnis stood stunned for a few moments. A shiver ran through his entire body. He stared at Shaukat as if he had just woken up from sleep. Then he burst out involuntarily, '*Chyaaalyaa*! What a big imposter you are, Dighe Bhau!'

'Yes, that's me. Vishwasrao Dighe.'

Vishwasrao and Raghunath Sabnis slapped palms and then turned their horses to the right. In a little while, they reached the outskirts of the Jawali township near the Moreys' palace. The treasure Vishwasrao had mentioned stood in front of them. Three thousand five hundred Bijapuri horses were corralled there.

The Bijapuri horsemen had been waiting anxiously for their master's bidding. Looking at the direction in which the battle was going, Khairiyat Khan had wanted to set off in this direction. He would then have picked up this cavalry and launched an attack on Pratapgad from its left wing. But he had met his end in the skirmish at Mahaar-tepa. Since this spot was quite close to Mahaar-tepa, the horsemen waiting here had got to hear of his demise too. Shaukat Khan roared loudly at the horsemen assembled there, 'Let's go, brothers. We shall play the last move of the battle now.'

The Bijapuri horses began galloping behind Shaukat, and behind them ran Raghunathrao's unit. It had started turning dark. The darkness made the jungle look terrifying. Many Adilshahi soldiers had begun fleeing in the direction of Wai. Many of them had lost their weapons; those who still had them had begun to find them excessively heavy. They had begun to lose sensation in their limbs. They clung to each other, these terrified men, and sat shivering in small groups. A number of them felt that being taken prisoners would be a better option.

The situation of the animals was not much different either. So many of the riders had fallen off their horses' backs. The coats of the animals were covered in blood. Without a rider, and often without any reins, these frightened animals had also begun to huddle together in groups, scraping their muzzles and their backs against each other. With the howdahs on their backs having toppled off, some seventy-odd elephants were roaming free, too. The camels had also got into similar huddles.

Just a little on this side at the foot of Radtondi, Moropant's infantry had gathered in large numbers. The clothing of these warriors had hardened with congealed blood and sweat. After the marathon slaughtering they had been doing since late afternoon, their limbs had begun to throb with pain. A rank, musty, unclean smell had settled upon them. The women and children of the hamlets in the hills had gathered about these soldiers and brought for them the best dishes they could rustle up in quick time. The hungry soldiers began consuming them as and where they stood.

A lot of tedious work still remained to be done. All the weapons, clothes and items collected from the kitchens of the enemy had to be gathered, separated and tied up in some rough order. Word had been circulating that the Raja had wanted them to move forward in some direction.

The grooms and the bullock-cart drivers had laid out fodder before their animals. Close to two thousand enemy prisoners were sitting in the dark in front with their heads bowed. They had been shattered by their crushing defeat, scooped out hollow by fear, and distracted to madness by the hunger in their bellies. Once Moropant was sure that he had properly pacified the hunger of his men, he signalled to his disciples. Soon, bhaakari and chutney began to be distributed among the prisoners.

Moropant himself took a round of the rows of prisoners and ensured that the food was properly distributed. Shivraya's instructions on this matter were very clear: as soon as the sardars had fed their own men, they should personally ensure that the prisoners had been fed too. Nobody should go hungry.

After the prisoners had been fed, Moropant announced in a loud voice, 'If some among you Bijapuris want to join our forces, they should assemble in the open ground on the other side.'

Moropant's captains set to work according to instructions. There were another forty or so captains, clerks and revenue officials standing there. 'Come along, men,' Moropant instructed them. 'Start taking stock of all the weapons, clothings, jewellery, horses, bullocks, elephants and everything else and prepare a proper list. I want no holes in the accounts.'

29

FUNERAL AND FELICITATION

The dreamy, soft light of the stars had just begun to glimmer. Many Adilshahi soldiers lay groaning and keening behind trees and bushes. A few hours ago, the jungles and hills of Jawali had reverberated with the shrieks and screams from a bloody hand-to-hand combat. Afzal Khan's army had suffered enormous hardships to drag the load of seven hundred camels, eighty-odd elephants and big and small cannons up to these dizzying heights. As it turned out, none of these hulking animals and objects had been of any use. Like the monkey-army of Hanuman, the Marathas had jumped down from trees and sprung out of bushes, sat on the enemies' chests, and beaten the living daylights out of them.

Shivajiraje had just about managed a thirty-minute nap when his eyes snapped open around midnight. He got ready and stepped out of his palace. Old Kanhoji Jedhe blocked his path. His white moustache and sideburns trembled softly. He blinked nervously as he entreated, 'I shall not address you as king, but speak to you as a father.'

'Kaka, your wish is my command.'

'Look, Shivba, for the past few months, your eyes have forgotten the meaning of sleep. You need to rest.'

'What can I do, kaka? Duty calls.'

'Yes, but how will it do for you to be so unconcerned about your health? After all, our body has its limitations. It needs a little bit of rest, doesn't it?'

'No, kaka. Destiny will mock the king if he goes to sleep in his palace while a war is on.'

Gomaji stepped forward to say, 'Raje, a few people here are of the opinion that we must have victory celebrations in our palace tomorrow.'

'It's too early to celebrate. When Raavan died, his entire Lanka sank with him; but the Adilshahi Sultan's Lanka is a large kingdom. Starting from our Rahimatpur on the bank of the Krishna, it stretches down south up to the ocean.'

'So, what does that mean, Raje?' Kanhoji resumed his theme. 'Put on your armour and set off in the middle of the night for your state-building exercise?'

'Yes, of course. This battle of Pratapgad is only the first chapter of the Mahabharat of us Marathas, you may say.'

As he stepped out of the palace, Shivaji said, 'I'll go straight to the crossing of the Paar village. I have to see to an urgent matter there.'

'We just worry, Raje, for your health.'

'We will have to act immediately. The enemy that we have bruised and battered will certainly come back at us with a vengeance in the next few days. Then, there are bound to be plenty of turncoats in our army conspiring with them.'

'That's true.'

In the darkness of the night, Shivaji climbed down the steps of the fort. The grooms had kept the horses saddled and ready. Shivaji came down the front slope with his unit. Further down, on the left became visible a bedraggled crowd of about a hundred-and-fifty men carrying flares and torches. They were the battered soldiers of the Bijapur army. Many of them had rags tied to their wounds. Pounded by their misery, they appeared to have gathered there with a purpose.

A bunch of constables had caught hold of them. One of them was shouting at the crowd, 'Go away all of you, and carry the corpses of your beloved ones with you to Bijapur!'

'Please, huzoor, have mercy on us.'

'Lift up your burdens and return to your homeland. If no mausoleum for Afzal Khan has been built there, dig a grave for him.'

That was when Shivaji's commanding voice reached his ears: 'What's happening here?'

'Maharaj, these fools want to bury their Afzulya Khan's body here, on our land. I've been telling them to go and toss it in the river there somewhere.'

'Shut your mouth!' roared Shivaji. 'Who gave you the authority to insult the dead?'

'It's not that, Raje, but—'

'You are a fool! An uncultured boor! It is the duty of the victorious king to honour the memory of a martyred soldier, and not to insult it under any circumstances, regardless of which side he fought on. We cannot forget this ethic of a soldier.'

The matter had stirred the king deeply. He called out in an imperious voice: 'Raghunathpant?'

'Your orders, Raje.'

'First thing in the morning, mark out a piece of land for these people to bury their dead. And, Gomajikaka—'

'Please command.'

'When the graves are built here, the responsibility of the prayers offered there and the expenditure on their maintenance will be borne by the state. This shall be a part of the monthly duty of the fort secretariat.' This gesture of the king impressed all those gathered there—friends and foes alike.

Raghunath Ballal Sabnis, however, was finding this generosity a little over the board. 'Raje,' he muttered, 'what you have declared shall, of course, be done. But why this magnanimity?'

Shivajiraja noticed the displeasure on the faces of some officials. He addressed them in a soft but firm voice: 'When Raavan met his death, Vibhishan asked the same question that you are asking today: what to do with the body? Prabhu Ramchandra performed the last rites of his enemy with his own hands. That's why, my valiant Maavalis, I have just this to say to you: when the enemy meets you on the battlefield, you must engage with him with your sharpest weapons, but the tenets of warfare and that of humanity demand that when he is dead, you should hold his body as you would a friend's.'

Shivaji's wisdom and grace touched the hearts of the enemy soldiers. Many of them broke down. The man who was sitting next to Afzal Khan's body stood up, bowed before Shivaji, who was still astride his horse, and said in a choked voice, 'Allah, this Shivaji is no mortal; he is an angel. Please grant him the remaining years of my life.'

Shivajiraje made to spur his horse on, but then suddenly turned it around to address Afzal Khan's soldiers. 'We respect the memory of your dead leader. The sanctity of the memorial you build for your leader here will add to the grace of our grand fort. Build a memorial here by all means, but do not attempt to extend your influence any further by using it as an excuse.' Saying so, he turned around and set off.

Riding through the jungle track along with his men, Shivaji reached close to the Paar crossing. That was where the customs office and the temple of the village goddess Vardayini were located. Citizens, soldiers and peasants had assembled there with flaming torches in hand. A camp had been erected there to take care of the wounded soldiers. Healers and physicians were busy attending to them. The wounds had been dressed with soft, thin cloth, and medicated oil was being applied on them. Turmeric, fat extracts from cow's milk, herbs, all possible remedies were being used.

On the other side, stock-taking of the loot from Afzal Khan's base camp was in progress. Around ten thousand bundles of cloth, big trunks and baskets filled to the brim with gold coins, diamonds and other precious stones—it was a big haul. Afzal Khan had brought with him from Bijapur wealth that would meet the expenses of his army for three full years. His own enormous wealth had also landed in Maratha hands as an unexpected bonus.

Shivaji was deeply aggrieved for the soldiers who had martyred themselves for the cause of the Hindvi swarajya. Appraisal of their contribution, therefore, began on a war footing. He began to move among the wounded soldiers lying in the camp. The very wonderment of their king coming so close to them and asking about their well-being lifted their spirits. They forgot their pains and miseries, even if for a little while.

The dead bodies of those whose villages were close by were handed over to the villagers present there. A list of the martyred men was being prepared. The relatives and fellow-villagers of soldiers—dead and alive—came before Shivajiraja and bowed respectfully. They were all aggrieved at losing a dear one, but were prouder that their loved one had sacrificed himself to the cause of Shivraya's swarajya.

'Moropant, how many of our men lost their lives?'

'The head-count is still not over, Raje, but the figure will be in the region of twelve to fourteen hundred.'

'Oh Mata Jagdamba! So many!'

'But, Raje, all our men fought with might and main. They sent five to six thousand Bijapuri soldiers to their doom.'

'Really?'

'Besides, we also have in our custody four thousand of Afzal Khan's men as prisoners of war.'

Shivraya did the rounds of the tents holding the wounded soldiers' hands and exchanging affectionate words with them. As he walked, he said, 'We adopted this policy after the battle of Purandar: when a soldier sacrifices his life for the cause of swarajya, his family becomes the state's family.'

'Absolutely, Raje.'

'Prepare a list of the martyred men. Then take the brothers and sons of the slain men immediately into the service of our government. If there's no man left to take care of a martyr's family, it should not feel orphaned.'

'For that, we have made the policy of *raand-roti*, "Bread for the Widow", to support the widows of martyrs.'

'Yes, of course. The policy must be implemented with the greatest integrity. Till so long as these widows of martyrs live, they should never be in any want. Their care is the swarajya's responsibility.'

Outside the camp, in an open patch on one side stood a large number of men, women and children. They were eagerly waiting to meet their king. Expressing his deepest gratitude to them, Shivaji distributed immediate compensation to the families of the wounded, ranging from twenty-five hons to two hundred hons. He declared rewards of elephants and palanquins for the brave sardars present there.

He distributed gold bracelets, necklaces, crests of pearls and medals to the soldiers in accordance with the courage they had displayed in the battle. The court administrators then handed over to him a sword with a jewel-studded hilt. He presented it to Kanhoji Jedhe and then embraced him. He said, 'Unfortunately, everybody cannot be honoured in this moment of hurry. A special durbar will be assembled soon to felicitate great warriors like Netaji Palkar, Moropant and Dighe. But the person who most deserves to be honoured for this victory is our Kanhojikaka

Jedhe. Right from my stint in Karnataka, I have had the good fortune to learn under his guidance. Today in the morning, when I started back from the pavilion for the fort, he himself came crashing down, like a ball of fire, upon the enemy soldiers who were chasing me. Kaka, I will never be able to repay the debt of gratitude I owe you and your family.'

Kanhoji accepted the sword with great humility. The king then summoned into his presence Gopinath Bokil. Giving him a robe of honour, he said, 'Any king who possesses an envoy like our Pantaji Gopinathkaka should consider himself extraordinarily fortunate. His astute judgement, his tact and maneuvers and his eloquence were put to great use in this war. If not for him, Afzal Khan, sitting in Wai like a tortoise with his limbs tucked in, would never have been persuaded to enter the hills of Jawali. In recognition of his intrepidity and ingenuity, I am gifting to him the village of Hivare on the Karha plateau.'

As per the instructions that Shivaji had given earlier, the lady *patils* of fifty-one villages were to be felicitated. Unfortunately, with the message having been received late, not all of them could make it to this meeting. Shivaji issued orders that their rewards be delivered to them at home. Then came forward the poor, illiterate, hard-working peasant women of various villages. Shivaji presented a sari, a blouse-piece and a gold trinket to each one of them. Expressing his gratitude to the hard-working women, he said, 'These jungles of Jawali and Pratapgad are said to be dominated by all kinds of wild creatures, ranging from huge tigers to tiny blood-sucking leeches. If these brave mothers and sisters from our villages had not rushed to our help, if in the torrential rains and in the battleground of today they had not supplied our fighters with food and sustenance, then our soldiers would have been reduced to dire straits in this merciless jungle. Hence, my dear mothers and sisters, we declare you today as honorary *patlins*, the village head-women of our swarajya. When the grand temples of our swarajya shall be built in the future, we shall never forget that the sweat and tears of our brave women lie mixed with the blood of our valiant soldiers in this soil.'

Shivaji had to leave in a hurry. He had received information that Netaji's army had crossed the Radtondi ghat and sped towards Wai in the evening. He once again made enquiries about the enemy soldiers that had fallen into their hands. He made sure that they were getting their meals. Not merely the Hindus among them, but also the Muslims were voluntarily joining Shivaji's forces. As he mounted his steed, Manaji and Annaji Datto approached him with mournful faces and whispered something in his ears. Shivaji immediately shot out into the darkness with his unit in the direction of the Koyna river.

The bodies of some of the martyrs had been recovered, but they were mutilated beyond recognition. Thirty huge pyres had been erected on the bank of the Koyna, on each of which were stacked five to seven bodies. Shivaji decided to light the pyres of these martyrs himself. Burning bunches of plant stalks were handed to him. He scattered bel and tulsi leaves on the flaming pyres. He was overcome at thus consigning the bodies of his brave soldiers to the elements.

Kanhoji and Moropant approached him with grief-stricken faces. Without uttering a word, Kanhoji held Shivaji's hand and pulled him along. Shivajiraja saw a pyre that had been arranged at a distance. The grave faces of his escorts created a lump in the pit of his stomach. The head of the man on the pyre had been badly mutilated by some sharp weapon. Deep cuts had drained the body of all blood, making it look shrunken.

Shivaji opened his eyes wide to examine the broad-shouldered, tall body that lay there. When he noticed the thick moustache and sideburns, his heart sank. A sob escaped his mouth as he croaked, 'Could this be Mambajikaka?'

There was no time nor leisure for much mourning. Somebody handed him a torch, and Shivaji lit the pyre.

He stood in the darkness under the trees on the bank of the Koyna river, tears streaming down his cheeks. Kanhoji was heartbroken at the sight. Holding Shivaji's arm tight, he said, 'Get a hold on yourself, Shivba.'

'Why, kaka? Doesn't a king have the right to shed tears?'

On the one side was the elation at having ground into the dust Afzal Khan, the very turret of the Bijapur Sultanate; on the other was his uncle, Mambajikaka, his own blood, who had deliberately crossed over to the enemy's camp. Fate, however, had finally dragged Mambajikaka to his death in the jungle of Pratapgad.

In a voice heavy with grief, he said, 'Kanhojikaka, here's the thing that makes me miserable. When my grandfathers, the two brothers Malojiraje and Vithojiraje, had set out from Verul, they would certainly have carried a shared dream in their hearts. Could they, at the time, have even fleetingly imagined that their family would split and scatter thus in the future?'

'Let go, Raje. The fire that did not spare the Kauravas and the Pandavas, that did not spare gods and goddesses even, why should you expect it to singe you any less?

.⸫.

A battalion of five thousand horsemen began to climb the slope of Radtondi that very night. They had to leave behind all their joys and sorrows, trials and tribulations, to get ready for a new battlefield. Heralds would often meet them along the route with the latest news. One such news was of the outstanding bravery displayed by his cousin Babaji Bhosale, who had been assigned the responsibility of defending the Radtondi ghat.

The horses had begun to froth at the mouth while climbing the near-perpendicular slope up to Radtondi. But they were striving on with tenacity. The cavalry was moving ahead at its best speed to render support to Netaji.

A herald informed Shivaji at one of the turns in the ghat: 'Babaji Bhosale is bound to meet you on the edge of the Radtondi cliff. He has been blazing away like a fireball for the past few hours. He must be made to rest, even if under duress.'

'Good you reminded me of that. In two months' time, he's going to get married.'

Shivaji was delighted at all the praises he had been hearing of Babaji from the heralds. He touched his chest to ensure that the valuable pearl necklace that he usually wore was still where it should be.

The wind at Radtondi was bitingly cold. In front could be seen the Met'tala crossing. It was at that ledge that Babaji was said to have shown many Bijapuri soldiers the way to Allah's house. On both sides of the track lay bodies, naked swords, broken shields, and the corpses of dead horses. Shivaji's unit waded through these bodies to reach the Met'tala crossing, where they ran into a wall of Maratha soldiers. But despite the resounding victory they had achieved, there were no triumphant cries to be heard.

A priest came forward and said in a subdued voice, 'Raje, we have been waiting with our eyes glued to your path.' The mournful voice of the man sent a shiver down Shivaji's spine. There was little doubt now that the hatchet of Fate had found the head of someone precious. On the other side of the Meyt, a pyre had been built. Shivaji dismounted and walked up to the pyre. Some of the experienced warriors present said, 'What do we tell you, Raje, of the valour of our young Babaji Bhosale? He was everywhere at once, with his sword dancing like a flame around him. Look at the enemy corpses littered everywhere. But finally, an enemy spear pierced his chest and brought an end to his gallantry. A terrible tragedy.'

Shivajiraja moved with leaden feet up to the pyre and kissed the forehead of the handsome boy that lay on top. He took off his pearl necklace and placed it on Babaji's body. The people assembled there broke into sobs, but Shivaji had turned into a pillar of stone.

Babaji Bhosale's pyre was burning in the jungle of Met'tala. Shivaji went down on his knees before the sacred pyre. Then, managing to stifle a sob inside his chest, he stood up and turned around, and mounted his horse.

Shivraya could see swarajya shimmering in the future. This was the time for him to gather together its victory flags. He spurred his horse and the spirited animal leapt forward in the early morning light towards Wai. It was critical for him to cross the jungles overnight and be there the next day.

Netaji Palkar had preceded in that direction much earlier with formidable assignments, the first of which was to raid Afzal Khan's Wai camp and take charge of all the enforcements the enemy had stored there.

There would be no time to stretch his limbs there either. He would have to race through all the land that lay in between and knock at the gates of the Bijapur palace on the morning of the third day. The thought of such a lightning advance was even more inconceivable because he would be doing so at the head of at least five thousand Maaval horsemen.

Galloping at top speed for two nights in a row without so much as a wink on the way and reaching the enemy's door on the third morning was an enterprise that would test the mettle of even an extraordinary warrior like Netaji. But there were two reasons why he had permitted himself no choice except to do the impossible. For one, he had given his master Shivaji his word. The second reason was far more compelling, compelling enough to have made him commit himself to this wild venture. Word in the air was that Shahaji was waiting at the other end with seventeen thousand fiery, frisky horses gathered in the Bijapur fort and in the jungles that surrounded it, in anticipation of the arrival of his compatriots from Maaval.

There the two intrepid armies would come together in a grand confluence. There it would be that sensational new lines of one of the most glorious chapters of India's future would be written.

The desire to transform the dream of his own independent country into reality had become the driving passion of Shivaji's existence.

Light had begun to break in the sky. The eastern horizon had gathered a tinge of ochre. The king's heart was heavy with grief for the men who had achieved martyrdom in the mountains of Pratapgad, but the journey that lay ahead of him was long and tortuous too.

As he galloped on in the company of his men, Shivaji pressed his horse's flank in an effort to infuse his fire and fervour into the animal. He ruffled its mane and whispered into its ears, 'Move on, my friend. No rest for us now. The siren call of destiny beckons.'

www.ingramcontent.com/pod-product-compliance
Lightning Source LLC
LaVergne TN
LVHW020417070526
838199LV00055B/3642